MORE

"You are unwise to tempt me further."

"But I like kissing you," she reminded him.

He stared a moment longer and then, rising, leaned forward to take her face in his hands, his callused palms rough against her flushed skin. His eyelids lowered as he covered her mouth with his, moving his lips gently as if to beg entrance. She yielded eagerly, but he hesitated, tracing her bottom lip with his tongue in a sort of teasing promise. Morgan rose on her tiptoes and encircled his neck in a silent plea for a more intimate touch.

BOOK YOUR PLACE ON OUR WEBSITE
AND MAKE THE
READING CONNECTION!

We've created a customized website just for our very special readers, where you can get the inside scoop on everything that's going on with Zebra, Pinnacle and Kensington books.

When you come online, you'll have the exciting opportunity to:

- View covers of upcoming books
- Read sample chapters
- Learn about our future publishing schedule (listed by publication month *and author*)
- Find out when your favorite authors will be visiting a city near you
- Search for and order backlist books from our online catalog
- Check out author bios and background information
- Send e-mail to your favorite authors
- Meet the Kensington staff online
- Join us in weekly chats with authors, readers and other guests
- Get writing guidelines
- AND MUCH MORE!

**Visit our website at
http://www.kensingtonbooks.com**

WICKED WOMAN

DENISE EAGAN

ZEBRA BOOKS
Kensington Publishing Corp.
www.kensingtonbooks.com

ZEBRA BOOKS are published by

Kensington Publishing Corp.
850 Third Avenue
New York, NY 10022

All Kensington titles, imprints, and distributed lines are available at special quantity discounts for bulk purchases for sales
promotion, premiums, fund-raising, educational, or institu-
tional use.

Special book excerpts or customized printings can also be created to fit specific needs. For details, write or phone the office
of the Kensington Special Sales Manager: Attn.: Special Sales
Department. Kensington Publishing Corp., 850 Third Avenue,
New York, NY 10022. Phone: 1-800-221-2647.

Zebra and the Z logo Reg. U.S. Pat. & TM Off.

ISBN-13: 978-1-4201-0121-8
ISBN-10: 1-4201-0121-8

First Printing: December 2007
10 9 8 7 6 5 4 3 2 1

Printed in the United States of America

*With many thanks to my critique partners for years
of faith and laughter:
Nina Singh, Robin Lawson, Debby Monk, and Katy Cooper.
For extraordinary support from my Moody Muses:
Cathryn Parry, Barb Wallace, Michelle Drosos,
and Karen Foley.
And with love for my heroes:
Tom, Sean, and Nat.*

Chapter One

Boston, Massachusetts, 1854

Shivering in the wind slicing across Long Wharf, Morgan Turner squinted up at Captain Montgomery's countingroom, which was, as promised, the last office in a long, tall brick building—last office, last hope.

A lump formed in her throat as she scanned the black windows. She took several short shallow breaths. Did she dare break in? If she was arrested, the police might connect her to the husband she'd left dead on her bedroom floor. A vision of a black-hooded hangman rose in front of Morgan, his eyes gleaming death as he pulled a rope over her head, gloved hands securing it tightly against her windpipe. Her throat clenched. No, she could not risk it—

Another icy gust penetrated her filthy cloak and once-pristine satin gown. The tangy ocean air mixing with the pungent smell of wet wood burned her lungs. Oh, but could she bear another night such as last, cowering in a damp alley, frightened by a roving gang of drunken men? If *they* found her—rape or hanging, which was worse?

The gang lived here, the hangman in Philadelphia.

Morgan slunk around to the back of the building where she found a shuttered window and an old, silvered board. She took a deep breath to stiffen her resolve. She could do this; how often had she and Amy laughed over similar escapades?

She shoved the board against the window. Wood splintered, glass tinkled, both sounds muffled by waves crashing against the wharf. Morgan stood on tiptoes and peered into the gaping hole. Silhouettes of furniture greeted her eyes, sleeping witnesses to the profitably employed. Respectable, honest people.

Wincing at the ugly comparison to her own character, Morgan wrapped her hands around the windowsill and pulled. Her feet fought for purchase against the rough stone. A minute later she slid through the window and fell to the floor with an undignified thump, thankful that the layers of stiff crinoline petticoats prevented shards of glass from cutting her. Pushing back her hood, Morgan rose and adjusted her itchy, blond wig. Her eyes fell upon a stove with a teapot and a box of coal. Heat!

In a trice, she lit an oil lamp and the stove. While warming her frozen fingers over the stove, she surveyed the well-appointed office. Captain Montgomery appeared to have prospered since she'd last seen him. Not surprising. During her disastrous voyage across the Atlantic two years earlier, he'd calmly sailed them through a hurricane and brought them into port ahead of schedule, master not only of his vessel, but of Poseidon himself. And still he'd found the time to offer her, a newly grieving widow, solace and assistance—rashly declined in favor of marriage to a man she scarcely knew.

Her heart lurched. A grieving widow then, she thought; the Wicked Widow of Philadelphia now. Her latest actions would surely revolt the soft-eyed, but ever-so-proper captain.

Her eyes passed over a globe and a gold-framed painting of Boston Harbor, hanging behind a flattop desk of black walnut. At the corner of the desk sat a jar of gumdrops. *Gumdrops!* Oh, oh, oh! Her hollow stomach jerked in excitement as she charged across the room.

She ripped off the top of the jar and shoved several in her mouth at once. Food, oh sweet, glorious food! Was there more? Sifting through the desk drawers, she discovered a tea box. A few minutes later, Morgan Turner, widow of Richard Turner, and of Charles Weatherly, and of Bart Drumlin, former Lady Morgan Reynolds of Westborough, sat down to a dinner of gumdrops and black tea.

Frowning, Ward Montgomery handed Rob his hat and cane, and stepped into his spanking new Piano Box buggy. "I'd rather have walked to the wharf, Rob."

Rob, Montgomery-tall and Byron-thin, merely shrugged, years of association having inoculated him against Ward's infamous scowl. "Your horses needed exercising, sir. Besides, what's the purpose of owning a buggy if you don't use it?"

"I purchased it because you insisted," Ward replied as he shifted several times in an attempt to fit his large body on the leather seats. Blasted things, he thought, were constructed for men on Byron's famous vinegar and potato diets. "Walking is good enough for Lowell and Cabot. It ought to be good enough for me."

"Surely not on such a raw day as this," Rob said, motioning to the leaden sky.

"Every day. It's a mere half mile to my countingroom, and I should have appreciated the exercise," he said. He settled his black-gloved hands in his lap.

"You took your customary row on the Charles this

morning, did you not?" Rob asked with a small grimace, for Rob, twenty-two, and seven years Ward's junior, disdained all form of exercise other than the mundane, a sad reflection on the younger generation. Or more likely, Ward thought as he stretched his legs in an attempt to ease his restlessness, a reflection on his own too-often restrained energy.

"Aye, Rob. And I dislike the formal address when we're alone. You're my cousin, for God's sake."

"As your clerk, I owe you all signs of respect." With a flick of the reins, Rob started them down Beacon Street.

Ward shook his head and sat back to watch the passing brick homes of Boston's elite to his left, and the common to their right, gray in the morning gloom, the limbs of its naked trees rattling with each stiff wind. "I suppose I ought to count myself lucky," Ward said, "that you drop formality when we play cards."

Rob smirked. "And much money, also."

Ward flashed him a faint smile. "I've warned you about my second sight. You refuse to heed it."

"I keep hoping that someday you'll be blinded."

"Not likely."

"You know, sir, if you ever wished to make your fortune at cards, it would be considerably less work," Rob said with a grin.

"And would send my grandmother to a premature grave. No, thank you. I prefer an honest living."

"There are days I think you'd prefer your grandmother in a grave."

Ward grimaced. "Occasionally. Most days, however, I enjoy her much more alive. She's a hard taskmaster, but she did her best to bring me up."

"She was a controlling harridan who refused to allow you to attend a decent school."

Ward flinched. Outwardly Grandmother Montgomery was a rigid, harsh woman, but inside she possessed a heart soft enough to understand the misery of a boy endlessly taunted by his schoolmates. "She thought it best for me. I liked my tutors well enough."

"Had you attended school, you might have gone to Harvard College."

"I still might have, Rob, but the sea called me, not Harvard. In that I disappointed her, which I regret to this day. She's had too many disappointments in her life."

"What disappointments? She has you at her beck and call!"

"Would you welcome a son like my father, Rob?"

Rob hesitated. The clip clop of the horses' hooves on cobblestones echoed along the empty streets. "No, sir," he finally answered. "Perhaps you're right. After all, she did a fine job with you."

Rob fell silent as Ward's mind wandered over his boyhood. For as far back as memory served, Ward had summered with his grandmother in Newport; from the age of twelve he'd lived permanently with her in New York. No doubt the prospect of rearing a child at her age had been daunting, but she'd never wavered in her commitment. Smiling a little, Ward remembered her occasional warm embrace and gumdrops silently slipped into his hand for work well done. He ought to take some time to visit her soon. Because of Rob's absence, he'd missed spending the past Thanksgiving with her.

"How was your trip to Worcester, Rob? Is your brother now duly married?"

"Yes, sir," he said. "Your presence was missed."

"You conveyed my apologies, correct? You told them I needed to attend business during your absence?"

Rob nodded. "It was understood."

Of course they understood. They all had Montgomery blood—Boston blood—running through their veins. There wasn't a born Bostonian who didn't understand the maxim "business before pleasure."

As they neared the wharf, the soft, tangy scent of the ocean filled Ward's nose. Another corner and there it lay, white-capped and gray, reflecting the sky. Ward took several deep breaths. As always, the salt air stirred his blood, the water sloshing against the wharf sang to his heart. Waves of yearning washed over him. Two years had passed since he'd swallowed the anchor, but he still missed sailing as much as when he'd stepped off the *Sea Gypsy* for the last time.

Rob pulled the horses to a halt in front of Ward's countingroom. As Ward took up his hat and cane, anticipation tingled in his blood, temporarily easing his heartache. "Make her fast there, Rob, if you please, then follow me. If I'm not mistaken, you'll want to see this."

A few minutes later they walked past the stairway to the storeroom, through Rob's office, and into Ward's. Ward's eyes flickered over the room. It was as expected.

"It's cold. Shall I star—" Rob's gaze fell on the small window in the back. "Sir! Your window's broken! You've been robbed!"

Ward nodded. "But if it follows the pattern of the past break-ins, not of much. A scoop of coal, some tea, and you see my jar is empty." He nodded to where he kept his supply of gumdrops. "I left a box of fudge on the desk last night. That also seems to be missing, although," he said, glancing into the wastebasket, "there's the box, along with what's left of my windowpane."

"You don't like fudge." Rob's eyes widened. "Your windowpane, sir? In the trash?"

"He appears to be a very tidy thief," Ward answered slowly, for the neatness disturbed him.

"A tidy thief?"

"Aye. I've had that window repaired three times in five days. Every time it's the same. He breaks the window, lights a fire, eats my gumdrops, and drinks a couple of cups of tea. At some point before leaving, he sweeps up the glass, cleans the teacup, and replaces the tea caddy. I believe he's living here."

"I'll inform the police immediately," Rob said, grimly.

Ward shook his head. Doubtless the thief was no more than a homeless boy, and not, he told his overactive imagination, a woman. "Not yet, Rob. For all his vagrancy, he's relatively honest."

"Honest! He's a thief!"

"Of food and coal only. I keep a hundred dollars in that drawer, and it's not locked. He's never touched it, nor the frame with my grandmother's picture, nor that gold paperweight. As desperate as he appears, he takes nothing but what he needs."

"All right," Rob said. "Instead of arresting him, we shall install a locking shutter and drop the key outside the window. At least it will save you the cost of replacing the pane."

"A fine notion, but I've decided to catch him," he answered and his stomach did a merry little jig. It had been months, perhaps years, since he'd indulged in anything half so exciting. "I suspect he's no more than a homeless waif; God knows Boston has enough of them. Captain Arnold needs a cabin boy. We'll put the waif to work and collect payment for the glass. I haven't the heart to charge him for the candy."

"You left the fudge for him, didn't you?"

"The lad needs something more substantial to survive on than gumdrops."

"Sir, you cannot save all the homeless waifs in Boston. Not even you have those means."

"No, but I intend to save this one. I like him. He's persistent and," he said as he settled himself behind his desk for a long day's work, "loyal. He disturbs no office but mine, no matter how many times I fix the confounded window. I plan to catch him tonight. Are you with me, Rob? I could use the assistance."

"You have one of Papanti's assemblies tonight. The Cabot girl and Miss Curtis will be there. Miss it and you risk offending Papanti and Mrs. Otis. You might lose your subscription."

"Damnation." Ward sighed in disgust. "Sometimes I wonder if that subscription is worth the effort. I've felt Papanti's blasted fiddle bow on my back more than once. My grandfather lost the use of his arm fighting English tyranny and what does Boston do but seventy years later? We engage an Italian tyrant to run our social lives!"

Rob grinned. "You've learned the rules well enough, sir, that you don't feel the bow anymore. And to lose the subscription, especially when you're contemplating marriage, would be a severe disadvantage."

"Sometimes I wonder if marriage is a severe disadvantage," he grumbled.

"Not if you consider the family name."

The family name, Ward thought as the holystone of duty once again settled in his chest. The once-hallowed Montgomery name, blackened by his father, and the Montgomery fortune depleted by the same. Long ago Ward had made it his mission to restore both and had spent the best years of his youth as a sailor, then captain, learning the business of his forefathers. A landlubber these days, he managed the business by day and used charitable deeds and impeccable manners to court Boston society by night. Fortune restored, family accepted. All he needed now to set "Montgomery" back among Boston's elite names was to marry a woman of long Boston lineage. The sort who attended Papanti's assemblies.

"All right, all right, point taken, Rob. I shall attend the blasted ball tonight. And tomorrow's Sunday. We'll come for the waif on Monday," he finished as a nagging little voice continued, *A proper Boston wife and a couple of sons—*

"I'm promised to Teresa on Monday," Rob argued.

"This should prove more interesting."

—and my life's work will be done. At twenty-nine. If I die, I shall scarcely be mourned, having accomplished all. At twenty-nine.

"All right," Rob said with a sigh. "Ought you to leave something else for him to eat? As you said, sweets won't sustain a growing boy."

Does life not hold more for me than that?

"I want him hungry enough to keep returning. We'll feed the lad better when we capture him."

"Sir," Rob said into the pitch-black office. "I don't think he's coming."

"Pipe down," Ward rasped. "We don't want to be heard."

"It's past three."

Crouched in the opposite corner from Rob, Ward shifted his pistol to his left hand and pulled his collar tighter around his neck. The stove's fire had long since ebbed and the deepening chill of the ocean air penetrated the building, seeping through the wool of his black frock coat. Outside a wind had whipped up, rattling the window-panes, an ominous sign to a seafaring man—and a danger to Ward's homeless waif. A nor'easter was brewing.

Frowning, he stared at the window across the room. Where was he? He'd come every night for the last seven. Had something happened to him?

The wind stopped crying for a moment. The sound of stamping hooves on wood and the jingle of reins filled the vacancy. His carriage. Stupid, damn fool, he'd bidden his driver to wait for them!

"Rob," he whispered, "send the carriage. First, though, enter through one door, then exit—quietly!—out the other. We want our intruder to believe we've left. Then hide yourself until I call you."

"The carriage! Of course! Why didn't I think of that?"

"Perhaps," Ward replied with a trace of humor, "because you weren't reared by a grandmother with a hawk's eye. Deception comes in handy."

Rob left. Fifteen minutes passed. Twenty. Twenty-five before Ward detected a slight scraping outside. A moment later a board broke the window far more quietly than Ward would have believed possible. He held his breath and watched as two small, gloved hands gripped the bottom window frame. The intruder grunted lightly and his feet slid along the brick. A minute later a figure pushed through the window, then fell to the ground with a thump, emitting a distinctly feminine, "Oh!"

Good God, it *was* a woman!

As she rose Ward did also, leveling his pistol. "Hold perfectly still, madam," he said calmly. "For I have my pistol aimed straight at your heart."

Chapter Two

Horror took Morgan's throat in a death grip, wrapping its long bony fingers around her cold flesh. Caught! She was caught! But that wasn't possible; he'd quit the office, quit the wharf altogether, she'd made certain of that. Oh but he hadn't, he'd tricked her somehow, and God help her, he'd send for the watch. She'd be facing the black-hooded executioner in no time.

"Rob!" The gun holder shouted in a devastatingly familiar voice, deep and masculine with a rasping edge—Captain Montgomery. Memory sent her pulses tripping as the man who'd climbed into the carriage strode through the door.

"Light the lantern, Rob, if you please. I warn you again, madam, I have a pistol," the captain said as Morgan stepped backward, wondering frantically if she might yet slip out the window. She heard the scratching of a match and the lantern came to life, creating a small halo in the middle of the darkness. Suddenly Morgan found herself staring straight at Captain Montgomery—and a large, shiny black gun. Good God, he wouldn't shoot, surely not? Her heart fluttered like a moth trapped in a young boy's hands.

"Good God, it's a woman!" the other man exclaimed.

"Aye," the captain answered. "Slip that hood back, madam. Let's have a look at you. Rob, there are two more lanterns in your office. Be so kind as to bring them in after you rekindle the fire in the stove. It's as cold as a blue flugen in here. Madam, I told you to drop that hood. I meant it."

With shaking fingers, Morgan pushed back the hood of her cloak and struggled to establish an outward sense of composure. Would the captain recognize her? She wore her wig and had lost at least two stone since last seeing him. She stood stock-still, her eyes following every movement of his hawk-like face with its high angular cheekbones and hard, aquiline nose. He passed his gaze over her curiously and even though she could not detect the color of his eyes in the semi-darkness, she remembered them well enough, deep-set, long lashed, and a breath-stealing liquid brown.

Seconds turned to minutes. She detected no flicker of recognition on his face and slowly, silently, she started to breathe again. The tension in her muscles eased, even as regret touched her heart, for she recollected *him* quite well. Her mind cast back to a picture of him standing on the ship's deck, the ocean spread all around them and the billowing white sails so tall they seemed to scrape the azure sky. His legs were spread to accommodate the ship's rocking, hands clasped behind his back, and his thick, wavy hair fluttered in the wind. In her mind's eye he wore his rare smile, complete with the left-cheek dimple, which fit so poorly with his general reserve.

Tonight, however, his face was as grave as the dead, and instead of his well-cut captain's uniform, he was dressed in all black—overcoat, trousers, satin waist-coat—chosen, she realized with a lurch of her heart, to conceal his large figure in the dark.

Rob, slighter and younger than the captain, with lightly oiled hair and a softer version of his counte-nance, returned with two lit lamps. Darkness fled to the corners of the room, leaving wavering shadows behind.

"You're shaking," the captain said finally, his voice cut-ting through wind rushing past the building. "Are you cold?"

"A trifle," she said, attempting to hide her British accent, one of the few correct facts published in the Philadelphia papers about the Wicked Widow.

"Rob, move my desk chair to the stove, if you please. And would you kindly hook the shutters again?"

Morgan glanced at the window. She'd broken the shutters a week ago. Apparently he'd replaced them. But why hadn't he locked them?

She focused on the pistol again. Because he'd planned to capture her, that's why.

"Madam?"

She lifted her gaze. The lamp light edged his face in shadows, making his expression difficult to read. Rais-ing one arched eyebrow, he nodded toward the stove. "No doubt you'll find that chair more comfortable than standing."

She obliged him, but her stomach complained loudly and she couldn't resist glancing at his candy jar. Empty, she saw with a wretched tug of her equally empty stomach.

"Here," the captain said kindly, withdrawing a silver flask and a small package wrapped in brown paper from the large pockets of his coat. With a trembling hand, she accepted the gifts. She placed the flask on the chair next to her, then opened the package. A *sandwich!* And beef, her favorite! After stripping off her gloves, she took several small, delicate bites. She dearly wished to stuff the entire thing in her mouth, but with the captain watching she ate slowly, like the proper lady she'd once been.

When she was about half finished, the captain said, "The flask contains brandy. It'll warm you some."

Brandy. Ladies didn't drink spirits. But then ladies didn't flee murdered husbands and hide out in wharf offices, either. She'd already sunk beyond reproach, what difference could drinking brandy make? Picking up the flask, she pulled the stopper, took a whiff, and jerked her head back at its potency. Rob, who'd positioned himself on the desk lightly swinging one foot, chuckled. She ignored him and took a small sip. She coughed at the harsh, deeply alcoholic taste, and her eyes widened when it blazed a fiery trail down her throat. Oh, it was perfectly vile! Then the fire subsided, leaving a soft glow in her half-frozen throat and belly. All right, she'd drink it.

"Feel a little better?" Captain Montgomery asked.

She nodded. "Yes, thank you." And then, because she'd never been one to postpone misery, she asked timidly, "Do you intend to summon the watch?"

He stared at her a minute. "The watch. You're English."

Oh no, it wasn't the watch in America! It was the police! How could she be so stupid?

"What," he continued, "is an English woman doing sleeping in my countingroom for seven nights in a row?"

"The hotels were full, sir," she answered, then cursed her unruly tongue, even as Rob snickered.

"I find no humor in this situation," the captain said. "You're in serious trouble. If you refuse to cooperate, I *will* send for the police. Do I make myself clear?"

Flinching, she nodded and finished the last bite of her sandwich.

"Then you shall answer the question," he said.

She hesitated. For a moment she considered laying her story upon the soft-eyed captain and trusting in his mercy. But she'd trusted in mercy before and born the bruises for it. What man could ever truly understand a woman's subjugation, a wife's plight? What man would ever accept her remedy, however unintentional? Certainly not master-of-the-seas Captain Montgomery.

"My family came to America searching for a better life. They didn't find it."

He frowned. "Dirty as it is, madam, your cloak is constructed of cashmere and silk. Your gown is of satin and fine lace and your gloves are fur-lined kid. Despite your present circumstances, you weren't always a pauper."

Her spirits sank. He was too clever by far, and she too unschooled in deception. *Oh, Mother, what good will all those years of French tutors do me now! Could you not have taught me anything about being common?*

After taking a fortifying sip of brandy, she said, "I stole the clothes."

"You stole them?" he asked with a child-killing scowl. "They fit you perfectly."

"I'm rather particular about my thefts," she replied.

"Fine," the captain snapped. "Rob, send for the police."

"No!" she gasped. "Oh no, please don't!"

"I'm certain they know better methods of extracting the truth than I do."

"I'm sorry! I promise to be honest! Please don't send for them!"

Rob shifted uncomfortably, saying in a low voice, "Sir—"

"Then answer the question, madam. First, however, honor us with your name."

"Morgan—" She paused to take a few deep sips of brandy as she recollected the false name she used at the

Tremont, Boston's most exclusive hotel and the only one that took Richard's Philadelphia bank money. "Brown."

He scowled, disbelief settling on his face. "Proceed."

All right, she thought wildly and took another long sip of brandy to forestall him. How could she explain silk on a vagrant? Only people of means could afford such a gown. Might she have a husband who cast her out in disgrace? No, Captain Montgomery would attempt to return her to him. A lover then! Perfect! A once-upon-a-time generous lover. "My family couldn't feed us all and so I—I was compelled to seek other means of support."

"No working girl could afford that gown."

"Not that form of support," she said, cringing at her own audacity. His eyes held hers for several heart-stopping moments, while a dreadful little thought wiggled through her brain. She'd always fancied the captain. Perhaps if she offered him—oh, but she could not!

"Rob—"

"No!" Oh no, he didn't believe her! "Not the police!"

He tilted his head slightly. "No, madam. Rob, would you excuse us for a few minutes? You might summon my carriage."

Rob quit the room, leaving her alone with Captain Montgomery, and with the brandy acting like fertilizer, those indecent thoughts took root in her brain.

"You were saying, Miss Brown? Or is it Mrs. Brown? Did you marry this form of support?"

She shook her head.

"Of course," he said in a light, conversational tone, as if he wholly believed her story—or fancied her a prime liar. "Was it just the one or have you taken many lovers?"

"Only—only the one." She hid her growing dismay behind sips of brandy.

"How old are you?"

"One and twenty."

"And when did you meet this man? Does he have a name?" His tone changed abruptly; he snapped out questions like she was one of his crew.

"Conrad Jones."

"Jones. Your age at the time?"

"Nineteen."

"And your family? Where are they?"

"They live in Boston."

"Does Mr. Jones support them as well?"

"Certainly not!" she cried, indignant on behalf of her fictitious relations.

"Then they've found lovers also?"

"They work!"

"Where?"

"In factories."

"What factories?"

"Textile factories."

"We don't have any textile factories in Boston."

"Then—then—" Hadn't she heard another name? It had stuck in her mind, for it was an English town— "Gloucester."

"Gloucester's a fishing town."

"Well, I don't know where they went! Why would I care a rap for that? I had Mr. Smith—"

"Mr. Jones."

Oh no! How could she have confused that? It seemed that while the brandy facilitated the melting of her conscience, it also fogged her brain. Attempting to drag it back to clarity, she said, "There were so many—"

"There was 'only the one.'"

"All right! So I lied! I'm a common tramp, can you blame me?"

He stared hard at her a moment, then turned. "I'm

sending for the police." He started for the door and horrified, Morgan jumped up and lunged toward him, snatching at his clothing.

"No! Please, no! I'll—I'll do anything. Anything you want, please—"

"Miss Brown!" the captain said, seizing her shoulder with his left hand. "Good God, woman, I have a gun in my hand!"

What did a gun signify when hanging threatened her? Ignoring his attempts to dislodge her, she lifted her right hand to caress his face, cleanly shaven except for a set of modest side-whiskers. He was taller and far broader than currently fashionable, but by her way of thinking he was uncommonly handsome—and she so frightfully desperate. "Anything," she whispered, squelching both tears and propriety.

The hard lines on his face softened to a curious v etched between his brows. He carefully shifted the gun, pointing it at the floor. Reaching up, he removed her hand from his face. The warmth of his bare fingers sent delightfully improper shivers down her spine. "I don't believe you're a common tramp, Miss Brown."

"I'll do anything," she whispered, lifting her left arm to wrap it around his neck. With a shudder of anticipation—oh, she was a tramp by nature if not by design!—she pulled his head down toward hers.

"Miss Brown," he said, gently, attempting to remove her arm. "I have no desire—"

"You'll see," she interrupted, and stood on her toes to press her mouth against his. As Bart had taught her years before, she slipped out her tongue and let it glide along the crease between the captain's lips, tentatively begging entry. When he didn't respond, she almost relented. But then a picture of the gallows slithered through her thoughts, and panicked, she continued stroking his lips until he yielded with a groan. Oh, he tasted like pepper! Pepper and brandy, a wonderful, heady combination. She tightened her arm around his neck, pulling him closer to drink more deeply of the kiss. He responded by sliding his soft, wet tongue over hers, exciting delicious sensations in her secret areas. Her brandy-fed legs weakened. Much more and they'd buckle—

He lifted his head abruptly, breaking free of her grasp. Her arm fell away, as he whispered, "You taste like brandy." She saw heart-pounding desire gleaming in his eyes. But was that her triumph or her dishonor? Oh, what did that signify? All she wanted was to kiss him again.

"You do, too," she answered.

"And yet," he said, using one strong arm to firmly set her back into her chair. "I must decline your offer."

Oh no, she thought, reaching for the brandy. What now? The police—

"And you'll drink no more of that," he said, taking it from her.

"I'm still cold."

"And," he said gently, "dirty. And half-starved. I'll have the truth now, Morgan."

The use of her first name, spoken in his deep, masculine voice, made her belly flip-flop. For so many years she'd been a lady; strange gentlemen never called ladies by their first names. "He—he dismissed me."

"Who did?"

"My lover."

"Oh, for God's sake! One more lie and I *will* send for the police. The truth, and now!"

"I'm not lying!" she protested. "I—I disgraced him. He became angry and sent me packing."

"Smith or Jones?"

"Neither. I'm not at liberty to provide his name. He's married and his wealth is derived from his wife's family. If they knew of my existence, he'd be ruined."

"Surely you don't believe I'd spread this story around town?"

"I've no notion what sort of man you are. Perhaps you'd resort to extortion."

Captain Montgomery's grimace expressed how little credence he gave her story. "If he has cast you to the streets, why do you care?"

"He may seek revenge. I'm afraid of him. He—he beat me."

"I see," Ward answered slowly, although he didn't really see, nor did he entirely believe her tale. To be sure, something about her struck him as familiar even under that horrendous wig. Might he have seen her on someone's arm? No, not if she feared her lover's family. Still, she was no unschooled farm girl; with one short kiss she'd ignited a fire down below. If not for the fact that her wet clothes had dampened his own, returning him to his senses, he might easily—

No. Impossible. What kind of man would take advantage of such a desperate offer?

"Sir?"

"Yes?"

"I'm hungry."

"I gave you that sandwich."

"And thirsty."

"You don't need any more brandy."

"And dirty, and damp, and tired. If you—if you take me home with you, I shall make it worth your while. I promise."

It wasn't her face, but her voice, too low to be precisely feminine, and marbled with a sort of irrepressible levity despite the most desperate of circumstances.

When triggered, he knew the amusement would come out in deep, melodious laughter, ending in a sound a little like the gurgle of ocean water running by a docked ship. But how could he know anything about a vagrant woman?

He heaved a sigh, and scowled at her. What in damnation was he to do with her? She appeared terrified of the police, and he could scarcely blame her. At best they'd haul her to prison. At worst they would heave her back to the street. Poor thing, her face was dirt-streaked with dried tears, and her eyes held the haunted expression of a back-alley cat, having learned to survive as prey and hunter, but frightened of both.

He sighed. He stood between the devil and the deep blue sea, for he couldn't in all conscience send her to the streets, nor could he with any sense of respectability take her home. But it was well past four in the morning and he hadn't slept all night. It would have been so damned much easier if she'd been a cabin boy.

Conscience beat respectability.

"All right."

"Herman, you're still awake?" Ward asked his butler as he and Rob escorted a sleepy Miss Brown into his house's dimly lit, mahogany-paneled entrance hall.

"Certainly, sir. I'd never go to bed before you returned home."

"Well, you ought to have," he replied. Sometimes well-trained servants were a distinct disadvantage. He'd hoped to slip the girl in unseen. "This is Miss Brown, a cousin of Rob's from Worcester. She's been in a carriage accident and requires assistance. Would you be so obliging as to find her a bedchamber where she may wash up and rest for the night?"

Herman's eyes flickered for the briefest of moments, but he nodded, took Miss Brown's dirty elbow, and proceeded upstairs. Rob stared after him, his eyes following Herman's progress up the curving staircase. Ward stripped his gloves and waited for the tirade that Rob's tight expression had threatened the entire ride home.

"*My* cousin! Good God, Ward," he snarled when Herman was out of hearing. "If my mother hears of this she'll hang me!"

"Worse," Ward answered, removing his hat and coat to lay them on a marble-topped corner table, "if it comes to my grandmother's ears." He crossed the hall to the library, his boot clipping business-like on highly polished marble.

"Your grandmother lives two states away!" Rob followed hard on Ward's heels. "My mother lives but two towns from here! Whatever possessed you to bring the woman to Beacon Hill?"

"You'd have me send her back to the street? Rob, it's freezing!" he spat back, closing the heavy library door behind Rob. A welcoming wood fire crackled in the grate, courtesy of Herman who regularly attended Ward's needs before he knew of them himself. Recently installed gas lighting bounced off the mahogany bookshelves of Ward's favorite room, bringing him a small measure of comfort—until Rob's next explosion blew it from his chest.

"Well, she can't stay with you!" Rob snarled, dropping his own outerwear on Ward's desk. "We should never live down the scandal!"

"Fine," Ward snapped, and marched toward a window. "We'll take her to your house." He yanked open its red velvet drapes to reveal an angry dawn and a small enclosed garden shaded in winter gray.

"Teresa would love me for that."

"Which is why it's infinitely preferable that Miss Brown be *your* cousin and *my* problem." As he'd suspected big, white snowflakes had started to collect upon the ground, turning it white. "At least I have no fiancées with which to contend."

"She's not my fiancée yet," Rob reminded him bitterly.

"That's none of my doing," Ward said, crossing the room once more to fall into his favorite easy chair. "I offered to set you up in whatever style you deemed necessary to marry Teresa. You refused."

"A man wants to care for his own."

"Hopefully before she dies from old age." He leaned forward to extend his numb hands toward the leaping flames.

"Oh, for God's sake!" Rob spat. "This is all beside the point. What do you mean to do with the girl now that she's under your protection?"

"For the love of God, Rob, sit down and warm yourself. I fear the cold has destroyed your brain's functioning."

"I'm not cold. I'm too worried to be cold. And you haven't answered the question!"

"I mean merely to assist the girl out of her difficulties, as you well know."

"Not in return for the payment she's offered, I hope!"

"Of course not."

"Although it shall certainly appear that way!" Rob replied, running fingers through his hair as he paced in front of the fire. "We must remove her from your home, and quickly too, before the other servants hear of it."

Ward sighed, and suitably thawed, leaned back, folding his arms over his chest. "They'll hear soon enough. I don't recall swearing Herman to secrecy."

"You ought to have."

"Only to have Mrs. Bartlett discover the girl asleep in one of the rooms later?"

Rob scratched his head and frowned. "There must be somewhere we can place her, some female who would take her for us."

"An excellent notion," Ward answered derisively. "We'll hand her over to Teresa. No doubt she'll be pleased to receive a ragamuffin off the streets."

"Not Teresa. Someone else."

"Think, man! If the woman you love won't take her, who else would?"

"Confound it, Ward, your grandmother will rake you over the coals when she hears of it! You know that! How long do you mean to keep her?"

"The girl or my grandmother?" he asked with a slight smile.

"This is not a laughing matter!" he snapped, shaking a finger at him. "You've pledged your life to clear the Montgomery name of scandal. Bringing a vagrant woman into your home isn't exactly the best way to go about it!"

The amusement riding through Ward's chest subsided, leaving behind his habitual heavy heart. "They'll say I'm my father," he said wearily.

"And your grandfather before that."

Ward rubbed his neck where the muscles corded. "We'll find her employment of some sort. A factory or mill work."

"She's already sleeping in your bed."

Narrowing his eyes, Ward replied, "She's not in *my* bed, Rob."

"It's your home. They're all your beds," he said, waving one hand in an arc.

"Then what do you propose I do? Send her to the

stables? Have her sleep with the stable boys? Aye, sir, that will quell the gossips!"

"Send her to sleep with the maids."

"It never stopped my father," he growled. An oily pit opened in his stomach at the recollection of his father's use of the maids, and the consequences.

"Fine," Rob said, leaning against the mantel. "If you insist upon following this course of action, then I shall stay as chaperone."

"Another excellent scheme! Instead of *one* man abusing the poor woman, it'll be both of us!"

"By God, we'd do no such thing!"

"Certainly not, but upon hearing of your stay, our families will expect the worst. Your mother will hang you, my grandmother will give me a sailor's blessing *and* a hanging party. And even if the story never went beyond this house, our families would never forgive us for such recklessness. That's no solution."

"Oh, for the love of God," Rob groaned, and finally dropped into a chair opposite Ward. "This is mad." He stretched his feet toward the fire and stared moodily into the flames, brow dark with thought, while Ward searched his weary brain for a solution. A hotel perhaps? But every hotel in Boston knew the Montgomery name.

"Well, then, what if you *are* discovered? What is the worst that can happen?" Rob asked after a time. "We are, after all, full grown men, Ward. This is nothing others haven't done before us."

"Not," Ward said icily, "in Boston."

"Your father did and your grandfather before that."

"And you wish to follow those examples?"

"No," Rob said, with a sigh. "Well then, we shall let her rest a few more hours while we search for somewhere to place her. Our two heads will doubtless devise some respectable scheme."

Ward glanced toward the window, and shook his head. "It won't be our two heads, Rob. Look outside. The snow thickens."

Scowling, Rob followed Ward's gaze to the blur of white outside the window. "It will ease."

"It won't. It's a nor'easter. By noon that wind will blow strong enough to unhair a dog."

"A nor'easter? But it's only November!"

"Nevertheless, you ought to shove off." Ward rose and walked to his desk where he picked up Rob's coat, hat, and cane. He held them out. "It falls, I suspect, at almost an inch an hour. If you wait much longer, you'll spend the night."

Rob's eyes widened. "Ward, you must reconsider—"

"I'm out of options. She stays."

Rob's shoulders drooped and he too rose. Silently he took Ward's offering, and shrugged into his coat. While Rob buttoned it, they walked together into the hall, still empty, although already Ward could hear the sounds of stirring in the sleepy house. The smell of java drifted up from the kitchen below. "All right," Rob conceded, "she may stay for this one night! For that," he said, putting his hat on, "you might still be forgiven, as such affairs are not a general practice of yours. Possibly you've built enough credit in Boston that it will be dismissed as a whim."

Ward flashed a small smile. "Even though, in truth, I've done nothing wrong."

Rob shrugged fatalistically. "It's not what we do, but what we seem to do that matters."

"You've missed your calling, Rob," Ward said, opening the entryway door to a curtain of falling snow. The street was deserted, the common across the road slowly taking on the fairy-tale atmosphere that only new-fallen snow could give. A half inch had piled up on his stone steps. "You would have made an excellent Greek philosopher."

"Certainly. I shall write the book tonight while the snow falls! Tomorrow morning, sir! Bright and early!"

"Not too bright, please, and not too early. Neither of us has slept this night."

With that Ward closed the door on the snow and Rob's stickler of a conscience. His eyes ran up the stairs. Which room, which bed, did Miss Brown presently occupy? *They're all your beds.*

He hadn't lied; he thoroughly intended to deflect all improper offers from Miss Brown. But when he remembered that kiss, he wondered just how successful he would be.

Morgan awoke, enraged, to the sound of a distant howling and, nearer at hand, the scraping of metal. Was Father unlocking her door finally? Would she be given a real meal today or would she be obliged to dine on bread and water yet again? Three days in her room for a few scarcely profane utterances was far too rough a punishment!

Oh, she thought, snuggling deeply in the feather ticking, her bed felt so incredibly soft this morning, even with hunger tightening her belly. But what *was* that incessant noise? She opened her eyes.

A maid stood at the stove in the corner, adding coal.

The howling came from outside. Another maid pulled back pink damask drapes revealing a cloud of white whirling powder outside the window. Snow. A snowstorm.

"Good afternoon, miss! The master bade us wake you and bring you downstairs."

The master—Captain Montgomery. Her stomach

quivered as the night's adventures rushed back to her. She was not at home in Sussex, but in Boston, Massachusetts, sleeping in the bed of a sea captain. Not a young girl furious over her father's tyranny, but a thrice-widowed woman, poor as a church mouse, who had offered the use of her person in exchange for food and shelter. She sucked in her breath. Well, she'd had the shelter already.

She sat up slowly and surveyed her surroundings having been too exhausted the night before to take much note. She'd slept in a large and sumptuously appointed room, with a thick crimson and gold carpet, rose-flowered wallpaper in the French tradition, and intricately carved rosewood furniture. Such a favorable comparison to Richard Turner's penchant for the spires, arches, and trefoils of Gothic design. And his equally Gothic treatment of his wife.

"Here, miss, swing your feet out," the servant said cheerfully, ordering her like she were a mere commoner. Which, Morgan supposed with sinking spirits, she now was. "And we'll take a look at you, Shannon and me. There, Shannon, I fancy she's more your size than mine. You'll have to lend her *your* gown."

Although approximately Morgan's height, Shannon appeared a good three stone heavier. With a smirk, she dropped a worn blue cotton gown on the bed, along with a threadbare corset and two tattered petticoats. "I'll lend her my clothes but not 'til she bathes! She'll wear her own to the kitchen."

A bath! Oh! Oh! They were taking her to *bathe!* Whatever came later little signified. If she could bathe, then she would gladly take on the world and Captain Montgomery with it!

A half hour later, hair and wig washed, Morgan sat scrubbing her skin all but raw in an enormous brass tub encased in mahogany. By some modern miracle it had both hot and cold water spigots, and steam drifted off the water. It was set in a windowless closet in the basement next to the kitchen where the delectable smells of dinner floated in the air mixed with rose-scented soap. Morgan's stomach growled angrily, and she dearly wished she could eat and bathe simultaneously. Bread or vegetables or meat—anything but gumdrops. She wished never again to behold another gumdrop.

Finished scrubbing, she dropped her sponge with a plop into the water, shifted until she was almost wholly submerged, and then leaned her head against the rim. Heaven, simply heaven! She wished she could bathe weekly, *daily*, even if Father did believe such practices indecent. Grimacing, she recollected his ire one day when she was fourteen and, because of an increasing interest in the male sex, found herself constantly primping—and bathing. "Bathing so often is not only unhealthy, but obscene!" he'd raged. "A decent lady avoids nudity as much as possible, but you seem to revel in it. Enough! You leave me no choice but to restrict your full-emergence bathing to once every two months. Between times, you shall use a bucket and sponge like everyone else."

The situation had not improved with Bart, her first husband, a sailor who fancied her penchant for bathing peculiar, or Philadelphia gentleman Charles Weatherly who thought it not only odd, but costly. His house possessed no indoor plumbing and carrying water to and fro wasted a servant's time. And Richard, wealthiest of all, had hated everything about her. She sucked in her breath, shoving pictures of his last moments out of her mind. With him she'd dared not indulge in an act even remotely pleasurable lest he use it against her.

But at least Captain Montgomery apprehended that weeks of dirt could not be entirely washed away with a sponge and bucket. Either that or, she thought with a quaking in her belly, he liked his women clean.

Oh good gracious, what had she gotten herself into? Had she truly made those vows? Surely the brandy had done her talking, not her? What sort of woman would offer the use of her person simply for food and shelter? A good woman, *a lady,* would rather starve to death, die of disease, freeze in arctic temperatures than sell herself. If she possessed even a scrap of decency she'd clothe herself right now and sneak out the back door before the captain collected on her promise. What signified a raging storm when her very honor was at stake?

A sudden gust of wind howled by the house, and she winced. What sort of woman made such a bargain? The sort who would elope with a sailor to escape a domineering father and the equally domineering constraints of London society. A woman who, widowed and destitute, would marry two more men, one old, one cruel, for the sake of food and shelter. How many others followed suit? Perhaps in the end the only difference between marriage and her offer to Captain Montgomery was a few lines from a book, a piece of paper, and a gold ring. And *this* way, she reminded herself with a lightening heart, no law compelled her to stay with him should matters get out of hand.

Besides, a wayward voice chirped in the back of her mind, *Captain Montgomery is* so *handsome.* His kiss had made her skin tingle. What if—

A pounding on the door interrupted her thoughts. "Miss Brown! Others are waiting for the tub!"

"I shall be just another minute!" she yelled back, and then emerged from the tub, toweled herself dry, and attempted to dress herself in borrowed clothes—the maids had taken hers for washing. But the corset was too loose around her waist to secure, and the petticoats' tapes wrapped twice around her, making them impossible to tie. Grimacing, she pulled the gown over her naked body—then groaned in frustration. Although the dress was the right length, her much-diminished bosom couldn't fill the huge bodice, which gaped open to allow a shocking view of all her charms.

"Miss Brown! Come out or I swear I'll knock the door down!" Shannon, the witch, yelled.

She sighed. The fit of the dress scarcely mattered. Decency had fled with the howling wind. She quickly arranged the hair of her wig into a simple chignon, then pinned it firmly on her head. With a few deep breaths, she collected her courage and opened the door.

Gas lamps on the wall held back the early evening gloom descending upon the parlor; a coal fire in the stove held back the cold—a waste of money. Ward's blood still burned from last night's kiss. Taking another sip of brandy, he shoved that recollection aside for the fifth time in an hour, and leaned forward in his armchair to peer at the parlor clock, a heavy brass ornament sitting atop a white marble mantelpiece. Half past five. Soon Miss Brown would join him. He'd ordered a late dinner and cancelled supper altogether. He planned to eat quickly, discuss Miss Brown's future briefly, and then retire—early. Very early, long before the lonely evening hours whispered to his faltering conscience that he gratify his desires and take the woman to bed.

He took several more gulps. Was it enough? Liquor was his only defense against the grievously overheated passion inherited from his father, held firmly in check for over a year. Hathaway, letch that he was, had told him many times that liquor dulled a man's ability to perform for a woman. Ro would know; before marrying Fran he'd drunk like a fish. No more, however. With such a wife he'd want to be in tiptop form at all times.

Closing his eyes, Ward sighed and leaned back. By God, he'd appreciate Ro's company tonight. Or Huntington's. Both would tease him to death over this situation, Ro encouraging him to "try the girl on." Edward would laugh, slap him on the shoulder, and advise him to drink more. With a name like Huntington, Edward understood the relentless pressure bearing down on Ward's shoulders. Ro understood nothing, but offered his friendship freely, never attempting to see inside Ward's soul, something Ward valued beyond words.

But Ro was with Fran in Marblehead, and Edward was an ocean away visiting his brother at Oxford. Ward had an open invitation to Ro's home, but given his own failed past with Fran he'd thus far declined. Tonight, however, if not for the storm, he'd cut and run without so much as a backward glance.

The door to the parlor opened, startling Ward. Slowly he rose from the yellow-striped damask sofa as Miss Brown entered the room. His breath caught in his throat. The dress she wore hardly fit, and from the way her breasts bounced as she shyly stepped forward, he suspected that she wore no corset. The skirt of the dress flowed freely without a single petticoat to hinder her movements, perfectly indecent. The blush on her face, however, and the way she held her hand against the bodice attested to a degree of modesty entirely at odds with her clothing—and her earlier proposal.

"They told me to meet you in here. For dinner."

The bath had uncovered a very pretty woman with a

pert little nose and skin as smooth as satin. He knew
from experience her rose-red lips were soft and yielding. If not for the brassy blond wig, she'd have been
beautiful.

"Aye, madam. I trust you slept well? You appear more
comfortable than last we met."

"Thank you, I am," she said and moved toward him
hesitantly.

Up close her eyes were a wild, sparkling sea-green.
They seemed to reach out to touch him, stroking the
part of his heart that yet mourned the ocean. Familiar.
Too familiar. He'd have sworn on the Bible that he'd
stood with her before, just this way, with those eyes
pulling at his heart, while all else tugged illicitly on his
passions, for she belonged to someone else. But who?
No man of his acquaintance would dare leave a woman
in such a predicament. No man of sanity would forfeit
such a treasure.

The door opened again. "Dinner is served, sir,"
Herman said.

At the interruption, Morgan dropped her hand and
turned her head toward the door, breaking their gaze.
Ward's treacherous eyes swiftly moved to her gaping
bodice. He sucked in his breath. Good God, he could
see straight down her dress, could see everything from
her rose-tipped breasts, to the curve of her waist and
hips, to the snatch of dark curls just below her navel.

She turned back to him, and he jerked his gaze
upward to catch those incredible eyes again. She raised
one silky eyebrow in question.

Damn, damn, damn. Having drunk two glasses of
brandy, he was but half seas over. He ought to have
gotten thoroughly bilged, because what he'd thus far
consumed had done nothing but dull his restraint.

"Thank you, Herman," Ward said, bracing himself for the longest dinner of his life. "It's rather chilly, Herman. Would you be so obliging as to procure Miss Brown a shawl? Miss Brown, if you would lend me your arm," he said turning to her with a light bow, "I should be honored to escort you to the dining room."

Chapter Three

A sea captain's deportment, Morgan decided as she relished each lovely bite of roast duck, resembled that of a gentleman in every way. In his deep, sea-salt voice, Captain Montgomery kept up an easy flow of conversation about the fickle Boston weather, the entertainments of the city, and current literature. When she'd dined on his ship she'd not noted his manners. Newly widowed and destitute, she'd been frantically attempting to engage Charles Weatherly's attention, a wealthy widower in need of a wife. Now, however, she had the captain's full attention with which to contend, an attention she'd brought upon herself by invading his office.

As the butler removed the second course, Morgan nervously sipped her claret. One more course and then—

Oh Lord, she thought, quickly shifting her thoughts and gaze to study Captain Montgomery's huge blue and cream appointed dining room, lit by a blazing birchwood fire and a hissing crystal gasolier. Like all the public areas of the house, the furniture was old-fashioned, but perfectly preserved, in the gentle curves of the Chippendale style. On one hand, the simple furnishings proved the captain, as she would have expected, to be only a moderately situated man, and the lack of gilt adorning the room bore that out. On the other hand, the wallpaper seemed expensive, a deep, vibrant blue accented in green and brown oak leaves, with a flocked and gold embossed border. The thick carpeting muffled the sound of the captain's exceptionally trained servants, who appeared as if by magic when needed, then faded into the background.

"If you wish to learn more about New England literature," the captain offered, "you might consider *The House of Seven Gables,* by Hawthorne."

"Perhaps I shall," she answered, focusing her attention upon the captain once more. Her breath caught in her throat. He was dressed casually, but elegantly, in a royal-blue frock coat and sky-blue silk waistcoat embroidered in silver. His pristine white linen shirt and cravat contrasted sharply with his black hair, and lovely, lovely brown eyes. In fact, she owned as she drained her glass of wine, everything about the captain far surpassed all three of her husbands, from manners to countenance. The more she drank the easier became the prospect of lying with him, submitting to his kiss, his touch, and anything else. At the start of the evening the contemplation had dug a monstrous pit in her belly, but now as the final course commenced, sparkling anticipation filled that pit. Her father was correct. She possessed the soul of a wanton. The wine made it easier to bear.

"Would you care for a glass of madeira with dessert, madam?" the butler asked.

Biting the inside of her cheek, Morgan nodded, although she'd drunk too much already. A lady ought to drink no more than one glass of wine at a meal, and that only when offered by a gentleman. She was no lady.

She took a sip of madeira and met the captain's eyes.

As had happened more and more frequently during dinner, when their gazes met her heart lurched, her nerves sizzled. His eyes, warm early in the evening, now glittered hot and dark.

Captain Montgomery had drunk a few glasses of wine, too, and while he didn't appear to be in his cups, she fancied that he'd also imbibed some brandy before dinner. As they ate dessert his eyes strayed more and more to her scandalous bodice, which she'd attempted to cover with an ugly purple shawl provided by Herman. And still he maintained that agreeable flow of conversation. His manners were better than a gentleman's. They resembled a saint's.

"Thank you, Herman," Captain Montgomery said to his butler clearing away the dessert dishes. "That will be all."

It was time.

Morgan's hands trembled, her stomach fluttered, her lips grew tender in expectation of his kiss. Those few short moments in the captain's office had sent her pulses racing. How would it be, she wondered feverishly, when he wasn't shocked into kissing her back? How would he kiss when he *wanted* to? How would it feel when he lifted her skirt—

What sort of woman *was* she?

A woman, some resentful part of her brain answered, who had scarcely been hugged or kissed since Bart's death. A woman starving for affection.

The butler exited, leaving only the blue brocade drapes and blinding white tablecloth to witness her final fall from grace. The captain shifted his chair backward and dragged his wineglass to the edge of the table, his fingers so tight around the stem she wondered why it didn't break. She lifted her eyes to his face to discover his hot, hungry gaze fixed upon her. Licking her suddenly dry lips, she asked, "Did you wish to retire, sir?"

He stared at her mouth for a moment, then caught her eyes again. "I wish to discuss your plans."

She swallowed hard, held those lovely dark eyes with hers, and rose. "Yes, sir," she said hoping not to sound as shy as she felt. As far as he knew she'd spent the last few years as a kept woman. She slipped the shawl from her shoulders and stepped toward him. Balancing her backside on the edge of the table, she reached for the ties of his cravat.

His eyebrows shot up. In a trice he shoved aside his wine and seized her wrists, bearing her hands downward. With a shudder—excitement or horror, she didn't know—she realized that his interest wasn't in his cravat. It was far lower.

"Not those plans, Miss Brown," he said.

Blushing she nodded and dropped her eyes. He released her wrists, and with shaking hands she reached for the fastenings of his trousers, her fingers brushing against his staff. A ripple of indecent excitement ran down her back.

He gasped and once more wrapped his fingers around her wrists, this time so tightly she winced. Could he be like Richard? Oh, he couldn't *enjoy*—

"Not those plans either!" he snapped.

She lifted her eyes and their gazes locked, his blazing with desire. Then his eyes fell once more to her bodice, for during her efforts she'd leaned forward, unconsciously offering him a clear view of her breasts. Her skin warmed where his eyes touched.

"Good God, woman," he gasped and shut his eyes. "Cover yourself."

Drawing a trembling breath, Morgan looked down at her imprisoned wrists. In all other ways the captain appeared a gentleman, but his hands were not the soft, exquisitely manicured hands of her former friends. His were strong, long-fingered, and callused—a man's hands.

"I cannot," she whispered.

He opened his eyes again, the tight muscles of his face testifying to his battle over the passion electrifying the air between them. "You must. I did not bring you here for this."

"We agreed—"

"It seems you mistook my meaning. I agreed that you were dirty and hungry and in need of assistance, nothing more."

But she'd spent the better part of a day preparing for this! And now with the combination of wine and attraction she truly wanted him. Her mouth longed for the feel of his lips moving against hers, her body for the press of his large, hard-muscled body. She licked her lips and said with the same foolhardy impetuousness that had begun her American adventure, "I liked kissing you. You taste like pepper."

He drew several more breaths and the restraint started to dissolve in his eyes, making her own breathing low and labored. She tried shifting her gaze upward, but it scarcely helped. The dim lighting of the gasolier turned his hair a gleaming blue-black. Her hands itched to run through it, to feel those crisp strands sliding between her fingers.

The fire's flames found a knot in the wood, spitting and sputtering in the lengthening silence. "You ought not to have said that," he said finally.

They locked gazes again. "I rarely say what I ought to, sir."

"That," he said with a glimmer of a smile, "I can readily believe." Another deep breath. "Do you ever behave as you ought to, madam?"

"Not often enough."

"What you ought to do right now is adjust that dress."

"Which way?" Oh Lord, she couldn't have said that—it was the wine—

His hands shook. "To conceal your—*damn*," he swore softly.

"It doesn't signify," she said huskily. "You still possess my hands."

He lowered his gaze to regard his fingers, so tight around her wrists her skin formed wrinkles. "If I release them, *I* may behave badly."

"Do you often misbehave, sir?" she quipped, tilting her head slightly.

"Rarely," he said with a wry twist of his lips.

"Regardless, if you're suggesting I escape when you release me," she answered, "it's pure folly. Cowardliness is not in my character."

"Nor is rape in mine, but I've drunk half a bottle of brandy and a full bottle of burgundy this night. I'm not entirely in control of my actions. You are unwise to tempt me further."

"I liked kissing you," she reminded him.

He stared a moment longer before, with another twitch of his lips, he said, "Then I suppose, madam, I should be remiss not to repeat it."

With that he released her and, rising, leaned forward to take her face in his two hands, fingers splayed against her cheeks, his callused palms rough against her flushed skin. His eyelids lowered as he covered her mouth with his, moving his lips gently as if to beg entrance. She yielded eagerly, but he hesitated, tracing her bottom lip with his tongue in a sort of teasing promise. She rose on her tiptoes and encircled his neck in a silent plea for a

more intimate touch. His hands tightened on her face
and he surged inside. The bold sweep of his tongue
transferred his pepper-and-port taste, and sighing in satisfaction she drank deeply, savoring every last drop.

A shudder ran through the captain's body, and he
lifted his head. His face carved in hard, desperate lines,
he searched her eyes as if uncertain of the honesty
behind her touch. Then a tight smile tugged at the
corner of his mouth and he dropped his head for another kiss, this one harsh, thirsty, demanding. Primed
with wine, her body reacted with a flood of desire, forming a hot pool between her legs. For a moment the
world slipped away and she felt nothing but the soft
courtship of his tongue and dark, wet welcome of his
mouth as he alternately encouraged, then demanded,
her own exploration.

Not enough, not enough, her nerves cried, and she slid
her hands down his back to grasp his taut, muscled but-
tocks. Standing on tiptoes she pressed against him, desperate to connect with the hard masculine areas so
perfectly designed to scratch the itch growing inside of
her. His staff pushed against her belly, and she groaned
in frustration.

He lifted his head. His hot breath fanned her flushed
cheeks. "Morgan . . . ," he rasped. "Quickly, we'll go to
my bedchamber."

Up a set of stairs, perhaps two, affording them time to
reconsider? Oh, never! Even now propriety hissed warnings to the wanton controlling her actions. And Captain
Montgomery appeared to be a high stickler in all things.
If he considered too long these actions, time might well
change his mind, leaving her with this horrible, aching
itch. "No," she said in a husky whisper, sliding a hand
along his hip to the front of his trousers. "Here."

"Here? What? Woman, if you touch me that way—Oh

God!" he gasped when she slipped her hand under his drawers to stroke his hot, thick staff.

"Here," she said, "on the carpet."

"It's dirty." With a backlash of his arm, he sent their goblets to the floor. Crystal shattered as, in one effortless move, he lifted her onto the table and pushed back her skirts, exposing her secret parts to his hungry gaze. Holding her breath, she shut her eyes against the heat rushing to her face and the persistent whisperings inside her head. *A lady never—*

His hand brushed across her thigh and his thumb flirted with the quivering bundle of nerves between her legs. Seconds later he slipped a finger inside her. She jerked in shock and her eyes flew open.

"You're ready." His sea-salt voice turned the words into a gentle caress, mixing oh so sweetly with the erotic thrills his touch ignited. He moved his now damp hand to her thigh, and spreading her legs, stepped between them. After releasing his staff, he carefully slid inside her. Morgan gasped, for her body easily stretched to receive him without any of the scratching to which she was accustomed.

"Damn," he swore, sucking in his breath as his eyes closed in tortured ecstasy. "Damn, you feel good."

After a couple of seconds, he opened his eyes to catch her gaze. Under the glitter of desire lurked that liquid-brown kindness, touching her shaking heart. "Hold on," he said, slipping partly out. She gripped the table as he grasped her hips with both hands, and he started a slow, easy rocking, rubbing against her swollen female parts with every thrust, transforming the itch into a sparkling tickle. The tickle spread through her body, making her skin tingle. *Wonderful, oh wonderful,* she thought, and wanted to reach out and draw the captain close, to share with him the amazing sensations tripping over her nerves. But the tightness of his jaw, the deep grooves around his mouth, discouraged it. He appeared somehow to be restraining himself.

Then the tickle surpassed enjoyment, transforming again, this time into craving for more and more stimulation. A sort of tormenting pleasure coiled low in her belly, increasing with each passing second. Her thighs shook and the world beyond them faded away. Morgan saw nothing but the captain's eyes, heard nothing but the blood pounding in her ears, wanted nothing but for him to bring an end to the torture.

Abruptly he stopped thrusting, and she whimpered in protest. A muscle in his jaw jumped as, holding her gaze, he slid his hand from her thigh to the "v" of her legs. He spread the petals, and then pressed on the tingling bud hiding there. Her body jerked; lightning flashed across her nerves. "Now, Morgan," he commanded in a rasping whisper as he stroked her with butterfly lightness. "Come." The coil tightened, then burst in writhing, rushing waves of pleasure, drowning her muttering conscience, washing away the last remnants of deportment and convention.

"Oh dear God!" she exclaimed, gripping the table desperately to prevent herself from falling over.

From somewhere far off, she heard the captain swear softly. Abruptly he started moving again, a wild, rough pumping, which brought her fresh thought-destroying spasms, ripping her breath from her chest. After several hard thrusts he shoved deep inside her and with a low triumphant growl spilled his seed, filling all the empty places he had left to reach. The pressure of his groin against her engorged bud and the feel of his hot seed flowing through her sent her over the edge again with a spine-tingling explosion that reached every last nerve, right down to her toes.

She fell forward, spent, and rested her flushed face next to the scratchy embroidery of his waistcoat. Enfolding her in his shaking arms, he invited her to lean into him, his quick short breaths fanning her neck. She wrapped her arms around his waist and snuggled deeper in his embrace. The fire crackled and the grandfather clock in the hall rang seven chimes in a low, booming voice. A gust of wind shook the window panes, a fierce reminder of the storm without and of the comfort and safety within. As she regained her breath, a feeling of contentment settled around Morgan, like a lazy summer morning, and she sighed. "That was incredible."

"Aye," he answered. After a moment, he shifted slightly to plant several tiny kisses along her neck. "But it wasn't enough."

"Not enough?" she repeated, surprised. It certainly felt like enough to her.

He straightened and slid his hands down her back, then up along her waist, halting just below her breasts. His eyes gleamed with lazy desire as he leaned forward to give her a long, melting kiss. Her still-wet female parts, as if starved instead of just fed, jerked excitedly. When he moved his right hand over her breast, his thumb grazed her nipple through the thin cotton of her gown, and her entire body flushed in renewed anticipation of more love-making. She played with the hair at the back of his neck, as with one more heavenly stroke of his tongue, he lifted his head.

"Not enough," he said, with a slight smile. He palmed her breast again, eliciting a shiver of delight, then stepped back to carefully remove his spent member. With a twitching of his pants, he hid it in his drawers, then fastened his trousers shut. His eyes flashed as he seized her waist and slid her feet to the floor. "We've scarcely touched. Come to my bedchamber. We shall have greater privacy there." He wrapped his arm around her waist.

"Can you?" she asked, surprised. "Again?" Bart had never attempted more than once, Weatherly had barely managed that, and Richard—but she wouldn't think of him, not right now, not after Captain Montgomery's magical touch.

"Once more at least," he said, guiding her to the door. A moment later they mounted the stairs. Her feet barely touched the rugs as they whisked past pictures hanging on the walls and delicately carved furniture. Gaslights lit the corridors against the night's gloom, along with astonished, white-faced servants who knew exactly what they were about. She didn't care. Captain Montgomery didn't seem to, either.

When they entered his room, she briefly noted several oil burning lamps and a huge mahogany bed, tall enough to require steps, draped in emerald and gold velvet curtains. A fire blazed in an enormous fireplace. Wood smoke perfumed the room. No coal? But she didn't like coal.

He shut the door and reached for her, swiftly pushing her oversized gown off her shoulders, letting it fall to the floor in a circular lump. Then while kissing her deeply, he yanked on her borrowed chemise. Old and worn, it ripped under his strength and joined her gown. Afterwards he stepped back, running his gaze greedily over her while pulling at the ties of his cravat.

Clenching her teeth against a sudden wave of embarrassment, Morgan looked over his shoulder, to find her image reflecting back at her from an ornately carved standing mirror in the corner. She was naked except for her frilly garter belt, torn white stockings and black boots. Her face was flushed.

As she took in other details, her eyes widened, for she hadn't looked at herself in weeks. It seemed that after six months of Richard's painful "suggestions" about dieting, and three weeks of living on soup, bread, and gumdrops, she now possessed the thin, pallid figure of a fashionable woman. Too thin. Her once rounded hips appeared angular, and each breath she took outlined her ribs. Stomach wriggling uncomfortably, she turned away from the imposter in the mirror and crossed her arms over her too-small breasts.

The captain had dropped his cravat and was pulling on the buttons of his frockcoat. He stepped forward to take her wrists and gently pull her arms back to her sides. "Don't do that. I want to look at you."

"You—you can't possibly. I'm so thin."

His eyes fixed on her breasts, he took a deep breath, tore off his coat, then started yanking at the buttons of his waistcoat. "You're beautiful. Remove your shoes and stockings. I want you entirely naked."

His words shocked her into paralysis. Every word out of his mouth was erotic, heating her blood. But every word was also a command, inciting rebellion. "No," she answered in a low, frightened voice. Frightened of what? Of him? No, of herself, wrestling to establish control over her person, yet dearly wishing to surrender every last inch of it to his touch.

"Very well," he said, two deep grooves appearing between his eyes. "Then you may help me out of my clothes." He dropped his waistcoat to the floor, then proceeded to unfasten blue and silver embroidered braces.

She wrapped her arms around her chest, fighting back tears of frustration. "No."

He threw his braces over his shoulder, then pulled his shirt from his pants. Eyeing her, he unbuttoned it and he yanked it over his head, revealing a muscular expanse of chest, lightly matted with dark, silken hair. He lifted one eyebrow. "It's a little late for shyness."

She merely stared back, incapable of forming so much as a syllable.

Hands on his hips, he studied her while continuing to speak in a soothing voice that belied the roughness in his words. "You offered yourself to me in my counting-room, Morgan, and again in my dining room. You made no complaints when I took you there, nor did you argue when I brought you here. If you're now changing your mind, you'd better cut and run, for when I've finished with my clothing, I intend to remove yours."

"Oh Lord," she whispered. "Must you be so dictatorial?"

His lips twitched as he stepped backward to sit on a green brocade divan tucked under a velvet draped window, and started to remove his boots. "I've captained a few ships in my time, madam." One boot dropped to the floor. "I'm accustomed to command." The other followed.

"I don't relish being commanded," she said, watching him yank off his stockings. Her heart sped up. He had only his pants and drawers left to remove, and then—

"You obeyed well enough downstairs," he interrupted her thoughts, as he rose to unfasten the buttons on his pants. The amusement in his eyes spread across his face in the wide, devastating smile she'd not seen since she'd crossed the Atlantic. The deep left-cheek dimple appeared, robbing him of years, robbing her of will. For a few seconds she could hardly breathe.

"I—I don't recollect following any commands," she answered when she could speak. Not fair, she thought, closing her eyes against the seduction of that smile.

"You came," he said, in a low, husky voice, "on my

command. Would you like that command again, Morgan?"

Flashing recollections of those moments, of his hands moving between her thighs, the teasing stroke of his fingers, brought a flood of wet heat in her private areas.

His pants slithered to the floor, and she heard the creaking of wood as he crossed the room. He stopped just inches from her, desire rolling off him in waves. Trying to ease her rising fever, she breathed deeply, but that only exacerbated the problem, for he smelled like a summer afternoon at sea, with the crack of thunder and the flash of lightning looming on the horizon.

The captain rested his hand on her shoulder. She opened her eyes. The flickering of the firelight cast the hard sinew of his arms and flat planes of his sparsely furred chest in heart-pounding relief. A tight black line of hair marched down his stomach, ending in a thick patch of midnight black curls, from which his staff proudly sprang. "Is that what you meant downstairs?" she asked, catching his gaze. "I've never heard such a thing. It's—it's a vulgar usage, isn't it?"

His kind eyes glinted with barely leashed passion as he slid his hand from her shoulder to her cheek, cradling it in his palm. Caressing her cheek with his thumb, he dropped chaste kisses on her forehead, the tip of her nose and her mouth. "To peak," he said in his harsh voice, "to climax, to come to orgasm." He slipped his other hand down to brush against the sensitive skin of her thigh. "Would you like that command again?"

"Yes," she gasped.

With a low rasping laugh, he bent his head to nibble her ear and her neck, while his hand slid up her thigh, over the curve of her waist to her breast. His thumb grazed her hard nipple. "Your skin is soft as a dove," he whispered in her ear. "Touch me again, Morgan, like you did downstairs."

"Oh, I can't," she gasped. "If I let go, I shall swoon."

"I'll catch you," he answered, then moved his mouth to take possession of her mouth, suckling her tongue while lightly stroking her breast. Her knees buckled and she slumped against his chest. After one last sweep of his tongue, he lifted her up to deposit her on the bed. It sank in soft acceptance as he knelt at her feet to remove her boots. Grasping the bands of her garter, he pulled her stockings over her knees, to her calves, to her ankles, and off. Then he reversed the caress, both hands working up her legs, stroking her sensitive skin as he shifted his position to slip his knees between her thighs. Afterwards he slid his hands over her bare thighs, his fingers so near to the apex that she groaned. Through half-closed eyes she watched him, her body moist and eager for his entrance.

His hands glided over her thighs and across her hips, while he leaned forward to kiss her mouth—hot, wet kisses, which traveled from her mouth to her chin, then blazed a trail across one trembling breast. Her skin burned where his lips touched, her private parts swelling as blood coursed downward. His tongue flicked out to circle her nipple, bringing incredible, glittering sensation. He licked it slowly, leisurely, and she whimpered, curling her fingers in his hair to hold him steady. In response, he covered her with his lips and she felt his hot breath seconds before he drew her deeply inside, sucking gently, transforming the glittering sensation into a rippling in her belly. While alternately laving and suckling one breast, his fingers caressed the other. Wild, wanton pleasure built, making her writhe. She couldn't bear it—she moved her hand from his head to his shoulder, thinking only to bring him forward, to convince him to enter her and end it.

Instead his hand slid from her breast downward, caressing her thigh before moving to part her trembling lips and touch the pearl hidden inside. He stroked it, combining the pleasure from his mouth on her breast with that of his fingers, bringing an eruption of hard, convulsing pleasure. Her head jerked forward and she cried out.

His fingers stilled and she fell back to the pillow. He shifted to speak in her ear, his voice low and amused. "You didn't wait for the command. Were you one of my men, I'd punish you. Instead," he said, bringing her hand to his staff, "I think we'll enjoy more of this."

She took several deep breaths, staring into his thickly lashed eyes as she tried to straighten her careening world. "More?" she protested in a whisper. "I fancy my body can't stand more, sir. It will kill me for certain." But when her hand closed around his pulsing erection, her body responded with renewed excitement.

He ran a finger across her protesting lips. "If this can kill us, madam, we shall both go to our final destination with smiles on our faces. First, however," he said, reaching for her head, "this must go." With that, he pulled at her wig and tossed it over the side of the bed. Then, as he moved in for another kiss, his eyes suddenly widened and with a rush of panic Morgan knew she'd been discovered.

"By God!" he gasped, jerking back to stare down at her. "You're that sailor's wife!"

Chapter Four

Morgan stared up at Captain Montgomery, biting the inside of her cheek as she attempted to settle her wildly thumping heart.

"Drumlin," he said. "No, not Drumlin. He hoisted anchor while on board the *Sea Gypsy*, and you married that other passenger, from Philadelphia. Weatherby—Weatherly. Good God, woman, what are you doing *here*?"

Oh no, what was she to do now? She could scarcely think with her mind fogged by desire. But she must take control of her reason, force it to fashion yet another tale. A simpler one, simpler and nearer the truth this time, to make the details easier to recollect. She was, some calm part of her thought ruefully, becoming quite adept at tale-telling. "He died."

Captain Montgomery's eyebrows drew together as he sat back on his heels. Morgan swallowed, wondering if he'd put the next puzzle piece in place. "Died, did he? Was it his heart?" When she nodded, a slight, self-satisfied smile curled his lips. "I expected as much. If you'd troubled to ask my advice, madam, I should have warned you that he wasn't the man for you. Did he die recently then? Is that why you're on beam ends?"

"On beam ends?"

A smile lit his eyes. "I apologize. It's sea-talk. Is that why you're in such a hard condition? He lived longer than I should have credited. I thought he'd be dead in six months."

Well, he'd more than doubled that, she thought with a touch of merriment. It'd been fourteen.

And three months later she'd married Turner—the merriment disappeared.

"Yes, sir. He left me without a farthing."

"But wasn't Weatherly fairly well-to-do? Not top of the trees on the social scale, but not a pauper either."

"He bequeathed his entire fortune to his children."

The captain's face wrinkled in disgust. "And left nothing to his widow? That's hard to stomach."

"He had six children, all grown. They thought his marriage to *me* hard to—to—" Stomach was a dreadfully vulgar word to use in a man's company. But after *his* use of vulgarity, how could hers be reproached? "To stomach, especially when it seemed—" She stopped completely.

He raised an eyebrow. "Proceed."

"When it seemed I'd provide him another."

The other eyebrow joined the first. "A child?"

"It didn't take."

A sudden softness entered his eyes, as he shifted his body to stretch out next to her. He propped his head up on one hand, gazing down at her. "I'm sorry." His harsh voice was streaked with gentle compassion, recalling to her mind his warm treatment after Bart died. "And yet, with this child on the way, he didn't alter his will? Did you think to ask?"

"I—I never considered it. He seemed in fine health to me, and I miscarried very early on."

"Were you ill?" he asked a frown appearing between

his eyebrows. "You've lost a considerable amount of weight since last I saw you."

"Yes, sir. I—I miscarried twice." Another fib; she'd had only the one with Weatherly, but Turner's would count as the second. Besides, it might enlist extra empathy, something she dearly needed.

"Still, I should have thought that knowing you were capable of having a child—"

"It seems—it seems not. I lost Bart's also."

His eyes widened. "When? Good God, not on board ship?" At her nod, he snapped. "Why didn't he inform me?"

She let loose a disbelieving laugh. "It's not the sort of situation a woman wants reported. Besides, it happened shortly after Bart's death."

Such warm brown eyes . . . He peered at her a moment, and she could almost see thoughts flowing through his brain. "Did Weatherly leave you nothing at all?"

Several trifling bits of jewelry, which she'd sold to purchase mourning clothes. After two months it became frightfully clear that Charles's relations would rather cast her to the street than settle any money on her—not truly a surprise as her conduct had given them every occasion to detest her. And so she'd sought another husband, this time making a far more dangerous choice. "Nothing."

"Then how could you travel to Boston? *Why* did you come to Boston?"

After a half-day's practice, lies slid off her tongue like melting butter. "I was desperate, so I stole some money and fled."

He tilted his head slightly. "How much?"

How much was too much to fear being jailed, but too

little to keep her in comfort? "Three hundred Pennsylvania dollars."

He nodded and her muscles relaxed slightly. "But why Boston? Weatherly has family here who, I imagine, know about the theft. Wouldn't another city be less dangerous?"

"Charles and I stayed in Boston for a fortnight before we traveled to Philadelphia, and I don't know any other American cities. For safety's sake I purchased the wig."

"Ah. Of course."

She suppressed a smile of triumph. But hadn't she missed her calling in life! She ought to have written adventure stories or those so-clever romances, like Alexander Dumas! Or, she thought with a touch of blighted spirits, murder stories. She'd proven shockingly capable of that, too.

"You ought to have told me the truth, Morgan."

"You had already threatened to summon the watch. I—I didn't relish adding fuel to that flame. You don't intend to send for them now, do you?" After what they'd done tonight, he could not possibly be so callous as to send for the police. Or could he? Was three hundred dollars much money to a sea captain? With the cut of his clothes, his richly decorated home, his full staff of servants, it seemed unlikely. But she'd fancied Charles to be worth considerably more also. What had remained after paying his debts had scarcely been worth dividing amongst his children.

He considered for a moment. "No, but I'm hanged if I know what to do with you."

She smiled mischievously. "You might," she said, excited color rising to her face, "teach me more of that vulgarity."

Ward drew in a breath as blood surged to his staff, which had softened slightly during the course of conversation. Parts of Morgan's tale rang true, other parts sounded no more credible than a sailor's yarn. He couldn't quite put his finger on where her story strayed from believability, but after staring into those sea-green eyes, he decided it could wait 'til morning. For now she lay naked in his bed, this beautiful, wild sea-maiden whom he'd secretly lusted after for that entire voyage two years ago. With another rush of excitement, he realized she was everything his imagination had conjured up during those three weeks—hot, passionate, uninhibited. Tomorrow he'd ponder all the possible solutions to her difficulties.

With a half-smile, he reached over to cup one rose-tipped breast. "I've not done half what I intend," he said, teasing her nipple with his palm. She moaned and the sea breakers of desire rose once more in her eyes, preparing for the inevitable crash. He leaned forward to cover her mouth with his and forgot everything but the need to satisfy the hot, sweet desire burning between them.

Clock-like, Ward woke early to a peculiar silence—the storm had ended. He opened his eyes to stare into the gloom of his shrouded bed. Curtains drawn for—what? He never drew his curtains.

His eyes adjusted and fell on the woman in bed next to him. For privacy. Memory came back in a flood of heat, stirring the embers of last night's passion.

Morgan. Morgan Drumlin—Weatherly!—curled into a "c." A fringe of her rosewood hair fell across her forehead, curling across the alabaster skin of a face which in sleep appeared young and innocent—in marked contrast to the heady images sailing through his mind. He pictured her naked between the sheets, the white skin of her rose-tipped breasts flushing as his thrusting brought her to climax. And later, the devilish sparkle in her ocean green eyes as she slid one of those slim hands down to waken his slumbering staff.

His heart jerked into a rapid beat as he hardened once more. As silently as possible he took several breaths to fill his lungs, suddenly desperate for air. With each breath came the musky fragrance of spent love, combined with the smell of sweet ocean air. Perfect, the perfect lover-like scent for a woman he'd wanted from the moment she stepped on board the *Sea Gypsy,* husband be damned. Fascinated by her abundant curves, enthralled by the full-throated laugh, he'd scarcely been able to take his eyes off her. Even after her idiot husband had fallen to his death while showing off among the rigging, even after she'd hooked Weatherly. But Montgomery men didn't marry sailors' widows, and three weeks later, heavyhearted, he'd watched her walk down the gang plank and out of his life.

And now she was in his bed. He frowned when he suddenly recalled the conversation earlier in the evening. Had she come out of desire or desperation? Last night, fueled with brandy, he'd believed the former. But last night he would have believed anything.

She opened her eyes. For a second she appeared puzzled, then she smiled sleepily at him. "Good morning."

"Good morning. Did you sleep well?"

"Well enough—for the time we slept," she replied wickedly.

He flashed his half smile and touched her cheek, so incredibly soft. "I confess I had rather too much drink last night. I'm not altogether certain I made my intentions clear. I didn't bring you to my bed in acceptance of your offer."

Morgan's eyes widened as a jolt of alarm shot through

her barely awake heart. "Are you saying I still owe you for the food and shelter?"

"Good God, no! You never did. I merely want you to understand that last night was purely about enjoyment. For me, at least."

She relaxed again. "And me also."

"You seemed—pleased," he said, eyeing her warily. "Some women, however, are adept actresses at this sort of thing."

"I shouldn't know how to play that part."

"No?" he asked. "Honestly?"

His voice sounded as hopeful as a child requesting a puppy, touching Morgan's heart. Her strong, reserved captain had surprising pockets of vulnerability. "Honestly, sir."

He slid his hand from her face to lightly stroke her breast. "Then perhaps we'll extend our evening a spell longer." With that he pressed his lips to hers in a hot kiss, which set Morgan's senses reeling. When he pulled her through the covers to lie on top of him, she shifted to straddle his body. Then she took the control of both the kiss and their passion, running her hand through the light fur of his chest to feel his heart's fast beat. Wet desire settled in her secret areas.

"I can feel your excitement," he rasped, touching the v of her legs, pressed against his rising staff. "With just a kiss."

"You kiss very well."

In answer he pulled her head down to kiss her again and again until breathless and dizzy, she slid sideways. She didn't realize she'd reached the end of the bed until, tangled in blankets and sheets, she fell through the curtains and to the floor with a thud.

She yelped. Seconds later a monstrous, yellow spider reached for her, sliding its long prickly arms across hers.

Screaming, she jerked away. When it followed her, she screeched again, seized the odious thing by its hair and flung it across the room.

A moment later the captain chuckled and she perceived upon further inspection that the spider was, in fact, her wig.

Face warm with embarrassment, she looked up at him. He'd shoved aside the curtains and lay at the edge of the bed, the silken fur of his chest dark against the sheets. "Flipped your wig, did you?"

"It's not funny," she said, even as amusement tickled her throat.

"Perhaps not from your perspective."

"I thought it was a spider," she said, with a laugh.

"A blond spider?"

"I didn't take the time to consider its color." She leaned forward to try to free herself from the sheets wrapped around her legs.

"Apparently." With that maddening eyebrow raised, he watched her a moment. "Are you coming back up?"

"That depends on if you're still 'up.' Oh!" she gasped, putting her hand over her mouth. "I can't believe I said that!"

His eyes sparkled. "Well, Morgan, I shall certainly be up if you come."

"Oh!" she said with another deep laugh. "Nor ought you to have said that!"

"We said much worse last night," he replied in a low, caressing voice.

"But that was last *night!*"

"We are as alone this morning as last night. What's the harm?" His dimple appeared and Morgan's heart fluttered. As always that dimple and the amusement in his eyes erased his usual gravity, dropping years from his countenance.

Without thinking, she blurted out, "I like your smile."

His smile softened. "Do you? I like your laugh."

"No," she replied. "You're quizzing me."

"I'm not."

"I have been often told it's too loud."

"I don't think so."

"Truly?"

"Aye. It's genuine." He propped his head upon his hands and said with a small sigh. "What *am* I going to do with you, Morgan?"

"I daresay," she said tugging at the sheets again, "you might consider lending me your aid."

"Certainly." Shoving back the blankets, he slid out of bed, stark naked, to kneel on the rug next to her. "Here, you'll need to roll to my left."

"I'll hit the bed."

"My other left," he said with a dimpled grin. "Don't you know your left from your right?"

"I know my right and left perfectly well, thank you. It's yours I've forgotten."

"Then be so accommodating, madam, as to roll to *your* right, toward the blond spider. Don't be afraid! It doesn't have teeth."

Laughing, she obliged him. Free at last, she sat up, smiling. "Blond spider. It's not nice to tease me so."

He grinned. "I enjoy it."

She leaned against the bed next to him and pulled the sheets across her legs. "You remind me of my brother."

"Your brother?" he asked as he reached up to pull the blankets down, too. "That's not exactly the sort of thing a man wishes to hear when sitting next to a naked woman."

"And what precisely does a man wish to hear when sitting next to a naked woman?"

"Moans and sighs," he answered, spreading the blanket over them. "And many yeses."

"Hah! Men wish to hear 'yes' from women continually, day or night, whether she be stark naked or clothed from head to toe."

"Some men, I suppose. And so, Morgan, tell me about this brother of yours," he said, the smile melting away.

"I miss him. He tried—" she stopped, frowning. Tried to ease her father's autocratic, domineering ways. Father had always been far more lenient with Reggie.

"Tried? To do what?"

"My father was a rigid disciplinarian and a stickler for the conventions."

"I see it had a great effect on you."

"It did, but the opposite of his expectations."

"And where are your people? Back in England?"

She sifted quickly through her mind for yet another tale. Lord, but it was all becoming so dreadfully tangled.

"Don't," he snapped. "When you hesitate in that manner, it means you're concocting another lie. I'd rather hear nothing at all."

"It's complicated," she said softly.

"No doubt. Have you no family to turn to at all?"

"None."

"No friends?"

She hesitated a fraction of a second, then shook her head. "No."

With a furrowed brow, he answered, "Well, I can't return you to the street. What about a job?"

A job? Heavens no! Just because the captain hadn't read the newspapers didn't mean others hadn't. And if either Weatherly's relations or Richard's saw her—

"I have no skills."

"Factory work requires few skills," he said. "Or per-

haps we might find you something in an office or countingroom."

"Could I not stay with you?"

He raised his eyebrows. "Here?"

Was she truly going to make such a proposal? Oh yes,
she truly was, even with the certain knowledge that
she'd burn in hell for it, or worse, destroy any shred of
reputation she yet retained. "I'll—stay and—and keep
you company, if—" She gulped as she perceived for the
first time that he might already have that sort of companionship. Perhaps even a wife. "If you'll have me."

Captain Montgomery sucked in his breath. When she
winced, he took possession of her hands and rubbed
them gently. "Morgan, I'm flattered, but you ought to
seriously consider the other options."

Stung, she yanked her hands from his. "Of course. It
was a foolish notion. Never mind."

"I never said that."

She flung back the sheets and rose before he could
see the tears, wretched, wretched tears filling her eyes.
Oh what had she been thinking? Rash, foolish, impetuous woman! "You don't desire my continued company,
wholly understandable. I am but a woman off the streets
and a thief at that."

"Nor did I say I don't want you. What are you doing?"

"Searching for my clothes so that I may take my leave of
you."

"I didn't say that either. Morgan, stop—"

"On the contrary, sir, you sent me packing," she answered. Unable to locate her clothes, she wrapped a
sheet around her shoulders.

"I merely requested that you review your options. For
God's sake, Morgan, belay that!" She stumbled toward
the door, desperate to hide the shame searing her face

and welling from her eyes. He jumped up and seized her arm, pulling her backward against his chest.

"Confound it," he growled. "Don't cry! I hate it when women cry."

"I'm not crying!"

"Then what's that in your eyes?"

"Not tears!"

"All right," he relented. "You're not crying," he said, carefully turning her to face him. "But you must understand, I didn't reject *you*. I rejected the idea."

"But I *am* the idea, so it's one and the same!"

"Good God," he breathed. Taking her hand, he led her back to the bed. "You're shivering. Bundle yourself up with those blankets there on the bed, and pull back the curtains while I stir the fire. Then we'll discuss your plans."

Chapter Five

Ward couldn't believe he was even considering her scheme. The whole blasted thing was ludicrous. If his grandmother found out, she'd start with lectures about his obligation to his name, then move on to painful words about her disappointment with him, ending it all with a well-fashioned keelhauling. But the devil of it was, he kept hearing Rob's voice, *We're full grown men, Ward. It's nothing others haven't done.*

Careful to protect his bare skin, Ward took the poker, stirred the fire, and added more wood.

He was a twenty-nine-year-old man. He owned and controlled a vast fortune and had done so for eleven years. In all that time he'd had only two sexual affairs, both discreet and short, since, for the sake of his family name, he kept his passions tightly reined. On the other hand, his father by twenty-nine had had one wife and one child, kept a number of women, and bedded countless others. He'd contracted syphilis, then spread it to three unwilling servant girls, one who killed herself, heaping scandal upon scandal upon scandal on the Montgomery name. In comparison Ward was a saint. After adding a final log, he turned.

Morgan lay dead center in the bed, the blankets pulled up to cover her breasts, her dark hair hanging loosely around her shoulders. Covered so, her temptation ought to have diminished. But she was damned seductive and Ward had never felt less saint-like.

We're full grown men, Ward.

Rubbing the muscles in his neck, he crossed the room to join her. "So," he said as he slid under the blankets and fluffed the pillows next to her. "Are you adamant about not pursuing these other options?"

"I truly don't believe it's in my best interest."

"And so . . . you would become my paramour."

She sucked in her breath as if he'd struck her.

"Was that not your offer?" he asked quickly.

"It was. It's only that the term sounds so—indecent."

He rubbed his neck. "You've never done this before, then?"

"Certainly not! Did you think I had?"

"I did last night," he said dryly. "I've never kept a mistress, either, and therein lies the difficulty. I'm uncertain as how to conduct such an affair."

"I rather fancied—a man of your apparent wealth— has not your father told—"

"No," he said harshly.

"Oh," she answered, and then smiled saucily. "I daresay, then, that we're both virgins in such affairs."

He smiled. "Oh, we're the picture of innocence, you and I. No doubt anyone who walked through that door right now would elect us to sainthood," he said, waving a hand.

"Saint Morgan! Oh, I rather like that! Do you suppose they'd fashion gold statues of me?"

"Draped in precious stones," he said, chuckling. "Morgan, are you sure about this?" he asked, shifting his body so that his eyes could follow the movements of her face. "It's not an easy road you propose to travel."

She stared at him a spell, fear or regret washing through her eyes as she searched his face. Then the indecision melted away, and she reached up to touch his cheek. "I'm sure."

He stared into her eyes, listening to the dissenting voices in his mind. They created a virtual cacophony, warning him about the madness of this adventure, that it would certainly end in a ballyhoo of blazes with everyone involved getting burned. But those voices couldn't see her sea-green eyes, had never watched the breakers crashing in them during a night's passion. "All right. We'll do it." He leaned his shoulder against the headboard as his well-ordered mind started flipping through the details. "I believe the first order of business is finding you a place to live."

"Then I shan't live here with you?"

He shook his head firmly. "That's impossible."

"Why? Have you got—a wife?"

He lifted an eyebrow. "Do you honestly believe I'd engage in such an affair as a married man?"

She shrugged fatalistically. "Many do."

Wincing as memories of his father stabbed at his conscience, he said harshly, "Not me. Good God, you've been here a full day and more! Where would I hide her?"

Her eyes twinkled as she answered, "Didn't Blackbeard hide a few wives in a closet?"

"Bluebeard, Morgan. I'm no pirate."

"No, but you are a sea captain," she pointed out.

Sea captain. Of course, how would she know he'd forfeited his captaincy? What could she know about him at all? For a minute he contemplated confessing the truth of it, but one of his two affairs had jumped ship when he refused her excessive demands of money.

Besides, Morgan hadn't been exactly forthcoming about her own past, either.

"At any rate, I have no wife. And so—"

"Mayn't a sea captain keep a mistress in his home, then?"

"Not this one. I'll discuss it with—"

"I would not put you to such expense, sir."

Scratch out, then, excessive demands on his money— at least as long as she thought he had none. "If I couldn't afford to keep a mistress, I'd not be discussing it with you. Now, as to—"

"But how can you know that, when you've never done it before?"

"Morgan," he snapped, "that is the third time you've shoved your oars in while I'm talking. The first thing you must learn as mistress is not to interrupt your master."

Her face turned to granite, and her eyes darkened to the color of an angry ocean. "No man is my master."

Raising his eyebrows, Ward answered slowly, "And yet, that is precisely the nature of this affair, mistress and master." The thought sent a hot thrill coursing through his blood—Morgan as a sort of sexual servant. Good God, he possessed some of his father's flaws after all—

"No man," she said through gritted teeth, "will be my master. Ever. Not you, not anyone. If you expect me to address you in that kind, I shall leave right now."

He scowled. "And if you expect, madam, to run rough-shod over me, you are sorely mistaken."

She tossed her head arrogantly, and even half-naked with her hair hanging loose, she had all the bearing of nobility. "I desire only equality."

"You cannot have it," he said flatly. "As much as you

dislike it a mistress is, at the heart of the matter, an employee." Harsh facts, and he flinched, yet refused to yield. If she couldn't accept certain rules, the entire affair was doomed to failure.

Wasn't it doomed, at any rate? To behave so in Boston of all cities—he could just about smell hell.

And yet, with careful planning, a man could accomplish anything.

The anger dissolved in Morgan's eyes as she tilted her head a little. "An employee?" she said slowly. "But not necessarily a servant. I may as well be a sailor on your ship."

Amusement dug at the corner of his heart. "No sailor ever had such a rig as yours, my dear."

"No? But I shouldn't be just any sailor, you apprehend. I should much prefer to be your first mate." Her eyes twinkled mischievously.

He laughed a little. "First mate, eh? May I have a second mate also?"

She shook her head and smiled. "As I shall have only one captain, I request—strongly—that you engage only one mate. But," she said, running her fingers through the hair on his chest, causing a hot shudder. "I vow never to disappoint you in my mating abilities."

"Mistress, you have the very devil sparkling in your eyes."

"Aye, sir. So you will be my captain," she said as her hands slid lower, "and I shall be your first mate, and your second mate, and your one-and-only able-bodied sea woman. And when you call 'all hands on deck,' I will *come* running." Her hand curled around his swiftly rising staff and another fiery shudder ran down his spine.

"By God, Morgan, you have a way with words and an especial talent with vul—" She'd slid her other hand down too, to stroke the rest of his male anatomy and he groaned. He responded by slipping his hand below the blankets to caress one soft round breast, bringing it to peak. She gasped and he smiled. "I believe, Mistress, we'll discuss the remainder of our arrangements later."

Morgan enjoyed a long, leisurely breakfast, savoring every delicious bite. The previous night, nervous about the activities to follow dinner and spending much time gathering the strength to endure Captain Montgomery's love-making, she'd not wholly appreciated the food. Now with her usual lively spirits revived, she filled herself to bursting, bringing a smile to Captain Montgomery's harsh face.

"Have you enough?" he asked, wryly, sipping his coffee—java, he called it. She must remember that. Didn't a proper mistress learn to speak her lover's language? "Ought I to send for more sausages? Another dozen eggs? Perhaps several more bowls of oatmeal?"

She laughed and daintily finished a piece of toast spread heavily with jam. "Oh please do! And you might bid them start dinner. I fancy I shan't rise from this table until well past supper!"

"You'll resemble one of those sausages, if you do that."

"Ah, but a happy sausage I should be!"

"Why then, I suppose I should also be contented."

"As my happiness is paramount to your contentment," she said with a delighted little sigh. She sat back in her chair, beaming at him.

His eyes rested warmly on her. "It seems it is today. Are you finished?"

"Yes, thank you."

"Good," he said and rose from his chair. He turned to the butler who'd appeared from nowhere to remove the breakfast dishes. "Herman, when Rob arrives, please escort him to the library. Morgan, will you accompany me?"

She nodded and walked with him across the marble foyer into his library. It was large, darkly paneled and thickly carpeted, lined with bookshelves. To her right sat a huge gleaming desk. In the center of the room, before a roaring wood fire, were two comfortable armchairs and a sofa. She chose a chair nearest to the fire as the captain settled himself at his desk. "Wood again," she commented. "Isn't it quite expensive?"

He pulled several sheets of paper from a drawer. "It is, and not efficient, either, thus the stove there in the corner." He nodded and she glanced across the room to where a small stove stood. "But I prefer the smell of a wood fire."

"Me too," she said, breathing deeply. "And so, sir, what do we discuss? Or do we wait for Mr. Montgomery?"

The captain dipped a pen in ink and started to write. "I intend to set Rob about finding you a home. I think, to avoid complications, you'll be known as Mrs. Brown, a widow. It will add respectability to your living alone. Unless you object?" When she shook her head, he said, "Excellent. And to more immediate circumstances— you'll need clothes."

She glanced down at Shannon's blue gown. "You dislike my borrowed threads, Captain?"

He continued writing. "I prefer my mistress to dress a little better."

"Do you?" she asked, tilting her head. "I should think you'd rather she not dress at all."

He lifted his head to regard her, a slow smile walking across his face as his eyes took a quick tour of her person. "I should like that very much, when I visit. Between times, however, you'll require *some* clothing."

"Goodness no!" she exclaimed, with a chuckle. "I shall remain in bed during those dreadfully long hours and pine over your absence!"

His dimple popped out, warming her. He leaned back in his chair, twirling his pen. "You'll pine for me, eh? But you'll need to leave your bed to eat, Madam Mistress."

"Nay! I shall live on love!"

"Nay?" he asked with a twitch of his lips. "I haven't heard that word used since my grandfather died."

"Oh," she said. "Don't sailors speak that way?"

"Did Drumlin?"

"No."

"At any rate, I don't wish you to speak like a sailor."

"But if I'm to be your first mate, oughtn't I to learn the vernacular of my profession?"

His eyes twinkled before he leaned forward to start writing once more. "I've shared accommodations with a number of sailors, and I can't say I've ever particularly enjoyed their vernacular. I much prefer your current manner of speaking. It's very pretty."

Her heart flipped. It was but a trifling compliment. During Morgan's one London season she'd become accustomed to larger and far more elegant flattery, yet none of it had affected her as these few honest words. For several minutes she watched her captain write, the scratching of his pen filling the room as she waited for her racing heart to return to normal. Today he'd dressed in a charcoal-gray morning coat, trousers of a slightly lighter color, and a silver satin waistcoat. His shirt was pristine white linen, his black silk cravat tied in a neat, no-nonsense bow. No checks, no stripes, nothing to detract from the excellent cut of his clothes or the exquisite black embroidery of his waistcoat. Nothing but simple elegance. It suited him.

Taking a deep breath, Morgan asked what he was writing.

"A list for Rob on the items we'll require for your new home. And another list of the items of clothing you'll need."

Her new home. A small tremor of trepidation passed through her. "Don't you mean our home?"

"I live here. This is for your house."

Morgan absorbed that slowly. She'd gone from penniless to a home-owner in a few short hours, merely because after a week of living on the streets she'd succumbed to the inevitable, the sale of her person. She attempted to swallow the lump rising in her throat at the sudden comprehension of what she'd become—and the words that could now be applied to her.

Then, list in hand, Captain Montgomery rose from his desk to cross the room. Her gaze followed his tall, broad figure, then rose to scan his face—his long-lashed eyes and the hard mouth that could turn soft in an instant, making her dizzy with his kisses. Was she truly selling herself? Oh, but she'd lie with him again merely for the bidding. Perhaps she ought to pay *him.*

"Here," he said, handing her the sheet of paper. "I believe this will do."

With trembling hands and carefully avoiding eye contact, she took the sheet. His neat script danced in front of her eyes, and she needed several deep breaths before she could shove aside recollections of the previous night.

It was a long and thorough list, complete with every article of clothing—and underclothing—that a woman could possibly wish for. "This—this is quite a list, sir, but . . ."

"But?" he asked as he sat in the second armchair. "What have I forgotten? Another cloak, perhaps?"

Oh Lord, it was too much to assimilate. From abuse to compassion, from cold black eyes, to warm brown ones, from starving and cold to—to— "You're overgenerous, sir. I shan't need half of this."

"New England has very cold winters. You'll need all, if not more."

"But seven walking dresses, Captain? Seven day gowns and seven dinner dresses? Do you expect me to change three times a day?"

"Only if you wish."

"One quilted cloak, one fur-lined cloak, ten pairs of gloves in various colors," she read. "How should I need two cloaks and seven walking gowns? I—I don't expect to go out that much," she said, lifting her head.

He frowned and leaned forward in his chair, holding her gaze with his. "Morgan, please understand," he said gently. "I have business interests that require my attention, and social engagements as well. You'll have many hours to yourself. You may wish to partake of Boston's entertainments."

She bit her cheek and dropped her gaze in abrupt comprehension. As a sea captain, he'd must necessarily be away for weeks, if not months, at a time. Boredom and loneliness must be a large part of her role as mistress. And yet, to walk the streets searching for excitement? To risk meeting a Turner or Weatherly— "No doubt I'll contrive to entertain myself at home. Truly, Captain, I'm something of a homebody."

His frown deepened. "Are you afraid of the Weatherlys? I could amend that situation. With your leave, I'll repay the money you stole."

Her blood turned to water, and it took all her fortitude not to snap a quick, fearful answer. Miss Weatherly would certainly know of her new title, the Wicked Widow of Philadelphia. "I daresay it's not only about the money. It's the crime as well."

"Once the money's returned, I doubt they'll pursue criminal charges. It was, after all, committed in Philadelphia."

Good gracious, how to deter him? "The Weatherlys never cared much for me. They might wish to prosecute for the sake of revenge. Besides, it's rather a lot of money, isn't it? I couldn't ask that of you."

"Not so much in the face of all else I shall be providing," he replied dryly.

She shook her head, hoping her fear didn't show in her eyes. "I prefer to pay my own debts, Captain. It's a matter of honor."

He peered at her a moment longer, then shrugged. "So be it. If your pride is worth so much that you'd rather suffer virtual imprisonment for its sake, I won't argue. Shall we say three walking dresses then?"

She nodded in relief, noting that his muscles seemed to relax also. Part of her congratulated herself for the small victory, but another slightly uneasy part wondered at it. She supposed Captain Montgomery to be quite clever, and her reasoning had been less than solid. . . .

They continued to discuss the list for a time. Morgan, concerned that if the captain found her too expensive he'd jilt her, plagued him to cut it even further until she'd finally worn his temper raw. "Enough!" he snapped, slapping the list down on the table between their chairs. "The list will stay *exactly* as it is, complete with all seven walking dresses! Good God, woman, had I not known better I'd think you were a born Bostonian!"

"I can't consent to wasting money—"

"It's mine to waste, madam, and as parsimonious as we Bostonians are reputed to be, I refuse to allow you to dress in rags." He glowered at her and Morgan sighed in defeat. She didn't particularly care to be referred to as parsimonious, but the ease with which Captain Montgomery tossed money about worried her, as if he possessed the financial resources of a wealthy landowner instead of a mere sea captain. "Are we agreed then, madam?"

She shrugged. "If you insist."

"I do. And there is one other minor thing I insist upon. You shall remove that silly wig before we leave this house," he said, waving a hand at her head.

"Never! It's my disguise."

He smiled grimly, his eyes glinting with determination. "You'll not require a disguise today. We received over a foot of snow yesterday, and I doubt Miss Weatherly will risk leaving her home until it has been well cleared."

Morgan rose uneasily and glided over to the fire, ostensibly to warm her hands. She presented her back to him, but kept her ears trained upon his every move. "She might send her nephew out, mightn't she?"

"Her nephew? Is one of Weatherly's sons visiting Boston?" At her nod, he continued. "Nevertheless, it's unlikely he'll visit a seamstress. I'll provide you with a hooded cloak to cover your head when we're on the streets."

But Turner's niece, sister to Kenneth Turner, Richard's heir, might very well visit a seamstress. She recollected meeting Kenneth at her wedding. The ice in his eyes had clearly conveyed his anger, frustration, and contempt for her. Then Richard's last moments cut into her vision— of his last breaths, of the pain he'd meant to inflict. Kenneth had Richard's eyes. Quite possibly he'd inherited Richard's brutality—Oh no, she thought as her muscles tensed, she'd not risk recognition by Kenneth's sister.

"You could ask the seamstress to visit here. That's the custom, isn't it?"

He hesitated before saying slowly, "Perhaps in most cases. In this instance, however, we'll visit her, and you shall travel un-wigged."

"I won't," she said, lifting her chin as she turned to face him.

The captain rose, his eyes darkening. His child-killing scowl creased his face. "You shall. That thing is not only filthy, but poorly constructed as well. No decent woman would be caught dead in it."

"But I'm not a decent woman, am I? As your mistress I've cast decency to the wind," she replied with a flick of her wrist.

"And as *my mistress* you've given me the right to regulate your dress. Take it off, Morgan! That is an order!" He spread his legs in his sea-captain stance, crossing his arms behind his back.

"I will not!" she said, a shiver running down her back at the coldness in his voice, the granite lines of his countenance. She'd have preferred anger. Richard had never struck in anger. "You may govern intimate matters, but not the dressing of me!"

His eyes narrowed. He stepped forward. She stepped back. "May I remind you that my money will do that dressing?"

A flush darkened his face, reminiscent of Richard's excitement as he raised a fist. Morgan rubbed her hands together and attempted to settle her quaking nerves with the intelligence that, thus far, Captain Montgomery had behaved with perfect civility. "You may remind me," she said, "but you cannot compel me."

He raised one eyebrow. "I'm half a foot taller than you and nearly twice as heavy. I can force anything I wish upon you."

Oh Lord, she'd been wrong! His civility was no more real than Richard's affability; monsters hid behind such façades. And Captain Montgomery was much larger than Richard. She could not even conceive of the pain he could inflict.

Menace in every step, the captain drew nearer. Her eyes tore around the room, searching for a weapon. A poker—a half foot away within easy grasp. She grabbed it and wrapped fingers tightly around the cold steel as he spoke. "And now, madam, I'll take that wig!"

From the corner of her eye, she saw him lift his arms. Every last nerve jumped to attention; tears stung her eyes. Whirling, she raised the poker, preparing to hit him waist high if he made another move, then slam it over his head. She'd bear no more pain, no more humiliation. She'd been a good wife, a respectful wife—

And then Captain Montgomery's words penetrated the fog of fear.

Standing still as a statue in front of her, he eyed the poker warily, his breathing fast and light. He'd lifted his arms in a defensive position to block her swing. Or to grab for her—knock her to the ground so that she might grovel at his feet, begging for mercy.

Except he didn't move.

He shifted his gaze to lock eyes with her. "Well, madam, do you swing?"

"I—perhaps I shan't if you put your arms down."

He let out a small, humorless laugh. "First drop the poker."

"Not, sir, until you lower your arms."

"Then we'll stand here for quite some time."

"You shan't beat me."

Confusion touched his eyes. "I should never hit a woman, but," he said, with a slight smile and a glint of levity in his eyes, "given the smallest chance, I swear I shall tear that wig from your head and stomp on it until it screams."

The vision of her staid and sober sea captain gleefully stomping on the mass of blond brought a tiny bubble of amusement to her belly. "You almost persuade me, sir, to drop the poker."

"If I cannot, the weight of it will do so soon enough."

The laughter gleaming in his eyes warmed her, dispelling Richard's memory and the fear that Captain Montgomery possessed the same demons. His passions, she remembered with a twinge of excitement, appeared perfectly normal in quality, if rather—excessive—in quantity. And yet thus far she'd matched that hunger with an equal and shocking appetite of her own.

Another minute passed as her skin warmed and her arms tired. "I own, sir, that my arms are indeed fatigued. I promise if you put down your arms, I shan't swing."

He lifted an eyebrow. "And if I don't?"

"I suppose I should call for assistance."

His dimple appeared. "By all means, madam, do so. The expression on Herman's face alone would be worth the embarrassment."

"Would it embarrass you, then?"

"Not enough to surrender to your demands." He stared at her a moment before saying slowly, "You know, I'm rather enjoying this. Something about that pose strikes me as seductive."

She laughed in spite of herself. "You enjoy being threatened with a poker? I must keep that in mind for the future."

His lips twitched. "I suspect my future will be fairly short if you actually swing that infernal thing. Do you mean to strike me in the head? Or in the chest?"

"I'm not certain," she replied with another chuckle.

"You know, Captain, I may be ignorant of such affairs as ours, but I fancy we may be proceeding incorrectly."

"Why ever would you think that?"

"Only that I've never before heard of a mistress threatening her lover with a poker."

"Aye, Mistress, but I seek originality in the women I keep."

"Then you've realized your wish, haven't you?"

Fire leapt in his eyes. "You've far surpassed all my fondest dreams. And now, what do you say we call this a draw? I'll count to three and we'll drop our arms together."

"That sounds logical enough."

"Excellent. One. Two. Three."

Relieved, she let the poker fall to her side. Seconds later the captain lunged forward, seized her wig and cast it to the floor to grind beneath the heel of his boot. "I win," he said softly. As she opened her mouth in protest, he pulled her tightly against his hard body for a rough, wild kiss. Afterward he moved his mouth to her ear, his hand caressing her backside. "From what I understand, Mistress, our affair should contain more hugging and kissing and much less poker wielding."

"Truly? Oh!" she gasped as his hand slipped lower to slide between her thighs.

"Less threats," he said, "and more moaning."

"Ohhhh," she moaned as his hand rubbed her rapidly heating secret areas.

"Less talk and far more action," he said and slid another hand over her breast as he bent his head for another kiss. She responded with abandon, all thought vanished save the mounting need to bring them both to climax.

"Sir," a male voice interrupted them. "The snow's just about cleared and—OH!"

Captain Montgomery started to raise his head, but Morgan, refusing to grant him liberty, encircled his neck with her arms. With a chuckle rumbling through his chest, he wrapped his fingers around her wrists and bore her hands down. Her body mourned the loss as, his eyes gleaming down at her, he whispered, "Enough. We shall finish this later."

He slid his arm around her waist and turned to greet the intruder. Robert Montgomery, Morgan noted through the mists of desire. With a deep blush, she concluded that he'd viewed all: the kiss, her response, and the captain's well-placed hands. Oh Lord, what would he think of her? Who would he tell? What would people *say*? Mother would be appalled; Father would lock her in her room for weeks, months—

"Rob," Ward said pleasantly, "you remember Mrs. Brown, correct?"

Except, she thought with a thump of her heart, neither parent was *here*.

"Mrs., Sir? Not Miss?"

"Mrs. Brown," he replied firmly. "We are becoming fast friends and, as such, I require your assistance in making various living arrangements."

What did Mr. Montgomery's opinions signify at any rate? Her spirits lifted as the heaviness of censure slipped from her shoulders. She was no longer Lord and Lady Westborough's daughter. She was a *mistress*.

Hot excitement flashed through her at all the connotations of the word. As the captain's mistress she was *expected* to kiss him and touch him and allow him whatever petting he requested. Shudders of desire heated her body. She'd forsaken all sense of propriety and she could do—could *bloody* well do, she thought, relishing the common indecency of cursing—whatever the *hell* she wanted with him. With a wide smile, she decided there were many advantages to the seamy side of life.

"Sir, are you certain this is the course of action you wish to take?" Mr. Montgomery asked. "The consequences might be—uncomfortable."

"The devil with the consequences, Rob. I'm a full-grown man in command of the piloting of my life."

Rob stared at him a moment, his face wooden. "Of course, sir."

Chapter Six

Sighing contentedly, Morgan surveyed her small drawing room, the jewel in her kingdom provided by her new king and captain. True, the decorating lacked—lacked—well it lacked everything. The cheap, maple furniture creaked when she sat upon it, and she feared it would break under Captain Montgomery's weight. The worn crimson and white striped brocade upholstery clashed with the milky lilac of the damask curtains, which when combined with a new, emerald and gold carpet jarred the senses. Fighting for domination, the wallpaper mixed all the colors in bright, flowered splotches.

But the chimney didn't smoke and with the drawing room door shut, the fireplace adequately warmed the room. Most importantly, her new home was located in the South End, a goodly distance from Beacon Hill and Boston's fashionable set, like the Weatherlys or Turners.

A knock rang through the room, followed by the door opening. "Mum?" a lilting Irish voice tentatively asked from the doorway.

Morgan gave Maeve, one of her two servants, her kindest smile. Maeve curtsied deeply.

"You needn't curtsy," Morgan said. "It's a small house, and we'll run into each other often, shan't we? If you curtsy every time, you'll wear your knees out before you're five and twenty."

Maeve's blue eyes held hers a moment before she glanced down, two red blotches brightening her pale cheeks. "I'm sorry for offendin' ye, mum."

Once more Morgan detected a cool, almost angry reserve, something she noticed even stronger in Fionna, her cook. Kingdom or not, it would take much restraint and careful consideration to make her subjects contented even without the Irish dislike of the English. For some reason Americans considered service an intensely humiliating career. "I'm not so easily offended, Maeve," Morgan answered. "May I help you with something?"

Maeve's eyelids flew up in surprise. "No, mum! I'm after helpin' ye!"

"Well then, how may I help you help me? Oh dear, that's rather confusing, isn't it?" she asked chuckling.

Maeve didn't laugh, but Morgan caught the slightest twinkle in her eyes. "We—Fionna and me—thought maybe ye'd be takin' yer tea in here?"

"Tea? Is it that late already? My, how the day has flown! Yes, in here, please. I should feel rather silly sitting in the dining room all alone, shouldn't I?"

"I wouldn't be for knowin' that, mum."

Morgan controlled a sigh. A well-trained servant would not have even considered answering a rhetorical question. Morgan didn't care, but Captain Montgomery might deem it impertinent. Ah well, she'd not scold the girl today. First she must develop a sense of trust and respect in Maeve. As for sour-faced Fionna, who knew what would turn that woman around? Good gracious, nothing at all, for how could either woman ever respect Morgan when she was a paramour?

"I shall take it in here, at any rate. Thank you, Maeve."

Maeve looked as if she was about to curtsy again, stopped herself, then left the room. A short time later Morgan sat sipping tea, her mind sifting through the day's events, from the pure pleasure of waking up next to Captain Montgomery, to the simple joy of eating a full meal. Later, after borrowing a hooded cloak from one of the maids, the captain had taken her for a short sleigh ride through the streets of Boston, pristine and sparkling white, like some sort of fairy tale. As promised, few others had braved the weather and they were the only customers at the seamstresses'. After giving Mrs. Fournier his list, the captain had sat back and quietly observed Morgan and the seamstress discussing materials and poring over dress patterns. Instead of expressing shock and disgust, he only smiled at Morgan's choices of too-tight dresses and shockingly low necklines. When she commented on it, he shrugged. "Wear what you wish. I'm only here to pay the bill and to ensure that the list is filled." With that he rose from the chair, reached into his pocket, counted out silver, and handed it to Mrs. Fournier. "This ought to do for you to begin work. I must leave Mrs. Brown here for now. Would you see to it that she's supplied with the other essentials, too? Fans, parasols, shoes, you know the thing."

After a few minutes' discussion—Mrs. Fournier didn't specialize in those items but agreed to assist in their procurement—the captain left, promising that Rob would arrive later to escort her to her new home.

Morgan had spent the next two hours ecstatically choosing clothes. Oddly enough, completely in control of her wardrobe for the first time in her life, her choices became relatively conservative. She changed her mind on most of her initial selections and in the end only three of her gowns truly befit her new role. But she did commission the making of several sheer negligees, which she fancied a mistress would wear.

Mistress, her mind repeated with deliciously wicked excitement. No longer a lady, no longer a wife, but a woman so far beyond respectability that she needn't adhere to society's rules; she was, in fact, expected to break them. A twinge of guilt tugged at Morgan's conscience, but she dismissed it, concentrating instead on how best to perform her new role. Her duties, as she perceived them, were to sexually satisfy her lover. She blushed at the words, themselves indecent and vulgar. Oh, but she must learn not to blush! Doubtless mistresses performed their duties gracefully, seductively. Blushing was *not* seductive.

Morgan glanced down at the black kerchief covering the low bodice of the only clothing quickly readied, a pink silk evening gown. She had pinned the kerchief around her shoulders when Robert Montgomery had escorted her around her new home. But Mr. Montgomery had long since quit the house, and the others must become used to her new station.

She unpinned the kerchief and laid it on the back of her chair. Biting her cheek, she stared down at the scooped neckline of her gown, rising barely an inch above her nipples. Oh dear, she would positively squirm in the captain's company if she must wear something so risqué!

But she'd already stood naked in front of him.

A knock sounded through the room. With a deep breath, Morgan bade Maeve to enter, and schooled her countenance to resemble the cool reserve her mother had taught her. Maeve's eyes swept over her, widening. "Oh!" she gasped, covering her mouth and Morgan blushed. Her mother hadn't taught her *that* well.

"Are you here for the tea tray?" Morgan asked.

"I—ay mum, if yer finished."

She nodded. "Yes, thank you. Would you please bring me a brush? I—"

Through the drawing room door came the sound of the front door opening. Morgan's eyes flashed to the mantelpiece clock. Five o'clock. Surely—

"Morgan?" Captain Montgomery's voice called.

Maeve's eyes became saucers. She and Morgan stared at each other and for the briefest moment Morgan fancied she detected pity in Maeve's expression. Then Maeve took the tea tray. "I'll be seeing to Captain Wyatt," she said, using the phony name Mr. Montgomery had assigned to his employer for purposes of privacy. Apparently Captain Montgomery had a grandmother who would object to his mistress.

As the captain and Maeve exchanged pleasantries in the hall, Morgan quickly rose and turned to check her hair in a gilt-framed mirror hanging over the fireplace. She'd had Maeve, yet untutored in hairdressing, pull her hair into a simple chignon, parted in the middle. Hands trembling, Morgan fixed a pin or two, then turned to glance around the room, blenching at the garishness. She pushed an ottoman forward and, careful to avoid creasing her gown, sat upon it, then spread the skirt around it gracefully. She pulled the bodice as low as she dared. Was that seductive? Good gracious, what did she know about seduction?

The captain entered, his eyes locating her instantly. Lifting an eyebrow, he slid his gaze over her leisurely. Morgan's breath caught in her throat. Lord, but he was handsome, perfect in every way, from the cut of his clothes to the hard, muscular body they concealed, from the harsh lines of his face to his kind eyes warming a woman's quaking heart—

"Mistress," he said, his gaze catching hers. He

closed the door as desire lit his eyes. "You do not *come* to greet me?"

Vulgarity. She ought to be offended; instead the gentleness of his voice and the amusement riding in it heated her blood. Tilting her head saucily, she flashed what she hoped was a titillating smile. "Oh no! I'm much too concerned with being pretty and seductive. Does it work?"

His smile spread as he propped his shoulder against the door. "You're always beautiful. As for seductive," he said, flashing his gaze over her person again, "at this point in our little affair no seduction is necessary." He jerked his head in a summoning motion and said in a low, husky voice, "Come here."

Oh, but how she loved that smile! That voice! A tiny thrill flew over her nerves. Perhaps she might contrive to be a seductress after all. It seemed as simple as flirting, only with sexual innuendos. Laughing playfully, she answered, "No, I don't think so."

"No?" he asked, raising an eyebrow. "It's not for you to refuse my orders. I've spent much money on you today. I expect payment." Rough words, spoken softly, belying the implied threat.

A little shiver of delight ran down Morgan's back and she tossed her hair. "It is all very well, of course, but I am now persuaded that I deserve more for my services."

"What more would you like?"

"Diamonds."

His eyes twinkled. "This morning you didn't even want to accept a few walking dresses. Now you want diamonds."

"Aye, Captain, after a day's contemplation, your first *mate* now demands payment in diamonds. And don't fancy that you'll fob me off with something as paltry as earrings! I demand a full necklace. Arranged in a water-fall, I think."

"How unfashionable of you, Morgan! Surely you'd rather have rubies or emeralds?"

She shrugged dramatically. "What do I care for fashion? A mistress only desires wealth. It is diamonds or nothing at all!"

He seemed to consider it a moment before answering. "All right, if you insist. I require service first, however." Pushing away from the door, he stepped toward her.

Her stomach fluttering, Morgan laughed and jumped up from her ottoman. Grabbing her skirts, she stepped behind it. "Oh, no! It would be shockingly ill-advised to render service without payment first, wouldn't it?"

Advancing upon her, he answered, "Obviously you know little of business practice. Payment is always made after service."

"Surely not in this line of business. Only consider how often a woman would be cheated!" Morgan shifted left, keeping the ottoman between them.

His dimple emerging, the captain shifted left too. Breathless now, she shifted right. He followed suit. She moved left again, but this time Captain Montgomery lunged forward. Having seen the move in his eyes, she quickly jerked back, stepped around the ottoman, and sprang for the door. Chuckling, he chased her and in three long strides caught her arm. With a slight tug, he twirled her around, wrapped one iron-strong arm around her waist, and pulled her against him. "I win," he gloated just before taking her mouth in a hard, ravishing kiss.

Afterwards she said breathlessly, "You always win."

Eyes gleaming, he slid his hand over one half-naked breast. "Ah Mistress, but in this, we both win."

The touch of his callused fingers on her bare skin ignited her senses. "Aye, Captain," she whispered and wrapped her arms around his neck to force his head down for another rough kiss, this of her own doing as she pressed her lips against his, eagerly thrusting inside to sweep his mouth as he had hers.

He responded by sliding his hand down her back to press her against his hardening staff. Presently he broke free. "I commend you, Mistress. You've learned the art of seduction well. I believe," he said, regarding her with glittering eyes, "I shall give my first mate a raise."

She laughed softly. "You already have! I feel it against my stomach."

"Aye, but in this case I meant to raise your skirts."

Hot, delicious desire shuddered down her spine. Oh, but the anticipation, the flirtation—that was indeed the best part of seduction. "First you must eat, my Captain. At your request, I ordered supper for seven o'clock."

"It's just five now. We've two long hours beforehand. Why do you think I arrived so early?" He brushed back her hair to press his lips to her neck, blazing a trail of shimmering kisses across the sensitive skin of her shoulders. Her knees weakened. "Will you come with me, Mistress?" he whispered in her ear. "To the bedroom?"

"Sir, I believe I would come with you anywhere," she replied weakly.

He sucked in a deep, harsh breath. "Enough of this," he growled. Seizing her hand, he led her swiftly up the stairs to her bedroom. After kicking the door shut, he pulled her to the bed and threw back her skirts and petticoats. In a matter of seconds, he was inside her, thrusting hard and fast, rubbing against her sensitive areas with each stroke. She cried out as pleasure built, peaked, and then washed over her in deep, rolling waves. Moments later he shouted her name in a harsh, guttural voice and spilled his hot seed, filling her with warmth.

"Lord, Morgan," he gasped, collapsing next to her, "you're incredible."

She laughed breathlessly. "I am scarcely displeased myself."

Grinning, he rolled her on top of him. "And now I want kisses. Many long, wet kisses. Let's see if we can do this again, slowly. Earn your diamonds, Mistress."

"How do you like your new home?" Captain Montgomery asked as he twirled his glass of port.

They sat in Morgan's small dining room, finishing the remains of supper. At first Morgan had watched the captain nervously as Maeve served them Fionna's plain cooking. Ham, potatoes, and peas, with apple pie for dessert. No soup, no removes, no other courses. The food was well prepared, but having eaten twice at the captain's house, Morgan concluded that he was used to more elaborate meals. Yet he smiled kindly at Maeve, ate his simple supper without complaint, and continued their conversation—about Boston's severe winter weather—as if nothing could have pleased him more than the company and food. Presently Morgan's uneasiness lifted, leaving behind a warm spot in her heart. No doubt Captain Montgomery was a favorite dinner guest among his set.

"It suits me well, thank you," she answered after swallowing her last bite of pie. "It has a bathing room."

His eyebrow lifted. "A bathing room? That's important to you?"

She grimaced. Oh dear, that wasn't a proper response, was it? "I—I like bathing."

His lips twitched slightly. "You've no notion how comforted I am to hear that. I should have thought, however, that you'd be a bit more interested in the décor."

She shrugged and studied the tablecloth. The linen, as the furniture, came with the house, and it was stained. "I'm interested in both. Only—" She lifted her head, narrowing her eyes. "Only, it's rather a strange thing, isn't it?"

"Strange? The décor or the bathroom?" he asked, clearly amused.

"I meant my penchant for bathing."

"I don't know," he said slowly. "That depends on what you mean by penchant."

She frowned. How had she stumbled onto such a subject, at the supper table of all places? Indecent . . . "My father believed my interest in full-emersion bathing to be wholly obscene. He restricted me to baths once every eight weeks."

"That sounds a little excessive. Current thinking, I believe, advocates weekly bathing."

Oh weekly baths! With perfumed water! She lifted her chin. "I'd prefer daily bathing."

"Then by all means, do so," he replied. "I don't understand the problem. It's your home. Do as you please."

"Some would consider such a luxury a waste of your money."

"How, if it makes you happy? By God, Morgan, of all the ways to waste money!" He shook his head. "Are you done eating? Shall we adjourn to the parlor?"

"Parlor?" she asked, surprised. She expected he'd wish to visit the bedroom after supper.

"Yes. Is that a problem?"

"But I'd presumed—" She stopped, blushing as Maeve entered the room to clear away the remains of dessert. Swallowing her confusion, Morgan smiled at the girl. "Thank you. That should be all for tonight, Maeve."

"Won't ye be needin' me later, mum, before bed?"

Morgan's face heated. "No. I shall see you in the morning."

"As will I," said the captain, rising. Morgan's eyes flew to his. In the morning? Did he intend to stay the night, then? She'd assumed that men took their pleasure from their mistresses, then quit the house. Oh Lord, she thought, her breath coming in fast, nervous spurts. She was in over her head, wasn't she? Perhaps she ought not to have started on this specific adventure. Oh, but of course she oughtn't; it was pure, rash folly. . . .

The captain offered her his arm. "Will you accompany me, Morgan?"

She nodded, permitting him to lead her to the parlor where she'd had Maeve kindle a wood fire in the grate. It burned merrily. In fact, it was hot. Or was her warmth caused by the captain's presence?

He nodded to a chair. "We have a few matters to discuss."

"Oh," she said, "that's why you didn't want to retire, then?"

"It's only eight o'clock, Mistress. I don't keep such early hours."

"I—" Feeling increasingly shy, she scanned his face. Laying with a man, she slowly apprehended, didn't necessarily encourage greater intimacy. She had—been—with the captain several times over the last twenty-four hours, but she had learned only trifling bits about him.

"You what?" he asked, perplexed. "Please, madam, if you would be so obliging as to take a seat?"

He continued staring down at her, his warm eyes setting her heart aflutter. With desire? No. These were entirely different sentiments, wholly unexpected. Love . . .

"Morgan? I'd prefer to have this conversation sitting."

His manners were asserting themselves again. Apparently they extended even to his mistress.

She nodded and made herself comfortable in an armchair. The captain chose a chair near to her, watching her with some puzzlement. "You seem distressed."

Was she distressed? No, for she could not possibly love Captain Montgomery. She scarcely knew him. It was merely the ill-conceived notion of a runaway imagination. "On the contrary, sir, I'm much pleased to have your company tonight," she replied. If he insisted upon formality, then she would return the obligation.

"So says your mouth, madam, but your eyes tell a different story. Perhaps you're reconsidering our arrangement? You seemed happy enough with it earlier."

"Oh no!" she exclaimed. "You've been more than generous. I'm merely a trifle—confused—about certain aspects of it. I'm—uncertain—about how to conduct myself."

A smile curled his lips, bringing the dimple out in his cheek. "I should never have guessed that, Mistress."

"You're quizzing me."

He shook his head, still smiling. "I'm attempting to reassure you. I'm not unhappy with your conduct. Did I say something that made you think it?"

She frowned, searching her mind for a way to express herself. "I presumed that after supper you'd wish to repair to the bedroom," she said blushing. "And I never considered that you'd stay the night."

"So that's it. Is staying the night unusual, then?"

She held up her hands in an exasperated shrug. "Goodness, how should I know?"

"I don't know either. At any rate, I enjoyed sleeping with you last night and thought to repeat the experience. Do you find that objectionable?"

"No! Of course not! Truly sir, in that regard I shall

gladly oblige your every request. That's my purpose, isn't it?" Her *only* purpose, she told her wretched, fluttering heart.

Regret touched his eyes before he returned, "You might consider using my name, then."

"Certainly. Captain Montgomery, I shall—"

"My first name, Morgan."

"But I don't know what that is, do I?"

He stared at her in surprise, before a chagrined smile graced his countenance. "No? It seems, Mistress, that we don't know each other well. That accounts for some of your uneasiness. We shall change that by and bye. My name is Ward."

"Ward," she repeated. "A strong name. It suits you."

He nodded graciously. "Thank you. Are you more comfortable now?"

A sudden touch of humor struck her heart, and she smiled. "Yes, thank you. A mistress ought to know her lover's first name."

"Good. Now, back to other arrangements." He glanced around the room, eyes falling distastefully on the furniture. "*Do* you care for this décor, Morgan?"

With difficulty, she suppressed a giggle. "It appears you don't."

"Not particularly," he said, amusement deepening his voice. "I chose the place for its size and location. If you wish, we could replace some of the furniture and," he grimaced, "those drapes."

Unable to control her mirth any longer, Morgan laughed. "I'm not sure. Your reaction amuses me."

His eyes bright with suppressed laughter, he said, "Then permit me to restate my point. If you expect me to spend much time in this room, you'll allow me to replace the furniture."

She tilted her head slightly. "And that, sir, is the whole

drift of our conversation, isn't it? Given our relationship, I quite naturally supposed we would spend our time together in the bedroom."

The humor in his eyes vanished. Abruptly, he rose to throw another log on the fire. After a moment he turned and leaned against the mantel, regarding her cautiously. "It seems we have different visions of this affair. No doubt that's due to neither one of us having ever participated in such an arrangement."

"Well then, perhaps you ought to tell me your vision."

"Fair enough. I expect to visit you several times a week. Sometimes I'll arrive in time for dinner, and occasionally stay for breakfast. My schedule is erratic, so I may only have an hour or two one day and a full night the next."

This time her stomach joined her foolish heart in fluttering. "And yet this morning you said you expected not to have much time for me."

"I meant during the day. We were discussing walking dresses."

"And so," she said, extrapolating out loud, "if I collect your meaning, on those occasions when you stay the night, we shan't spend all the hours in bed?"

His smile didn't touch his eyes. "Not all of them. You know, if I didn't enjoy your company, my dear, I should never have agreed to this arrangement."

A man like the captain—like Ward, she corrected herself—a man with his countenance, manners, and amiability need never pay for a woman's companionship. He would draw women like flies to honey. But if they could not hold his attention, their loss was her gain, for she enjoyed his company, too. "All right."

His smile broadened. "Excellent. It's settled. The furniture goes."

She laughed. "All that to rid the room of the furniture?"

"You see," he said, as he crossed the room to take his chair once more. "I really hate it."

"So I perceive. Will you change only this room?"

"The dining room table may stay, since it's covered most of the time. As for the linen," he shook his head, "that goes. And the bed, and the mattress, and definitely those drapes!"

"You'll cause quite a stir, won't you? Will the landlord object to your plans?"

"No doubt he'll be grateful for having the place redecorated. As for a stir," he said frowning, "I'll insist it all happen in one day."

"One day?" she exclaimed in surprise. "Is that possible?"

"I'll make it possible."

He spoke with conviction, and a shiver of dismay ran down Morgan's spine. In spite of the uncommon compassion that lived in Ward's eyes, she occasionally glimpsed traces of hardness in him. Might she, before their time together ended, have cause to regret that? Oh, but she wouldn't even contemplate that occasion. It struck fear into her heart, for when this ended, she'd be at the mercy of the streets once more.

"As to other arrangements," he said, appearing slightly discomfited, "you'll require a household allowance."

"Mr. Montgomery said he'd manage the finances."

"The large ones, yes, but household expenses, such as food, I shall leave to your discretion." He withdrew two gold coins from his waistcoat pocket. "Thirty dollars a week ought to suffice. You may keep anything that remains beyond those expenses. If you require more, let me know."

She stared at the money in his hand. "More?" she said, raising her head. "You must fancy me a shocking spendthrift, sir. I could hold house with a quarter of that. It's too much, isn't it?"

Shaking his head, he turned her hand over and dropped the coins in her palm. "No. It's yours."

"But—" She stopped. His jaw muscles tensed and abrupt comprehension struck her. He was *paying* her! Mortified, Morgan flushed and dropped her eyes, unable to confront him. The rental of the house, the clothes, the servants, and the furniture she'd naturally taken for granted, since the captain stood to benefit from those expenditures. But this, to be actually paid in gold coin for the use of her person—the shame of it pierced her newfound joy, ripping at her heart. "I can't take this," she said and leaned forward to drop both coins back in his lap.

His hand caught her wrist. "I insist. I have no interest in purchasing food."

Face burning, she snapped, "No! You shall not—"

"Damn it," he swore, and with one strong hand, took her chin and lifted it until she met his gaze. His countenance was somber, his eyes grave. "Had I a wife, I should make the same arrangement. Didn't either of your husbands provide you an allowance?" he asked, removing his hand.

"But that is a wholly different matter! As husbands they were obligated—"

"And I am less obligated to you?"

"Of course you are! Legally and morally and—"

"Legally, madam, no man need make his wife an allowance. The law considers a wife little more than property. Morality is a matter of interpretation and changes from generation to generation. At all events, I'm paying you an allowance because I *want* to."

Her shaking eased slightly. "I don't expect it."

"I'm aware of that. You expect next to nothing."

She gulped. "You only wish to salve your conscience."

"My conscience? What have I to feel guilty about?"

"Why because—because—you've made me your mistress."

His frown deepened to a black scowl. "I haven't *made* you anything. To be sure, madam, *you* suggested this affair, not me. I gave you every opportunity to seek other employment, and you refused. It's *your* choice to stay."

Breathing lightly, she stared back at him as half-formed thoughts whirled through her mind. Run—stay—become an apprentice—a factory worker—but she could be recognized—and she'd be without her captain—but she ought to be without him—this was wrong—but it felt incredibly *right*—

"Do you want to leave? Do you now wish to explore those other options?"

To go where? To hang—several more breaths and she shook her head.

"Then take the money," he said, squeezing her hand gently. "It's neither guilt nor payment. Consider it a gift. Use it for household purchases or to provide yourself with whatever trinkets might strike your fancy."

"You strike my fancy," she said softly.

Emotions crossed his face—surprise, joy, regret. His eyes softened. "You've had a difficult time, my dear. Once you've recovered, you may see it differently."

She stared at the coins, one double eagle, one single, flashing liberty in the firelight. She'd never had such a large allowance. Her father, like Richard, hadn't believed women capable of managing money. Bart had earned scarcely enough to keep them both in room and board. Charles, most generous of all, had bestowed upon her five dollars a week, which she'd spent frivolously. She no longer had any use for fashion. What could she possibly do with so much money?

Entertainment. She'd have to entertain herself somehow. That's what she would spend it on.

She nodded. "All right."

Chapter Seven

Squinting at the closely printed words of the receipt, Morgan read aloud, "'If you do not bake under the meat in a dripping pan, pour it into a well grefed'— goodness no, that's one of those foolish f's in place of an s. 'Pour into a well *greased*, shallow baking dish and bake in a hot oven.' Oh for heaven's sake! Of course one would bake it in a hot oven! What would ever bake in a cold oven?"

As she was alone in the parlor no one answered. Exasperated, Morgan dropped the book. She'd been living under Ward's protection for two weeks now, and she'd grown wholly bored of Fionna's plain Irish cooking. When she'd mentioned it—as tactfully as possible—and offered her the recipe book, Morgan had discovered to her dismay that neither Maeve nor Fionna could read, something Morgan had every intention of correcting. In the meantime, she must study the etiquette and cookbooks that Robert Montgomery had kindly provided. Unfortunately their lack of details frustrated her, the term "hot oven" only the latest example. How did one determine how hot an oven needed to be? How did one ensure that the oven remained evenly "hot" during the whole cooking process? Good gracious, how did one *ever* learn to cook at all?

From a mother, she thought disgustedly. But as a well-bred lady, her mother had never considered teaching Morgan anything about cooking. That was the servant's job; hers was to plan meals. *English* meals. Americans ate differently from the English, she'd learned quickly, and within America one region ate differently from another. Worse still, the Irish ate differently from all of them!

She glared at the book. Well she was an American now, in action if not in truth, and she'd learn how to cook like one or—or *be damned*.

Oh, but how she loved to curse! she thought with a smile as she lifted the book. Loved cursing, vulgarity, and sheer negligees like the one she now wore, along with the indecent freedom of spending hours liberated from corset and conventions. For that, she thought, peering at the receipt again, she *would* learn to make Yorkshire pudding for Ward. Christmas was but a week away, and she was determined to serve him a traditional dinner, complete with roast beef, Yorkshire pudding, and mince pies.

If he meant to spend Christmas dinner with her at all.

Once more she let the book drop into her lap. She'd no reason to believe her captain would spend any part of Christmas with her, although contrary to his warnings he'd visited her nearly every night over the past two weeks. And stayed till morning, even on Sundays, although he left earlier to attend church, chuckling when Morgan teased him about the hypocrisy of it. Eventually he'd brought clothes from home, along with an impressively fashioned silver and gold chess set, which he'd spent hours patiently endeavoring to teach her to play.

A smile flitted across Morgan's face. The game was monstrously dull and dreadfully complicated but she'd persevered. Truthfully, she'd apprehended the essentials rather quickly, but continued her erratic play merely for the pleasure of hearing Ward laugh. Goodness, but she could not get enough of that laugh—or, she mused, any other part of him.

Through the half open door, Morgan heard the front door open, heralding Ward's arrival, early as usual. Her heart and stomach fluttering in anticipation, Morgan shut her book and placed it on a table with three others. After patting her hair into place, she arranged the shimmering skirts of her black and gold spangled silk negligee and turned toward the door with a welcoming smile, just as he strode in.

"Damn Cabot!" Ward spat angrily. "He's the biggest goddamned idiot in all of Boston!" He whipped off his gloves and dropped them on a table. For a minute she sat stunned by Ward's rare exhibition of temper. Seconds later, the absurdity of the situation wrung from her peals of ever-ready laughter.

"What? I find nothing humorous in this situation!" Ward snapped as he yanked off his coat and flung it on a chair.

"It's not the way a mistress expects to be greeted," she said, swallowing her humor long enough to speak. "Especially when robed in a black, and shamefully sheer, negligee. But if we must damn Cabot then by all means we shall. Damn Cabot! Damn him to hell and back again!" she said, attempting to lower her voice to a man's depth. The laughter bubbling in her throat made it difficult.

"Well," Ward said, his eyes running over her appreciatively. "He's still a goddamned idiot, but I like the negligee."

"It's positively indecent."

"Which you seem to revel in."

She laughed. "Aye, sir, but," she said her voice deepening once more, "that's of no import right now. We are busy damning Cabot! Damn him. Double damn him. No, triple-dog-damn him!"

"Dog damn?" Ward asked, his smile broadening until that magical dimple appeared. He seated himself across from her.

"That's not a curse?"

"I've never heard it before."

"Oh," she said, disappointed. "And I was so certain it was an intensifier of sorts, as in dog-faced or dog-drunk."

"Perhaps. Not, I think," he said, chuckling, "in dog-damned. But I do appreciate you entering into the spirit of cursing, if not the cursing itself."

She laughed. "Any time you desire cursing, sir, you may count on me! But, uh, you might want to teach me a few first."

"Mistress," he said, reaching for the arm to pull her from the chair and into his lap. "You'll learn no cursing from me. The vulgarity I taught you has taken on a life of its own. I shudder to consider what you would do with cursing." Running his hand down her back he kissed her gently on the mouth.

She sighed. Passion meandered languidly through her veins as she started to unbutton his waistcoat. "Ah, now I have your full attention. Or do I?" she asked wickedly, sliding her hand down to touch the hardening area between his thighs. "Perhaps not so full yet?"

"Not quite," he said with a laugh, and pulled her hand away. "Nor will it be this night. I'm here for dinner only. I have an engagement I cannot miss."

"Oh no!" For the first time she noticed his formal dress, complete with black tail coat, white silk waistcoat, and white cravat, all adorned with gold—studs in his shirt, sleeve links, and a shining watch chain. The effect took her breath away. "It's formal, isn't it?" His clothes were cut exquisitely in, as Reggie would say, bang-up style. What manner of engagement demanded such dress of a sea captain?

"Very," he said dryly. "I apologize, Morgan. I ought to have warned you. Will you wear the negligee for me another time?"

"I shall wear it for you tonight, sir."

He smiled tenderly. "This engagement will run very late. I shan't be returning."

"I don't care how late it is. You may wake me when it's over. As your mistress I may sleep all morning if I'm inclined."

"I'm not so inconsiderate. I promise to visit again tomorrow, however."

She peered at him a moment. Over the weeks she'd practiced various seduction techniques on him, taking especial note of what pleased him. No doubt she could coax him to return, if not stay. Her mouth twitched as she slid her hands between his thighs, eliciting a groan of pleasure from him.

"Morgan, belay that!" he said, clamping strong fingers over her wrists.

Smiling wickedly, she touched her lips to his ear, kissing, then nibbling on the lobe.

"And that too!" He twisted his head away, flashing her a chagrined smile. "I must attend this ball, Mistress. You shall not seduce me!"

"Try to stop me," she whispered against his mouth, as she moved to kiss that too, passing her tongue slowing over his lips before entering.

Laughing slightly, he jerked his head back. "I'm not certain I can, but if you insist in continuing on this course, I shall leave. And I warn you, I won't visit you before such an engagement in the future."

Morgan froze, eyes widening in hurt surprise. "No! Ward, I've waited all afternoon to see you!"

He lifted an eyebrow. "Have your days been so barren of entertainment?"

"Your visits would be the highlight of my day had I a house full of company and a whirlwind of parties to attend."

A sweet, hopeful sort of yearning settled on his face. He brushed his thumb across her cheekbone. "Honestly?" he asked.

A tiny lump rose in her throat as she nodded.

The yearning changed to deep affection. "Well then, it would be an even greater inconsideration for me not to return."

"I should miss you dreadfully," she said in a low, tight voice.

"No more than I," he said, before touching his lips to hers in a long, leisurely kiss, setting her pulses flying. She wrapped her arms around his neck, reveling in his peppery taste and the soft, luxurious stroking of his tongue. When he broke off the kiss, he said between deep breaths. "That was not very prudent. It would be best, Mistress, if you were to return to your chair."

For a moment she could only stare into his eyes, gleaming with desire, yet soft with affection. Her heart lurched, then turned to mush. Oh it was true! She was in love with him! But she oughtn't be shocked. Didn't most damsels in distress fall in love with their saviors? And yet her sentiments went far beyond mere gratitude. She'd been grateful to Weatherly. And she'd loved Bart. With her captain the two emotions combined and deepened.

On feet lightened by newfound love, she moved to

the sofa and seated herself as Ward rose to straighten his clothes, brushing out creases. Amusement flashed through her as she pictured his friends noticing those creases and wondering how he'd gotten them.

He nodded at the pile of books. "What are those?"

"Those? Oh—cookbooks. And books on American etiquette."

He raised an eyebrow and strolled over to flip through one. "Cookbooks? Etiquette! Good God, why?"

"I requested them. Neither Fionna nor Maeve possess much knowledge of New England cooking."

"And you'd like to try brown bread, I gather. I'm not particularly fond of it myself," he said, frowning. "Where did you get these?"

"From Mr. Montgomery."

He lifted his head in surprise. "Rob? When?"

"This morning. He supervised the replacement of the furniture."

"Ah," he said, glancing around the room. "I hadn't noticed."

She smiled mischievously. "Perhaps my negligee distracted you? Or was it this Cabot whom we were damning?"

"Your negligee is much more distracting and far more pleasurable than Cabot," he said wryly. "Do you like your new furniture, Morgan? Nothing Gothic as you requested."

"No, it's rococo, isn't it?" she said, running her hand appreciatively over the light blue upholstery and the smooth curving rosewood. "And beautifully carved. It looks a trifle—expensive."

He smiled down at her as he dropped the book back on the table. "It's made by an American named Belter."

"Oh," she said relieved. "Then I do like it. Is he from Boston?"

Ward controlled a smile at Morgan's relief. Belter's craftsmanship was much in demand and consequently, quite costly. These pieces were some of the best he'd ever purchased. "He's from New York."

"New York? Wouldn't Boston-made furniture have been more practical?"

"Perhaps," he said, sitting on the sofa next to her. "But I prefer this."

"I wonder, then, that you don't use it in your own home, and furnish this one with your old furniture."

Picturing the shocked expressions of his circle, Ward smiled. "If I did, I should be tossed out of Boston."

She tilted her head quizzically. "For buying furniture? How absurd."

"For replacing the old with new, my dear. Bostonians revere tradition and look with suspicion upon anything new."

"You have gas lighting and running water."

"We make exceptions for invention and cleanliness."

"All of which explains," she said slowly, "the Chippendale of your public areas and the rococo style in your bedrooms. Do you prefer newer styles, then?"

He shrugged. "Some of it, although I can certainly do without the gilt. But enough of that. Are you telling me that these books have been your sole source of entertainment when I'm working? Or has Rob provided you with anything a little more, uh, lively?"

She laughed merrily, spreading warm ripples of delight through his chest. "You don't fancy etiquette to be lively? For shame, Captain!"

"I think," he said dryly, "that it would be entirely wasted on you, Mistress, with the possible exception of informing you precisely how *not* to behave on every occasion."

"Oh no," she said with another deep-throated gurgle.

"I'm not so ignorant of the proprieties as to behave poorly on *every* occasion. Surely if I were presented to the Queen or King I should prove to be the very pattern card of ladylike conduct."

"Unlikely, as we have no royalty in this country. Have you discovered any other occasions for proper behavior in your reading? Dinner with President Pierce, perhaps? Is this something you wish me to arrange? I warn you, a negligee may impress me, but would be considered inappropriate by others."

"Truly?" she asked grinning. "But perhaps your president would enjoy my negligee?"

"No doubt, especially with you in it, but I believe I'll insist that you reserve such clothing for no other eyes than mine," he said, flashing her a dark scowl. "And that includes my esteemed cousin, Robert."

Her eyes sparkled. "Aye, aye Captain! Only for you. For Mr. Montgomery I choose my stiff-necked walking dresses. Anything else and I fancy he'd fly into hysterics."

He doubted that, but if Morgan presented herself to Rob in a negligee, Ward would receive one ranting, raving lecture on Morgan's lack of propriety, decency, and general conduct. "Just a touch of discretion, Mistress. As for livelier entertainment, I've a fairly well-stocked library. Shall I bring you something?"

Her eyebrows gathered together. "I'm not certain. What do you consider lively?"

"Hawthorne, perhaps, or Dickens."

"Yes, well, one must own that they're morally illuminating, but . . . I confess I should fancy something a trifle warmer."

"Warmer? A romance, then? Sir Walter Scott or Miss Austen?"

A touch of color rose to her cheeks. "I wouldn't consider Miss Austen warm."

Ward said slowly, "Warmer still . . . Would Richardson satisfy you? *Pamela* perhaps? Or *Clarissa?*"

Her eyes lit up. "Oh yes! My father positively refused my reading of them. And also, do you perhaps possess something rather less moralistic?"

"Ah, now I understand," he said, uncomfortable. As much as he enjoyed Morgan's company, her increasing interest in vulgarity disturbed him, reminded him, actually, of his father. "I have such material, but those sort of books aren't written for ladies. Moreover they're illegal."

"I'm not a lady," she said lifting her chin. "I'm a mistress and I fancy those novels are *exactly* the sort of thing mistresses ought to read."

"Boston sent a man to prison in the '20s for selling *Fanny Hill.*"

"Not to you I hope!" she said laughing. "I should relish reading *Fanny Hill.* As for illegality, what does that signify? Am I not illegal also?"

But, he reminded himself, shaking his head ruefully, her interest in vulgarity had yet to cross into depravity. Nor could he believe it would when her eyes sparkled with such amusement. "Aye, and my family has had some experience on that score, too. I'll bring them tomorrow, then. Now, if I'm not mistaken, Maeve's coming to announce dinner. Is that your robe on the chair? Black velvet, how appropriate," he said dryly as he helped her into it. "A witch's color and God knows you've cast a spell over me. If we lived in Salem during the old days you'd no doubt be tried for witchcraft."

"Salem?" she asked, her eyes brightening. "Where is that? And what has it to do with witchcraft?"

He dropped a kiss on her forehead. "We'll discuss that over dinner. And I'll send you a book on Salem too for a little taste of education in the midst of all the debauchery."

"Aren't the others educational? But that," she said wickedly, "is precisely why I wish to read them!"

Smiling affectionately, Ward re-read Edward's words, hearing his laughing voice in his ear.

Sir Captain!
Yes, to wed! You've heard the news! Imagine me, can you, no longer a licentious rake, but a staid and proper married man, and to a noble woman at that, Lady Amelia Cunningham! But it's what I shall be come January 25. And you must be there, sir! Ro can't—Fran is in confinement and he refuses to leave her—turned into a regular milksop. You can be sure I will never be such. Except, perhaps in a year's time!
Ward, you'll love my Amy, I promise you. Not too much! I know how the women fall for all that injured gravity and your black scowls. Hah, hah! But she's wonderful—that such beauty and spirit can be wrapped in one woman. Ah, but I won't go on, lest you accuse me of poetry.
Come—you must! January 25. I expect you, and you'll captain us back on one of your clippers. My love—spirit though she has!—is afraid of steamers since the Arctic went down. I have assured her that with my good friend— my kind, compassionate, wonderful friend!—at the helm she need not fear. Come, convey us, Sir Captain, back to the states and I shall forever be in your debt. We'll entertain you, that I promise! Amelia and I plan to honeymoon in Boston, to haunt you, old friend, and Ro. If Mohamed won't come to the mountain, the mountain will tease Mohamed until he cries Uncle.
Fail me not, faithful friend!
           Your servant—in a general way, you understand—
                                             Edward.

January 25. Three weeks out, a week in port, three weeks back. Six joyous weeks with a ship's deck rolling once more under his feet. Ward's blood quickened. He'd take the *Sea Gypsy*. She was currently in port. No doubt he could find enough cargo to at least make the voyage break even, if not profitable. Calculating sums, he rose from his library desk to send for Rob. While he was away for those weeks Rob would need to keep everything in order and care for Morgan—

He stopped in his tracks. Morgan. Six weeks' voyage. Perhaps more if the weather was bad. As much as eight weeks—two long months away from Morgan. A sudden dark cloud settled over him and his shoulders drooped. Eight weeks without her kisses and smiles, eight weeks without her soft skin, her infectious laughter. No soft, yielding body to warm him at night, no sweet cries of surrender when they joined in passion's embrace.

He'd take her with him.

To Edward's wedding? His *paramour*? Damn, if Edward so much as heard of Morgan he'd spare no words persuading him to end the affair. Ward had no desire to spend eight weeks attempting to explain the unexplainable—why he had engaged a mistress in the teeth of Bostonian respectability. All worse if news of Morgan's company on board ship spread through town—no, he couldn't take her.

By God, he thought, heart sinking, two months was a dog's age when a man had a mistress. But he must go. Without Ro, Edward would stand at his wedding with only the spirited Amelia to lend him support, for Edward's family inspired little love in him.

Ward rubbed his neck, sighing. He'd have to leave before the New Year. How would Morgan react? With relief at being free of his attentions? She always responded ardently to his advances, but he scarcely understood women. It could easily be a façade. On the other hand, she might very well feel abandoned after only three weeks together. *That* he could easily remedy with a gift. Women loved gifts, especially expensive ones.

Except for Morgan. Perhaps women didn't confuse him so much as Morgan did.

Well the devil with that, he decided and stepped forward once more, purpose in his stride. Someday he'd marry a proper Bostonian woman who would no doubt count every penny spent. He didn't need his mistress to do so also. Confound it, he worked hard. It was time to enjoy the fruits of his labor.

Chapter Eight

With a peculiar shudder, Ward watched Morgan draw a gleaming blade across the roast beef she'd, much to his dismay, cooked for him. Dismissing a stab of foreboding as she wielded the knife, he smiled, "It looks perfect, my dear, although I must say again that you needn't have troubled yourself."

"Aye," she answered merrily, as she sliced the rare beef. "It's done to a turn, isn't it? I confess, however, it wasn't all my doing. Fionna and Maeve lent me their aid before parting for their own Christmas dinners. Along with helping me with the Yorkshire pudding," she said pointing to another serving plate, "and a mincemeat pie too, right there! And there's—"

"I see it all," he said smiling affectionately. "I should never have expected my mistress to double as kitchen help."

Morgan blushed as she passed him a plate and sat across from him. "If you dislike it, I'll stop."

He took a bite, swallowed and smiled again. "This is excellent. If cooking entertains you, then enjoy it, by all means. I'm only reminding you that your women are paid handsomely to perform that service."

"*No* one is paid enough to miss Christmas dinner with their family." She took a bite, then asked casually, "Do you have family, Captain?"

Ward chewed slowly, controlling an expression of alarm. Morgan never spoke of her own family; he assumed she'd not concern herself with his. "No siblings, if that's what you mean."

"Mr. Montgomery says you have a grandmother."

Now what in the name of God's creation had induced Rob to tell her that? "I do. And Rob's my cousin, as you might suppose. My grandfather was his great uncle."

"Yet, you're spending Christmas with me."

"It's where I'd rather be."

"Oh," she said, fell silent for several minutes and then, with a lightening in her voice, thanked Ward for the books he'd sent her. "I've read them all."

"All? Good God, Morgan, *Clarissa's* fifteen hundred pages long!"

"Yes, well I must own I read only the warmer parts of that one. It irritated me with all its wretched attempts at morality. What does it signify that Lovelace dies in the end? Clarissa dies too, doesn't she? Both rapist and victim die, where's the morality in that?"

Muscles relaxing at the change in subject, Ward answered between bites, "Perhaps Richardson hoped to show the consequences of brutality toward a daughter. Until her death neither Lovelace nor her family fully comprehended their mistake in attempting to force Clarissa into marrying a man she hated."

"Yes, well I have personal experience as to cruel relations, but to die to spite them all is beyond folly! It's perfect stupidity! No doubt Clarissa's readers thought it wholly proper she die a slow and lingering death after being ravished, but personally *I* should have married the bastard and made his life so miserable as to wish for hell. She ought to have stabbed him with the scissors when she had them instead of threatening to stab herself, of all the idiotic notions. And I *don't* believe Richardson was writing morals. He wrote to entertain men who are excited by brutalizing women, which I cannot at all comprehend! What is the joy in a woman's subjugation when men already possess all the authority? It's like kicking a dead dog!"

Ward's lips twitched at her analogy. "A dead dog, eh? I don't know about that, but in all honesty, Morgan, men don't control everything. Women control certain notable aspects of living that men find, uh, entertaining."

"Entertaining! Good God, raping women isn't entertaining!"

"I never said that—"

"And I'm damned glad you didn't!" she said slamming down her fork.

"Morgan," Ward said mildly. "Richardson wrote fiction. If you don't like—"

"It's not merely fiction. Men read these tales and are persuaded it's perfectly acceptable to brutalize women! It's barbaric!"

Ward couldn't quite make out the gleam in her eye or the rough tension on her face. Something was wrong here. For all the mercurial quality of Morgan's moods, he'd yet to see her overreact. "Then consider *Pamela*. In that book the hero not only resisted temptation, but married the woman he threatened to abuse."

"Lovely. Threaten rape; get married. That's an offer a girl can't refuse!"

He shrugged and pushed aside his plate. "All right, Richardson was a brute." Reaching across the table he took her small hand in his and caressed the smooth skin with his thumb. "On another subject—"

"I don't wish to change the subject. I'm enjoying this one."

"I promise to return to it later. I have other plans to discuss with you."

"Do they include brutalizing women?"

He chuckled. "No, Mistress, they don't. I recently received a letter from a friend of mine. He requests that I attend his wedding."

She frowned. "And you wish my permission? It's perfectly fine with me, as long as it's not your wedding."

"It's in England."

Her mouth opened, no doubt to make some quip, but closed after a spell to form a tight, hard line. "I see."

"I expect to be away seven or eight weeks."

Avoiding his eyes, she reached for her wine with her free hand. "When do you leave?"

"Around the first of the year. You're distressed."

She shrugged. "I shall miss you."

"Most mistresses would find the prospect of having so much time to themselves enthralling."

"Yes, well." She took a sip of wine. "This mistress rather enjoys her captain's company."

"I'll leave you plenty of money—"

"I don't care a rap for that," she snapped, flashing angry eyes at him before her face turned stoic once more. Her eyes focused on some point past his left shoulder. "I'm sorry. I've forgotten my place. As your employee, I'm obligated to accept your whims without comment."

He sighed. "It's not a whim, Morgan. If you must know, I'd rather not go."

She focused on him again, and Ward's heart tightened when her face twisted into that hollow expression he'd first encountered when she'd broken into his countingroom. "Because, I'll warrant, you'd rather not leave your business interests."

He raised an eyebrow. "Because I'd rather not leave you."

"Truly?"

"Truly. If it eases your mind any, I've arranged my schedule so that I may devote the intervening five days entirely to you. Would you care for a short holiday? Perhaps escape the city for a few days?"

Her eyes lit up and the hollowness started to melt away. "A holiday? You and me?"

He nodded.

"Where? Oh, it doesn't signify, does it? I'd travel to the North Pole with you!" she said. Excitement replaced the tightness on her face.

Ward laughed, his heart warming at her unrestrained affection. "Not quite that far, Mistress. I thought we'd travel up the coast. Weatherly's family lives in Boston and west of the city. If we journey north, you need not worry about encountering them."

"I could go wigless."

"I'd prefer it."

"Oh, Ward!" She sprang from her chair to throw her arms around his neck. "I should love it above all things! It's the best Christmas present ever!"

Automatically his arms curled around her waist, reveling in the gently yielding curves, while her joy shot tiny cupid-like arrows into his chest. He hoisted her into his lap as she asked enthusiastically, "When do we leave?"

"Tomorrow afternoon, if that's convenient for you."

She beamed at him, laughter gurgling through her voice. "Oh, I fancy I can fit you into my schedule. Five days! It's not terribly long, is it, but far better than just nights."

"I enjoy the nights too," he said grinning.

"Captain," she said impishly, "if you wish to find an inn somewhere and never leave the bed, I shall most willingly oblige you."

"You credit me with far too much stamina."

"You're a sea captain," she said cocking her head slightly. "You have vast amounts of stamina. Oh! I'd almost forgotten! I have a gift for you, too!"

She slid off his lap, her backside rubbing against his half-hardened staff. He smiled at the reaction and watched her race from the room, her blue negligee dancing behind her. By God, she was amazing—enthusiastic child, raging reformer, and wild wanton all in one woman. Leaving her damn near tore the heart out of him.

His *heart*, he thought as he rose to follow her into the drawing room. Was that the way the wind blew? Aye, so it seemed. If questioned, he'd have sworn that over the course of the last three weeks the sun had shone all day, every day, and the moon and stars lit the heavens at night so brightly he could not tell the difference. So this was love—not a violent, breathtaking passion but a soft, gentle joy.

He seated himself on the sofa as Morgan retrieved a small package wrapped in brown paper, hanging from her Christmas tree on a table in the corner. She practically skipped across the room. "Merry Christmas, Captain!"

"You needn't have gone to all the trouble, Morgan. I hold you under no obligation—" He stopped when he noticed a jar also under the tree. "Gumdrops?" he asked. "Feeling nostalgic, my dear?"

She sat next to him, her pretty little nose wrinkling in disgust. "No! If I never eat another gumdrop, it'll be too soon. They're for you, and the fudge in the box, also."

A lump rose in his throat. "Why, thank you," he said.

Clearing his throat, he continued, "Although, I confess I'm not particularly fond of fudge."

"No?" she asked. "But you kept it in your office."

"I bought it for you."

She stared a moment, her face still. Then unshed tears brightened her eyes as she reached up to caress his face. "Thank you."

Such a simple gesture, yet it touched his heart. "It was then, Mistress, and still is, my pleasure to serve you."

Smiling, she shook her head. "A captain doesn't serve his mistress."

"This one does," he said grinning roguishly. "Sometimes, at any rate."

Mischief sparkled in her eyes. "Well, now *that* is a wholly different matter, isn't it? Aren't you going to open your present?"

He took a moment to drink in the shimmering expectation on her face, the bright, unsullied pleasure in her eyes. Never had he known a person who could so completely immerse herself in a moment, entirely dismissing all other matters be they large or small. Without a doubt that trait had brought Morgan to ruin—but it also lifted the persistent heaviness in his soul.

He turned to the package in his lap and carefully pulled on the twine. Her burst of laughter tickled his heart. "Oh Ward, you are forever too precise! Just tear the paper!"

"Why destroy it when I could as eas—"

"Good gracious, it's only paper! You aren't actually *planning* the opening of your gift are you?"

He smiled. "I'm merely practicing economy."

"Economy! About opening a present? Whoever heard of such unnatural behavior? Obviously you're dreadfully unschooled in such matters," she declared gaily, brushing aside his hands. "Here, let me demonstrate. Watch carefully now! You might wish to take notes!" She leaned forward to pull at the corner of the paper. Her scent filled his senses. "First you must rip the paper—"

"Fine," he said chuckling and dropping a kiss on her head. "You open it."

With a silly little gurgle, she obliged him, tearing the paper while he watched, both enchanted and aroused as her fingers brushed against his thighs.

"Here," she said and withdrew a small sculpture. He looked at her a spell longer. Prepared to utter false gratification, he glanced swiftly at her gift—then dropped his eyes to stare. Stunned, he took it from her hands, carefully turning it this way and that. It was a perfect miniature of a ship, in whalebone. Not any ship. Etched in the bow were the words *Sea Gypsy*.

"My God," he breathed. "Where did you get this?"

"It's the *Sea Gypsy*, isn't it? Mr. Montgomery said it was in port, so I contrived to commission a man on Park Street for the carving of it."

He ran his finger along the tiny bow as his heart skipped a beat, then seemed to expand. "But you rarely venture out, and Park Street lies quite a distance from here."

"I employed my wig," she said, eyes narrowing. "You like it, don't you?"

"Good God, Morgan, it's wonderful. Did it cost you much?" he asked, peering at her again.

"Not too much," she answered. She lifted her shoulders in a shrug that was too stiff to be casual.

"You're lying. Inducing the man to drive to the waterfront, to draw the ship in detail, and then carve it must have cost you quite a bit." He frowned. "It's not how I expect you to spend your allowance."

"It's my money, isn't it?" she asked with the touch of

the haughtiness that fit so poorly with her sketchy back-ground.

"Of course, but this—Morgan did you spend it *all*?"

"Not—all. I purchased scarves for Fionna and Maeve, too."

He shook his head in awe and rose to place the sculpture on the mantel. "I think this is the perfect place for it."

"You don't wish to take it to *your* home?" she asked, hurt darkening her brow.

Sitting on the sofa again, he smiled and brushed her soft cheek with his lips. "I haven't slept in my own bed but twice in the past three weeks. I should never see it if I kept it on Beacon Hill. I brought you a present, also." He withdrew a long, slim box from his frock coat pocket.

"A present? But the trip—" she started.

"We shall both benefit from that. I bought this for you." He laid it in her lap.

"Oh," she said, then lifted it carefully and shook it in her ear. "It *sounds* like jewelry."

"Open it," he commanded, anticipation of her delight flickering over his nerves like a warm, mellow fire.

"Not so fast!" she exclaimed with her large smile. "Truly, Captain, you've no notion of how to make the moment last, do you?"

He raised an eyebrow. "With you, Mistress, I endeavor to do so at every opportunity."

Her eyes twinkled. "And you do it well too. All right, I'm opening it," she said lifting the lid slightly. "Oh no! It closed again!"

"Woman, you'd try the patience of a saint."

"All right, I'm trying again! No! It's shut again. Captain," she said lifting her eyes slightly, "there's a tiny troll in there, I'm certain of it. It keeps pulling the box shut every time I pry—"

"Fine, Mistress, hand it over and I shall open it."

"No!" she shrieked as he stole it from her lap. Brushing aside her groping hands, he opened the box, then laid it in her lap.

Morgan's heart jerked to a halt as her eyes widened. There, in the center of a bed of blue satin, glittering in the yellow lamplight, lay a necklace of diamonds, arranged in a waterfall as she often teased him for. Lord, she thought, they couldn't be *real*.

"Do you like it?" Ward asked, his deep voice rumbling over her shocked nerves. "You've asked often enough."

She shook her head. "They're paste."

"Then my jeweler's a thief. Go on, take it out."

"I'm afraid."

"It won't bite," he said, and reached forward to take the necklace from the box. The sparkling stones threw patterns of light on the wall and ceiling. "Turn around and I'll put it on."

"No. If I wear it, I shan't be able to see it," she said, biting her cheek as she reached for it with trembling fingers. She held it up to the light. A rainbow of colors flashed through each stone. "Oh, Ward, it's lovely!"

"But not," he said softly, "nearly so lovely as its owner."

She shifted her gaze, tears welling in her eyes. Overwhelming affection glimmered in his, causing her heart to leap. He cared for her, she knew that, but not—surely not enough to warrant *diamonds*. "I can't accept this."

"Of course you can."

"But Ward, you can't possibly afford such expense! Not for your mistress, and certainly not on a sea captain's wages!"

"Morgan," he said taking the necklace. He leaned forward to clip it around her neck. It felt cool against her throat. She reached up to touch it, running her fingers along the smooth jewels, the rough settings. "You ought to have guessed by now that I'm more than a sea captain." She frowned at him as he sat back and took her hands in his warm, capable hands. "If that were my sole source of income, I shouldn't have had this last month to spend with you."

"I supposed that you were between voyages—"

"Not four weeks between, love. I swallowed the—I relinquished my captaincy after the voyage you were on. That's one reason that carving," he said nodding toward the mantelpiece, "is so especial."

Not a captain? she thought with a tiny chill. Had he borrowed the money then? "I don't understand. How do you have such wealth?"

His lips twisted and something flashed through his eyes, too quick to see. "I own the *Sea Gypsy*, my dear, and several more ships."

Owned ships. *Owned* ships? "I don't wholly comprehend business matters, Ward. Might a man earn much money owning ships? Enough to purchase—diamonds?"

He eyed her speculatively, as if considering how best to answer her question. After a moment he said slowly, "Many things can go wrong on a voyage, and ships are lost at sea all the time. However, a year's run to San Francisco, the Orient, and Liverpool, could pay for this house. Several such runs would pay for another ship."

"Another ship?" she asked, stunned. The import of it set her nerves to quaking. "Oh Lord, you've done just that, haven't you?"

"Aye, several times in past years, but recently the trade with San Francisco has ebbed, along with the profits. I've stopped purchasing new vessels."

"Then you're spending the profits, instead? On me . . . Ward, I can't allow—"

"I've invested them in other areas. Railroads, land, banking."

Several ships, she thought. Four? Five? "Have you had many good runs?"

More hesitation. "I've been lucky."

"Or careful," she said, for Ward was careful in everything. And with several ships earning that sort of wealth— "You're quite rich, aren't you?"

Another twisting of his mouth. "I know many who are wealthier."

"Many?" she asked, with a chagrined smile.

"Some," he said. "Will you now stop worrying about my spending habits? It would take a severe turn of fortune to put us on the streets."

"More than the purchase of precious gems for your mistress," she said. Then, amusement ripping through her nervousness, she tilted her head slightly and surveyed him a moment. "I ought to have asked for the earrings, too!"

The seriousness melted from his face, replaced with a broad smile. "Never. Didn't you listen? The money is tied up in railroads and land."

"Oh, you're hoaxing me! You have plenty of the ready, as Reggie would say, and now I want the earrings too! And sapphires and rubies!"

"And I ought to have clapped a stopper on my tongue, Mistress Greed."

"Yes indeed, for I shall never stop plaguing you for pretty things now, you know!" she said with a laugh. "And so, this trip, where shall we go first? Have you a plan? Oh," she said laughing again, "of course you do! You do nothing without a plan."

"Except for engaging one impudent mistress, with nary a trace of decency in her soul. As to my plan, I thought we'd spend our first night in Salem."

"Oh!" she exclaimed. "The witch town?"

"The witch town. Then a night in Gloucester, a couple in Portsmouth, one in Newburyport, and home again."

"It sounds like a whirlwind. What is there to see in all these places?"

"The ocean," he said softly. He leaned forward to press his lips against hers before whispering, "And you, Mistress, all day, every day."

Chapter Nine

Morgan leaned against the dock's rail, pulling her cloak tightly against the cold ocean breeze as she listened to Ward's deep, harsh voice explaining the uses of the different sails on the ship being built in front of them. Through breaks in gray and white clouds, the sun's rays bounced off the gray-green water of Newburyport's shipyard. "—and I must be boring you half to death," Ward finished ruefully.

She shook her head. "Not at all. It never before occurred to me how much a captain has to know."

"The knowledge isn't the difficult part. It's directing the men that's difficult, knowing when to push them hard and when not to. It's learning the vagaries of the ocean and deciphering the signs of changing weather. Raising and lowering sails is relatively easy."

She watched his face as he scanned the ship critically. "She'll be a beauty, that one," he continued. "Not quite up to McKay's standards, but close enough."

He looked, she decided with a pained thump of her heart, like a man in love. Bart had worn a similar expression when talking of the sea, but with him it had been excitement. With Ward the sentiment was broader, more intense.

"Who's McKay?"

"Donald McKay, out of Charlestown. The best builder of clippers in the world. I tried once to commission him, but the price was too dear and he not available at all events."

"Have you ever captained a steamer?"

Ward shook his head, his eyes following a huge mast being lifted onto the deck via ropes and pulleys. It took several men to do so, combined with much shouting and cursing. "Never. They're too noisy, they smell, and they require too little—I don't know, finesse, I suppose—to captain. For traveling they're faster, and will continue to become even faster, than any sailing ship. But for beauty, steamers offer no comparison."

"I hear they're pretty enough inside, with all manner of luxury."

"Aye, so has the *Sea Gypsy* if you recall, and McKay's vessels. No, it's a sailing vessel or nothing for me."

"It must have been," she said with a tightening in her throat, "very difficult to give up." With a tiny little prick in her heart, she conceded that she needn't worry his love for the ocean would take him away. But could being second—

He turned abruptly to her. Her heart skipped a beat, for the regard in his eyes didn't change. His gaze traveled swiftly and, oh Lord, *lovingly* over her face, before settling on her eyes. "I thought I should spend my entire life longing for the ocean. But lately," he said with the slightest catch in his voice, "lately that emptiness has been filled."

Her heart fairly flew, her face flushing with wild, fearful emotion. Not true, it couldn't possibly be true. . . .

"You have the very sea living in your eyes, Mistress," he said softly.

Good God, what did he mean by that? Nothing, for if he meant a thing, he'd kiss her. And yet he wanted to kiss her, she could see it in his eyes. He made no attempt to do so, however, playing the perfect gentleman as he had through these last three days. In public he treated her, his mistress, with utmost respect, touching her only when custom demanded it. But in private—in their well-padded carriage or alone in their room—he kissed and caressed like a man starved for affection, filling her nights with hot, sweet pleasure. But that was both his strongly ingrained manners and lust. Not, surely not something—

"It's growing late. Shall we return to the inn for dinner?"

He could not *love* her. "I suppose."

He nodded and they fell into step together. After a few moments' silence Ward said, "And so, Morgan, if you would be so obliging as to satisfy my curiosity, we've discussed many pieces of literature these past days, but you've yet to mention *Fanny Hill.*"

At the recollection of *that* book, nervous excitement bubbled through her veins, snatching her away from other thoughts. "Oh heavens! Ward, I swear I never— never knew people *did* such things, never mind wrote about them!"

"Ah, so you did read it. Was it warm enough for you then?"

"Warm enough! I wonder it doesn't burst into flames!"

He flashed her a bemused smile. "Did you dislike it? You've developed rather strong opinions on Richardson."

"Dislike it? I—I don't think that's the proper word. It

was—illuminating. It certainly gave me a different notion of a mistress's role."

His mouth twitched. "As in?"

As in mistresses rarely stayed with one man for more than a few months, she thought with a pained tightening of her heart. At least Fanny Hill hadn't. Did he love her, or was the trip a farewell? "Are you leaving?"

He halted abruptly, eyebrows forming a straight line of confusion. "Leaving?"

Facing him, she said with pained breathlessness, "Yes. Her lover left her, to go to sea. I thought, perhaps, you gave me the book as a sort of—warning. You're going away—just like he did."

"Morgan," he said gently. He lifted his hand as if to offer comfort, then dropped it. "No, it's not a warning. Didn't her lover return at the end?"

"After she'd been with many many, different men. And," she said with a touch of amused hysteria, "and a woman or two! You are *not* considering that, are you?"

He shook his head, his eyes crinkling at the corners. "Nor any of the other more perverse, and sometimes painful, aspects of that book."

She chuckled in spite of her twisting heart. "I daresay I'm relieved."

"Although," he said, "I remember a part with a young Italian count that could be—interesting."

"You mean," she said flushing under his now-smoldering gaze, "when she put her mouth on him?"

"Aye. Such an action can bring a man to his knees."

"Or," she said with a little laugh, "a woman."

"Aye." He grinned. "A woman has more than one set of lips to kiss."

Oh Lord, the visions his words created! A rush of excitement washed over her, leaving her weak. "Ward," she said in a low voice, "do you really think the street is the best place for such a discussion?"

His eyes flashed wickedly. "I confess, I should prefer the discussion in the privacy of our room."

She nodded mutely and started forward on legs so wobbly she stumbled, and Ward took her elbow to steady her, then swiftly guided her over the cobblestones to their inn. A moment later they entered their room, a crackling fire casting flickering light through the deepening gloom of late afternoon. With hot recollections of the fire's light and shadows dancing upon Ward's broad chest, Morgan tripped across the room to a huge four-poster bed, shedding gloves and cloak as she moved. When Ward didn't follow, she turned to find him leaning against the door watching her. "I thought we were going to discuss *Fanny Hill*," he said.

She swallowed. "I thought you wanted me to *be* Fanny Hill. Or at least the count's woman."

He shook his head, a mischievous smile playing upon his lips as he slowly stripped his gloves. "Tonight you shall play the count, and I will kiss your second set of lips."

His words were a tidal wave of excitement. "Ward—" she said, feeling for the edge of the bed. Finding it, she sat, and tried to speak. "How—you—"

"Hush," he said and crossed the room. He fell to his knees in front of her. Shuddering in sweet anticipation, she closed her eyes and held firmly to the bedpost as he slipped his hands under her gown. He caressed her ankles, then slid his hands slowly toward her thighs, lifting her skirts to expose her to the comparative coolness of the room. He spread her legs, and a moment later she felt his warm breath seconds before his mouth closed over her. His tongue flicked slowly over the pulsing bundle of nerves within, exciting a high-pitched gasp of delight. A short time later, her body rocked with hard, pleasure-filled contractions. She called his name, burying her hand in his hair as she fell forward limply.

"I ought to—," she rasped lightly. "You'll want—"

"Morgan," he said softly. "I'm fine."

"But—"

He rose and kissed her temple. "I enjoyed it."

"All—all right," she said and let him guide her to the middle of the bed, where she cuddled up under his arm, nose against his neck, taking deep breaths of his sea-salt smell. Oh, how she loved his scent, how she loved the feel of his arms around her. She could spend a lifetime here, just like this. "Ward," she asked dreamily, "do you think mistresses often fall in love with their keepers?"

"In love?" he asked, his body stiffening. "Are you in love with me, Morgan?"

"Very much," she sighed.

"Because I pleasured you?"

"Because of everything."

Relaxing, he gave her a gentle hug. "Sometimes. Occasionally captains fall in love with their mistresses, also."

"And so you love me, too?"

"Aye," he said softly. "It's an incredible feeling, isn't it?"

"The most beautiful," she said. So it was true, he loved her, and the deep satisfaction in her private places spread like warm honey up through her heart. She reveled in it for several minutes, as the last of the sun's rays slid past the window. "I never knew a man and woman could give each other so much pleasure," she eventually offered.

Ward's fingers tightened on her waist, and he answered in a controlled voice, "Well I suspect Weatherly was too old for you, and Drumlin too inexperienced. And it is not a subject talked about in polite society."

"My family didn't talk of it at all."

"But your mother explained the basics."

"She explained nothing."

Ward sucked in his breath. "Surely when your monthly flows started she told you *something*."

"She told me," Morgan replied bitterly, "that it happened to all women. More than that was for a husband to teach."

"And so when you married Drumlin . . ."

"I was hysterical. I thought Bart had mortally wounded me. When he finally perceived the extent of my ignorance he carefully explained the limit of all he knew, which as you suspected, was little."

"I'm sorry, Morgan." His arm tightened around her as he added, "We've had much different experiences. My education started when I was but seven years old."

"*Seven!* Good gracious! How could you understand anything so young?"

"No doubt my father thought it best to explain what I saw with my own eyes," he paused a minute, then continued tightly. "My mother had recently died and my father started bringing women home. He had no compunction about using them anywhere in the house."

Morgan jerked into a sitting position. "*Your* father! No, I can't believe it!"

The tension lines creasing his face made his nose appear larger, his cheekbones sharper. "Believe it," he said flatly.

For all his harshness, the hunger in his soft eyes touched her heart. She ran her hand over his whisker-roughened jaw. "Was it difficult, then?"

He shrugged, a casual gesture that did nothing to

relax the tight muscles of his face. "I thought it was normal."

She pillowed her head against his chest, comforted by the beat of his heart, the deep rumble of his voice. "And so you found him with a woman—"

"With two."

"And he explained it, then? My goodness, he didn't demonstrate, did he?"

Ward chuckled, and thankfully she felt him relax. "He still had some sense of propriety at that point. He sent me away, and came to my room later to explain—in gratuitous detail—exactly what they'd been doing. From that time on he talked about it often and gave me books such as *Fanny Hill.* I knew more about women at twelve than most men know in a lifetime."

"At first I found it disgusting, later interesting, and finally infuriating. My father never considered the consequences of his actions. Eventually he contracted syphilis, which shrunk his pool of available women. He took to the servants, willing or not, passing the disease on to three, one of whom hanged herself. Eventually Boston employed the eighteenth-century Puritan Laws, and had him arrested for fornication, thus destroying his reputation and the Montgomery name."

"And with your mother dead. . . ."

"My grandmother brought me to New York. He died, thankfully, three years later."

"Good God," Morgan breathed. "I should never have thought it of your family."

"It is actually a family trait, but my grandfather, and his father before him, were both seamen, and discreetly kept their philandering to other ports of call. The sea never interested my father. He desired, rather, to squander his inheritance."

"But you took to the sea."

He nodded. "My grandmother insisted I attend college, but I," he drew in his breath, "I could not stomach it. I ran away at sixteen, signed on to the *Sea Gull*. I worked hard, made second mate in two years, chief the next, and gained my first captaincy when I was one and twenty."

"And yet you've settled in Boston."

"Montgomerys have called Boston home for two hundred years. My father destroyed our reputation; it is my duty to restore it."

"Is it so important to you? The memories must be painful."

"It is two hundred years, Morgan. It must be that important."

Morgan snuggled deeper into Ward's arms, consternation wiggling through her happiness. Ward loved her, but it appeared that for all that in the end, he could not keep her. A name, a family line, meant nothing to her—it meant everything to him. On the outside Ward represented all his father did not. He was cool, considerate, reserved, but on the inside he had his father's hot, passionate blood. Her heart ached because for the life of her, she could not see how he could reconcile both.

Chapter Ten

In the seven weeks of Ward's absence, two things occurred. First, Morgan became certain that she carried his child. She wasn't overly concerned, as experience had proven that a man's seed easily planted itself inside her, but could not grow.

The second occurrence was longer and more insidious. Boredom, deep, depressing boredom. While she passed many happy hours learning to cook from Fionna and teaching Maeve to read, her body required exercise. Finally she uncovered her wig and took to walking early every morning before most people were awake.

Neither activity stimulated her brain, however, nor did gossiping with Maeve and Fionna. Initially the prospect of indulging in such common behavior thrilled her. In actuality, though, as much as she enjoyed hearing about Fionna's children, her "drunken-Irish-bum" husband and Maeve's attempts to meet decent, steady men, even those stories became old.

Finally one morning she donned her wig, a large poke cap and a hooded cape, then sent Maeve for a hackney cab. Heart pounding lest she encounter a Weatherly or Turner, she directed it to the Athenaeum, a private library to which Mr. Montgomery had kindly purchased her a subscription under the name Mrs. Brown. Keeping a watchful eye for intruders, she scanned the stacks. Fortunately at this early hour the library had few patrons. She selected several books, giddy over the far-from-enlightening *Three Musketeers* and *Count of Monte Cristo,* and returned home. Delighted, she read them in three days and returned for many visits, always disguised, always very early.

A few days before Ward's expected return she made one such visit, cheerfully poking through the books for something her captain might enjoy. Preoccupied, she didn't notice another woman in the stacks until she'd run headlong into her, spilling the woman's books on the ground. Apologizing, Morgan bent down to retrieve them, reading the titles automatically. *Wuthering Heights.* With a sudden tug of longing, she recollected it had been Amy's favorite.

Rising she handed the books back, then froze. The woman, wearing a cornflower blue gown and exquisite little blue cap on her light brown hair, stared back at her with familiar blue eyes. "Amy!" Morgan gasped.

A puzzled expression on her face, Amy said frostily, "Do I know you?"

"Well of course you do, silly!" Morgan replied, lowering her voice as she glanced around. They were alone. Beaming at Amy she continued, "It's me, Morgan."

For a moment Amy stared, and then her eyes widening, she clasped a blue-gloved hand to her mouth. "Morgan! It is you! Oh, what happened to your *hair?*" she asked, slipping into a soft breathy voice.

"Shhh!" Morgan hissed, glancing around again. "It's a wig, isn't it? I'm incognito."

"In—incog—what?"

"Disguised."

"But whatever—oh, Lord, of course you are!" she whispered, tears welling up in her eyes. "But how? Oh Mo, my dearest friend, I have heard such *rumors* and it has been ever so long since you've written! Oh, pray tell me that they are mere fabrications!"

She shrugged, smiling lightly. "I can't tell you a thing if I don't know what they are."

"Oh," Amy said with a tiny sob of a sigh. "About murder!"

Morgan winced. "Oh, those rumors. They're true."

"No!" she gasped. "No—you could never do such a thing!"

"It's amazing," she said in a low voice, "what desperate actions one would perform under desperate circumstances."

"Was he so horrible, then? Oh Mo," she said, wiping the tears from her eyes. "The gossip, the whispers . . . And you disappearing without a trace! But when last you wrote you lived in Philadelphia and—oh goodness, how do you come to be *here?*"

"I thought it prudent to leave Philadelphia under the circumstances. And you? Whatever are you doing in America, Amy? In Boston?"

Eyes brightening, she grasped Morgan's hand. "I am married! Can you believe it?"

"No!" she gasped. "When? Where—" she stopped, realized where they were, and grimaced. "Oh, bloody hell, Amy, we can't talk here, can we? Come visit me, you must, at my home where we shall be most private, I assure you! Here," she said, turning to a blank end page at the back of the book. She took a stub of a pencil from her bag and scribbled her direction. "This is where I live. Come in half an hour? But take great care, Amy, to cover your face and even your clothes for you mustn't allow anyone to recognize you, promise me?"

"But—but why?" Amy asked, staring down at the address. "Is it a bad part of town? Morgan, never tell me that you live in a—in a—slum?"

"Never fear, darling," she said, kissing her friend swiftly on the cheek. "I am much past that now. I am living with a man. Amy, I've become a mistress!"

Forty-five delicious minutes later, Amy and Morgan sat together on the sofa in Morgan's drawing room, sipping tea while Amy, eyes wide, voice breathless, asked a dozen questions at once ending all by glancing around the room and commenting, "But this isn't so very bad, is it? The furniture is quite handsome. Does he—does he pay for it?"

Morgan laughed and answered, "Oh Amy, how delightful it is to see you again! I've missed your company dreadfully! It's been how long, two years?"

"Two years. *And* nine months since you wrote that you *would* marry that Richard Turner, whom I heard was a vile, odious man and that you *killed* him. And you say it's true! Oh Mo, I promised I'd find some money! Why didn't you wait?"

Morgan shivered at her recollections of that time, recalling Richard paying court to her even while she wore widow's weeds, even while grieving for Charles. She'd loved him, in a fashion. "I couldn't. I was being dunned, threatened with prison by bill collectors. And Richard seemed so genteel, and as handsome as the devil with, I discovered too late," she said bitterly, "the soul to match. But that is all past me now. Oh Amy, I simply adore being a mistress! Only consider, I wear whatever I wish, read positively indecent novels and speak without censure! Vulgar words," she said with an airy toss of her head, "fairly roll off my tongue!"

Amy laughed, her eyes sparkling. "Never say so! Your lover has much to say about that I'll warrant!"

"But he *taught* me them! A lover is not a husband," she said, confidentially. "A husband governs his wife, chastises her when she disobeys, keeps her ignorant of all things vulgar, and pets her for proper behavior. A husband treats his wife like a child! A lover," she said, smiling mischievously, "treats his mistress like a woman. I daresay if I'd known earlier I'd have been a mistress long before a wife!"

"But the humiliation! The degradation! No, I refuse to believe you can relish such a thing, being so well bred as you are!" she exclaimed, blushing profusely.

"But it's not humiliating!" Morgan answered. "I'm happy, truly I am! Amy, his kisses fairly make me swoon."

Abruptly, Amy's stiffness melted and a devilish sparkle took over those wide, innocent eyes. "Do they? As much as Mr. Drumlin's?"

"Oh, far more," Morgan said. "Bart knew nothing in comparison. I live in complete comfort and yet need never attend parties or soirées or any of those monstrously dull balls. No obnoxious men or goat-faced matrons ready to pounce on me for the least indiscretion!"

Amy smiled and patted Morgan's hand. "And I know how difficult it has always been for you to avoid the least—if not the most!—indiscretion."

"Just so," Morgan said sprightly. "And now, do tell me how you heard of my—troubles so far away as London!" she said. Her nerves tightened and a sharp pain ran through her teeth. If Amy had heard of Richard in England, how could Ward have missed it in Boston? How could anyone have missed it? "And, of course, about this husband of yours. It's Howell, isn't it? But first," she said, biting her lip, "tell me of Reggie."

Amy grimaced. "Your father refuses our association, but I hear he's well."

Morgan sucked in her breath. "Oh no! Heavens, not because of me!" she exclaimed, putting her hand to her clenching heart.

"Partly because of my role in your elopement. Then I—I broke off my betrothal to Howell and now your father believes I am beyond redemption."

"No!" Morgan gasped. "You could not! Amy, everyone has expected your marriage forever!"

"Yes, but I never loved him, Mo, and how could I marry a man I never loved? My parents and I had row after wretched row over it, and I fancied myself sunk beyond all hope until I met my Edward. Oh and Morgan it was just as you said! As soon as he kissed me I *knew* I'd found my one true love! He is an American and you *must* recollect how I have forever *longed* to meet one, for they are so free-spirited, so respectful of their wives, not like our stuffy Englishmen! Edward's brother Gregg went to Oxford with Gareth. When Edward was visiting Gregg and cholera broke out what must Gareth do but bring them home to avoid illness. Before I knew it we were engaged, and now married. But it is also," she said with a pained sigh, "how I heard of your circumstances. He is from Philadelphia and at our wedding his sisters could talk of nothing but the Wicked Widow. Oh Mo, tell me it's not true," she wailed, "for now I shall live in Pennsylvania! I thought we might be friends again, but now you're under this man's protection and—oh at least tell me he is good to you!"

"He treats me like a queen. Wait, I'll prove it you!" Grabbing her skirts, she ran upstairs to retrieve her diamond necklace. A few minutes later, Amy's eyes all but popped out of her head as she took it from Morgan.

"It's lovely," she breathed, running her fingers over

the jewels. Oh, they cannot be real!" When Morgan nodded, Amy gasped, "But how did you ever meet a man with such wealth? Does he have a wife? Who *is* this man?"

"He captained the ship that carried me to America. He owns several of them. He's away on such a journey right now."

"A sea captain? From Boston?" Amy asked, alarmed. "How long has he been away?"

"He went to see a friend's wedding in London, two— two—" She stopped as realization dawned on her.

"Oh my God," Amy said, gloved hand to her mouth. "Oh never say so—It's not possible—"

As Morgan formed a reply, the front door opened and Ward's deep, beloved voice called out. "Morgan? I'm back."

Amy's eyes widened in dismay. "Dear God, Morgan, you must hide me!"

"But he said he'd not return 'til Thursday at the earliest!"

"We had uncommonly good sailing weather. Oh, Lord, this is a nightmare!"

"Morgan?" Ward called, entering the room and Morgan's heart flipped. His eyes found her, gleaming dark and sinful before falling on Amy. Then his smile faded and he raised one eyebrow as he slowly stripped his gloves. "Morgan. And Mrs. Huntington, I see."

Chapter Eleven

A dreadful silence controlled the room as Amy, eyes wider than Morgan would have thought possible, stared back. Finally she stammered, "Mr.—Mont—Mr. Montgomery?"

"At your service," he said with a bow. His eyes went to Morgan, perched on the edge of the sofa. "My dear," he said silkily, "I expected a warmer welcome after seven weeks' absence. Do I receive even a kiss?"

Heart beating like a frightened bird, Morgan turned to Amy, "It was your wedding, then, Amy?"

Amy nodded, saying slowly, "And Mr. Montgomery is your *master?*"

A spark of anger flashed in Morgan's heart. "No man is my master."

"I am," Ward said, taking a chair opposite them, "her captain."

"Captain? But—no," Amy said, hiding her blushing cheeks between two hands. "Oh, this is impossible! Of all the horrible coincidences . . ."

"Since we are here together, it appears entirely possible. Morgan, you owe me an explanation. How are you acquainted with Mrs. Huntington?"

"Yes!" Amy exclaimed, regarding her friend. "And how are you—mistress—to Ward Montgomery? Lord, Morgan, he is my husband's dearest friend! He's all the reason we are in Boston!"

A sudden case of shaking possessed Morgan's nerves as she clenched her hands together. "Dearest friend? But how could that be if Mr. Huntington is from Philadelphia?"

"Edward attended Harvard," Ward answered. "When he graduated he boarded the *Sea Gypsy* for his grand tour and we became friends. He met Miss Cunningham's brother while visiting his own at Oxford. I ask again, how do you know each other?"

"Morgan has been *my* dearest friend since we were children," Amy said, lifting her chin haughtily.

Morgan winced, and rasped, "Amy, please, he doesn't need to know."

Ward frowned. "Did Morgan's parents work for you, then?"

Amy's eyes hardened. "They did not!" she snapped. "We were neighbors. Her father is the Earl of Westborough."

"Earl!" Ward exclaimed, stiffening. "Good God, woman, you're English *nobility?*"

Everything, all the long weeks of careful artifice, was falling to rack and ruin before her eyes. Why, oh why hadn't she just ten more minutes alone with Amy to explain it all? How dreadfully stupid of her, how rash and reckless for a lowly paramour to invite Lady Amelia Cunningham for a morning call! "It's of no great significance. My family refuses to recognize me."

"I can well imagine that! Why didn't you tell me?"

She flinched at the suppressed anger in Ward's voice. "I was persuaded that a mistress's background was unimportant to her lover."

His jaw worked as he clenched his teeth. "I should never have made you my mistress if you'd informed me of this."

"You'd rather see me living on the streets?" she spat back.

"Far better options exist for a woman of your breeding than life on the streets or in my bed!"

Amy, her dear, dear friend, cringed, but said, nonetheless, "You may not speak that way to my friend!"

Ward's eyes darkened. "With all due respect, madam, her situation affords me the liberty to address her in any manner I please."

Amy sucked in her breath, blood drained from her face. Turning to Morgan, she snapped, "You shall not remain here one minute longer. Pack your things. I'm taking you home with me."

"Excellent," Ward barked. "Edward will no doubt revel in the notion of his bride foisting his best friend's paramour on him. By all means, take her with you!"

Amy glared at him, then patted Morgan's hand. "Go on, dear. I'll wait."

Trembling, Morgan shook her head. "No. I haven't anything to pack, at any rate. Everything belongs to Ward."

"Then come as you are. I'll lend you some clothes, and we shall send these back," Amy said rising.

With a twist of her heart, Morgan shook her head again. "No, but you go on Amy. Find your Edward. I shall be fine."

"Don't be absurd! You cannot remain here!"

"It's my home."

"It's his home!" she said, dramatically flinging her hand toward Ward.

Morgan swallowed, emotions warring in her breast. She loved Ward with her whole heart, but she had missed Amy terribly, far more than she'd admitted even to herself. In a husky voice, she replied, "His home *is* my home, isn't it?"

"A mistake that we shall correct, you and I." Unshed tears brightened Amy's eyes, and she pleaded. "Oh, Morgan, I can not leave you in these circumstances! It's unconscionable!"

Narrowing her eyes, Morgan said in a low pained voice, "I shall be fine, truly. Just, please, keep my secret," she said, passing her tongue over suddenly dry lips. Putting all her faith, all her fear into her eyes, she begged, "Please, Amy, not even your husband. I—I rely upon your discretion."

"I don't know. I—" Amy said on a quivering little sigh. "All right. All right. But *you* must vow that you will be *careful!* And if—anything—should occur, should you need *anything* at all, you shall contact me!"

Tension seeped from Morgan's shoulders and a trickle of levity infiltrated her frightened heart. "Oh yes, and Philadelphia is the ideal location for such contact!"

With a laughing sob, Amy replied, "It's a large enough city from what I understand. I should be quite discreet."

Morgan smiled softly as she squeezed Amy's hand. "As always, my dearest friend. And now you'd better take your leave. No doubt your husband misses you!"

She glanced at Ward. "Yes, I imagine he's returned to the Tremont by now." She nodded and quit the room. With the click of the front door the only friend Morgan had in the world departed.

Silence filled the room as Morgan fought back hot, aching tears. After a moment, Ward spoke in that deep-throated tone guaranteed to send thrills tripping across her raw nerves. "And now, Mistress, I await that kiss."

She turned to him. He sat on the edge of his chair, facial muscles taught with anger, but his eyes glowed with desire. She crossed to him and leaned over to touch his lips with hers. His arm wrapped around her waist to drag her into his lap. His mouth took possession of hers, forcing entrance, delving deeply. She responded by pressing her lips hard, first to suckle his tongue, then to dance with it as she demanded entrance of her own. He refused, tightening his hands on her head; her fingers crushed the fabric of his jacket as she fought for control of the kiss. Finally, with a rumble of a laugh in his chest, he relented. She surged inside, sweeping his mouth, relishing the peppery taste of him, sighing with pleasure when he welcomed her with hot, velvety strokes.

Eventually, he lifted his head and his eyes laughed at her. "You're a little firebrand, aren't you?"

"Aye, Captain. Would you like to put my fire out?" she asked huskily.

Smiling tenderly, he ran his palm across her flushed cheek. "I doubt that's possible."

"You do it well, sir."

A shudder shook his large, muscular body. "Lord, Morgan, you ought not to talk that way." He sighed. "Nor should I have taught you such things had I known of your connections."

"Bloody hell! Does that mean no more diamonds, too? Damn Amy!" she said with a chuckle.

"You ought not to curse, either."

She tilted her head. "But I enjoy cursing."

"Aye, Mistress, you enjoy anything improper or indecent."

"Mmm," she said, reaching for the buttons on his waistcoat. When he tried to draw back, she held firmly to the material with one hand, while caressing his hard chest, warm through the fine linen of his shirt. "I enjoy working for my diamonds you know," she said huskily.

"Wanton," he accused between deep breaths. "Damn, how did a woman like you get born into nobility?"

"No doubt," she said as she halted her attentions to untie his cravat. "My mother had a love affair with the butler."

"I doubt butlers have such skill at seduction."

"It is just a freak of nature, then."

"You are no freak, Mistress," he said, reaching up to grasp her wrists. "That is enough. We must talk, Morgan. You ought to have told me the truth. You know I never should have engaged in this affair had I known it."

She smiled saucily. "Perhaps that's why I never told you."

"You ought to have taken one of the other options," he said severely, guilt darkening his eyes.

This, she thought with a heavy heart, was one of the reasons she kept her background to herself. "It matters little, Ward. My family disowned me."

"And what did you do to deserve such hard treatment?"

She shrugged. "I married a sailor."

"A sailor? Good God, you forfeited family and fortune for *Drumlin?*"

"Aye, Captain," she said ruefully. "Was that a mistake, do you think?"

With a humorless bark of a laugh, he replied. "I think that's a severe understatement."

"Especially since he died shortly thereafter."

"Did you love him so much? I recall you grieving, but, forgive me, it seemed not overmuch."

"I loved him, although truthfully I should have married almost any man to escape my father."

Ward remembered too well Morgan's bitterness of her parents and the hard constraints they'd imposed upon her. Fools, he thought as he rubbed the muscles cording in his neck. How could they not see that the tighter their hold, the more she would rebel? "Understood. But surely you could discover some gentleman of society more suitable for your escape?"

"My father had already found me a suitable husband who shared his views on women. He believed only Randolph would administer the discipline I needed. He betrothed me to Viscount of Arlington against my will. And so," she said with a sigh, "during my only London season, I resolved to enjoy some freedom before prison life. While my family planned the wedding, I slipped away to venture everywhere unsuitable to a lady. On one such adventure I met Bart, fell in love, and with Amy's assistance, eloped."

Ward's eyebrows drew together as he said softly, "She assisted you? I wonder if Edward knows that." In a louder voice he continued, "And then Drumlin died, you married Weatherly, who died also, leading you to me. I repeat," he said, harshness entering his voice, "this is no position for a woman of your birth. Damnation, when I consider the demands I have made of you, the lessons I have taught you—" He sucked in his breath. "Things no decent woman would know. Had you but told me the truth—"

"I relish my lessons," she said, sliding her hand across his chest, to his belly, and then below. His breath caught in his throat, his face creased in tortured guilt. "I'm not so unhappy."

"You ought to be."

"Would you have me leave?" she asked, leaning forward to kiss him, running her tongue along his bottom lip.

"Morgan, please, I'll have a promise from you before this continues."

She frowned. "What sort of promise?"

"That you have no further congress with Amelia Huntington. I'm sorry," he said, his heart aching at the pained longing in her eyes. "She's your friend and you have damned few, I know, but it's the path you've chosen. Consider her reputation, and Edward's, if it were discovered that she visits with my mistress."

"Is the society of sea captains so strict?"

He hesitated. "Edward's people are that strict. If it matters that much to you, we might still search for another, decent form of support for you."

She shook her head. "No."

"Are you certain, Morgan?"

In answer she kissed him deeply, her small tongue flicking through his mouth, setting his body on fire once more. With a small groan he yanked her hard against him, running his hands down her back. After a time his mouth left hers to slide across her shoulders, then down to the crevice between her breasts. She gasped and after that, all other conversation centered upon the sensual.

"Amy!" Morgan gasped as she turned the corner of a book stack.

"Oh Morgan," her friend cried out, then flung herself into Morgan's arms. "I thought I should find you here! But ought you to come?" she said lowering her voice. "These people," her eyes swept the small room, "are part of—his—set."

"I'm disguised. But Amy, you must not seek me out! We aren't to be seen together. If your husband's people discover our friendship, you'll be ruined."

Amy shrugged fatalistically. "It is probably inevitable, at any rate. I've never been a paragon of respectability."

"No, nor I!" Morgan whispered, chuckling. "But at least you have toed the line, when I crossed it."

"Lord, Morgan," Amy whispered, giggling. "You've

passed it by a mile at least! And still I don't have the whole story."

"'Tis very long," she said with a sigh.

Amy smiled, hooked elbows with Morgan and said, "Then we must discover a quiet corner where we can be private."

"If my captain or your husband learns of it, they'll be enraged."

"And how could that happen with you in that odious wig?"

She smiled. "I suppose if we could conduct my affair with Bart under my father's nose, we can do this." As they exited the stack, they glanced furtively around, then moved swiftly toward a back staircase. "I know just the place, in the basement."

"You would! Oh, Mo, how I have missed you!"

"And I you. How long do you stay in Boston?"

"Six weeks before we leave for Philadelphia, but in two days we leave to visit another friend of Edward's. Your captain is to accompany us."

"Is he?" Morgan said disappointed. "But he has already been away so long!"

"Morgan," Amy said, pulling to a wide-eyed halt. "You're in love with him!"

"Deeply," she said softly.

"Oh Lord, what a coil you've found yourself! All right, off to this corner of yours to tell me the whole."

After two wonderful hours of whispers, muffled laughter, and tears, they planned to meet again the following day. After all, Morgan had never specifically promised Ward anything.

Chapter Twelve

"Well then," Ro said, smiling as he reached the end of the joke, "says the woman, 'I've been fucked!' To which the sailor replies, 'That's just what I was saying, madam!'"

Edward burst into laughter and a few seconds later, Ward emitted a few guffaws. After the humor died down, Ro and Edward exchanged glances over the dinner table, and Ro reached out a foot to kick his friend's chair. "What's the matter, Sir Captain? Did the vulgarity escape your understanding? Do you require an explanation?"

Ward flashed him a small grin and shook his head. "Not from you, I don't."

Edward frowned. He'd spent two months now with Ward, but he'd swear he'd not had his full attention for more than five minutes during the entire time. In the beginning he hadn't cared a rap, not with his bride eagerly awaiting him in bed. But as Amy's spirit had exerted itself in other areas of marriage, he'd become increasingly aware of Ward's unusual preoccupation.

"All right, man, out with it! What's got you acting so demmed mutton-headed?" Ro asked.

"Mutton-headed?"

"I'd employ more descriptive vocabulary, but I daresay you'd get your back up about it and read us a lecture."

Ward gave Ro his sideways smile, poured himself more port, and asked pleasantly, "Should I?"

"Bloody hell," Ro said in his most comical English accent as he reached for the port. "Do you ever answer a straight question, or just ask new ones? I won't scruple to tell you, *Mon Capitaine*, that it's frightfully fatiguing."

Ward shrugged.

"He's been this way since my wedding," Edward said. "Couldn't get a rational word out of him no matter how hard I tried. He's beat me to a standstill."

"Indeed?" Ro asked slowly, casting a knowing eye over Ward. "Why then, the cause is obvious enough. He's cunt-struck."

Ward spit out his drink and knocked over the decanter, while Edward laughed. "Damn, Ro, marriage hasn't changed you one whit." And Amy had thought that women and men ought to retire together after dinner! Why could she not understand that a man needed private time with his friends?

Ro's eyes gleamed devilishly. "What's she look like? Red-headed and buxom? Or blond with pouting red, uh, lips?"

"Hell, Ro, Ward's never been a petticoat chaser. Could be he don't like petticoats," Edward replied with a chuckle. "Always wondered about that."

"Aren't they called crinolines these days?" Ward replied, making a deal out of cleaning the spilled port with his handkerchief. "I've heard that some ladies in England are wearing hoops again."

"How shocking, Sir Captain! Where would a prim and proper fellow as yourself come by such improper information? I should have thought you'd conduct such affairs in the dark."

"And current information, at that. The last woman you spoke of was," Edward calculated, "two years ago. That blond actress. What was her name, Ro? Emma?"

"Esmerelda, from New York, I recollect, a year after I married Fran."

Ro's cynical amusement softened on the last word, stabbing at Edward. He'd loved Amy as much two months earlier. Now he wondered how in hell he'd gotten himself into a marriage with so uncontrollable a woman. Spirit was all well and fine in bed, but a woman ought to be obedient outside of it.

"Two years without a woman. Egad, man," Ro said with a laugh, "you've all the sensuality of a saint!"

"A most damning statement from a man who's never been known to keep his equipment in his pants for more than a day at a time," Ward replied mildly.

"Point scored, Ro," Edward said.

"Quite so, Sir Captain," Ro said bowing his head briefly in mock agreement, "because the women kept taking it out."

"Which is a sorry reflection on the sort of female you've associated with, and the use of the gold in your pockets."

"I protest! I've never once paid them in gold!" he said slamming his fist on the table. "It's strictly silver from me or nothing at all!"

Edward laughed and Ward smiled slightly before his eyes glazed over again.

"Confound it, he's gone again!"

Ro negligently scanned Ward's face. "Sure he ain't foxed? Been hitting that port rather hard."

"Hell no, he spilt half the damned bottle out when you—" Edward halted, eyes widening as the truth struck him. "By God, it's true! Ward's found himself a woman! Well if that don't beat the Dutch!"

"No!" Ro exclaimed. "Are you contemplating marriage and begetting yourself a household full of junior sailors, old man? It's not Penelope Curtis, is it?"

"Never," Edward teased. "She's entirely too pretty to fall for that hawk's face. How about Cornelia Howard? With that hook nose, she might not notice Ward's beak."

Ward grinned and shook his head. "You men veer far off course."

"Why, then she's a member of the New York set," Ro said with finality. "A Livingston, I presume. Or perhaps a Morris."

Edward shook his head. "Impossible. If he was chasing petticoats in New York, why would he be here with us?"

"Edward, I'm shocked! He'd much rather drink my port than dance attendance on a mere petticoat!"

"Aye," Ward said with a chuckle. "Or a crinoline for that matter. But, I'm sorry to say, your company isn't preferable to the figure that fits into either. Gentlemen, I make sail tomorrow for more interesting shores."

"Make—Good God," Ro exclaimed, whistling. "It's true."

Ward shrugged. "She's neither blond nor redheaded, and," he said, narrowing his eyes in a damnably peculiar way, "not someone either one of you knows."

Ro lifted his eyebrows over laughing eyes. "You're sure of that? Between the two of us, I daresay we've known most of the women in Boston in some form or other."

Wards eyes gleamed. "Not this one."

Edward cocked his head slightly. "Not this one? She's not one of us, is she, Ward?"

Ward hesitated a moment, confusing Edward. There was something disconcerting in all this, something Ward was concealing, not that that was anything new. He'd never been forthcoming about his private affairs. Sometimes it seemed to Edward that all of Ward's life was a private affair.

Ward sipped his port, fixing his eyes first on one, then on the other. "She lives in town, under my protection."

"Bloody hell," Ro whispered, and Edward started coughing, dragging Ro from his astonishment. With a sudden burst of laughter, he belted Edward on the back, accusing good-naturedly, "See what you've done, *Mon Capitaine*? I dare swear you've killed Edward and with such splendid port too, weeks on the boat straight from the home country herself. There, there, Edward! We've got milk if that suits your head better!"

"Get your confounded hand off me, you lout!" Edward gasped. "Damn, Ward, does your grandmother know of this?"

"Not to my knowledge."

"Well I'd like to be a fly on the wall when she hears of it!"

"Would you?" Ro asked. "No doubt she'd swat you dead, dear boy! If ever that woman allowed a fly to live in her home, I'm a bloody monkey."

Ward grinned. "No doubt some of those silver-paid women would agree with that assessment."

"No doubt," Ro agreed with a grin as he sat back in his chair. He twirled his glass and watched Ward with sharp, amused eyes. "So, *Mon Capitaine*, tell us about your paramour. By God, but you've pulled the wool over us! How long?"

"Three months give or take."

"And when do we meet this paragon? Or is she bacon-faced and you're afraid we'll laugh?"

Ward's grin grew to a broad smile, alarming Edward. Ward never smiled, damn it. "She's fairly pretty, to be sure. But you won't meet her," he said, fixing his eyes on Edward. "You've neither of you heard of this? Not a breath?"

"Never a word," Ro said, placidly. "And you know I should have, for as holed up as I am here in Marblehead, I have my contacts."

"Don't see why we shouldn't meet her, do you, Ro?" Edward asked, grinning in spite of the worry marbling his amusement. "We're placid married men now! Not likely to steal the wench away from you, Ward, not that it wouldn't be easy. No doubt she'd fly at the first sign of a smile from another man! That's it, isn't it? You've locked her up! There," he said slapping the table with his hand, "the mystery's solved!"

"Or our venerable captain wishes to keep her existence secret from his grandmother," Ro agreed. "We wouldn't tell a soul. Word of a gentleman and all that."

"All the same, she may discover it," Edward answered. "Someone's bound to see the girl on your arm and it'll get back to her. She'll—what's the expression he used to use Ro? 'Ride you down as she would the main tackle!' Be sure you've got your phaeton waiting and a train ticket in your pocket!"

"The lady doesn't go out much."

"Good God, you are keeping her under lock and key!" Edward said.

"She's rather—shy."

At that Ro burst into laughter, his eyebrows raised over humor-filled eyes. "Shy? Who but you, Sir Captain, would engage a shy paramour? Is she religious to boot? Does she recite Bible passages in bed? Or perhaps she lays still as stone?"

At that Ward truly laughed, which made Edward's

muscles tense. "No, she doesn't recite Bible passages. If she's read the book at all, it was in search of the warmer passages."

"Ah, so she's hot for you, then?" Ro asked. "No doubt 'twas pitch black when first you met her."

Ward smiled slightly, eyes twinkling. "She's paid for that, isn't she?"

"In gold or silver?" Ro asked.

"Diamonds," Ward said, chuckling. "And now, gentlemen, I'll bid you good night. Edward, shall I see you in Boston before the week's out?"

"But Ward it's early hours yet!" Edward complained.

He shrugged and rose. "I mean to shove off before the morning tide."

"Come, now, not that early! What's she have we don't?" Ro asked.

"Petticoats for one thing, and no whiskers!" Ward said as he strode toward the door.

"Well that's better than Esmerelda!" Edward called just before the door closed behind Ward. "Still," he said frowning at Ro, "I don't like it."

"Let him be, Ed," Ro said crossly. "The man has a woman. Who cares if she's shy, or bracket-faced, or a monkey in disguise? He likes her, that's clear, and he allows himself little enough pleasure."

"He has his name to consider."

"His name, his name! That's been his soul consideration for twelve bloody years. His father's lechery isn't his fault! Ward's a flesh and blood man and for the first time since we met him, he's acting like it. I say bravo!"

"His grandmother will hand him his head on a platter."

"Hah! I'd like to see anyone hand Ward his head. He's not as mild-mannered as he pretends to be, Ed. He was captaining ships when we met him, one-and-twenty, with the cool head of a man ten years his senior. And we three years older, Harvard men at that, and *he* saved *us* from more than a few tight scrapes. If there's a man better able to captain his life, I don't know him."

"But Ward's family expects him to marry well, and if Boston hears of this it could destroy those prospects. You know full well, Ro, how this town frowns upon such actions."

"They'll be scandalized no doubt, but Boston loves Ward and the women adore him, little though he knows it. He'll have this little affair, then send her on her way and settle down with a proper Boston woman. Ease up, Ed. Let the man sow a few wild oats first."

"Right. You know what I think? I think you're ignoring the consequences of these actions to salve your conscience for stealing Fran from him, that's what I think," Edward said savagely, ignoring the tightening of Ro's mouth.

"Fran came to me of her own free will—"

"You all but kidnapped her while she was engaged to Ward!"

"She never loved Ward, you know that, and his own feelings for her were lukewarm at best. My conscience, sir, is quite clear. You, however, seem to harbor rather a lot of anger for a man newly married. Could it be your own wife that concerns you?"

Edward breathed in deeply at the stabbing in his chest. "Damn, but she's hard to control, Ro. She cares little for conventions, less for a husband's rule."

"Perhaps you oughtn't try to rule her then," he said, pouring another glass of port. "Sit back," he said grinning, "and I'll tell you my philosophy of wives."

"No doubt full of vulgarity."

"Certainly. Ward's gone."

* * *

"Oh, Maeve, can you not lace it any tighter?" Morgan pleaded, staring at herself in the mirror as Maeve pulled on the tapes of her corset. She turned her head this way and that, inspecting the plaits running along both sides of her head and coming together in a knot in the back. Rob had brought a message from Ward that he'd returned to town earlier than expected and demanded 'a good English tea' around four. Only an hour to wait, and she so much wanted to present herself at her very best!

"Any tighter, ma'am," Maeve answered, "and we might be hurting the wee one, so we might."

"Oh," Morgan said, a tremor wriggling through her stomach. She winced at Maeve in the mirror as thoughts of hairstyles slipped from her mind. "How did you know?"

"Ye've not been handin' us any rags for washin' since we came here."

"And," Morgan said turning slightly to examine her figure, "I have added some more weight, haven't I? How quickly it has come on, in just two weeks!"

"So it happens."

Morgan grimaced. "Perhaps you ought to loosen the stays, then. Tie them just tight enough so I can fit into my gown."

Maeve obeyed and then proceeded to help Morgan into petticoats and bustle, venturing gently, "Have ye told the Cap'tin yet?"

Morgan frowned. "I never thought to. I supposed it would go away."

"Babies aren't after doin' that, if you don't mind my sayin' so."

"Oh, Maeve, but mine *do*. I've lost three already."

"*Three?* I *am* sorry, ma'am."

Morgan shrugged. "They all terminated before the

quickening. I hadn't any opportunity to become attached."

Maeve tied the tapes of the bustle and drew Morgan's blue velvet dress, trimmed with pink embroidered flowers, over her head. Its scooped bodice proudly—if a trifle indecently—displayed Morgan's breasts. As Morgan adjusted it, Maeve circled her, tugging at the gown's skirts to spread it evenly over her underclothes. "I'm thinkin' ye be past the danger point now."

Her last monthly had been in November while she'd been staying at the Tremont. She was entering her fifth month. "I suppose I am." And just at that minute, something bubbled in her stomach. A strange sensation— "Good gracious! It moved!"

"Moved? No, ma'am, it can't be doin' that yet. 'Tis early days, still."

"I swear I felt a movement!" she insisted as Maeve retrieved a bouquet of pink violets to string through Morgan's hair. "Oh, forget that Maeve, and help me out of my petticoats! I wish to feel it with my hands!"

"Ye won't," Maeve said with a wisdom beyond her years. "'Tis too soon, so it is."

Alive! It was alive and living *inside* her! Not dead, not another miscarriage, but a baby. But she'd never expected this! "Oh fudge! I'll try, at any rate."

"The Cap'tin will be here soon. Ye know he's always early."

"But he'll wish to feel it too!"

"Will he?"

Morgan froze. Would he? Oh God, she'd not considered—but mistresses didn't have children, did they? No. They—a tiny little chill settled in her stomach—they had abortions. Suddenly frightened, she hugged her stomach. But she could not! It was her baby!

"Morgan!" Ward's voice rang out through the house.

Morgan swallowed hard and said in a quivering voice, "I require a few moments to compose myself, Maeve."

Maeve, eyes full of pity, said kindly, "Ay, Miss. I'll be tellin' the Cap'tin ye'll join him shortly."

Morgan, entering the parlor, heart fluttering, found Ward casually garbed in charcoal gray, sitting on the sofa reading a newspaper. When he lifted his head upon her entrance, the frown on his face transformed into a full, dimpled smile adding longing to her apprehension. Dropping his paper on the table, he strolled forward to sweep her into his arms for a breathtaking kiss. Dizzy, confused, she almost swooned. He chuckled slightly, moving his head to nibble her ear. "Miss me, Morgan?"

"Always," she said as her heart pleaded his case. A man who kissed thusly could not possibly order her to end the life growing in her belly. In all their time together Ward had never once displayed signs of cruelty. "It's early for tea."

"Aye, Mistress," he said, lovingly running his hands up and down her back. "I hoped first to visit your bedroom."

"But I only finished dressing!" she protested.

"I don't know why you troubled yourself. I sent word I was—coming."

How could one simple word contain so much meaning? It created visions of his passion-taut face looming above her, breathing heavily as he entered her. Her whole person reacted with a flood of heat coursing downward. She shut her eyes and tried to shove it aside.

"Morgan," he teased. "You hesitate? Need I persuade you?"

He slid his mouth down her neck toward her breasts

and she gasped, arching her back to allow him further access. Wanton, oh she was a hopeless wanton without a drop of self-control. "Oh, when you do that I am yours! You may command me at will."

He chuckled as he kissed her breast. "You disobey those commands with regularity." Then, grasping her wrist, he led her swiftly upstairs where, upon shutting the door, he yanked at her stays to free her breasts from their confines. He suckled one nipple, causing a wonderful convulsing down below as she frantically pulled at his trousers. Moments later they were on the bed, Ward taking her quickly, with deep, hard thrusts, to a sparkling plateau and beyond. It lasted only minutes, leaving them laying at odd angles across the bed, still partially dressed. Ward chuckled in her ear. "That's not precisely how I imagined our first meeting in two weeks."

She smiled, caressing his dear, rough cheek. "It's generally the way such meetings are with us, though."

"Generally," he said, his eyes crinkling as he balanced his head on his hand. "We'll make up for it this evening. First, however, I wish to hear how you passed your days. I spent mine in conversation with two obnoxious men who believe they are the heart and soul of wit. They are not. Come," he said, pulling himself up and reaching for her hand. "We'll discuss it over tea. Do you wish me to re-lace your corset? You seem to be tying it loosely these days."

"Yes," she said, blushing as she rose to retrieve it from the floor and pull it around her breasts.

"Aye," he repeated, bewilderment rifling through the levity in his voice. He stood, then leaned over to gently pull on the laces. "And hesitation in the parlor. You've always been wont to present yourself at your best for me. Are you starting to take my love for granted, Mistress?"

"You—you've always before opposed tight lacing."

"It's unhealthy, but I don't remember you ever following that piece of advice. Or, in truth, many other pieces," he said, tying the laces loosely. Afterwards he frowned and ran his palms down her waist and over her hips. "It seems you've added more ballast, love."

Oh no, here it came. Strength. Strength. How to present this? *Oh Mother, there's so very much you never prepared me for!*

"Not that it matters to me," he added quickly, grasping her waist to turn her toward him. She lifted her chin to hold his gaze, unable to control a flinch of fear as his eyes searched hers. "But you'll require a seamstress if it continues."

Morgan drew a deep steadying breath and collected her courage. "I shall require a whole new wardrobe, and soon. Ward, I'm carrying your child."

Chapter Thirteen

Ward stared, momentarily paralyzed. A child? Impossible. He hadn't planned for it. "You're mistaken," he said flatly. Pain shot across her face, and for one furious minute it left him with a deep sense of satisfaction.

"I've been in this condition three other times. I'm not likely to miss the signs, now, am I?" she said acidly.

Satisfaction evaporated. His world swung and swayed, floundering like a ship in a hurricane. *Steady, old man,* he told himself, closing his eyes. *Hold fast to the wheel.*

He opened his eyes. She was now sitting on the bed, hurt accusation on her face. "No, of course not," he said. "I've never contemplated such an occasion, that's all. You lost the other three."

"Would you prefer that? Do you wish me to destroy it?"

The words sank in slowly, then turned into a dull knife, ripping a hole in his heart. "No! Good God, do you believe I'd have you risk your life?"

"I've no notion of what you might bid me do."

"Well you ought to after these last four months," he growled. Damn it, damn himself for his foolhardiness. A good captain left nothing to chance, planning for the worst while praying for the best. Instead he'd permitted his passions to control his actions.

"How a man treats his mistress when she pleases him, and his conduct when she does not are two wholly different matters."

"God damn it!" he yelled, pain and shock flaring into self-righteous anger. "Your insults are entirely unjustified! I've always treated you with the utmost respect!"

"As I have always pleased you. And now as you are certainly *not* pleased," she said, her eyes turning to ice," you yell and curse. What will you do next? Beat me? No doubt if you struck hard enough you would have that abortion."

His chest tightened, and he clenched his hands into fists as alarm and anger battled for control. What the hell was the matter with her? He'd never even threatened to mistreat her. He loved her, for God's sake! Gritting his teeth he snapped, "I never wished for that. How should I, when I am only now discovering the situation, which, by the bye, seems to have progressed far past the point of first knowledge. Why is this the first I hear of it?"

She rose and stalked to her bureau. "Like you, I assumed it would end spontaneously." She opened the door and pulled out her black dressing gown.

"But it didn't. How far along is it?"

"I'm entering my fifth month."

His mind automatically calculated the timing. "November then. It took immediately. Damnation, Morgan, you ought to have informed me earlier. Like you ought to have told me of your parents, like you ought to have told me of Weatherly! Do you have any other surprises for me?"

"No. Would you like your dressing gown? Fionna will be serving tea shortly."

He grabbed his pants. "These will do," he said, buttoning them up. "We'll continue this discussion in the drawing room, then, if you can be civil."

"Tea," she snapped, "is eminently civilized."

"Fine." He rose, jerked open the door and motioned her through. He followed her stiffly, calling for Maeve.

As they waited for tea, Ward wrestled with the pounding in his chest, attempting to confront the situation with some measure of calm. It proved remarkably difficult, as the consequences struck him over and over again. Thus far, with infinite discretion, he'd kept this affair hidden from the eyes of the world. Even if he'd been discovered he'd believed in the possibility that many would turn a blind eye to the situation. But for that same mistress to walk the streets heavy with child? He had his share of enemies. He easily envisioned the whispers, the disgusted expressions, and God save him, his grandmother's disappointment. He'd have the very devil to pay and no pitch too hot.

Maeve entered the room with the tea tray just as his stomach took a queasy flip. Years, literally years, of exemplary behavior lost for a few weeks of stolen passion. How could he have been so stupid?

Rubbing the muscles cording in his neck, he glanced at Morgan at the parlor table preparing the tea. Several tendrils of dark hair had escaped their pins and hung in soft curls around her face, which was pinched and pale in the sunlight streaming through the window. When Maeve left, Morgan brought him a cup of tea, her eyes catching his briefly. Incredible sea-green eyes, as deep as the ocean, now red-rimmed with hurt. In clearer moments he admitted to himself that he'd known more classically beautiful women—Fran for example—but in his heart no more beautiful woman existed in the world.

As Morgan made herself comfortable on the sofa, he

sat back and asked, "You are four months along, correct? The child is due in August." She nodded. "You understand," he continued as his heart clenched, "that this has progressed too far for you to end it."

She sipped her tea and answered, "It can still be done."

"Not safely. If you'd wished to follow that course, you ought to have done so earlier."

She sucked in her breath as if he'd struck her. "I never said I wished for that."

"Do you?"

She turned and lifted her head, her gaze catching his. Her eyes, the color of a frightened ocean, shimmered with pain. "It's your *child*, Ward," she said and her voice cracked.

His child. Their child, conceived in love. The thought wriggled into his heart bringing with it soft visions of Morgan, baby to her breast. Red hot desire shot through him along with a fierce, bittersweet love, temporarily driving out all recriminations. Taking a shaky breath, he put his cup on the table next to the sofa, and held out his arms. "Come here, love."

With a strangled cry she laid aside her cup and dove into his arms, burying her head in his chest. He waited for tears; they didn't come. Instead she held tightly to his shirt, fingers crushing the material as she took deep breaths.

After a time she shifted to snuggle under his arm. The sweet fragrance of her hair drifted under his nose, making him smile. "So, we're to be parents, then."

"Aye," she said happily. "And we must choose names, mustn't we? I fancy something nautical. What about, hmmm, Star, as in starboard."

"Aye, madam," he said chuckling. "And if we have a son, we shall name him Lars, for larboard."

"Goodness, no!" she said with a little laugh. "What a vile name for an American born son! If we want something foreign, we ought to name him Porthos from the *Three Musketeers*. Only consider, Captain, we might call him Port, both for the land and the wine!"

Amusement spreading through his chest, Ward grinned and shook his head. "Morgan, no! Our child would run away from home—"

"Oh, oh! Better still, Leland!" she exclaimed, really laughing now. "We should call him Lee and when we combine your names—"

"It would be *LeeWard!* Good God, woman, what will you think of next?"

"Not much," she admitted, twinkling up at him. "I don't know any more nautical terms."

"Nor will I tell you any, lest you find worse names. Perhaps, my dear, we're putting the cart before the horse. We ought to be planning its birth."

"What is there to plan? A baby arrives on its own schedule."

"True, but with luck and good care it needs its parents for eighteen years or more."

"Oh," she said, frowning. "I'd not considered that."

"Yes, well luckily it has a father to plan for its future."

"If," she said carefully, "you intend to remain in its life that long."

"Of course I do. Do you believe I'd abandon my own child?"

"Eighteen years is a long time."

"Not so long for a parent."

"But my child's surname—" she paused, "won't be Montgomery."

Ward stiffened as the next wave of shock slammed into his battered heart. "No," he answered slowly, "it will be Weatherly."

She shrugged casually, but her face tightened, bringing shadows to her eyes.

"Eighteen years," he said softly, further ramifications settling in, "*is* a long time." Especially for two people with no legal commitment between them.

"You may wish to marry during that time, Ward."

"You may, also."

"Oh yes," she answered with rough sarcasm, "I shall have *so* many offers."

"Blast it," he exclaimed, rising, suddenly miserable and restive. Rubbing his neck he went to the sideboard to pour himself a brandy. "For you?" he asked holding up the bottle.

"A little sherry, thank you."

He nodded grimly, poured her the drink and handed it to her. Then he sat in an armchair and sipped his brandy, attempting to picture his future with his perfectly eligible Bostonian wife and perfectly *legitimate* children. He'd always intended to present to the world a picture of himself as a devoted father and husband. But could he love another woman after Morgan? Could any woman ever take her place? And did it matter, at all events? He'd never included love in his plan; he never expected to find it. Instead, he'd fought for, longed for unimpeachable respectability, to stand head and shoulders with the leaders of Boston society.

But, he thought with a terrible wrenching, what honor was there in fathering a bastard child?

The remedy to that . . . damn it, the remedy . . . but Morgan didn't have a respectable bone in her body.

Heart tight, Morgan watched Ward, his face one large frown as he swirled his glass. Sipping her sherry, she rubbed her belly as if the baby could feel the caress. His baby. Her baby—the child of a fugitive murderess. Oh Lord, eighteen years was a very, very long time.

He took a sip of his drink and looked up at her, his eyes narrowed as if in pain. "Do you wish to marry me, Morgan?"

She sucked in her breath. For a moment she could not breathe, could not think.

Then her brain jerked into action, running along at a frightening speed. In her few short hours of knowledge, she'd not considered *that*, an offer of marriage. Oh but what sort of offer was it, at any rate? Not a heartfelt offer. Not "will you marry me," but "do you wish to marry me?" Oh God, she thought breathing out slowly, oh God, it was his own, desperate solution to a desperate situation. He didn't truly want her as wife. If he knew the truth, he wouldn't wish her as mistress, either. "No."

"All right." Was that relief in his voice? She couldn't tell with the blood pounding in her ears and her heart turned into a storehouse of gunpowder, each new reality setting off yet another bloody explosion. A lifetime with Ward—a lifetime of passion and laughter. Not for her, never for her.

He smiled ruefully. "We didn't plan this very well, did we?"

She swallowed hard. "I don't generally."

"I do."

"I know."

"Well I can make some amends. I'll have my lawyer start the paperwork tomorrow to create a fund for the child. It won't want for money, nor," he said with a breath, "will its mother. I shall do the same for you."

And that was it, she thought as the final explosion shattered her heart. A settlement of money before he cast her aside, gave the mitten, jilted her—a thousand different ways of expressing that one monstrous thing—

"Oh Lord," she said in a cracking voice. "If you please,

Ward,—I can't, I truly can't discuss this any more tonight."

He stared at his glass. "Morgan, I'm sorry. If I could do it all over again . . ."

"You'd not have done it at all," she filled in.

"You mistake me." He lifted his gaze, his forehead wrinkled. "I should have planned it better. I don't regret a moment spent with you. I love you."

Oh Lord, he loved her—still. But not enough. Enough for what? He could never marry her. Amy had informed her that her captain was not just a captain, nor a captain of captains, but a high standing member of Boston society with connections, through his grandmother, to New York society. And the rules for this American aristocracy were even stricter than that of London.

"Morgan?"

She lifted her head.

"No answer to that?"

To his love? To what purpose? She shook her head.

"All right," he said looking back at his glass. "Do you wish me to leave?"

She swallowed. "Not—not quite yet. Please, would you just hold me?" she asked on a sob. Immediately he put down his drink to join her on the sofa. He pulled her against his hard, strong body as she searched her mind for comfort. Eventually Fionna entered to clear the tray away and add wood to the fire. Beyond the window the sun sank into night.

"Captain Wyatt, sir?" Fionna asked after pulling the curtains.

"Yes?"

"Would ye be stayin' for dinner, sir?"

He looked down at Morgan. "Should I?"

She hesitated. If she were smart she'd force him away

now, before he broke her heart even further. But if she'd been smart, she'd never have left England.

"Yes."

Ward flashed her a smile and nodded to Fionna. After a time he said gently, "You'll be fine."

"I know. The money. I'd—" she swallowed. "I'd rather have you."

He looked down at her and for the first time in hours, his expression softened to the warm affection she'd grown to love, to crave. "You have me. I'm not going anywhere."

"But those funds—"

"Are to ease your mind, not end our arrangement."

And the pain did ease, although it surely didn't disappear. "You'll marry, someday."

He hesitated. "It's expected."

"And you said that first night that you'd never have such an arrangement if you were married."

He drew in his breath sharply. "Damn, Morgan, must we discuss that now?"

"It will happen. I'm merely attempting to—plan."

His mouth twisted wryly. "Well, you've chosen an extremely inconvenient moment to practice that skill."

She smiled back, digging deep inside for the stubborn optimism that had guided her through—and frankly, into—so many storms. "It seems a little absurd to plan the planning, Ward."

The twisting of his lips turned into a full-fledged smile. "But, Mistress, that's precisely what we're going to do. We've dealt with enough for the night. What about playing a game of chess with me?"

"Chest?" she asked impishly.

"No," he said with a laugh. "Chess. And that is *all* we shall do, my dear, until you see a doctor. I suspect he'll limit certain activities for the health of the child."

Her stomach dropped. "But why? Surely it can't *hurt* the baby?"

"I can think of a number of ways it might."

"But—"

"I won't risk it. Neither shall you. Tonight, it is chess. Or cards. Or some other purely platonic form of entertainment. Tomorrow we'll send for the doctor."

She grimaced. "My bed has been cold and lonely for two weeks, and now I must wait upon some misogynist doctor who's never been in an 'interesting condition' of his own?"

He grinned as he rose to pull the chess table between the two wing chairs. "I promise that whatever doctor I find will positively love women."

"Will you?" she asked, tilting her head slightly. "And how many doctors will you have to choose from, Captain Wyatt?"

Ward groaned. "Another complication. Tomorrow, however. Tonight it's parlor games and yes, Mistress, I'll stay the night."

She lifted her eyebrows as her heart flipped. "Truly?"

"Truly. I wouldn't wish your bed to grow too cold or you too accustomed to sleeping without me, lest you decide to keep me out forever."

"Now that, I assure you," she said with a flirtatious smile, "shall never happen."

Chapter Fourteen

"Pregnant!" Rob shouted.

Ward scowled. "For God's sake, pipe down! Do you want the entire building to know?"

Rob, sitting in a well-cushioned leather chair in front of Ward's office desk, shook his head vigorously. "It can't be so."

Ward leaned back in his own chair and folded his hands in his lap. "I have a number of arrangements for you to attend to in this matter with, as you'll expect, the utmost discretion."

Rage disrupted Rob's normally cool composure. "She'll have to get rid of it."

Over his dead body. In one short night he'd become attached to the little tyke. "You forget yourself," he ground out. "This is my child, my affair, and I have the captaining of it, Rob, not you."

"With all due respect, this *affair* could have repercussions for your entire family."

"How so? Do you expect to care for the child?"

"Damn it, Ward, this is a scandal in the making," he snarled, stabbing the desk with his finger.

"And, as you insist upon every occasion, you are but

a distant cousin. Should this come to the public eye, which I trust it *won't*, no one will include you or your family in the scuttlebutt."

"Except that my name is Montgomery!"

Ward snatched up his pen and dipped it in an ink well. "The child's shall not be," he growled, with a stabbing of his heart. "You'll follow these instructions. I want two funds set up. . . ."

He continued for a few minutes, writing it all down. Afterwards, he set the paper aside to dry. "Understood?"

Rob nodded grimly. "Those are rather large sums."

"Overcoming the stigma of 'bastard' will tax the child hard enough. The trust fund at least ensures that it never wants food."

"Nor anything else. What you're doing is providing for both mother and child for life."

"I am. I made a mistake and I'll pay the shot."

Rob peered at him. "But it's an excessive correction. Didn't Mrs. Brown make the same mistake? What if she decides to marry?"

Ward shrugged to dislodge the weight bearing down on his shoulders. "That's her prerogative."

"This allowance will support a husband also. Is that your intention?"

Ward rubbed the crick in his neck, attempting to shove aside thoughts of Morgan laying with another man, pledging herself to another man for life. It yanked at his heart and set his chest on fire. "No."

"Would you withdraw the money in case of marriage then? What about the child?"

"I don't know. Damn it!" Ward exclaimed, smashing the desk with his fist. "I'm between the water and the wind, here, Rob! Instead of arguing with me, you might consider bearing me a hand!" Frustration propelled him out of his chair to pace the room.

Rob sighed and reached for the paper. "I'll discuss it with Higginson. He's been an attorney for a dog's age. Quite possibly he's dealt with similar issues."

"For legal purposes, he'll need to use the name Morgan Weatherly."

"Weatherly? As in *Amanda* Weatherly?"

"Aye. Morgan was married to her brother, but wishes it to be kept quiet as she has had difficulties with the family." Ward heaved a sigh. "And for obvious reasons, we'll also wish for utmost discretion. I expect Higginson will abide by it as well."

"Why did you not tell me of this before?"

Ward shrugged. "It didn't seem important, and she was adamant about keeping it private. Now, however . . ." He shook his head and stared out the window at Boston harbor.

"We have other business to attend. It's—it's about your grandmother."

Ward continued staring at the ocean. Not a cloud graced the sky, and the sun sparkled on the bouncing waves turning the ocean aqua-green traced with gold. Like Morgan's eyes when lit with laughter. Would she re-marry? She'd refused him, although in all honesty he'd made but a lukewarm proposal. Marriage to his mistress—impossible. His grandmother and a hold full of cousins depended upon him to uphold the Montgomery name, not drag it deeper into the mud. "I've made bad weather of it haven't I, Rob?"

Rob hesitated and Ward winced. Rob's anger originated from a deep loyalty to Ward, to a friendship beyond cousinship.

"We'll come about, sir."

"We shall try to, at all events. I doubt that I can keep this from my grandmother. You'd better schedule time for me to visit."

Rob hesitated again, and when Ward turned he saw helplessness on his cousin's face. He spread his hands in supplication and said, "That's what I've been trying to tell you. She's already here, staying at the Tremont. She sent you a—" He gave an uncomfortable laugh. "A summons this morning."

"Oh, good God," Ward said, the ache in his neck worsening. "Send back, tell her I cannot see her today but I shall—no, *she* may wait upon *me* tomorrow."

"Oh no, you would not do that," Rob said, shaking his head in dread. "You cannot return a summons with a summons. She'll tear you to pieces."

"She's heard something, you may count on it. Better to meet her on my own deck."

"And what will you tell her about Mrs. Bro—Mrs. Weatherly?"

"I'm open to suggestions."

Rob had no suggestions and the interview with Ward's grandmother went as expected. In his house or hers, the tall eighty year old woman had a mast-stiff spine and the character to match. Perched on the sofa in Ward's parlor the following day, she shot questions at him about Morgan for fifteen minutes, appearing increasingly agitated with his answers. Finally she snapped, "At the very least, tell me that you have no serious intentions toward this female!"

"I haven't."

For a moment she stared at him, her keen black eyes attempting to read his face like a newspaper. He kept his poise however and her face relaxed a bit. A touch of warmth entered her dark eyes as she said in a calmer voice, "It is unlike you, son, to engage in such practices. Would it not be easier to find a wife? It is two years since that scoundrel Hathaway stole Miss Sheridan from you. Surely you've recovered."

"Seeing Fran and Ro together remedied that."

"And yet you remain unmarried."

Ward hesitated, suddenly guilty at his lack of effort in securing the wife that his name and family demanded. "It's only prudent to be thorough in such a search."

"And has your search yielded any serious results? With whom do you contemplate marriage, Ward? You must know this mistress will not be tolerated by any decent wife."

"No one as yet, but I am no fool. I should never attempt to keep both."

"And so when you marry, you'll turn her away."

The thought cut at his heart and for a moment he couldn't answer. Finally he said with as much certainty as he could muster, "I will."

As she searched his face, her own softened slightly. "Perhaps you ought to accompany me back to New York. Or join me in Newport this summer," she said gently. "Boston women may be too—cold—for you."

Smiling, he took her soft, dry hands in his. "Few New York women would be happy in Boston. It just takes time. Try, Grandmother, to have some faith in me. In the end I trust you'll be pleased with my choice."

Sighing, she dropped her stiff shoulders. "I should be pleased to see you happily settled. However, if you promise to maintain discretion I shall say no more about this woman. Do you go to Mrs. Otis's ball tonight, Ward? I wish you would escort me."

"I would be honored."

Chapter Fifteen

"And so, with all the expenses paid, you retain a profit of thirty-five thousand dollars, sir. A handsome sum, I'd say, for a year's work," Rob said.

Ward studied the books Rob had laid out on his desk. Through the open windows an early summer breeze drifted, carrying with it the tangy smell of salt air. Were it sweetened with perfumed soap, it would perfectly match Morgan's scent when his touch stirred her passions. Ward's thoughts drifted over this morning's loving, her soft, red lips and the heady sounds of her pleasure.

"Sir?"

Ward hauled his mind back to his small waterfront office, and leaned back in his chair. "Handsome indeed, Rob. Thank you."

Rob shrugged. "I merely recorded the numbers, sir."

"You underrate yourself," Ward replied firmly. "You executed many of the arrangements that brought the voyage to a successful conclusion, as always. You must accept some of the credit. And you deserve some of the profit."

Rob shook his head. "I only carried out your orders."

"You always carry out my orders, and devilishly well, too. When was the last time I raised your wages, Rob?"

Rob flashed him a grin, his sternness melting into boyish humor. "Just last month, sir."

Ward shook his head, rose and stretched. "It's not enough. Write in an expense for ten percent of the profit."

"Ten percent, sir! No! I've not—"

"Are you arguing with me, Rob? You know I brook no arguments from my employees. I shall dismiss you, cousin or no."

"But I've never invested even a pen—"

"You've invested hours of work, far beyond what I expect. And it's only the shipping business. The income from my other interests still belongs to me." He wandered over to the window and, leaning against the wall, stared out at the ocean. Sun-tipped waves rose and fell, then rolled over each other like children at play. The gentle splashing became light, sing-song voices, beckoning him. *Too much work, Ward, too little laughter.* By God how he missed sailing! But not nearly so much as a year ago, he thought with a slight tug at his mouth. Not nearly so much as before Morgan.

". . . so perhaps, sir, after the repairs are completed on *The Dolphin* the profit may shrink a bit. Do you wish the repairs completed before its next voyage?"

Rob continued to harp on about business and the endless amount of details to attend to if they wished to keep the coffers full to overflowing, leading not to enjoyment, but merely to the need for new coffers.

"Of course. Send her to Newburyport. You know I never put a ship to sea without her being in top condition."

"No, sir, but in this case we have a charter interested that could bring you quite a bit of money if you chose to forego the repairs this once."

"And risk the loss of both the ship and the souls on board? No."

"Yes, sir," Rob answered obediently, but his voice registered disappointment. Over these last few months Ward had come to believe that Rob cared more for the Montgomery fortune than he did. Since meeting Morgan, Ward mused as he watched the sun bouncing on the waves, everything inside him seemed to shift. All that had once occupied even the corners of his mind was now mere shadow—

"Sir?"

Ward closed his eyes, summoning up patience. "What is it now, Rob?"

"The profits from *The Dolphin?* Where should we next apply them?"

He sighed. "Let's let it ride for now."

"Let it ride? You don't have some investment interests?"

He opened his eyes to stare at the ocean again. "Rob, do you ever wonder what the use of it is?"

"Use of what?"

"The money, the work."

Silence, stunned silence filled the room. Finally Rob said slowly, "For your future sir, and that of your wife and children. For all of us."

Wife and children. Like Cordeilia Howard, a good, respectable wife, bred to marry and bore a man so relentlessly that he'd escape to the office at every opportunity, claiming the need to earn more money to fill even more coffers. It was the Boston way.

In the distance Ward spied a small yacht, sails full as she skipped across the harbor. Today the wind would blow cold upon the ocean, but soon enough full summer would arrive. If not for Morgan's pregnancy, he'd take her sailing. Down the coast for another holiday, full of heat and passion, laughter and lazy conversation.

His gaze following the yacht with longing, he asked, "When was the last time you took a holiday?"

"Why, last November, sir."

"Your brother's wedding, correct? How long were you gone? I forget."

"A week, as you insisted. As you do with all your employees."

Of course. He'd learned long ago that a well-rested worker performed much better than one constantly running under full sail. He advocated paid holidays for all, something his associates thought madness, but then they'd not increased their own fortunes by tenfold in ten years. "I've only taken the one. With Morgan."

"Didn't you go on holiday in England? With Hathaway and Huntington?"

"A little time here and there, when I wasn't acquiring goods for the return voyage. A sort of working holiday." He paused a moment, comparing the nights spent carousing with Ed and Ro—or saving them from yet another scrape—to the days spent with Morgan. It scarcely compared at all. Those precious hours had marked him permanently, bringing warmth to his heart and relaxation to his muscles. Were all holidays accompanied by women similar?

For a moment Ward supplanted it with the image of his mythical wife. It chilled him to the bone, finalizing the decision he'd struggled with for several weeks. "Do you think, Rob, that you could locate a copy of the *Peerage*? I believe that's the name of it. The book that lists the estates and family lines of the English nobility."

"The English nobility? I suppose Teresa might have one. That sort of thing interests her. I'm not sure it would be current, however."

"Current over the last several years will suit me, thank you."

"Are you thinking," Rob asked timidly, "of taking a holiday? To England, perchance?"

Reluctantly, Ward turned from his view of the ocean. Forehead wrinkled in puzzlement, Rob sat at his desk, pen in hand, watching Ward carefully. "England? Why should I go there?"

"The *Peerage*, sir. Is there someone you wish to visit?"

"I count few friends among the nobility," Ward said mildly. "You mistake me with Hathaway and Harrington."

He blinked and then nodded. "Of course."

Dismissing Rob's confusion, Ward sifted through various plans. "I must, however, write a letter to a certain earl."

Rob's frown deepened as he nodded slowly. "Of course. I'll see to it."

Another lengthy silence passed, while Ward leaned against the wall, focusing his gaze on the floor. His next words would anger Rob, but of late he'd become increasingly certain he was charting the best course—into the northern storm to avoid a southern hurricane. "Have I ever told you that Morgan's father is an earl?"

"*What?*"

Ward lifted his head, his eyes slits as he gazed at Rob. "The Earl of Westborough. Her family disowned her, but she may still claim noble blood."

Eyes wide in disbelief, Rob stuttered, "When—when did you learn of this? Are you *certain?*"

"Morgan confessed it a few months back under, uh, duress. A reliable source confirmed it."

"But, sir, she's—she's your—Good God!" Rob whispered as he sat back, the enormity of the situation settling on his face. He rubbed his forehead in consternation. "What did she do to be disowned?" he asked. "Good God, Ward, tell me you're not the cause of her ruin!"

Taking a steadying breath, Ward crossed the room to a standing chest in the corner, from which he withdrew a bottle of brandy and two glasses. "I had no involvement with that whatsoever. She eloped with a sailor."

"A *sailor!* But you said she married Weatherly!"

"Aye, after Drumlin died. She believed the sailor to be her only method of escape from her father's tyranny. From what she told me he's fanatically conservative," Ward said, pouring them both drinks. He sat at his desk once more and slid a glass of brandy across to Rob.

After a couple of sips Rob found his voice again. "Conservative and tyrannical. Those traits would ill suit Mrs. Weatherly," he said dryly.

"An understatement. From the little I've gleaned, her mother isn't much easier. They dealt badly together and so she married Drumlin, who died aboard the *Sea Gypsy*. She met Weatherly on the same voyage and married him within the month. Quite a history, wouldn't you say, Rob?"

"And this is the reason you want the copy of the peerage? You intend to write to this earl? I doubt, sir," he said wryly, "that he wishes to receive correspondence from his daughter's protector."

"I doubt," Ward said swirling his brandy, "he cares to hear from me at all. However, Morgan misses her brother and I've resolved," he said and took a long sip of brandy, "to put the entire situation to rights, come what may. I shall ask Lord Westborough for his daughter's hand in marriage."

"Oh hell," Rob swore and then drowned his other words in several gulps of brandy, adding dark amusement to Ward's anxiety. Rob's would be but the first in a long line of shocked faces. With effort and handsomely planned deception, he expected to avoid the worst of the scandal, but not all of it. Hopefully Boston would temper its disgust with recollections of his years of hard work, charity and propriety.

After a moment Rob spoke in a liquor-roughened voice, "Are you sure?"

"Aye."

Rob drew a number of breaths before saying, "She loves you very much."

Ward's heart leapt. "Does she? How can you know that?"

He shrugged. "It would be difficult to not notice. Her face lights up whenever your name is mentioned. And you, Ward? Do you share these sentiments?"

He smiled as a lump formed in his throat. "Aye, Rob. She is everything."

Rob's eyes warmed with amused affection. "Thus the reason for your distraction of late. And so," he said with a sigh, "you'll marry her. I anticipate many difficult months ahead."

Ward passed a gimlet eye over his cousin. "Yet I observe little distress on your part considering your hostility toward Morgan two months ago."

"Her situation shocked me, as you are habitually conscientious in all matters. But despite Mrs. Weatherly's high spirits—and her troubled history—she displays the best of manners when called upon. To be sure, her attachment to English nobility increases her attraction in the eyes of Boston. With some restraint she might prove a good wife for you. And to own the truth, Ward, for all your intentions to the contrary, you've never formed a lasting attachment to any other woman, despite the way they throw themselves at your head. Not even to Fran Sheridan."

Ward smiled, lifting his eyebrows. "Throw themselves at me? What, have I missed something? I'm not aware of such a thing."

"Miss Curtis practically pants after you."

"Miss Curtis? She and I are merely friends with similar interests in housing the indigent Irish. Romantically, she casts her cap in Lodge's direction."

Rob smirked. "Of course. As to Mrs. Weatherly—ought I to obtain a license?"

Ward shook his head. "First I wish to try for Lord Westborough's permission."

Rob frowned. "If he's disowned her, why trouble yourself? She's been married twice already. She's scarcely a gently bred maid at this juncture."

"Still I dislike marrying her without at least knowledge, if not consent, from her family. Anything less strikes me as dishonorable."

"Even sir, when they've disowned her?"

"Even then. I don't answer for her family's actions, only my own."

"Understood, but it shall take at least five weeks before you receive a reply, and the baby is due in August. Perhaps, for expediency's sake, you ought to marry her first and inform them afterward."

Ward rubbed the tightening muscles in his neck. "Morgan might prefer prior consent, also."

Rob studied him. "You haven't asked her yet."

"She rejected my petition."

"Good God," Rob said with a deep sigh of weariness, "she can't have."

"I admit the proposal lacked enthusiasm. She'd just informed me of the child's existence, and I wasn't certain of my course. I hope that gaining her father's approval will aid in persuasion on my next attempt."

"But with all you have to offer, what persuasion do you need? And she loves you!"

"Aye, and one would expect that to be enough. But

Morgan rarely does the expected. My best bet is to leave her no reasonable alternative."

Rob's forehead creased and he nodded his head wearily. "Well you know her better than I do. Write your letter, sir, and I'll deliver Lord Westborough's direction to you by tomorrow afternoon. In the meantime, I'll start devising a way to present the entire situation to society."

Ward grinned wryly. "And to my grandmother, which will undoubtedly require some handsome navigation. I have some ideas on that issue, if that helps. . . ."

Chapter Sixteen

"You have visitors, sir," Herman said as Ward entered the comparative coolness of the house, breathing a sigh of relief after the heat of the July sun. Herman took his gloves, cane, and hat, then handed him the post.

"Visitors? Who?" he asked, sifting through it quickly. Invitations, a letter from his grandmother in Newport, requesting his time no doubt, a letter from Aunt Ellen Montgomery in New York, still hiding from her brother's indiscretions thirteen years after his passing. Grandmother considered her weak. Ward thought her plain stupid.

Nothing from England.

"It is Mr. Huntington, sir, and his wife. I said you wouldn't be home for long, but they insisted. They're in the drawing room."

Ward nodded with a quick smile of approval. "Perfectly correct, Herman. Thank you," he said handing him back his mail. "Would you be so kind as to put this on my desk? How long have they been here? Have you rung for refreshments?"

"Yes, sir. They've been here closing in on an hour.

And sir," he paused and Ward noted an unusual tightness around his butler's eyes.

"Yes?"

"At the risk of appearing presumptuous, sir, they seemed a little agitated."

"Agitated?" Ward asked.

"Yes, sir. I've heard some shouting."

"Thank you, Herman," he said glancing at the clock. It wanted a few minutes to five. Had Edward skipped dinner? An Edward with an empty stomach was an ugly Edward indeed. But what circumstance would possibly have caused him to do so, or, more importantly, to arrive in Boston without proper notice?

He strode to the drawing room door, braced himself for the hot wind of Edward's temper, and pasted a smile on his face. He opened the door, exclaiming, "Edward! Amelia! What a pleasant surprise. I'd no notion—"

Edward spun away from the mantel, his face ablaze. Ward flinched as he closed the door. Edward conversational, amused, or even bilged, Ward enjoyed immensely. But when the man's temper flared, he could enrage even the most level-headed man. Any bystander, innocent or not, would do well to set sail—and fast.

"I've just arrived," Edward snapped. "My wife has some important information for you. Tell him Amy!"

Alarmed, Ward turned to Amelia, who sat on the sofa in travel-stained clothes, her brown hair in disarray, her eyes red and swollen. His own widened as he swiftly scanned her for signs of Edward's lamentable temper. To his relief he found none. To the best of his knowledge, Edward had never hurt a woman, but Edward had never before been married either.

Amelia started sobbing, tears rolling down her cheeks. Shaking her head, she concealed her face in her hands.

"And long may you weep," Edward snarled, "for placing my friend in mortal danger!"

"Mortal danger—for God's sake, Ed, what's the matter with you?" Ward exclaimed. "She's your wife!"

"She's a damned fool," he spat. "Tell him, Amy!"

Ward, tension knotting his neck, sat next to Amy and offered her his handkerchief. "Hold your temper, sir! You've better manners than this!"

"You have not heard. Do you tell him, Amy, or do I?"

Taking Ward's handkerchief, she continued sobbing and with a disgusted tsk, Edward fixed his gray eyes on Ward. "Then I shall open the ball! Apparently, Ward, my wife is well acquainted with this mistress you've kept so damnably secret."

"Secret? I told you about her."

"Precious little. You don't appear surprised. Perhaps in your family it is usual for gently bred women to associate with whores?"

Ward jerked at the insult, then clenched his jaw a moment, fighting to hold fast to the reins of his own temper. "Have done, man!" he snapped. "You insult three with one blow."

"Three—you mean that harlot of yours?"

A picture of Morgan dressed in her black negligee, her eyes gleaming with desire, rose in Ward's mind. His hands formed fists and it was only due to years of training that he kept himself from hauling off and belting Edward as he seemed so determined to invite. "You'll lay aside the insults or you'll leave my home."

Muscles jumping in Edward's cheek, he stared at Ward. By and bye, his expression relaxed. "I apologize. It's for your welfare that we've come."

"Aye, 'mortal danger' so you said. So mortal, Edward, that you couldn't change after your travels?"

"So mortal."

"No!" Amy cried out in a tight, watery voice. "Not so, Edward! Morgan would not hurt Ward for all the world! She is so entirely attached to him that even contemplating such a prospect would overpower her spirits beyond redemption! She loves him! She does!" she exclaimed and started sobbing lightly once more.

Ward slowly looked from one to the other. "Not hurt me? Why do you think Morgan would hurt me?"

"Have you read of Philadelphia's Wicked Widow?" Edward asked.

"Wicked Widow?" he asked, allowing a small laugh in an effort to ease the increasing tension. "Are there so few that you name them?"

"I'm not joking. This woman is responsible for the death of at least one husband, and is suspected of killing another. Her name is Morgan Turner."

"Morgan Turner? Are you implying that Morgan—*my* Morgan—is this woman? That's absurd, Edward. I saw Morgan's first husband fall to his death from a top mast."

"Did he?" Edward asked, a tight note of sarcasm in his voice. "Was she behind him at the time?"

"Edward!" Amy cried. "How *can* you be so monstrously hard? Oh tell him, Ward! Tell him how tenderhearted and uncommonly droll she is!"

Ward's chest tightened. It could not be possible. Edward was confused. "Her name isn't Turner. It's Weatherly."

"It *was* Weatherly. And before that it was Drumhill—"

"Drumlin," Ward provided as an uncomfortable tightening in his stomach followed his chest.

"Drumlin. Then Weatherly, then Turner."

"Turner. Are you sure?"

"Dead sure."

"Oh," Amy wailed. "Don't *say* that!"

"The truth is," Edward said, watching Ward's face with sudden, weary compassion. "The truth is she killed Turner almost a year ago, bashed in his skull, then fled. Here, Ward. Here to Boston. Morgan Turner, murderess, is your mistress. And you'd better damned well have her arrested before it's your head she bashes in next."

Chapter Seventeen

Unreal, a completely impossible situation. Morgan could not have harmed a soul, not his Morgan with her laughing eyes. And yet she was terrified of the police . . . and, until recently, held fast to that wig as if it were her savior . . . "What proof do you have?"

"The hired help's testimony, by God! One minute they heard shouting, then a groan of pain, then silence. Mrs. Turner bolted ten minutes later, summoned a hack and was never seen again. Two hours later her maid found Turner dead, blood pouring from his head."

"But why?" Ward asked.

"He beat her," Amy said, swollen eyes pleading with him for understanding. She could have saved herself the trouble. His own heart did that just fine.

"What difference that?" Edward shouted. "Many men beat their wives. They don't kill 'em!"

"You don't know Morgan," she said, with a defiant toss of her head. "She has far too much strength of spirit to bear such brutality for long."

The man had beat Morgan. The haunted expression in her eyes those first few weeks suddenly made sense, as did the incident with the fire poker. *You won't beat me!*

Damn the man! His mind created horrible pictures of Morgan in pain and his heart seemed to explode. His breath came in hard, pained gulps, and he fought to keep his cool.

"Spirit doesn't necessarily incite murder," Edward snapped at Amy.

"It *wasn't* murder. She was merely defending herself against a beast of a husband. One must make allowances for that!"

"Really, Amy? Was she afraid he'd kill her?" Edward asked savagely. "Because if she's not afraid of dying *at that very moment,* it's still murder."

"No one would consider it any great occasion were a man killed during a bout of fisticuffs!"

"But they found no evidence of fisticuffs," Edward answered, tight-lipped. "He had no sign on him—"

"Enough!" Ward said, rising. "You speculate without facts. Only Morgan can supply the full details."

"Exactly!" Edward turned toward Ward. "We shall obtain the truth from that little witch if we have to throttle her!"

Ward, frustration, anger, and anxiety bursting inside his chest, warned, "Have a care, Edward. You threaten the woman I love."

"You cannot possibly! She—"

Through a tight jaw, Ward ground out, *"I—love—her.* Understand?"

Edward, his entire profile wound into action, flinched. "Ward," he said lowering his voice. "All right."

"I shall have a dead reckoning from her before we discuss this any further." He started toward the door, mind working over this new information, this new betrayal. She'd lied to him. Again. "Leave Herman your direction, unless you intend to stay here. You're welcome, of course. I'll contact you—"

"The devil you will!" Edward swore, brushing past Ward to reach the door first. "I'm coming with you."

"You shall not!" he snapped. He'd no desire to expose Morgan to Edward's temper—or expose his own stupidity at swallowing her lies over and over again.

Edward set his teeth. "She's a suspected murderer. I'll not allow you to enter a murderer's den alone."

"Then I'm accompanying you!" Amy said, jumping up. "*I'll* not allow either of you to bully Morgan!"

"Stand aside, Edward. The woman won't harm me. Confound it, man, she's a month shy of delivering my child! If she's capable of rising from a chair without assistance, it's cause for celebration."

For once in his life, Edward was speechless.

Morgan sat on the sofa, book resting on her belly, which the baby bounced occasionally. "You're an active little thing, aren't you?" she whispered, rubbing the side of her belly where a foot or a hand kicked her, then settled into a little lump. "That's all right, darling. I love you." She had no notion of whether or not it could hear her. Soon enough, though, in six weeks or less, it would hear her with perfect clarity. In six weeks or less, she'd cuddle her baby in her arms and tell it to its face how she loved it with her whole heart, how much she'd longed for its birth. Even, she thought with sudden lowering of spirits, even though it was a bastard.

But this is America, she reminded herself and the apprehension wiggled through her heart. It was a shockingly large country. With so many cities, so much land, such a stigma wouldn't signify, would it?

Not for a son, but what of a daughter?

She's not nobility, Morgan reminded herself. She may marry whomever she pleases. Not, she thought swallow-

ing, within Ward's set—she'd be banned from them—
but within other circles. America was for everyone,
wasn't it?

Even sons and daughters of murderesses?

Even those. Had not the state of Georgia once been a
penal colony?

Laying her book aside, she frowned and rubbed her
belly. For almost a year she'd evaded capture and arrest.
During that time she'd neither read nor heard any mention of Philadelphia's Wicked Widow, except from Amy.
Could they possibly have forgotten about her? If she hid
for the next several years could she, in fact, remain at
liberty permanently? Oh, if it kept her baby safe, she'd
stay in these rooms forever!

Through the open windows came the sound of foot-
steps climbing her front steps. Odd. Ward had quit the
house a little over an hour ago, with no plans to return
until evening. And he never brought—

The front door opened. Ward shouted in a rough
voice, rimmed in steel, "Morgan! Where are you?"

Other voices followed: two voices, one male, one
female. Amy—oh Lord, Amy! She clasped her hand
over her mouth.

Ward strode through the door, his face dark with
anger, his eyes black as jet. Amy entered behind him,
followed by a strange man whom Morgan concluded,
with a sharp intake of breath, must be Amy's Edward.
He, too, wore an expression of anger—rage. Amy's eyes
were red and swollen. They'd been discovered!

"Morgan," Ward said in a clipped tone. "You know
Amelia. No doubt you've guessed this is Edward Huntington—"

"Yes—"

"Do not *dare* to interrupt me!"

Irritation flared in Morgan's chest, but the granite in Ward's voice warned her to hold her tongue.

"Nor you, Amy!" Mr. Huntington growled, pulling the drawing room door shut. "You have much to explain, Mrs. Turner."

"T—Turner?" Morgan asked, eyes flashing to Amy as fear hatched like snake eggs in her stomach.

"Turner," Ward answered in a frightfully cold voice. "Mrs. Richard Turner. Do you deny it?"

Breathe deeply, go slow. "I should like to know why you believe it so."

"You, madam," he said, spreading his legs and clasping his hands behind his back as if upbraiding one of his men, "will answer my questions without further prevarication! Are you, indeed, Mrs. Richard Turner?"

Her heart fluttered like a captured bird. "Richard Turner is dead."

"Not an answer! Shall I summon the police for questioning?"

"No!" Amy exclaimed. Hand against her throat, she sank down on the sofa next to Morgan.

"Ward," Mr. Huntington warned, "have some sense. Such action will only add fuel to the gossip mongers."

"And place your child in peril," Morgan whispered in horror.

"You, Mistress, have placed my child in peril. Answer the question!"

She'd never yet seen him in such a passion! Oh, but to be anywhere but here, to have any reasonable answer but the truth! She drew a deep breath and admitted shakily, "My legal name is Turner."

"There!" Mr. Huntington snarled triumphantly and sat in a chair. "She confesses. And now you'll hand her her marching orders, Montgomery!"

Ignoring Edward, Ward snapped, "Did you kill him?"

"Oh no," Amy said leaning forward to take her cold hand.

"None of that!" Mr. Huntington snarled, eyes flashing to Amy. "She'll receive no comfort from you!"

"She is my friend. I owe her my allegiance!"

"You owe her nothing."

"It is you," she said, raising her chin proudly, "that I owe nothing."

"You owe me everything. You are my wife."

"Morgan," Ward interrupted, "answer the question."

The rage flowing between Amy and her husband disturbed Morgan even more than Ward's scarcely restrained temper. Concern for Amy dragged her mind free from icy shock. To see Amy abused was more than she could bear under any circumstance. "You, sir, are an abominable husband," she snapped at Mr. Huntington.

"You, madam, you are a hellish paramour!" he returned. Morgan gasped. For Ward to address her thus was one thing, but for another man to use such terms sank her lower than the snakes writhing through her stomach. What sort of man had Amy married?

"Morgan!" Ward's voice rose. "Answer please!"

"Yes," she confessed, "I killed him."

Amy cried out in protest; pain shot through Ward's eyes, squeezing Morgan's soft heart. Dismissing his rough treatment, she instinctively rose to console him. He stepped back. "Sit down," he said. The ice in his voice spread frost over her heart and she slowly sat back down, trying to swallow the pain in her throat.

"There," Mr. Huntington said, his eyes narrowing maliciously. "I told you."

Amy started weeping, while Ward studied Morgan as if he could read her mind. Oh Lord, how had this happened? How had she never foreseen her discovery? Ward was far too clever not to have learned the truth eventually and now—now he must hate her. How could he not? "You've lied to me from the beginning," he finally said.

She bit her cheek. "Not always."

"What truth is there in anything you've told me? I wonder, after all your tales how you expect me to believe a word you say."

Sorting through her various lies, she stuttered, "I—I did marry Charles."

"Which you admitted only when I pried the information out of you."

"He did die of a heart problem."

"No doubt after you poisoned him!" Edward interjected.

She shrugged as casually as she could and answered Edward, while holding Ward's gaze. "There's no accounting for a man's expectations."

Ward regarded her a moment. "I requested that you have no further correspondence with Amelia. I now discover that you've exchanged letters all these past months."

"As I recollect, you requested I have no further congress with Amy. Letters aren't meetings."

His eyes flashed a moment's hope. "And you obeyed that request?"

She hesitated. "No."

"No. Have you *no* regard for my wishes, Morgan?"

Memories of steamy, passion-filled nights rose in front of her—his demands, her wanton response. "For some," she replied bitterly.

He winced, rubbed his neck, then seated himself in an armchair opposite Morgan. After a minute he fixed his gaze upon her and stated in a low voice, "Amelia says Turner beat you."

Her spirits took another deep plunge, shocking her,

for she'd have sworn they'd hit bottom. They appeared, however, to find depths she'd never imagined existed. She tried to collect the strength to face further humiliation as Mr. Huntington growled, "I can damned well see why!"

Ward glared at Edward and answered, "You're not helping the situation."

"The only help for the situation is an immediate end to the entire affair. Why trouble yourself with further questions? You cannot trust her! What will she tell you but lies?"

Ward rubbed his neck and sighed disgustedly. "Perhaps, Edward, you ought to make sail."

"And abandon you to her company? Never! I've come to save your bacon, Ward, and I mean to do it!"

"Then clap a stopper on your tongue, sir."

Mr. Huntington glowered at Morgan, then rose to pour himself a brandy. Ward focused his attention on her once more, the anger melting in his eyes as he asked gently, "Did he, Morgan?"

Her face burning with embarrassment, she lifted her chin in defiance. She set her teeth. "Yes."

"Often?"

"Yes."

"Badly?"

Out of the corner of her eye, Morgan saw Amy wipe tears away. Mr. Huntington took a seat and swirled his brandy, seeming to concentrate on it. Should this continue, both would become witnesses to a period in her life that she scarcely relished reliving. "Why do you ask?" she snapped. "Are you contemplating it also?"

Ward grimaced. "I've never struck you."

"Mr. Huntington believes you ought to."

Mr. Huntington lifted his eyes to shoot arrows at her. "I said he ought to throw you to the streets."

"And that's better?"

"It's what you deserve."

Her muscles tensed with the desire to slap him. He reminded her of Richard at his worst. A vision of Amy bruised and cowering at Huntington's feet arose and wrapped around her throat, temporarily making it difficult to breathe. Oh, if he had hurt so much as a hair on Amy's head, she'd kill him!

"Morgan?" Ward asked, his eyebrows raised as he waited for an answer. She stared back mutely, refusing to continue with this sham of an investigation. No doubt he and Huntington meant to employ her humiliation as a form of punishment; no doubt they'd hit upon the scheme shortly after the latter had beat Amy until she wept.

But no, she told her wild imagination, willing back the tears that rose so quickly these days. As despotic as Ward might be, he'd never be so beastly as to stand by while Mr. Huntington kicked and punched his wife. What was wrong with her that she could accuse him of such a thing?

Mr. Huntington swirled his drink one more time, took a long gulp and answered Ward's question. "Badly enough, Ward."

Ward never shifted his gaze, as if afraid that a minute's inattention would allow her to perpetuate the lies. He needn't worry. In the face of Mr. Huntington's damning testimony, creativity failed her.

"So you've speculated, but it seems that only Morgan knows the truth."

"This is the truth," Mr. Huntington said slowly. "I wasn't in town when Turner died, nor did I know the man personally. Our circles rarely met. Still rumors floated about." He took another sip. "I even saw her once at a charity ball. Mrs. Turner was talking to a friend of mine, and when she bent over to hear some snatch of conversation, her gown slid down her back. She had a bruise about the size of a grapefruit along her spine."

Morgan's heart lurched as she turned to Mr. Huntington. His dark eyes held hers and she fancied she saw compassion flickering in their depths. "You don't remember me, do you?"

"No," she admitted, "but I do recollect the ball. I didn't attend so many parties after marrying Richard that I would forget it."

"As you ought to have expected," he said, his voice hardening once more. "A woman with so little propriety as to marry three months into mourning isn't likely to receive many invitations."

The swift changes in his sentiments took her breath away—then felt like a slap in the face. Oh, how could Amy have married such a man! "You are too quick to judge. You know nothing of my situation."

"I know you lack any sense of honor."

"Honor is a concept devoid of meaning without money to support it."

"Honor knows no bounds and requires no wealth."

"Spoken like a man who has never known a night's hunger."

"Good God, am I supposed to pity you now? Your fishing for compassion, ma'am, falls wide of the mark. You forfeited all right to it when you married your second husband, also after a notably short mourning period."

"Oh for the love of God!" Ward interrupted. "Enough of this. It moves us nowhere. Morgan, would you please oblige me by relating the entire story without," he snapped at his friend, "unnecessary interruption."

"And where, precisely, do you wish me to start? From the moment I married Charles and cast aside all sense of propriety? Or, as my father fancies, when I was born without any?"

"I wish to hear about your marriage to Turner."

"Do you wish to hear *all* the details or only the ones that support Mr. Huntington's conclusions?"

"For God's sake, you are no better than he! I want the truth, and now if you please!"

"Well I don't please! Not in front of him!"

Ward ground his teeth. "Considering how well Edward has supplied the pieces that you have neglected to offer me, that's no wonder."

"He is here," she spat out, shaking a finger at Mr. Huntington, "merely to witness my humiliation."

"And Amy is here," Ward answered coolly, "to console you."

Morgan glanced at her friend in the corner of the sofa, pulling her handkerchief through her fingers. Amy returned a quivery smile of encouragement.

"All right! All right!" Morgan surrendered angrily. "Richard was an odious husband! He beat me, he did it often, and it hurt! Does that please you, Mr. Huntington? Does it satisfy your sense of decency that I paid for my rashness? Contrary to your assessment, as Richard's wife I received plenty of invitations. Richard had wealth, and wealth buys company. I didn't attend them because," she said focusing on Ward again, "as your friend so *agreeably* described, I wished to avoid embarrassment. Society views such punishment, by and large, as a wife's disobedience and a husband's correction."

"And so you killed him!" Mr. Huntington snapped.

She glared at him, then looked at Ward again. "I tried to be a good wife, as much as you disbelieve it."

"Hah! As you were to Weatherly?" Mr. Huntington asked. "Such a wife would provoke any man to violence!"

Ignoring him, Ward shook his head. "I've made no such judgment."

"Sir, you judged me before you entered this room."

"I judged you untrustworthy, nothing more, and you've given me ample proof of that, Mistress," he said, his voice gentling on the last word.

"It's much the same! If you don't trust—"

"Morgan, please. Your story veers off course again."

A course of which she wanted no part. Recollection burst in her mind, horrible pictures that had battled so long to become part of her—Richard's clenched fist, driving deeply into her tender belly. Her crying out as she doubled over in pain—and anger flaring in her heart. The voices in her brain willing herself to endure the torture as his blows rained down upon her head and back and legs, for in the end fighting back only excited more violence.

She drew in a trembling breath and focused on Ward. "I married Richard because Charles left me without a farthing, which," she sighed, "in retrospect ought not to have been so shocking. Mr. Huntington is correct. I was not the best of wives. I behaved appallingly in public. I flirted with any interested man, drank too much wine, and dressed outrageously. After his death, I thought it entirely possible that my conduct contributed to Charles's attack. When Richard proposed, I vowed that I would behave with the utmost propriety—" Richard's voice, *I'd rather you obey me as a good wife ought to . . .* Her faltering reply, *I'm sorry. I mustn't have attended well enough. I shall in the future . . .* "—and prove an exceptional wife, lending neither him nor the world even the slightest cause for censure. And I tried, truly I tried, but Richard was not as he appeared to me during courtship. He—he had some peculiar," she said, searching for wording, "idiosyncrasies regarding the more intimate aspects of marriage."

Her eyes met Richard's eyes, hot with lust. His face was flushed a dull, lewd red. Breathing heavily, he spun her around and shoved her into the lovely Gothic bureau. The marble edge of the dresser cut into her chest as he tore her gown open, sending pearl buttons flying. To control her growing rage, she focused on a statue of a half-naked woman fashioned from ivory and gold—a woman free from pain, from suffering . . .

Edward's low voice interrupted the horror replaying in her brain. "He had such a reputation, Ward." His eyes flashed a brief apology to Amy before he continued. "He frequented the rougher brothels and not, if you take my meaning, as a recipient."

Ward sucked in his breath; his face twisted in pained revulsion. "Damn, Morgan," he swore softly. "I'd no notion. Ed, I could use that glass of brandy."

His friend, eyes warming when they rested on Ward, nodded and poured a drink while Ward said gently, "Go on."

Biting her cheek, she looked down at her hands laying on her belly where the baby—their child—now slept. "It started on our wedding night. Richard couldn't—perform. Because of his age, Charles had had similar difficulties. I— I wanted to be a good wife, and so I offered him the sort of assistance I'd lent Charles." Her recitation, the necessity of remembering all, scratched and tore at the scabs of old, festering wounds, wounds she'd spent months trying to ignore. "Richard took my efforts as an insult to his virility and he—hit—me. Several times. And after that," she said with a shaky breath, "after that everything worked just fine. Over the next few months his—needs—escalated until six months into our marriage, I could bear no more."

Richard's eyes met hers in the mirror as, with a cold, brutal smile, he found her nipples and squeezed. Pain flashed through her body, dragging a scream from her throat. Oh God, what was he about now? He'd never hurt her in that manner before! He squeezed again, his eyes lighting up with amusement as tears sprang to her eyes. Amusement at her pain.

No more. No more! NO MORE!

Blinding fury ripped through Morgan's control. She reached for the statue; her fingers curled around the cool ivory. . . .

Morgan jerked herself back to the present, focused on Ward and said in a hard voice. "I hit him with a statue. He died. I fled."

Ward's eyes held hers, full of liquid brown compassion. Her heart snatched at that compassion, using it as a salve on newly bleeding wounds. "That's rather an abbreviated ending to your story," he replied. "Thank you, Edward." He took the drink his friend offered, glanced at Amy, and asked kindly, "Would you care for a glass of sherry, Amelia? Edward will pour you one."

Edward glared at Ward, glowered at Amy, but complied with the request.

Ward turned back to Morgan. The kindness in his voice reminded her sharply that he rarely indulged in fits of anger, nor did that anger last long. "Edward informed us earlier that a presumption of self-defense requires that the killer acted in the belief he was defending his life. Did you believe Turner meant to kill you that night?"

"No."

"Oh, but you did, Morgan!" Amy burst out. "You have only forgotten!"

"Don't put words in her mouth," Edward said, handing her the sherry. Amy scowled back.

Morgan held Ward's gaze. "I never believed he wished to kill me, only hurt me enough to—" Oh Lord, she couldn't say it. It was too terrible. "I didn't mean to kill him. I only wished to end the abuse."

"Which you did permanently," Edward commented sarcastically.

Ward, irritation creasing his face, jerked around. "Confound it, man, show some compassion! Brutality comes in forms other than the physical!"

Edward's eye twitched. "I'm merely stating a fact."

"A fact," Ward returned, "that we all knew. If you cannot speak civilly then for God's sake hold your tongue!"

"I'm here to support you."

"Your support ought not to entail insulting the woman I love."

Morgan's heart jumped. Did he love her still? How, after her deception, after her shame? Mustn't such a past forever darken that tender emotion?

"You cannot love a woman who would lie to you!" Edward exclaimed.

"No?" Ward asked softly. "Are you so very certain of that?"

Edward stared a moment, then studied his brandy once more.

Ward turned back to Morgan. "This statue, was it heavy?"

He loved her. He'd not say it without meaning it, would he? Suddenly her arms ached to hold him. "I lifted it well enough."

"And you hit him on the head?"

"Yes."

"And he died after that? How?"

"How?" she asked, confused. "Why, he fell."

"Immediately? Think hard, Morgan."

Richard stumbled backwards, reaching for his head. Blood seeped through his fingers, but that unnatural amusement increased. "So, you fight back," he said. "I like that."

Oh dear God, she thought, dropping the statue. She'd made the situation worse—

His expression changed. His hand slipped down to his chest, a groan escaped his mouth and fright creasing his face, he sank to his knees. "Oh no," he whispered. "Oh, not yet."

Horrified, she stepped forward. He fell on his arm, then rolled to his back. A second later a dreadful gurgling erupted from his mouth, and she fell to her knees next to him, holding her hand to his head to stem the flow of blood. Darkness encroached upon the lust in Richard's eyes, and, terrified, he stared back at her. "Doctor," he gasped. "Send—send—" A deep intake of breath, and pain creased his face. "Too late—too late—"

The darkness overtook his eyes. His breathing stopped.

He was dead.

"No," she said, dragging herself away from the horror of those moments, "it took a minute or two."

"Did he say anything? Yell? Shout?"

"He requested a doctor."

"That's all?"

She frowned. What did it signify? "He said, 'not now.' Then he died."

"And how did you react?"

She grimaced. "I attempted to stem the flow of blood."

"Did you call for anyone? Send for help?"

"N—no. I'd killed him and—" She sighed. "I'm not even an American, Ward. I panicked."

"But it appears to have been at least partially accidental," he pointed out.

"He was very wealthy and the servants knew about our problems. I didn't mean to kill him, but who would believe me? So I stole the little bit of money I found on his person and took a cab to the train depot, where I stayed until the morning train for New York City arrived. You know the rest."

"You bought a ticket on the packet to Boston. What did you intend to do once you arrived?"

"I didn't know. I thought something might present itself."

"And so," he asked a tiny sparkle of amusement lighting his eyes. "You had no plan at all?"

"Other than to stay alive, no."

"That, my dear," he said with the slightest twist of his lips, "is ultimately everyone's plan."

She tilted her head. "To keep me alive? How kind of everyone!"

His eyes glinted in reply, as Mr. Huntington said flatly, "It is not the plan of the Philadelphia police department."

Morgan glowered at him. He had all the grace of a bull in a china shop, and less wit. Why on earth would Ward want him as a friend?

"As always, Edward, your ability to hold fast to a subject astounds me. Had you been born canine, you'd have been a bulldog," Ward said wryly. "And so we ghost along. Apparently Amelia and Morgan have been corresponding behind our backs. How is it you discovered this deception Edward, and why so much haste? You might have written me a letter."

Amy glared at Edward and answered for him. "I overheard some people discussing the Wicked Widow at a party a few days ago." Her soft blue eyes fell on Morgan and once more she leaned forward to take her friend's hands. "I'm sorry, darling," she said. "It appears someone of name in Boston has seen you. The Boston police telegraphed Philadelphia, and they're now preparing to conduct a citywide manhunt."

"Oh good God," Ward whispered.

Morgan's mind reeled—oh Lord, they'd found her. How? Because she'd been lulled into a false sense of se-

curity. . . . "I ought to have continued wearing my wig,"
Morgan said to herself. "It was just so *hot* and I'm so—
large. I never thought anyone would recognize me. . . ."

"Apparently," Edward added with his viper's tongue,
"you were wrong. And that very condition has prompted
many, including the police, to conclude that you carry
Turner's child."

Morgan's head shot up and she stared in dawning
horror at Ward. His expression remained cool, com-
posed. When it didn't alter, she set her teeth and said,
"Come now, ask the question."

"I have no enquiries on that subject."

"I'll answer it at any rate. The child is yours. Should
you require the details on *that* Mr. Huntington? I shall
gladly oblige you!" she snapped.

He had the good grace to flush. "I need none."

"I never doubted it, my dear," Ward said.

"It's worse still. To add another nail in the coffin," Mr.
Huntington continued, "Turner's will left his fortune—
it's rumored to be about four hundred thousand—to
his progeny." Ward winced and Amy's eyes grew large.
"Should he die childless, the entire fortune is held in
trust for Mrs. Turner, with this clause: if *she* dies within
five years, it reverts to Turner's only nephew, Kenneth
Turner. Consequently, Kenneth is quite obsessed with
seeing Mrs. Turner caught, tried, and hanged, *before* she
delivers this child. In the meantime, it is in *Mrs. Turner's*
best interests to claim that the child *isn't* her former
husband's, thus inheriting all."

Morgan snapped. "How could you accuse me—Good
God, I have more honor than that!"

"Do you? But how can you," he reminded her maliciously, "when you have no money?"

Ward took a sip of his drink and said, "Pipe down,
Edward."

"It's a moot point. The child will bear Turner's name," Edward continued, sitting back in the chair, "and the money, my dear, will not be yours."

Ward, speculation creasing his forehead, sat back to study Morgan. After a moment, he said in a cool, even voice, as if making no great statement. "Not if he carries my name. Would you do me the honor, Morgan, of becoming my wife?"

Chapter Eighteen

Heart in his throat, Ward followed every movement of Morgan's face. Amelia cried out, "Oh yes!" while Edward sputtered, unable to form a coherent phrase. Morgan stared back at Ward in stunned silence, her throat working as she rubbed her belly. Even from this distance Ward could detect their baby kicking. He—Ward had long since stopped referring to his child as "it"—seemed to grow more powerful daily, Ward thought proudly.

"You can't possibly mean that," Morgan said.

"No ma'am!" Edward shouted. "On that we agree! This is preposterous, Ward. You can't marry the girl!"

"I am in perfect earnest, Morgan."

More heart-pounding silence as Edward started a sort of incoherent ranting, which Ward easily ignored. Edward specialized in ranting. Morgan, however, unaccustomed to Edward, turned to watch him with an expression of bewildered astonishment.

"Edward, would you please," Ward finally said, "belay that."

"But this is madness! You can't marry your mistress! It's not done!"

"No doubt it's been done many times."

"Not in Boston, it hasn't! Bostonians don't even keep mistresses! And your grandmother—by God, Ward, I'll not consent to this!"

"Fortunately, I don't require your consent." He leaned forward and held Morgan's gaze with his eyes. "An answer, love?"

"No! Of course not. Have you gone mad?"

His heart fell in his chest with a large thud, and he clenched his jaw against the ensuing pain. "Why not?"

"Oh Morgan!" Amy said, taking her other hand now, her eyes gleaming with unshed tears. "Why ever not? You must marry him, you must! Only consider, my dear, you will regain your position in society and we may be friends once more!"

"Over my dead body!" Edward shouted.

"That," Morgan said, amused anger glittering in her eyes, "I can arrange."

"Are you threatening me, madam?" Edward asked, his voice tight with rage.

"Do you take it so?"

"Damn it, Ward!" Edward said, slamming his hand on the table. "This is more than enough. You'll give her the mitten, and now, before this all blows up in your face!"

Ignoring him, Ward searched Morgan's face for some sign of love. "Why not, Morgan?"

"Why, because of all the reasons Mr. Huntington so inelegantly detailed! You have a duty to your family, especially after your father's conduct. You are obligated—no, *compelled*—to marry a woman of unimpeachable character. Oh, Ward, I'm not so ignorant as you think! Amy has written me about your position in Boston society, and you are no mere retired sea captain. I'm not the only one dancing, sir!"

Ward frowned. In the beginning he'd concealed his

status from her out of fear of being milked, later out of convenience. Over the last few weeks he'd come to congratulate himself on the small deception. Morgan disliked society. Persuading her to marry him would prove far easier if he could slowly bring her to the knowledge of his social standing. "I thought it better that way."

"So did I," Morgan answered.

In his scheming he'd never considered Amelia. The devil take her, he thought as Morgan's jaw tightened stubbornly. Was Amelia so stupid that she could not foresee Morgan's reactions? And now, damn it all, now with a murder charge on her head, he not only wished for Morgan's consent to marriage, but her safety depended upon it. With as much composure as he could summon, he answered coolly, "Marrying me is the best solution to your problems."

"Is it? How so?"

"For one thing, your child will bear his rightful name. That should relieve Kenneth Turner's desire to see you swiftly hanged, while providing us time to devise a strategy for your defense."

"But should it be named Turner, Kenneth would have *no* interest in my death, since the entire fortune would belong to the child."

"I suspect the will specifies that in the event of your death Turner becomes the child's trustee. It's a common enough provision."

"What does that signify? The money still belongs to the child."

"In fact, but in truth as trustee Turner would control the use of it for the child's welfare. An unscrupulous man could live very well under those circumstances. Moreover, the money doubtless reverts to Turner if the child dies."

Her eyes widened as she shook her head slowly. "Oh no, Ward! Oh no, he would *not*."

"I'm not accusing the man of a murderous temperament. I don't know him. But eighteen years is a long time, Morgan. Consider how many ways a child can die."

Her face tightened and she rubbed her belly. "I'd rather not."

"Should the child bear my name, the problem disappears."

"Should the child bear your name," Morgan snapped, "the money becomes yours until I hang, which, once the marriage license reveals my true identity, will happen in a trice. Marrying you merely puts the money into Kenneth's pocket earlier."

"Do you honestly believe I'd allow that?"

"It isn't for you to decide! The Philadelphia justice system controls it."

"As my wife you'll possess all my resources to battle that system."

"Good God, Ward," she exclaimed, her eyes bright with unshed tears, "can you not imagine the *scandal*?"

With a sick twist of his stomach, he said softly, "I can."

"Then you must realize the folly of this scheme!"

"You're already deeply embroiled in scandal. Marrying me can't possibly exacerbate it."

"Not for me! For you! And my baby—" She sucked in her breath. "For it to live with such a legacy as murder—"

"He'll live with it, nonetheless. As a Montgomery, he'll evade more allusions to it than as a Turner."

"That assumes I'm caught. I don't intend to be."

"How can you hope to evade capture with a manhunt in progress?"

Her jaw worked a moment. "I shall leave town."

He raised his eyebrows as his muscles tightened in alarm. "Leave town? Impossible! You're but a month away from delivering! Travel is entirely out of the question!"

"I'm perfectly well."

"You could deliver at any time, Morgan!"

"Better," she snapped, her eyes glittering, "to do so on a train than in a prison cell!"

"You shall not go to prison."

"You can't prevent that."

"Once you become my wife, I most definitely can, and will."

"I haven't agreed to become your wife. In point of fact, I rejected you."

Ward's heart clenched. For all his bravado, he could too easily picture Morgan weeping and alone in a musty prison cell. "You must change your mind," he snapped.

"Impossible. It is set."

"You're trying to whistle up the wind, Morgan. I've offered you the only plausible solution to your difficulties."

"It's no solution at all. Marrying you will very likely get me hanged."

"In truth, it's the only way you may reasonably expect to avoid such punishment."

"By announcing to the world, 'Here I am! Come and get me!' Unless you intend to marry me under an assumed name?"

"Don't be an idiot. Such a marriage would not be binding."

Her eyes narrowed. "I am *not* an idiot!"

Fear for her safety added fuel to his own anger. "You're behaving like one."

"Tell me, sir, is this how you propose to *all* the girls? I can perfectly appreciate why you remain a bachelor!"

"I remain a bachelor," he said, gritting his teeth as

he rose from his chair, "only as long as it takes me to obtain a marriage license and a reverend!"

"You cannot force me into marriage, Ward!"

His eyes narrowed as he peered at her; his voice became a low-toned threat. "I can. Need I remind you, Morgan, that you're living under my protection? That you and your child presently depend upon me for the very food you eat?"

She sucked in her breath, and her eyes turned hurricane gray. "That can be remedied!"

Edward, gaze flashing from one to the other, leaned forward in his chair. "Ward, you're not thinking clearly. Give over, man."

"No! You're perfectly correct!" Amelia interjected. "Morgan, you must consider—"

"Shut your damned mouth, wife!" Edward snarled.

"Don't you curse at me, Edward!"

"You, sir, are no gentleman," Morgan threw in.

Ward, ignoring all, started for the door.

"Where are you going?" Morgan asked.

He yanked open the drawing room door. "Prepare yourself, Mistress. By the end of this week, you shall be my wife."

"I will not! Drag me to church if you wish, but consenting words shall *never* leave my lips!"

"They most certainly shall, madam. I'll use any means, be they fair or foul, to that issue."

With that Ward quit the room, leaving Morgan staring after him, her muscles tight, her stomach heavy with dread.

Edward jumped out of the chair. "Ward! Come back here, man! Damn it! Amy, we're leaving!"

"I am not!" she snapped. "You cannot force me, either!"

"Oh," he said taking a step toward her, his eyes hard.

"I absolutely will force you, wife, if it means dragging you out by the hair for all the world to see!"

"You shan't lay a hand on her!" Morgan snapped, awkwardly rising from the sofa. "To do so, you must pass me!" she snarled although she could scarcely consider herself an intimidating figure—except to a man brought up to be a gentleman. Rage reddening his face, Edward glowered at her. For a short moment she thought he would ignore his breeding, push her aside, and seize Amy. But the moment passed and throwing Amy one last scowl, he stalked from the room. Seconds later, the slamming of the front door reverberated through the building, making Morgan flinch—and Amy fly into hysterics.

Chapter Nineteen

"Ward!" Edward yelled as he ran down the stairs and out to the street. Standing as cool as you please in the shimmering summer heat, Ward waved down his carriage. Edward, fury all but choking him, could only huff and puff and swear profusely. "Damn that woman! Damn them all!"

With a face as hard as marble, Ward glanced at him. Disdain rode high in his voice. "Restrain yourself. She's my responsibility, not yours."

"Not your mistress, you ass! My wife! Do you think I'd dare damn Morgan?"

"I shouldn't think so, but your temper is all in the wind right now. Edward, you fool, have you no better notion of a wife's management than that? You used to be so cool with women!"

"I return the compliment, Montgomery! At least when I made up to Amelia she accepted my suit!"

The carriage stopped. As they entered, the coachman asked to where they wished to be conveyed. "To hell," Edward spat back, picturing Amy laughing with Morgan over his poorly controlled temper—and poorly controlled wife. Damn her, damn her!

"Do you still belong to the Somerset?" Ward asked.

Sitting back in his seat, Edward growled affirmatively. Ward nodded to his driver and a minute later the carriage started down the road. The interior burned like the inside of a furnace, and Edward unbuttoned his frock coat. "I thought you were going to find a reverend," he snapped.

"First I mean to feed you dinner. Hunger frays your temper."

In fact, his stomach yawned. Was Amy hungry also? They'd eaten only a roll before leaving the hotel. He'd been too damned angry for more.

He was still damned angry. She didn't want to accompany him, so she could stay hungry. She could die of starvation for all he cared, the little bitch!

"How is your mother?" Ward asked after a minute or two.

"Fine!" Edward shot back. "Why the devil do you care?"

"She's rarely fine. Does her arthritis still nag her?"

"It's nagged her since the moment I was born. No doubt that's my fault as well as every other blasted misery in her confounded life."

Ward stared out the window. "And your father?"

"In Baltimore, visiting Aunt Martha." A code in the family for his father's paramour. In truth they did have an Aunt Martha in Baltimore, but during such visits it was merely his father's address, not his sleeping accommodations.

"And Roxanne?"

"My sister is well also, as is Sally and Gregg and the rest of the goddamned family. What the deuce does any of it matter *now*?"

He shrugged. "I'm making polite conversation."

"You're irritating the hell out of me."

"It's unlike you to curse so much."

"Not when I'm provoked!"

Ward sighed. "You want food."

"I want an obedient wife."

"Then you ought—" Ward stopped abruptly.

"What?"

"Nothing."

"What? You meant to say something, what was it?"

"Nothing important."

"You meant to say," Edward snarled, rage ripping through his chest once more, "that I ought to have married one! Well you haven't done so well in your paramour, sir!"

"Perhaps not, but I don't complain."

"You ought to! That woman needs schooling!"

Ward turned from the window. Judging by the impassive expression on his face, Ward was completely unaffected by the scene in Morgan's home, a harsh contrast to Edward's own reprehensible temper. Guilt and envy lit his heart, for Ward rarely succumbed to anger. The man could have been a saint.

"On the contrary," Ward replied, "that very 'unschooled' quality in Morgan is what attracts me most. If you searched your heart, Edward, you might discover a similar sentiment."

"My heart," Edward replied as the carriage halted, "has been destroyed by my wife." Upon his remark that very organ tightened painfully. Not destroyed at all, but sore and aching and bewildered at a turn of events he'd never foreseen.

Ward's mouth twisted into the thin smile that signaled all his warmer emotions. Not for the first time, Edward wondered what demon ate at the man's soul that he couldn't grin like a normal human being.

They entered the club, found a table, and within a

short time sat killing a bottle of brandy as they waited for their meals. Finally Ward broke the silence. "You loved Amelia when you married her."

"Before I knew her well," Edward said, urging that soft, sweet emotion to flee his heart, for a man oughtn't love a woman so lacking in basic decency.

"You called her spirited."

"Spirit isn't all it's cracked up to be."

Ward emitted a disgusted tsk. "Edward, you behaved atrociously."

"You know nothing about it."

"I know she loves you."

"You," Edward said, gritting his teeth, "don't know beans!"

"It's as plain as that beak on your face."

"If she loved me, she'd obey me."

"Love and obedience rarely travel hand in hand."

"No?"

"Does your mother obey your father?"

"That's living proof, isn't it?" Edward said, and turned to blindly survey the room. His parents' marriage was a sham, two people without an ounce of liking for each other, who had joined together purely for financial and social reasons. How did two such people beget four children when he and Amy had not yet conceived one? His heart hurt so much he could hardly breathe.

Dinner arrived, beefsteak and peas and potato croquettes. After the waiter left, Ward asked in a low voice, "Have you struck her, Ed?"

The question snatched Edward from his misery. For a moment he could only gape at Ward. Hurt a woman? His *wife*? Enraged though he was, the notion of striking Amy turned his stomach. "No!" he cried. His eyes flickering around the room to see who might have heard the exchange, he hissed, "A gentleman does not hit a woman!"

"I'm aware of that."

The irony wasn't lost on Edward. After swallowing a few more bites of rare beefsteak, he replied, "I never said I approved of Turner's methods of control."

Ward's jaw tightened. "In truth, sir, you stated it very clearly. As I recall, you claimed to understand why Turner beat Morgan."

With the food taking the edge off Edward's temper, he reluctantly admitted that Ward's accusation contained some merit. "She irritated me," he protested sullenly.

"You were enraged before leaving Philadelphia. I suspect you heaved insults and general bearishness at everyone along the way."

Edward shrugged sulkily and, shoving aside the peas, cut into a croquette all the while silently making excuses for himself. None held up under the weight of his shameful conduct. Slowly his rage faded to miserable, black guilt, digging a hole in his stomach.

"Huntington! *Mon Capitaine!* I thought I might find you here!" a merry voice called. Edward lifted his eyes to see Roland Hathaway approaching, his eyes laughing, his mouth wreathed in smile lines—and a fresh growth of whiskers. "Have you forsaken your third?"

Edward's tension instantly subsided. Rising, he clasped hands with his old friend. "Ro! By God, it's good to see a smiling face!"

Ward, slower to rise, bowed. "What brings you to town, Hathaway?"

As Ward and Edward reseated themselves, Ro dragged a chair to the table, turning it around to lean his long arms across the back. "I heard Edward was visiting. I knew he couldn't bear your company too long,

Capitaine, without a smile to alleviate all that brooding gravity. But never fear, dear boy!" he said and gave Edward a playful punch in the shoulder. "I daresay I can provide enough levity and general uselessness to make your stay enjoyable!"

Edward shook his head ruefully. "From whom did you hear? I only arrived last night."

"And in a bloody pelter too, so says the very British Mr. Grumland. He's a neighbor of mine who happened to be in the Tremont when you, uh, stormed in. Apparently you pelted him and everyone else in sight to such a fit of temper as to disturb even the placid and ever amiable Grumland. So I 'made sail' as Ward would say, for I couldn't possibly be expected to miss the opportunity to watch you pelt."

"Pelter? What the devil is a pelter?"

"Do you like it? It's British. As to definition, why it's you, dear boy, when you've been crossed or left unfed. I see *Mon Capitaine* is remedying the latter."

"Is there nothing English you don't like?" Ward asked with a trace of amusement.

"I never could stomach their cooking. It is most likely the reason we won the war."

"Which one?" Ward asked.

"Both."

"From what I understand they say the same about American cookery," Edward commented.

"Because they've no taste left, man. And so," he said, slapping Edward on the arm with his gloves. "What returns you to the homeland, Edward? And in a pelter too? What, don't they pelt in Philly?"

"Boston is not my homeland, and that name's an abomination of the city of Philadelphia which, I remind you, was once our capitol."

"You've reminded me so often, it enters my dreams."

"I thought Fran entered your dreams."

A light gleamed in Ro's eyes as he opened his mouth. Ward lifted his hand. "Belay that. We don't require any further elucidation on your prowess in bed."

He laughed. "Ward, how shocking that you think I'd discuss such a topic!"

"Discuss? Boast, more like!"

"About my own wife? I've better breeding than *that*, I hope."

"I hope constantly, but you generally disappoint me."

"Not, I trust, about Fran." His eyes threw a subtle threat.

A shadow of a grin crossed Ward's face. "No, sir. I'm sorry."

"You ought to be, old man. Edward? You've no answer to my inquiry?"

Finished eating, Edward sat back and took a little wine. "I came for Ward."

"Ah . . . then Sir Captain inspired your peltering."

Edward chuckled. "Ward hasn't the fire to inspire anger." Ward lifted one cool eyebrow. Abruptly recalling a series of embarrassing details from earlier in the day, Edward squirmed. "Not much, at any rate. I've come upon more urgent business, the matter of a certain female."

A slow sparkle entered Ro's eyes. "A woman? You intrigue me. Pray tell, sir, who is this woman?"

"We've discussed her before."

"Hmm," Ro said and turned to Ward. "Have we?" He lowered his voice. "Would this be the Paragon? The shy, Bible-reciting one?"

Ward shook his head, his mouth thinning in displeasure. "This is not the place for that conversation, Hathaway."

Ro's grin spread. "What?" he asked, glancing around

at the men in the room. Several were involved in deep conversations, a few laughed in a corner with Harcourt Carleton, a man famous for a ribald sense of humor. "I fancy they'd be quite interested in your mistress."

"By God," Ward snapped. "Pipe down!"

The humor in Ro's eyes dimmed, replaced by the well of compassion he reserved only for his friends, carefully concealed under his rakish façade. "They already suspect it, *Capitaine*," he said gently. "You must know that. And," Ro said, glancing derisively at Edward, "the world neither stopped spinning nor slammed their doors in *Mon Capitaine's* face."

Ward sighed, his eyes narrowing. "You—and they— know but half the truth."

"Half?" Edward said with a tight laugh, picturing Morgan's swollen belly. Lord, what a pickle they were in! "A quarter is more likely."

"By Jove, have you *four* women now, Ward? You're bamming me! With that hawk's face? No doubt they're milking you dry!"

Lowering his voice, he replied, "It's worse than that."

For the first time concern creased Ro's face. "Worse? You know, I dislike that tone in your voice, Edward. Perhaps," he said, standing, "we should repair to Ward's home."

"Repair? Good God, man," Edward said, rising also, "why can't you talk like a normal American?"

"Why should I? Normal Americans are dull. At any rate, English customs are all the crack in Boston! How shocking if I became unfashionable! By the bye, do you like my beard, gentlemen? It's on the cutting edge of fashion."

"It's abominable," Ward replied mildly.

"And that is *precisely* the reaction I expect from the older generation. But come, come, my carriage awaits us."

"You haven't kept it waiting all this time!" Edward exclaimed.

"Why, what else should I do with it? You didn't think I meant to stay at the Tremont with you, did you? After you pelted? I'm accepting Sir Captain's hospitality," he said slapping Ward on the back as they started for the door. "I daresay I'm particularly curious to hear about your grandmother's reaction to your latest hobby. You've kept your head, I see. I ought to have taken a bet on that, Edward."

"She ordered my continued discretion," Ward answered.

"Good advice, entirely ignored as always," Edward said.

"Ignored? When has Ward ever ignored good advice?"

"He always ignored our advice."

"Yes, but ours was never good, now, was it?"

"Oh, he's a vile, vile man, worse than Heathcliff in *Wuthering Heights* by far!" Amy moaned as she wiped her eyes, her enormous heart broken right down the center. "I hate him! Why, oh why did I ever marry him, Mo?" she asked.

Mo surveyed her warily, and for a moment Amy fancied that she didn't believe a word Amy said. Oh, but she must, for Morgan was her very dearest friend in all the world! To be sure, after meeting Edward she'd fancied those sentiments might change, for Edward had been every bit as tender, thoughtful, and understanding of all her trials and her parents' odious attempts to 'control her waywardness' as Mo had always been. *He* didn't think her wayward or a hoyden. *He* admired her spirit, her courage. But that was before marriage had transformed him into the very pattern card of all she despised.

"He is rather—forceful—but you loved him once Amy. You must have seen some good in him," Mo replied doubtfully.

"But he's changed!" she wailed. "It's exactly like *Beauty and the Beast* only backwards! I wrote you so in all my letters."

"I could scarcely decipher half of them, splattered as they were with tear stains."

"And that is hitting the nail on the head, Mo, for I could never think of him but to weep!"

Amusement touched Morgan's eyes. "Tears have always come easy to you, my dear."

"No, never say so! Only when I am beset upon by malicious, *malignant* opposition to perfectly *reasonable* requests."

"Which were?" Mo asked suspiciously.

"Nothing, *nothing* of import. Merely to cast off my corset on occasion."

"Oh you're bamming me, Amy. You couldn't wish to do something so vulgar. Why, you'd jiggle about like jelly!"

"It's *not* vulgar! It's liberating. *You* don't wear one all the time, do you?"

Morgan laughed and patted Amy's hand. "I'm a mistress, my dear. By definition I am vulgar, and I am *paid* to jiggle!"

"And pray tell why I mayn't adopt the ways of a mistress?" she asked. "I have experienced the—the—intimacies of marriage!"

"Because you are *not* a mistress. You're a young woman married into a well-connected family. You must abide by the conventions, mustn't you, or face censure. Good gracious, Amy, haven't I set you the perfect example of how *not* to act? You'd not like being ostracized, believe me. I advise you to obey Edward."

"Obey!" Amy said jumping up to pace the room. Oh she could see it all so perfectly well and felt the boiling of her blood again. Edward, his face black with rage, his hands fisted as he explained in a voice as cold as winter that she must obey him, must follow his directions implicitly! "Obey, obey, obey!" she cried. "That's all I ever hear nowadays! Edward scolds me constantly and reads me lectures until I fancy I shall run mad! I swear I'd liefer not attend anything he says at all! Why should Edward guide me? Why should he command me? What knowledge does he possess that is better than mine own?"

"You know how I view these issues—"

"And you killed that vile, detestable man because of it and I congratulate you with my whole heart! *I* think you are heroic!" she exclaimed, clasping her hands to her heart.

Morgan sighed and rubbed her aching temples. In her mind's eye she saw Richard lying on the floor, blood seeping from his head, his hands clutching at his chest as if attempting to force life back into his dying heart. "You don't understand."

"On the contrary," Amy said, her eyes snapping. "I *wholly* apprehend the *constant* oppression of women. There's a movement afoot, Morgan! Women shall no longer accept a man's superiority. Such lectures as I've attended—"

"Lectures? What lectures?" Oh Lord, this couldn't be good . . .

"Lectures on women's rights! We will be heard!"

"Amy," Morgan gasped, "never tell me you're following that Bloomer woman's example!"

"They are *monstrously* comfortable."

"Oh dear God," Morgan sighed, closing her eyes, once more seeing Edward's face red with rage. He scarcely seemed the sort to forgive such foolishness . . . "Did you truly purchase a pair?"

"Certainly! And I wore them, too. Do you reproach me? I thought you'd support me on this!"

"Well I don't," she said, once more fixing her gaze on Amy. "Besides being dreadfully ugly, bloomers—indeed wearing any men's clothing!—merely provoke them, thereby opening *us* up to ridicule. The whole matter is shockingly ill-advised and you're far too clever not to apprehend that, Amy! Women will never obtain any degree of equality if we wrangle with men over silly matters such as clothing."

Her face twisting with grief, Amy's resolution crumpled. Flinging herself to the sofa, she buried her face in Morgan's shoulder and indulged in another round of weeping. "Oh Morgan, I merely wished to prove to him that I'd not be bullied. I didn't mean to behave badly, but he was enraged! We had row after dreadful row and the things he *said* to me—you would never believe it!"

"Amy, oh darling, it will be all right," Morgan soothed, wrapping her arms around her friend's shaking shoulders. Although only a year separated them in age, Morgan suddenly felt many years Amy's senior. Such a fuss over nothing! Try, Morgan thought, living with a husband who beats you for sexual pleasure.

A recollection of Edward's face as he cursed Amy before taking his leave rose in front of Morgan's eyes. His color had been as high as Richard's had before he'd first struck her, his eyes as cold. Did Edward's angry words sometimes turn to angry blows? He hadn't a forgiving nature. . . . Just because Amy had an hysterical temperament didn't mean she never suffered.

"Oh, my dear, dear friend," Amy continued, "how did

you ever bear his domination? His brutality? I cannot! I cannot! I swear, I will never submit! Never!"

Morgan's mind re-drew a picture of Amy cowering at Edward's feet, and suddenly the experiences of Morgan's last three years crystallized, forming one hard, clear picture. Edward, well-dressed, well-groomed, so perfectly civilized in all outward appearances, beat his wife—*her* friend! She'd not allow it! Amy would never experience the long, bitter months of pain and humiliation she had withstood! "No, my dear, you shan't. We're leaving."

Amy lifted her head, sobs halting. "Leaving?"

"Yes. You and I. I cannot possibly marry Ward, and under no circumstance shall you remain with that—that *beast* of a husband! We shall carve our own way in the world, Amy. We possess all the cleverness and cunning required, I assure you!"

"But—but Ward *loves* you Morgan!"

"How deeply can a man ever love?" she asked bitterly.

"Why, as much as a woman I should think."

"If Ward truly loved me he'd not insist upon placing me in imminent peril; he loves himself," she replied, trying to ignore the sudden wrenching in her chest. "We'll head west. The North has too little industry, and south leads us to a world where not only women, but men as well, are enslaved. Our fates lie to the west."

"Just you and me?"

"Just you and me."

Amy bit her lip. "To Chicago, then. It's the largest city in that direction."

"Chicago it is. Uh, where is Chicago?"

Amy chuckled, wiping her eyes as she sat up. "I've no notion. I'll warrant a train conductor could direct us."

"Certainly," Morgan said smiling. "We'll require money. I've saved most of the allowance Ward provides me. When that's gone, I shall—I shall sell my diamonds." She swallowed hard, attempting to shove aside recollections of him giving them to her, of that night's pleasure when she'd worn nothing but her diamonds to bed. Could she really sell them?

The baby kicked. Her baby. She wasn't merely escaping Ward, but providing her child a better life, a life in which names like Turner or Montgomery, Huntington or Reynolds didn't signify. For that she could part with her diamonds—and her love.

"I have money also," Amy interrupted her thoughts. "Edward's given me an allowance, and other than the bloomers, I haven't had anything to purchase."

"Did you bring it with you?" Morgan asked, surprised.

"I did. Upon hearing of the manhunt, I fancied you might have need of it," she said, then added in a small voice, "I've never lived on my own, Mo. Is it dreadfully difficult?"

Morgan smiled bitterly, old age settling in her heart. When did one and twenty become old? "Not when you have money."

Chapter Twenty

"And so," Ro started as Ward propped an elbow on the library mantel and stared into the dormant fireplace. "Your mistress is not only a Bible-toting, shy, thrice-married, pregnant, 21-year-old, but a murderess as well. Egad, Captain, I shouldn't have believed such a woman existed. Don't you find her fatiguing?"

Ward lifted his head to look at Ro. His long-limbed body lay sprawled in an armchair, his cravat untied and hanging loose. A cigarette, his latest hobby, dangled from his hand. Edward, on the other hand, sat upright in his chair, scowling with revulsion at his counterpart's slovenliness. The friendship between the two—so similar in spirits, so different in attitude—had always fascinated Ward. As boys they'd become fast friends while attending Andover, which had continued through perdition at Harvard. The fact that they'd adopted Ward as friend and compatriot still surprised and gratified him. What had he, with such a lack of spirit and education, to offer them?

"And," Edward added in a harsh, tight voice, "he next intends to crowd the mourners by marrying the wench."

Ro froze, all pretense at negligent male rogue melting away. Slowly he straightened in his chair. "What?"

"Exactly," Edward said. "He's out of his flugin' gourd!"

"You're quizzing me."

"I'm not," Edward replied. "He proposed to her in front of us. When she categorically denied his suit, he vowed to *force* her into shackles, though God only knows how. You can't make her say what she doesn't want to, Ward."

"*Force* her? Good God, man, have you taken leave of your senses?"

Ward shrugged. "It's the best solution."

"It bloody well isn't! God damn it, I'll not allow it!"

Ward raised an eyebrow. Edward turned to eye Ro, whose face resembled granite. "What could you possibly do to prevent it?" Ward asked.

"All that lies in my power," Ro replied, stubbing out his cigarette. He fixed his gaze upon Ward and spoke in his most serious tone. "In the entire time I've known you, Ward, the only thing you ever cared for was the restoration of your family name. Marrying this woman will ruin it for good."

Ward flashed a grin. "Only for a generation or two."

"A generation! That's your entire life, man! Your grandmother will never speak to you again, nor will any of society ever receive you."

"That's exactly what I've been saying, Ro," Edward interjected.

"In actuality," Ward reminded him gently, "you've said very little about it, Edward. Mostly we discussed your mistreatment of your wife."

"Which is none of your business!"

"I shall make it my business if I discover that you've brutalized her in any way."

Ro peered at Ward, then shook his head. "You shift

subjects, sir, to distract us I think, but I'm not so block-headed as that. We're discussing you, not Edward."

Ward eyed him warily. "You don't think that as his friends we ought to prevent him from making a misery of his wife over foolish pride?"

"I think," Ro said severely, "you know dashed well that Edward wouldn't touch a hair on that woman's head."

"But I don't know that," Ward replied, raising his eyebrows.

"Then I know it. At any rate, we must consider what's to be done with your mistress. It seems we must first remove her from the city or risk her capture. I'll talk to Fran. We might take her in until—"

"Oh no, you won't! Foist my mistress on you, Ro? What kind of man do you think I am?"

"I think you're a man gone mad."

"And then?" Edward asked, glancing between Ward and Ro. "I presume that after she delivers the child we'll move her out of state. Where, though?"

"California," Ro said resolutely. "Can't get farther than that, can we?"

"It's an awful long trip for a woman with a baby."

"Right. We'll send someone with her, then. Hire a lady's maid or something. It'll cost a pretty penny—"

Ward, listening to this exchange with amusement and growing alarm, interjected with a well-timed chuckle. "Thank you, sirs, both, for being so obliging as to enter into my problems, but I assure you, I require no aid. I'll marry Morgan and that's the end of it."

"No, confound it, you won't," Ro snapped. "Not even if I must bribe every last city official in Boston to deny you a license."

"Good God, you don't even know for certain that the child is yours!" Edward exclaimed.

Which, Ward decided with a sudden burning in his

chest, was the last insult he was going to take from Edward and his foul temper. "I'm as certain as a man can be."

"How can you be? How do you know she hadn't been scheming for months? First she inherits Turner's fortune, and then some years down the line, she takes yours when you, too, die 'accidentally.'"

"You overstep your bounds, Harrington," Ward warned, clenching a fist.

"Does he?" Ro asked. "Good God, man, we've known you for seven years and in all that time you've never acted so recklessly." Ro ran his hand through his hair and leaned forward, his forehead furrowed with rare concern. "You've fished Ed and me out of enough peccadilloes, God knows, but you never once entered into any of your own. Nor did you ever offer a word of censure or expect a whit of gratitude, not even when you laid down your own hard-earned brass. In answer we, swine that we are, used every device available to mankind to drag you down to our level, supposing that by doing so we'd triumph in some depraved game where the winner loses all. Well we failed, much to our better good. You're a dashed good friend, Ward, better than we deserve." He paused to take a breath then continued, "It's time we proved it. Whatever hold this woman has on you, we'll break it. Your name is all that ever mattered to you, and I'll be damned if I'll allow you to destroy it."

And, Ward thought, in all those seven years he'd never once believed Ro or Edward cared a whit for him beyond their own lazy, self-absorbed interest. It seemed he was wrong, proven both by Ro's speech and Edward's frantic travels. Anger melting, Ward turned to Edward, who sat with a broad smile on his face. "Same as he said."

Shaking his head, Ward grinned. "Whatever made you miscreants think I didn't enjoy rescuing you? A man needs a hobby."

Ro raised his eyebrows. "A hobby? Is that all we are to you?"

He shrugged. "You always made me laugh. I never knew a pair so raring for trouble in my entire life. On some occasions devising a way to extract you from it stretched my brain almost beyond its limits."

"Not too difficult, that, its limits being so small to begin with," Edward said, laughing.

"Much more difficult than the stretching of the puny thing inside your skull."

"At any rate," Ro said, "you're the one in trouble now, and we shall certainly extract you whether you wish it or not."

"By sending Morgan to California?"

"If that's what it requires."

"Then you'd better book passage for two. We'll call it a honeymoon."

"Damn it, NO!"

"You forget, Ward," Edward said, leaning back in his chair with a gleam in his eyes, "she refused your offer. We might actually have her on our side, Ro."

"Then she'll agree to California?"

"I don't know," he said, mulling over it aloud. "She seemed concerned about money."

"She'll find a protector there, no doubt. California—"

"She shall not!" Ward snapped, the sense of warm companionship replaced by flashes of stomach-wrenching jealousy as he envisioned Morgan in another man's arms.

But Morgan had never actively sought her current position, he reminded himself. It had been thrust upon her after Turner's death. A situation that had been thrust upon her after Weatherly's death, which had followed Drumlin's. Marriage—a woman had few other choices for survival. Morgan had no other choices. "I will marry Morgan. And you shall not interfere, understood?"

"Over my dead body!" Ro growled.

"Confound it," Ward snarled back. "Are you the only ones allowed happiness? Do you expect me to keep bachelor hall all my life?"

"No!" Edward exploded. "But you shall choose an acceptable wife, by God! If you don't care for the women you've met, we'll introduce you to others."

"I choose Morgan."

"Then you choose to spend the rest of your life alone," Ro cut at him, angrily. "Because no one will accept you other than Edward and me, and Edward lives in Philadelphia. And as for business dealings, try to conduct them without your club. Do you think the Somerset will renew your subscription after this scandal? What about your charities, Ward? Do you think they'll want the husband of a murderess as spokesman? And your children? What kind of lives will they have? Even if Morgan is acquitted, there will always be that doubt in people's minds. The taunting—"

Ward growled, "I know about taunting."

Ro stared a minute, then sighed. "I meant no offense, but you must see reason."

"Do you think being born a bastard will be easier?" Ward challenged. "If Morgan stands trial and is convicted, my child will be both a bastard child *and* the child of a murderess."

"She could be convicted, marriage or not."

"But," he started, dismissing the notion from his mind. Morgan would never stand trial. He'd see to that—somehow. "At least one title will be removed. It is the best, and the least, I can do."

"It's not. With our plan, she'll reside in a state so far detached from Pennsylvania, they'll never find her."

"With your plan, I lose her entirely."

"If she's hanged you'll also lose her."

"Oh for the love of God! They don't hang women, Ro, and you damned well know that!"

"I own it's rare, but it *does* happen, and will in this case if Kenneth Turner has his way. Even if he doesn't, she'll serve time in jail and you'll *still* live without her. Under those circumstances, you'll have no wife!"

"And if I have *my* way she'll avoid prosecution completely."

"How? What prevention can you possibly offer?"

"I don't know yet. I must investigate it."

"Investigate it! Good God, man, it's clear enough that she killed the man. She admitted as much."

"Something about her story seemed fishy to me."

"It was a confession! What can be fishy about that?"

Ward stared a minute, then shook his head as his eye fell on the mantel clock. "Gentlemen, this is getting us nowhere. Believe me, I appreciate your interest, but your assistance is more dangerous than helpful. Edward, it's been hours. Your wife has probably returned to her room by now."

"Hah! Do I care?"

Ro frowned at him. "You ought to."

"You haven't lived with her these past months."

"Does living with her lead to the annihilation of your manners? Good God, man, you can't bring a woman to a new country, drag her unceremoniously from her home within months of marriage, and leave her entirely to her own devices, especially when those include visiting with Ward's paramour! You concern yourself with Ward's reputation, but forget she has one to maintain as well!"

"She cares little enough for it. The damned fool's intent upon ruining herself, and I'm just about ready to hand her her marching orders."

"Marching orders? What the deuce do you mean by that?"

He sighed. "Damn it, Ro, she wore bloomers to a tea. Can you believe it?"

Ro whistled and poured himself another drink. "Bloomers? A little out of style aren't they?"

"That's not the point and you know it!"

"All right. Ward, we'll forget your mistress for now and discuss Mrs. Huntington's less than laudable conduct. It seems," he said with a large grin, "that the only one of us who understands the handling of women is me, which is no great shock. Had you both marked me years ago, you'd have had fewer difficulties. . . .

Flowers in hand, Ward stepped just inside the door to Morgan's house and took a deep, calming breath. He'd proposed to her twice thus far and blown afoul both times. Both offers he'd made rashly, with no strategy at all. This time, however, he was prepared with flowers and a short speech. If not for the baby, he'd use seduction—but if not for the baby it wouldn't be necessary.

He frowned. Would he have married Morgan if necessity hadn't prompted it? If he'd met her as Morgan Reynolds, daughter of Lord Westborough, he'd have exchanged places with Drumlin in a heartbeat. But as Morgan, his mistress, . . . perhaps. It didn't matter at any rate. She was the Wicked Widow, and he would marry her to protect her from Philadelphia's justice system.

Can you not imagine the scandal? He could, all too well. It had kept him pitching and tossing all night, envisioning the harsh faces and the angry words from those whose favor he'd spent years currying. It dug a pit in his stomach with teeth as sharp as a shark's, for he imagined more than the scandal of the Wicked Widow. He imagined Morgan, with her disregard for convention, worsening the situation, making it unbearable. . . .

"Captain Wyatt?" Maeve greeted as she passed out of the drawing room. "May I take yer hat, sir?"

He shook his head. "No, thank you. How is she today?" he asked, lowering his voice as he dropped his hat, cane, and gloves on a table. Over the last months Morgan's health—and her careening moods—had become a sort of secret conversation between him and her two maids.

Maeve averted her eyes as she replied, "She's a wee bit worn today, sar, after havin' guests yesterday and all."

And arguing heatedly with those same guests. He nodded. "Thank you."

"Will ye be stayin' for supper, sar?"

He grimaced. "I don't know yet."

Morgan lay on the sofa, legs propped up on pillows to prevent swelling in her ankles as the doctor had advised. She read a book, no doubt containing many passages about brutality against women to whet her appetite for argument. Why she read such balderdash, he couldn't understand, especially after having been a victim herself.

"Morgan, my dear, I brought these for you."

She glanced up from her book to look at the flowers disdainfully. "Why didn't you give them to Maeve to put in a vase?"

An ill wind indeed blew today, he thought, his stomach sinking. "I thought to present them to you first. They're a gift," he said, dropping them on an armchair.

"I don't require any gifts."

As she occupied the entire sofa, Ward dragged another armchair over and seated himself in front of her. "We need to talk, love," he said in his most cajoling tone.

"I'm reading."

"Lord, but your voice could freeze blood. We have plans to make."

She eyed him warily, her eyes a cool ocean green. "What sort of plans?"

"Marriage plans," he said, leaning forward to dangle his folded hands between his knees. "I must apologize for yesterday's indiscretion. I ought to have made such an offer in private. And yet, I was no less sincere than if we'd been alone. And so," he took her hand, held her gaze and continued, "I love you, Morgan. You know that. In twenty-nine years I've not met a woman who suited me as well as you. Will you marry me?"

Emotion flickered through her eyes, but he couldn't name it. She had the unfortunate ability to conceal her thoughts and feelings when she wished. With a tightening of his muscles, he wondered if that came as a consequence of Turner's brutality.

"As I recall, sir, you ended the conversation by informing me that I had no choice in the matter. Why you ask me now is beyond comprehension."

He sighed. "May I at least plead my case?"

"You may if you wish to waste both your time and mine."

He peered at her a minute, attempting to discover some way to penetrate her cold reserve. Failing, he said, "It's a matter I've been contemplating for some time. I wish our child to carry my name."

"Excellent. We shall name it Ward."

He narrowed his eyes. "I want you as my wife."

"Why, that will be more difficult, sir, as the Philadelphia police may challenge your suit."

He took a moment to study her, trying to anticipate her rebuttal to each comment he might make. The wrong words would end in an explosion of temper or a final, unremitting denial. Although he'd resolved to use force to win her hand, he'd rather have her willingly, especially since no evil genius had presented him with an idea on precisely what manner of force would accomplish his purpose. By and bye, he settled upon a question instead of a remark. "Is that your only objection?"

She emitted a hollow laugh, a painful shadow of the levity he cherished. "Isn't it enough?"

"That's not an answer."

"As it is an insurmountable obstacle, I don't see the object in answering. We must live the life we're given, mustn't we, not the one we wish for."

He smiled tenderly and squeezed her hand. "Come now, Morgan, you've never once settled for the life you've been given. If you had, you'd not be here."

"If I had, I should be married in England, with at least one child to love," she said, a hint of wetness in her eyes.

"If I'd known you then, love, if I'd met you before Drumlin, I should have spared you these years of suffering."

"You would have married me then, an incorrigible girl of eighteen lacking even a dram of sense? I think not, Ward."

"I should have without a second thought."

"But you give every decision a second thought, don't you? And when I was on board your ship, you never made any attempt to fix my interest."

"You displayed not even a token interest in *me*, madam. Your eyes were all for Weatherly."

"Because, Captain, only he looked back. Admit it, you wanted nothing to do with the widow of a sailor. I took Weatherly because I had no other choice."

"And would my Lady Reynolds have accepted the suit of a mere sea captain?"

"Sir," she said with a tiny hiccup of a laugh, "I married a sailor."

"Point taken," he conceded with a smile. "Had I known the truth, I should have cast Weatherly overboard and taken you as my own."

"What truth would that be? That my father is an earl? Oh my, but how that eases my heartache!"

"Does your heart ache, love?"

Morgan turned her head, unable to look him in the eyes. Her heart more than ached, it sat dying inside her chest. At this very moment Amy was procuring train tickets for them. Tomorrow morning she'd quit both Ward and Boston to start a new life out West. "It does. I love you, Ward," she said. "You know that."

"Ah, but Mistress," he said as he cupped her chin, turning it so she faced him once more. "I don't know it. I need to hear it, and often." His eyes, soft with love, searched her face a moment before he leaned forward to kiss her. She responded with all her heart, shifting her legs to the ground to lean into the kiss, to prove her love with her lips. When he lifted his hand to stroke her breast, she moaned, and her skin warmed to a wonderful tingle. Oh, to touch him, to feel his touch, to join together in that most incredible union of heart and body.

And then the baby kicked. Pressed against her as he was, Ward laughed and leaned back. His eyes gleaming with budding passion, he stroked her cheek, then slid his hand to her belly. "Feisty little thing, our son."

She smiled and placed her hand against his, feeling the proof of life together. "Aye, Captain. Could you expect less from your child?"

"No, because he is *your* child."

"You're so certain it's a male? Is this some sort of connection men have?" she asked with a trace of amusement.

"I love him already, Morgan. Male or female, I care not, but referring to him or her as an 'it' strikes me as cold."

She smiled wickedly. The doctor had lately restricted their passion, but with desire burning in her veins and the knowledge that Ward would never satisfy it again, she asked, "And you, sir, are hot?"

"For you, Mistress, my blood fairly boils," he said with a grin.

Holding his gaze, she slid her hand along his thigh toward his staff. "I could cool it."

His grin slowly broadening to a dimpled, breath-stealing smile, he dropped his hand over hers. "I never doubted it. I will, however, remain warm today."

"Unnecessary," she said moving her other hand up his other thigh. "I will cool you."

He chuckled and took hold of that hand, also. "Has no one ever explained to you that men, not women, are supposed to be the aggressors in such activities?"

"Aye, sir, but I choose to ignore it. I should make a frightfully bad mistress if I didn't."

Squeezing her hands, he said softly, "I love you as mistress. I should love you more as wife. Marry me, Morgan, and we shall have many years of heat between us."

She sucked in her breath, then pushed from her mind the images he attempted to create there. Foolhardy images, without a prayer of ever becoming real—so much prevented them. "I cannot, Ward. It's impossible."

"I don't deny it'll be difficult, but impossible? No. With the assistance of a land shark or two, we shall manage well enough."

Morgan shook her head. "You insist upon ignoring the consequences. Setting aside the murder charges, you still must consider the difference in our stations. Without titles it is difficult to follow your American aristocracy," she said, frowning, "but from what Amy says, your family is very important. As your mistress I could not care less, but it is everything to your wife. Surely you must see that! Oh Ward, you cannot bind yourself to a woman like me! Think what it would do to your name!"

He shifted impatiently in his chair, his eyes darkening as his face formed grim lines. "I've considered deeply, madam. It remains our best choice."

"Bloody hell!" she swore, trying to swallow the lump in her throat. "How can you be so dreadfully blind? I am a woman completely devoid of reputation! I'm—"

"Morgan," he said taking her hands once more, refusing to release them when she struggled. "I've heard these arguments—"

"And you must listen to Edward and Rob—"

"Rob," he said with a slight smile, "is in the process of obtaining a license."

"No! He's not so stupid!"

Ward shrugged. "Rob dislikes scandal more than most, and yet he believes I've charted the only honorable course. As for other issues, you are nobility, Morgan, and Bostonians revere English nobility."

"Even," she asked bitterly, "noble murderesses?"

"Even those," he said firmly, but his expression wavered.

"Oh Ward," she asked, pain scorching her heart, "why must we do any of this? Why not continue as we are? Aren't you happy with me?"

Hurt flashed across his face, and he shifted from chair to sofa to fold her in his arms. With her face pressed to his chest, she could hear his heart. "Very happy, love," he rumbled. "That's why we must do this."

"But there's no reason for marriage!"

"I remind you of the authorities in Philadelphia."

"I shall hide! They haven't found me yet—"

"Where? Shall we stuff you in a cupboard? My dear, in your present condition I fear you wouldn't fit."

She laughed and lifted her head, tears in her eyes. "It's abominable of you to provoke me to laughter when I'm perfectly serious!"

He smiled. "I love the sound of your laugh."

Warm, comforting words to take with her should she fail in persuading Ward to abandon this scheme. *Oh, Ward, I should never leave, not even for Amy, if only you'd see reason!* "I'm well enough to leave town for however long is necessary."

"Kenneth Turner will never stop hunting you."

She swallowed. "He will in five years, won't he? And it's a monstrously large country to search for one female."

"The country is, my dear, but not Boston and its environs. Traveling is out of the question during your confinement. Worse for you, Boston has recently commissioned detectives under the police department and if they possess any intelligence at all, they'll interrogate all the doctors in the area about their obstetric patients. They *will* find you, love. I repeat, marrying me is your only option."

Biting her cheek to prevent the pain from escaping her mouth, she stared down at her hands. Leaving was her only option, but she owned his company for the next few hours. Did she truly want to spend that time in a row? She could not dissuade Ward, for he'd charted his course and would stick to it like any good sea captain. It was best, she thought with a slight lilt in her heart, to lie and spend the time in comfort.

"I'd rather not quarrel. If I swear to consider your proposal, might we dismiss this topic for today?"

Silence and then he commanded, "Look me in the eye and promise first."

Lifting her head, she held his eyes steadily. "I promise to consider your proposal."

He frowned. "I'd prefer your consent."

"Would you have me lie?"

Eyeing her wearily, he shook his head. "I think we'll continue the discussion."

"What more could you say?"

"Plenty," he said wryly.

She sighed. "I wholly comprehend your offer. You possess wealth, name, manners, and breeding, all that a woman could wish for in a husband. You know my situation and you intend to correct it. Most importantly, you're the father of my child. I should be a bloody fool not to give such an offer serious consideration."

"Put that way," he said with a grin, "I don't see what you need to consider. Accept me and we'll be done."

Oh, but she'd never known a man so stubborn! "All right. I'll marry you."

The grin blossomed to a full-fledged smile, eyes sparkling with triumph. "I win," he said softly, making Morgan laugh in spite of her pain.

"You always win."

"Aye, Mistress. But in this we both win. A kiss then, to seal it," he said, then took her into his arms and sealed the bargain quite thoroughly.

Chapter Twenty-one

Ward sat sipping his coffee and scanning the morning paper when Ro came down for breakfast, wearing a red smoking jacket and grumbling under his breath. Lifting his head, Ward greeted him with a grin. "Bit of a head, Hathaway? I'd thought you'd quit hoisting brandy altogether. Sticking to port, so you told us."

"Bloody cheerful this morning, Montgomery, ain't cha?" he growled as he poured a cup of java from the sideboard. He slumped into a chair. "I quit brandy in Fran's company, but she wasn't here last night."

Ward chuckled. "Not physically, but you mentioned seeing her once or twice."

"I was merely keeping Edward company in his misery. If you'd had any regard for his friendship, you'd have followed suit."

"As a friend, I provided the brandy."

Ro groaned and, elbows on the table, leaned his head in his hands. "If you cared one whit for *our* friendship, you'd stop repeating that damnable word."

"All right. I have some mercy in my soul," he said cheerfully as the front door knocker sounded. Ward glanced at the clock. It was late for breakfast, and he didn't expect any morning callers. It seemed far too early for Edward, who'd been three sheets to the wind not five hours earlier.

But it *was* Edward. Face white under a day's growth of beard, he entered the room shouting, "They're gone!"

"Oh for pity's sake," Ro hissed lifting his head. "Must you be so bloody loud? Can't you see I'm in agony, you damned fool?"

"Who's gone?" Ward asked, sitting forward. Rob entered the room also, his face grim as he reached into his pocket to withdraw a folded sheet of paper.

"Amy and that witch of yours, that's who! Oh God," Edward said, sinking into a chair, heartache darkening his eyes. "She's left me."

Ward shook his head. "You're mistaken. Morgan agreed to marry me just yesterday. She wouldn't jump ship now. You've slipped your cable, Edward."

"I'm afraid he hasn't," Rob said, offering Ward the sheet of paper. "I went to pay Morgan's women this morning, and we found this on the drawing room mantelpiece."

With a lurch of his heart, Ward recognized Morgan's carefully formed letters.

My dear, dear captain,
I am sorry that I must bid you good-bye in such a manner, but you are so very stubborn, sir. I cannot possibly marry you, Ward. You must know that. Both my own life and my child's are at stake. You believe you possess the resources to correct that, but your heart and pride have misled you. Therefore, I have taken Amy, whose husband has abused her cruelly, and we are leaving for other parts, where we shall be safe. Perhaps in time, love, we shall meet again, under better circumstances, and you will become acquainted with your child. For now, give us leave to go in peace and know that I shall, in my heart, always remain,

Your loving mistress,
Morgan

Good God, he thought, swallowing several times. Why had he not seen it? For Morgan to agree so easily to his proposal . . . but she'd not agreed easily. It had required much persuasion. Morgan never persuaded well.

He'd find her.

Lifting his head, he peered at Edward, whose eyes were red-rimmed and puffy from drink. "Morgan accuses you of abusing Amelia."

Edward frowned. "It's a lie. I never touched her in anger."

"Why would Morgan lie about something like that?"

"How the devil should I know?"

Ward rubbed his neck, working his brain hard to suppress the pain bursting in his chest. She'd left him—

He'd find her.

"Did Amelia leave you a message?"

"Yes, but it's largely indecipherable. She was crying when she wrote it," he said, pulling two crinkled pages from his pocket.

"Did she offer any indication of their direction?"

"None," he said as he suddenly rose and started pacing the room. "Just two blasted pages of recriminations and accusations. And she's perfectly correct," he said, his voice cracking. "I've been a terrible husband, and now I've driven her away. Oh God," he said, leaning his head against the mantelpiece to stare into the dormant fireplace. "I can't bear this."

Ro stood and crossed the room to lay a hand on Edward's shoulder. "It's all right, old boy. She'll return."

Ward rose also. "We'll find them. Rob, be so kind as to join us in the library. I believe we shall require your services," he said as he crossed the room to place his own hand on Ed's other shoulder. "We'll find them, Edward. I promise you."

* * *

"It's begun, sir," Rob said, tossing the morning newspaper on the dining room table three days after Morgan's defection. Ward, heart in his throat, pushed away his half finished breakfast.

"Begun?" Edward asked with a wince as he sucked down the last dregs of java, heavily laced with rum.

"Ah, bloody hell," Ro swore, also shoving his plate aside as he leaned forward to peruse the paper upside down. "Well she left town in time, at any rate."

Ward ignored both to read the glaring headline. *Philadelphia Widow Woman in Boston!* Below it, in smaller print *Manhunt Begins For Wicked Widow.* The contents of Ward's stomach soured. "When you gentlemen are done eating, you'll find me in the library. Rob, mug up if you wish, then join me. The java's on the sideboard."

"We'll come now," Ro said shoving back his chair to follow Rob and Ward. Edward, face creased with misery, shuffled along behind.

In the library Ward seated himself at his desk while Ro and Edward took the chairs they'd made their own over the last three days. "Well, Rob?" Ward asked as his cousin sat in a chair closer to the desk. "We could all read it, but I suspect you've done so already. A brief synopsis, if you please."

"Well they don't appear to know much more than we've already guessed," he said. "Weatherly's sister claims to have seen her months before, but she's at least two hundred years old and no one attends her. Turner's cousin, however, they are listening to. She saw Morgan twice, once in June and again in July. She took note of her," Rob said with something between a grimace and a grin, "because Morgan was obviously far along with child, and it disgusted her that a woman should be abroad in such a condition."

"Bloody hell," Ro said. "They printed that?"

"They did, sir."

"No doubt," Edward said with a resigned sigh, "they'd print anything that made Morgan appear disreputable."

"And," Ward added, "Morgan's tendency to disregard the conventions only compounds the situation."

"You ought to have taken her in hand," Edward said with a viciousness that lost its bite when he heaved another weary sigh. "Then we shouldn't be in this situation and I should have Amy in my arms."

"If you'd behaved with any manner of sensibility," Ro scolded, "you'd not be in this situation."

"You have no notion of how it is!" Edward snapped. He leaned forward in his chair as fire sparked in his eyes. "With Fran—"

"Gentlemen," Ward interrupted calmly, "we've discussed this thoroughly several times. Doubtless we'll discuss it several more times, but presently it merely serves to irritate. Rob? Anything else of import in the article?"

"It contains a brief, poorly detailed description of the gowns she wore when seen. And," he said, taking a deep breath, "a sketch of her on the fourth page." He flipped through the pages. "It's rather good, I'm afraid."

Ward peered at the sketch. The artist had drawn Morgan's oval-shaped face correctly, along with the delicate arching of her eyebrows. He'd drawn her nose too long, however, her eyes too wide, and her mouth too small. Moreover, it lacked definition, Morgan's vivacity and, of course, color. Even the description of hazel eyes and dark hair misrepresented her. Morgan's eyes changed with the color of her clothes, her mood, and the weather.

"Granted he has some talent, but this picture and description could be many women. And the height is wrong. It claims she's average, but Morgan's no more than five feet two inches," he said, handing it back to Rob.

After pouring himself a drink Ro wandered over to take the paper from Rob's hands. Rob frowned at him. "A little early for drink, isn't it, sir?"

Ro sprawled in his chair once more. "Not when the police are conducting a citywide manhunt for Sir Captain's murdering mistress."

"Sir!" Rob exclaimed, eyes brightening with indignation. "Morgan is—"

"Belay that," Ward said mildly to Rob, and treated him with a quick smile. "He means no insult. We must act fast to control the damage, Rob. For the time being we'll transfer Fionna and Maeve's services to this house, and I shall as a matter of course explain to them the necessity for discretion. They're devoted to Morgan and will do all in their power to keep her from harm's way. First, however, they must destroy those gowns. Burn them, cut them to ribbons, whatever is necessary so that they cannot possibly be identified. Is that clear?"

"As crystal, sir."

"Excellent. We shall break the lease on her home using the explanation that Captain Wyatt found a berth on a ship sailing out of New York. His mistress has joined him there."

Rob smiled. "Well done. Next?"

Edward asked tentatively, "Has there been any news of my wife? That investigator Ward's hired—what was his name?—Adams or Richards or something. Has he found anything?"

"Allen. Thomas Allen, sir," Rob said, turning to him. Pity filled his voice. "No, sir, not yet. He's still interviewing train depot employees. You understand he must proceed with the utmost discretion."

"For which you ought to be bloody grateful, Edward,"

Ro said, flipping through the paper. "If she had been identified so easily, then so would Morgan. I hate to say it, but we'll be better off if neither are discovered for at least a fortnight."

Ward nodded, even as the loneliness in his heart grew. Only three days missing, and yet his arms ached for her soft body, his lips for her kiss, his ears for her laughter. "Even if Allen learns nothing, Edward, I suspect that we'll receive some manner of communication from Amelia fairly soon. She loves you, and she loves Morgan. Eventually her anger will abate. When it does, she'll realize the stupidity of flight and have a change of heart."

He sighed. "She hasn't had a change of heart in the last six months."

Ro gave a ghost of a laugh. "From what I've heard she's had a severe change of heart! Buck up, dear boy," he said, leaning forward to slap Edward on the back lightly. "*Mon Capitaine* is correct. Console yourself. Her heart will indeed change back."

Edward, eyes dark once more with grief said in a low voice, "I'll console myself with Amelia. Lord, but if I only knew she were safe!"

Chapter Twenty-two

Amy sat at the kitchen table watching Morgan skillfully spread out bread dough. She'd rolled the sleeves of her cheap muslin frock up to her elbows, and her forearms where white with flour. "Can you check the oven?" Mo asked. "To see if it's hot enough?"

Swallowing, Amy shook her head. "I don't know how. It would be simpler to buy from the baker, wouldn't it?"

Setting aside the rolling pin, Morgan dipped her fingers in the flour, then pinched the ends of the dough. "We must exercise the strictest economy."

"But we still have plenty of money. We've yet to sell your jewelry. I fancy we can afford a few luxuries." She'd spoken the last with an attempt at levity, but Morgan didn't laugh as she began rolling the dough again.

"We have plenty *now*, but you'll see how quickly it goes. Besides, I've been considering our situation. Chicago suits us currently, but I fancy we ought to travel further west when the baby's of an age."

Amy's heart clenched; her stomach flipped. She didn't want to go west. The homesickness she'd experienced when arriving in America was nothing in comparison to the last two weeks in Chicago. Not only did she miss home—Philadelphia of all places—but she particularly longed for Edward, for his hard, hungry kisses, his warm arms, and, oh she thought with a lump rising in her throat, she even missed his tiresome lectures. As much as she loved Morgan, she now perceived that setting up house with a woman lacked the comfort of living with a husband, especially when the former proved shockingly tightfisted and the latter generous beyond all things.

"Where should we live that is better than Chicago?" she asked as Morgan folded the dough into something that resembled bread and dropped it into a baking dish.

Morgan smiled broadly, her eyes sparkling as she began the same procedure with the next loaf. "San Francisco. Now don't panic, my dear!" she said, lifting her head. "For it's not nearly so frightful as it may first appear!"

"But we should have to travel by ship, and you know how I *hate* ocean travel!"

"I do, dear," she said, her eyes smiling sympathetically. "But afterward we shall be much better off. Only consider, Amy, we'll be living an entire continent away from them." She spoke the last word bitterly, but Amy detected a note of sorrow too. "I've read that the opportunities there are virtually limitless."

"What opportunities?" Amy asked. "Never tell me you wish to be a gold miner."

Morgan laughed. "Of course not! But there are very few women from what I understand—"

"I'm already married."

"—and men can't cook. I suppose that if we open a restaurant advertising home-cooking, we should be rich in no time."

Edward was already rich enough to suit Amy and, oh, how she despised the shabby row house that Morgan had insisted they rent, with only four rooms—two up-

stairs bedrooms, a parlor, a kitchen and an outhouse—
an *outhouse*—instead of a water closet. *She* suspected
they resided in the slums, even though Morgan had
laughingly declared this neighborhood as far a cry from
poverty as Westborough had been from White Chapel.

Even less did Amy relish doing their own housework,
although she owned that Morgan excelled at it. In all
her life, she'd never expected to see her dear friend
Lady Reynolds perform such menial tasks as would
break her nails and flour her clothes.

Worse for them both, the birthing day drew ever
nearer, exciting more dread in Amy than she'd ever
known. Even though they'd found a midwife, they had
no other women acquaintances, and what Amy understood of birth could fit on the head of a pin. What
would she do if the baby came so quickly that the midwife didn't arrive in time? Then *after* the birth, if Amy
survived it, she must of a necessity carry on the managing of the house, which Morgan had tried ever so patiently to teach her. She'd not grasped even the smallest
of instructions. She didn't wish to. She wished for home
and Edward.

And Morgan? Although she'd tried to hide it the last
two weeks, Amy fancied she concealed her true sentiments behind a countenance of determined merriness.
Several times she'd heard Morgan crying late at night
when she supposed Amy to be fast asleep.

"Don't you miss him at all, Mo?"

Morgan placed the second loaf into a pan, then
dropped into a hard-backed chair, mopping the beads
of un-ladylike sweat from her brow. "Miss who?"

"Ward. I—I miss Edward."

Morgan's eyes narrowed, grief flickering in her gaze
and flashing across her countenance. "After he treated
you so brutally, I wonder you think of him at all."

Amy cringed as what had once seemed but a trifling fib wriggled through her conscience. "I suppose he was not quite so wretched a husband after all."

"A man who would hit a woman," Morgan snapped, "is a perfect monster."

"But—but he didn't really—not truly—hit me."

Morgan froze. "What do you mean 'not truly'?"

"I own that his words *felt* like slaps, but to be sure, he never actually laid a hand on me, Mo, except—except," she said, her voice breaking, "in love."

"Good God, Amy, are you saying you *lied* to me? That you fled your marriage merely because Edward *shouted* at you?"

"I suppose—I supposed that 'brutality' should follow angry words, eventually. *You* thought it had, and I let you believe it, for I was enraged."

Morgan, her face tight with anger, shook her head. "And I thought I was saving you. Do you wish to return to him, Amy? You may. I shall be fine on my own."

"Would you continue on to San Francisco?"

She nodded grimly. "In time."

"Is not—is not returning to Ward a better idea?"

"No."

It was perfect folly for a young woman and baby to travel alone to a foreign coast peopled by rough, crude men. And to bear a baby alone, with only a midwife for comfort. *Oh, Morgan, we were such fools, my friend!*

"Then I shall stay. San Francisco sounds wonderful," she lied, because if her friend apprehended her true thoughts, she'd flee. Morgan, she resolved, would not bear her child alone, nor would either of them live another week without their men to care for them, as men were supposed to do!

* * *

—I've written the direction at the bottom of this page. Please hurry, Ward. The baby's arrival is imminent.

Your servant,
Amelia

Ward lifted his head, not attempting to suppress a smile. Scowling over a game of solitaire, Edward threw another card on the library pedestal table. "Damn, I can't win for anything today! Ward, aren't you done with your confounded correspondence, yet? I swear I've never known a man more enamored of work than you. I ought to have joined Ro in Marblehead." Edward turned to Ward and, seeing his expression asked, "What is it? Have you swindled some poor soul out of another million?"

Chuckling, Ward shook his head. "No. You'll like this much better. It's a letter from Amelia, complete with three paragraphs begging your forgiveness. *And* their direction in Chicago."

Edward sprang up to cross the room in two huge strides. He yanked the three sheets from Ward's hands. Ward sat back in his chair, folding his hands in his lap as relief relaxed his muscles. For the first time in three weeks he breathed easily. He had much to plan, but for a few minutes he'd sit and gloat.

"She still loves me," Edward whispered in a hoarse voice. "Did you read that, Ward? She still loves me, even after I scared her away."

And Morgan loved him. Amelia had said she believed it to be perfectly true, not that Ward had ever doubted it. Morgan had flown from fear.

He reached for paper and pen to write a note to Amelia requesting a short, clandestine meeting before he confronted Morgan. His next few moves required intricate planning and delicacy. "Ring the bell there, Ed.

I must send for Rob. We'll need train tickets to Chicago and hotel arrangements, maps, all that sort of thing. And you, my friend," he said, smiling as he wrote, "had better start packing. We shall have plenty of time on the trip for you to choose the best words to win back your wife's goodwill. Not," he said with a small smile, "that it sounds necessary!"

Edward's face broke into a huge grin. "Aye, aye, Captain! Just as soon as I send a message off to Ro."

Ward controlled a grimace, for Ro had resolved to meddle in his schemes. Edward would also, if his wife's desertion didn't occupy his mind so completely. "After packing, Ed. With a little luck, Rob might have us on a train today."

"Today? Do you think it's possible?"

"If it is, he'll find a way. Rob is very, very good at his job."

Morgan lay on her side on the sofa, rubbing her belly. So peculiar. Just yesterday she'd had enormous amounts of energy, baking four loaves of bread, dusting, sweeping, and cleaning everything in sight. This morning, though, her back ached and she wished never again to stir from her spot on the sofa. Across from her Amy sat in a frightfully ugly purple wing chair, embroidering a blanket for the baby although she despised embroidery.

"Oh, for heaven's sake!" she spat, dropping it on a table. "I fouled it all up again!"

"You're rushing it, dear," Morgan said gently.

"Well, it is a rush, isn't it?" she snapped, gesturing to Morgan's distended belly.

Morgan raised her eyebrows as the ache became a cramp. "The baby will love his Aunt Amy whether or not the blanket's completed."

A rush of guilt crossed Amy's sweat-dampened face, pinching at Morgan's conscience. She oughtn't have included Amy in this adventure. For all her stubbornness, she hadn't the strength for such escapades. Abandoning her husband was a far cry from wearing bloomers to tea.

"I'm sorry, Mo!" she said, and crossed the room to sink down to the floor next to Morgan's head. "I'm a witch, aren't I? But you'll forgive me for you must know how this waiting wears on my nerves, and the heat has always made me dreadfully cross. The air is so thick! Shall I fetch you a cool drink?"

Morgan smiled. "I'm fine, but I shouldn't scorn a nap if you—"

A rapping on the front door interrupted her.

Amy jumped up, a sudden blush darkening her cheeks. Her hands fluttered nervously. Morgan frowned. She'd behaved oddly these last three days, ever since venturing out to purchase some small items for the baby's arrival. With a sense of foreboding Morgan asked, "Who do you fancy that might be?"

"The midwife, perhaps, come to inquire as to your health?" she ventured as she scurried from the room.

Morgan shifted into a sitting position. The baby seemed to shift slightly also, and the ache in her back strengthened, making her wince. Voices drifted through the doorway. Not the midwife's. Male voices. Two of them.

Oh Lord, no!

A moment later Amy returned, her arm linked with her husband's. Guilt rode high in her eyes, even while her chin stubbornly tilted up.

Ward followed them. "Hello, Morgan."

Tiny bubbles of joy rose in her fickle heart as his hungry gaze flashed over her person, settling on her face. Then comprehension struck her. Morgan jerked her gaze toward Amy. "You sent for them!"

"One of us needed to come to her senses, for you must know by now, Mo, that you can't possibly bring up that child on your own."

"Oh Lord, Amy, how could you?" she asked, tears burning her eyes. Whatever was the matter with her that she wept so easily these days? It appeared that carrying this child had blighted her senses, as well as her spirits and mental strength.

Edward pulled Amy nearer. "I agree. Two ladies rearing a child on their own! Why, it's not to be thought of!"

"It's thought of all the time," Morgan spat back emotions careening through her heart. "Have you no notion how many women are forced to bear and bring up children alone?"

"Not you," he said icily. "Ward is a man of honor. He'll provide for his child."

She'd never doubted Ward's interest in his child. It was marriage she'd hoped to escape. But was it possible that he'd changed his mind?

She turned to regard him, her heart leaping hopefully. His eyes were as soft and kind as she had dreamt of these many nights, but resolve lined his beloved face. Her spirits sank. A changed mind? Her captain? Once he'd laid a course not even a hurricane would steer him from his goal.

"Perhaps, Edward," Ward said, gaze fixed upon Morgan, "you and Amelia wish to return to the hotel?"

Edward frowned. "Aren't you and Morgan accompanying us?"

Something flickered in his eyes. "I've engaged a doctor who wishes to examine Morgan as soon as possible. He'll be here within an hour or two."

"A doctor? But I already have a midwife," Morgan said.

"Is that what you were doing these last three days, Ward?" Edward asked. "Ought I to send the carriage back for you?"

"No. I'll find transportation later."

"In this area? Really, Ward—"

"I'll manage," he said, his voice suddenly sea-captain stern.

Edward shrugged, then turning his wife around, headed toward the door. Flinging one last glance of contrition and stubbornness over her shoulder, Amy went with him. A minute later the front door shut behind them.

Chapter Twenty-three

Morgan watched Ward strip off his gloves. After laying them aside he seated himself next to her on the small, shabby sofa, his warm thigh brushing against hers. She shifted away.

"Afraid of me?" he asked, raising an eyebrow. "You know I'd not hurt you."

Her back started aching again. The pain radiated to her stomach, causing a slight cramping there. "You oughtn't have pursued me, Ward, nor do I appreciate your meddling in my medical needs. I don't want your doctor." But, she thought rubbing her belly, she might require the midwife quite soon. Was this true labor, or merely more of the false pains that had plagued her these last days?

After a short pause, he asked, "How have you been, love?"

The gentleness in his voice sent a warm shiver of delight down her back. How could he sound so loving after she'd lied to him, fled him? "Well enough."

"Excellent," he replied, reaching for her hand. "Neither distance nor time has altered my feelings. I still request this hand in marriage."

She averted her eyes, biting her cheek in hope that the pain there would replace that in her heart. But the stabbing in her belly did that better—

True pain. A tightening, a cramping, a stabbing—oh, it *was* labor! Excitement and dread clutched at her heart. It was time!

"Morgan?" Ward asked in alarm. "Are you all right?"

A knock rang through the house. Ward's doctor, no doubt.

"It's too late, Ward," she said. Triumph filtered through her pain, mixing with regret, for some small part of her dearly wished for Ward as her husband.

"Too late?" he asked, rising slowly, his eyes calculating.

"The baby. It's time."

He stared hard, then a tender smile spread over his face. "Wait here. I'll answer the door."

After he left, the cramping passed and Morgan leaned against the sofa back. She'd hear no more talk of marriage now. The child would be a bastard despite her captain's best intentions. And then perhaps—was it possible?— Ward might take her back as his mistress, after the excitement over Philadelphia's Wicked Widow died away. Might they, she wondered with a lightening of spirits, return to their former relationship?

Ward entered the room accompanied by a balding man of indeterminate age, carrying a battered leather book instead of a black valise. In fact he wore all black, Morgan noted with dismay.

Ward's eyes glowed. "Permit me to introduce the Reverend Howard to you, Morgan. Sir, this is my fiancée, Mrs. Turner. The reverend, my dear, is an Episcopalian rector, whom I commissioned to marry us."

Morgan's eyes widened, speech momentarily stolen. Reverend Howard wore a wrinkled frock coat, shiny on the elbows with wear. Red eyes peered at her from a florid, heavy jowled face, the product, no doubt, of the silver flask peeping out of a pocket. "Mighty glad to meet you, ma'am," he slurred, with a bow. "You want the full service or the short version? I'm 'quipped to pe'form either."

Disbelieving, Morgan fixed her gaze upon Ward. "Good God, Ward, I require a midwife, not a priest!"

"A midwife?" the Rector Howard asked, glancing down at her belly.

Ward shrugged. "If you wish, I shall send for one as well. However, my doctor will preside over the delivery."

"He shall not! I have this all arranged. You've no right to interfere!"

"I have every right to make decisions in the care of *our* child."

"*My* child, by law!"

"Not," he responded in a silky-smooth voice, "after the rector has completed the service."

She knew that tone; not resolve, but decision. Chest tight, she grasped for straws. "But he's drunk!" she exclaimed. "Such a marriage could not be binding! And you must acquire a license first, at any rate."

Rector Howard shook his head. "Just a bit damaged is all."

"I have a license."

Before she could argue further, another pain seized her attention, which began in her back then crept forward to harden her belly. This time she took fast, panting breaths as the midwife taught her. Ward watched impassively, arms over his chest. When the contraction passed, he commented gently, "You're running short of time, my dear."

The priest, his gaze moving between the two, scratched his head. "Am I understandin' this right? Ma'am, are you having that baby?"

"I am."

His eyes widened. "Unusual," he said, grasping for his flask. "Highly unusual."

A tiny bubble of laughter rose in Morgan's throat at the shocked disapproval on the rector's face.

"You see, sir," Ward said, "the necessity of a quick ceremony."

"It's yours I reckon?" He took a deep swallow from the flask.

Ward nodded.

"Well, then. Well then, I'd suspicion you need a doctor."

Morgan chuckled. "And if it weren't his baby? Should I then summon a veterinarian?"

Ward cast Morgan a scowl before replying, "Aye, sir. I've sent for Dr. Marlow already."

"When? I never heard it."

"Before you arrived."

"Never heard of Marlow, neither."

"Which scarcely matters. You must marry us regardless."

"Not under these circumstances, I won't! I might have had a nip or two, but I've not completely lost my morals!"

"Why then, please feel free to drink until you *have* lost them. But be quick about it!" Ward said.

Morgan chuckled again.

"This ain't no laughing matter, missy, you being in this situation without a husband—it's purely immoral!"

She lifted her eyebrows. "It is, isn't it? Oh dear! Perhaps I consumed too much liquor prior to conception. But the lesson won't be lost on me, I assure you. In the—"

"Now that's just the matter!" Howard interrupted, waving his flask at her. "This here goes against all Christ's rules, and she don't even regret it!"

Ward took a deep, stabilizing breath. "You are trained to correct immorality, Reverend. You must consider this the perfect opportunity."

Another pain gripped Morgan. Lord, so quick! The intensity made her gasp and Ward flew to her side, taking her hand as she panted. The pain peaked, then passed. Relaxed, once more she lifted her head to discover Ward smiling softly. "It's time to bring you to bed."

Soft smile, but she distrusted the cunning behind the glint in his eyes. "I've time, still."

"Are you certain?"

She bit the inside of her cheek. Her pains were progressing rather faster than expected. And the cramping *had* begun hours earlier. "All right."

A short time later she sat, dressed in her chemise, in a chair in her room. Ward stood near the door, watching while she breathed through another pain. A light breeze stirred the curtains, and as the pain passed, she noted thunderclouds gathering in the distance, promising relief from the heat. But not, she prayed, impeding the doctor.

As if in answer, a knock sounded on the front door. Ward glanced out the window. "It's the doctor. I'll see to him," he said and quit the room.

Thank God! Morgan thought. She'd prefer her midwife, but at this juncture she'd welcome any professional. Thus far she'd not permitted herself to consider it too nearly, but women were forever dying in childbirth. . . .

Ward returned. Alone. The door closed behind him with an ominous click. "The doctor awaits your decision in the parlor."

She tilted her head as a dreadful thought gnawed at her brain. "My decision? For heaven's sake, Ward, you must bring him to me!"

His eyes narrowed. "Certainly—after you bid me summon Rector Howard."

"After—Ward, you cannot possibly mean—"

"The doctor shall only attend Morgan Montgomery."

"Then," she said carefully, "if he refuses me, you must send for my midwife."

"Doctor Marlow doesn't refuse you, madam. I do."

"Oh no, you would not!" she spat back, her hands shaking in anger—and fear. "Have you lost your mind? I am having a baby!"

"I'm aware of that."

Frantically she cast her eyes over his face, searching for some measure of mercy. She found none. His jaw was as tight as a steel band; his eyes as hard as diamonds.

Another contraction struck, dragging a hoarse cry from her throat. This time the breathing exercises scarcely helped ease the agonizing vice around her belly. Through it Ward appeared unmoved, standing between her and the door with his arms crossed behind his back and his legs spread like a man at sea—a devil of a man, wholly impervious to her agony. "Damn it, Ward," she said between gritted teeth. "I'll not listen to any more of this nonsense. You call that doctor *now!*"

"Will you marry me?"

"No, damn it! I refused you before, and I *will* not change my mind under such ramshackle circumstances as these."

"Had you accepted me earlier, we should not find ourselves in such circumstances."

"We? I bear the pain not you!" When he merely held her gaze, not budging, fear marbled her anger. "Oh, Ward, how *can* you treat me so shabbily? You must know women are forever dying in childbirth! You hold my very life in your hands. Would you sacrifice it for pride?"

A smile flashed across Ward's harsh countenance.

"Now that's absurd. You're far too healthy to die from childbirth."

"What does a man know of such matters?"

"The doctor is a man, too."

"But trained, sir! Are you trained?"

"I know enough to trust that you'll neither die nor suffer any debilitating aftereffects of childbirth. You shall, however, bear this child without medical attention if you continue in your obstinacy."

"I am not being obstinate. That is you, sir."

He sighed disgustedly. "I merely wish to save you years of misery. You think I don't value your life? I stand here because I value it so much. I've explained this to you over and over again. I've employed reason, compassion, and love, but it seems nothing will convince you but compulsion."

"And *I* have explained my refusal, but you refuse to listen!"

"I've listened well, Morgan, and weighed your fears against my ability to correct for them. Marriage remains the best answer."

Oh God, she thought closing her eyes and rubbing her temples. This could not be possible! *Amy, you little fool, how could you have brought me to this pass? I was so near to escape. A few months more and I should be living comfortably in San Francisco, and Philadelphia none the wiser.*

But married—the police, oh *God*—. Her eyes flew open as her nerves jumped to attention. "Ward, the license—it refers to me as Turner, doesn't it?"

"It does."

"Do you know what you've *done*? You've all but told the Philadelphia police where I am!"

"You place far too much faith in our justice system. I doubt they correspond regularly with Chicago. At all events, that's for the future. Presently we must remedy this situation."

She pictured her body swinging from the gallows, dead eyes bulging, face ghost white as Kenneth watched, a smile of smug satisfaction gracing his weasel face. "How could you do this to me?" she gasped. Then her belly tightened again, squeezing horribly until tears burst from her eyes. Oh no, this couldn't be right! Not so much pain—women would never—oh—

The contraction peaked, sank, then peaked again, stealing all thought, sapping her strength. When it finally ended, she panted, looking at Ward with bleary eyes. He passed his gaze over her thoughtfully, then spoke in a devilishly enticing voice, "You should know Dr. Marlow is quite proficient with ether, chloroform, and opium."

For a moment she could not believe her ears. Then rage propelled her from the chair and she lunged for the door. As she did Ward's hands shot out to grasp her shoulders, holding firmly while she struggled. "Let me go! Damn you, let me go!" She slammed her fists into his chest, then reached to scratch his face. Releasing her shoulders, he took possession of her wrists and pushed them downward in a dreadful parody of their first night together, when she'd been a starving wretch named Miss Brown and he a mere sea captain. Tears streamed down her face, as her breath came in sobs of frustration and heartache. Desperate, she searched his face for traces of her soft-eyed captain. Gone, those eyes transformed to stone-cold flint.

A stabbing pain, then something tore deep inside her private regions. Warm liquid slid down her legs, and then, as she stared down in horror, it gushed from between her thighs, splashing before her and forming a pool at her feet. A frightfully strong contraction followed, pumping the liquid from her body. Morgan sagged against Ward, smothering screams in his waist-coat.

Ward dropped his arms around her waist, holding her steady. She leaned into him, sobbing, "I hate you. I hate you." And for the first time since seeing her, guilt yanked at Ward's heart. Damn it, what kind of man was he? A man like his father, forcing himself upon a woman he professed to love. He was an animal, no better. He ought—

"All right," she said, sucking up a sob. "Call Howard."

And with those small words, guilt fled, replaced by love, triumph, and pure, perfect joy.

Chapter Twenty-four

Morgan had wed three different men in as many years, twice in a church, the last in the drawing room of her dead husband. For pure peculiarity, this wedding beat the others to flinders. Instead of a wedding gown, Morgan wore a nightdress. Instead of standing before a priest, she lay in bed, covered in a sheen of perspiration brought on by the sticky August heat and the laboring of her body. Beside her stood the groom, holding her hand and admonishing her with each contraction to squeeze his hand tightly. Their two witnesses stood at the door, the doctor and his nurse, the former swearing under his breath as he watched her helplessly, and the latter growling about the pure immorality of the situation. In the middle of the confusion the priest performed the ceremony in a long slur, skipping passages, then returning to them out of order until, compelled by pain and pure frustration, Morgan let out a long, high-pitched scream. The doctor lurched forward, but Ward held up his hand. "Not yet."

"For the love of God, man, let me assist her!"

"Not before she is my wife."

"If you cared one whit for her, you'd permit me to do my job!"

Morgan, furious with everyone—for being pain-free, for daring to speak—screamed louder, gasping at the end, "I hate you all."

Reverend Howard shook his head. "Can't say that, not being as how you just vowed to love, cherish—"

"Damn you," Ward said through gritted teeth, "stop reading her lectures and for God's sake marry us! You'd have long since accomplished the task if you'd just get on with it!"

"Get on with it? Well, why din't you tell me you wanted the short ceremony? Here 'tis. We did all this, right? Vows, vows, prayers, vows, prayers, ah ha! And now, I pronounce you man and wife. You may kiss the bride."

"If I did, she'd belt me. Hand me that blasted license. Morgan, you must sign this."

"You're joking," she ground out through a red haze of fury.

"You must."

"Damn you!" She yanked the paper from his grasp, scribbled her name, and flung it at him.

Ward dropped the paper on the table with a satisfied, "Done. Doctor, your patient."

"Finally!" the doctor snapped, and lunged forward to pull the sheets up.

Ward jerked his head at the preacher. "I've left a bottle of rum in the parlor. Drink what you wish, but be so obliging as to refrain from vomiting."

While a new ribbon of pain gripped Morgan, the doctor commanded her to lift her legs. She swore at him and he said, in a gentler tone, "Please, madam. I only wish to help. Splendid. Hilda, my bag if you please. Mr. Montgomery, you may leave now."

Through half closed eyes Morgan saw Ward scowl. "I'm staying."

The doctor's eyebrows snapped together. "You will not! Men are prohibited from my deliveries!"

Hilda shook her head as a clap of thunder heralded the arrival of the storm. "It's unseemly!"

"I was there at the creation of the child, and I've been here during the labor thus far. I intend to see the end."

"Are you aware of the fact that I may refuse my services?"

Ward smiled slightly. "I understand that you have too much honor to leave this poor woman alone with such a monster as me."

As the contraction subsided, another one came on, harsher but with a different feeling, a sort of crunching sensation. And the urge to push—"It's coming!" she gasped.

The doctor turned swiftly and shoved back the sheets to uncover her completely. "You're right, but don't push—I must check—"

His slid his hands between her legs and her face grew hot with embarrassment. But the need to push controlled her, and instead of protesting, she cried out. "I can't—I can't help it."

"Excellent, you're fully dilated. Push, madam, go ahead—harder."

And so it went for an indeterminate amount of time, the contractions racking her body, the doctor commanding her to push, as lightning flashed, thunder crashed, and cool sweet air flowed through the windows. Ward, ignored now by both doctor and nurse, knelt on the bed next to her. He held her hand and murmured tender words of comfort between contractions, the words he'd withheld before she'd married him. At times she wanted to box his ears, or toss him from the bed, or scream and yell and beat him senseless. But then he'd bathe her face with a cool moist cloth and brush soft kisses across her forehead. Oh, she loved him then, begged him to stay—and how she hated him when the pain struck again, all a perfect duplication of her sentiments towards the baby splitting her apart, making her beg for chloroform, ether, opium—

And then the baby's head emerged. Another contraction, a long, agonizing push and the shoulders came through. Her baby slid into the world.

"A boy!" The doctor exclaimed as if he didn't deliver babies all the time, as if it were a miracle. He raised a doll-sized creature up by its chubby red legs and slapped its bottom gently. Her son howled indignantly.

It *was* a miracle. The pain had ended; a life had begun.

"Healthy?" Ward asked as Hilda brought swaddling clothes.

"Very," the doctor shouted over the howling.

Ward smiled—the broad, heart-stopping smile that had stolen Morgan's heart. "A son, Morgan," he said, stroking the back of her hand with his thumb. "Leland Reginald Montgomery."

"Montgomery," she repeated, shutting her eyes against the fear rippling through her.

"Ma'am?" Hilda asked, perplexed. "Are you still in pain? Doctor Marlow?"

"The afterbirth is coming," he said. "A moment please—"

Morgan sighed and opened her eyes. "I'm well enough. May I see my baby?"

Smiling, Hilda laid him on the bed between Ward and her. His shock of hair was dark as night, his little crossed eyes sky blue and staring at her as she touched his soft red cheek. His howling stopped as his brows drew together in a frown shockingly similar to his father's. She chuckled. "Angry, sweetheart?" she whispered. "Oh, but you are perfectly lovely." A tightness gripped her heart, her throat—warmth, wonder, and bittersweet love.

"Excellent," the doctor said from his position at the end of the bed. "Everything is intact. You may put down your legs, ma'am," he said, pulling the sheets down to cover her. "Hilda, would you be so kind as to find Mrs. Montgomery something clean to wear? And perhaps some clean sheets. Mr. Montgomery, if you please, I require a few minutes' conversation."

"In a moment," Ward answered, lifting his son's tiny hand, his face a picture of awe as he watched the tiny fingers curl around his thumb. An uncommon brightness lit Ward's eyes. "He *is* perfect, love. He has your eyes."

"And your hair. And your name," she said with a hiccup of pain.

Wariness flickered in Ward's eyes, stubbornness colored his voice. "As is only proper."

"He won't inherit Turner's fortune," Morgan said, ripping her own heart apart as she tore into his. "Instead he will inherit the Montgomery name, the Montgomery fortune, and," she said on a sob, "one hanged mother."

Ward sucked in his breath. "Never."

"Say what you will, you cannot prevent it. This is what you've presented your son today. I hope you're happy." Tears dripped from her eyes, and she waved at her new baby. "Take him away. I need rest."

After passing on myriad instructions to Ward, the doctor insisted that Morgan stay abed a fortnight. When

Ward inquired about removing her to more comfortable surroundings, he glanced around the small room and replied, "These rooms appear adequate. If you move her, sir, you do so against my advice. She had a simple enough birthing, but she's not yet out of danger of fever. Moreover he's a fairly large baby and if she's to supply enough milk for his needs, she must be well rested." He snapped his bag shut. "I shall return in four days to see how she progresses. I trust that you won't cause my patient any further distress."

"My wife need never fear any harm from me."

Morgan, exhausted, fell asleep upon those words. Hours later a mewling cry awakened her, followed by Ward's voice. "Morgan, love, it's the baby."

Bare-chested, he squatted down next to her bed. In the mellow lamp light, sweet love shone from his eyes, turning her heart to mush. Then, with a flicker of pure, stubborn anger, she remembered his betrayal. "Here, allow me to help you sit up," he said, "and I'll bring him to you."

Seething once more, Morgan shoved his hands away and pulled herself up to lean against the wall. The baby's mewling turned to a cry. "Do you retrieve my son, or does he starve?"

Frowning, Ward rose. A short time later he laid her baby in her arms. Lee's tiny face was screwed up and red, and he flailed his arms about in anger. Morgan bit her lip in consternation, staring down at the tiny human being that hours earlier had been living inside her. No doubt he was hungry and wanted to suckle but she'd little understanding of how to go about it. Taking a deep breath, she drew the strings of her nightdress and freed one breast, then shifted the baby to bring his mouth near her nipple, crooning, "Shh, shh, here, sweetheart, this is what you want."

It wasn't. He rooted for a few seconds but quickly became frustrated. As he wailed, she again attempted to guide him to the nipple. Arching, he cried louder. Tears sprang to her eyes. What was the matter? Oh, she was doing it wrong, that was his point! Motherhood, it appeared, didn't come naturally to her. It appeared that only vulgarity came naturally to her.

"Morgan?" Ward asked. He sat at the end of the bed, watching her. "Is there a problem?"

"He doesn't care for me."

"You're his mother. He loves you."

"I'm an unnatural mother. I can't even suckle my own child."

"Of course you can. You need only show him the way."

"I'm trying," she snapped, pushing the baby's face against her. "He won't take it!" In fact, he screamed. After two days of strained nerves, with her body aching from childbirth, her heart broken with betrayal, Morgan, too, wanted to scream, scream and gnash her teeth. "Bloody hell, Leland! You're driving me to distraction! Take the thing." But he refused, for she'd no more understanding of motherhood than of being a wife, both roles thrust upon her by the monster sitting not five feet away, compassion warming his traitor's face.

"Do you require assistance?"

"And what would you do, hold a gun to his head? Threaten death should he disobey?" When Ward scowled, she exclaimed, "Why, it's much the same as you did to me, isn't it? Here, take him away! He doesn't want me. If he won't suckle, I can do nothing for him," she said on a sob, holding the baby out to him.

"He wants you, Morgan, not me," Ward replied mildly. He rose and took a turn so that he knelt on the bed beside her. "Put him to your breast."

"I did! That's not what he desires."

"He's but a few hours old. That's all he desires."

"Perhaps he's ill."

"No sick baby could cry that loudly."

"He's in pain!"

"He's hungry."

"Not for anything I can provide," she said, holding him once more to her breast. Screaming, he twisted his little head in her hand, sending feelings of inadequacy racing through Morgan's heart. "Do you see? He won't take it!" she cried raggedly.

"You must put it in his mouth."

"If he wished for it, he'd take it himself."

"He's not yet a day old, Morgan. He's incapable."

"Oh you're mad," she said, fighting to force the baby's head back toward her breast. "Such matters come naturally. It's me that's unnatural. Oh, he won't take it!"

"Then put it in his mouth."

"If I did, I should smother him!"

Ward shook his head, leaned forward, and brushed her hand aside. Laying one firm hand on his son's head, he used the other to squeeze her breast near her nipple, thereby making it smaller. When he brought the two together, Leland, mouth full, stopped screaming. Unable to do anything else, he rendered a tiny suck. Morgan gasped at the sensation. Another tug, then another, and he sighed softly, his breath brushing her breast as he settled down to enjoy his first meal.

"Oh!" Morgan whispered, lifting her head to regard Ward gratefully. "How ever did you know?"

He shrugged and leaned back on his heels. "It seemed logical enough."

Pain creased her heart. "You've done this before, haven't you? You have another child somewhere."

His face twisted, not, Morgan fancied with some distracted part of her brain, unlike his son. "I have only one child and only one wife."

Anger shot through her, combined with more wretched heartache. Trembling, she looked down at her baby. "Against my wishes."

"Nonetheless, you *are* my wife."

But a murderess of a wife and a murderess of a mother. Despite her long attempts at avoiding it, she'd be caught, tried, and hanged. Inevitably Ward would be a widower and her son, motherless. How much misery and scandal must they endure first?

Ward chuckled abruptly, a warm, incredulous laugh, shooting rays of light into her weary heart. "He takes to it well, doesn't he? I'd considered them mine but it appears I must surrender use for a spell."

"They're my breasts, not yours," she said mulishly.

Ward sighed disgustedly. "I'm attempting, my dear, merely to conduct a polite conversation. Might you at least try for a little cooperation?"

"There's nothing polite about discussing a woman's breasts."

"Very well. You choose the subject."

"I choose nothing. I only want sleep."

With another sigh, Ward slid off the bed to take up residence in Amy's, dragged from her room earlier. "When he's finished, call me. I'll put him back in his cradle. The doctor ordered complete bed rest for you."

"What if he needs changing?"

"I'll do it," Ward said, pillowing his head.

"You're a man. You cannot."

"I'll learn."

She wanted to snap that she'd not teach him, but suppressed her wayward tongue. Tears burned her eyes as she watched her baby suckle, his tiny fingers fisted against her breast. Ward would eventually have the total care of Leland. Biting her cheek to keep from sobbing, she brushed her fingers against Leland's cheek, his skin as soft as down. Oh, but he had the tiniest feet, tiny toes, tiny fingers, everything so exquisitely perfect in miniature. That such a miracle had grown inside her for nine months! How would she ever gather the courage to leave him? Impossible, impossible, but her only alternative consisted of tearing the hearts from husband and child, for the longer she stayed, the stronger would grow their attachment, the more wrenching her departure. She could bear that far less than losing them forever.

From across the room, a smile floating on his lips, Ward watched mother and son—his wife and baby. Nothing in the world could warm his heart more than the expression on Morgan's face when she looked at their son. Beautiful, both of them, perfectly, amazingly beautiful. He'd made the correct decision. Presently Morgan's anger poisoned her heart, but that would wane by and bye. She loved her son, and that love would whittle away at her anger until she came to love the father as well. All it needed was patience. Fortunately he'd been gifted with vast amounts of it.

Chapter Twenty-five

"Morgan, we have visitors," Ward said, sidling into their bedroom—torture chamber in truth. It was another hot, humid day, with a low, dirty-gray sky, dotted here and there by white puffs of steam pretending to be clouds. The thick cover turned the sun into an impotent white ball, strong enough to warm the air, but not to dry anything. Consequently, everything Morgan touched was damp and sticky, from her pink cotton bed-clothes, to the scratchy sheets, to the walls of her cell, once red but now faded to a vomit-colored orange. The windows, flung open to catch any stray breeze, proved useless. She was hot, tired, and disgusted. She wanted out of this bed, out of this room, out of this bloody city. Three wretched days had passed since Leland's birth, during which Ward had refused to let her out of bed other than to care for her most basic needs. To that purpose he'd hired a servant, one Mrs. Donovan, who brought her food and assisted her in dressing and washing. She also cared for Leland's needs other than feeding, Morgan's only duty.

"I don't care," she snapped.

If he had any consideration for her at all he'd not

look so well, with his neatly trimmed side-whiskers and clean-shaven face. Although he wore full day-dress, including a frock coat, no sweat beaded Ward's brow. Only a slight darkening under his eyes testified to three sleep-disturbed nights and three tension-filled days, whereas *she* undoubtedly looked a fright, like some dark fury from the depths of hell.

Ward's jaw tightened, but he replied with formidable patience, "Amelia's arrived, along with Edward and another friend of mine you've yet to meet. They've come specifically to see how you're faring."

"I'm neither in spirits nor state of dress to meet your friends."

"Amelia is *your* friend."

"She ceased to be so when she allowed your entrance."

His dark eyes crackled, and for a tiny space of time she thought he might snap. Instead, he grasped the reins of his temper and shook his head. "You're allowing pride to overrule your heart."

"You've left me nothing else."

Drawing a deep breath, Ward turned and spoke to those outside the door. "She declines all visitors."

Morgan flinched when she heard Amy's reply, the traitor. "It doesn't signify what she wishes. I'll see her all the same!"

Ward shrugged and stepped aside. Amy swept in, crisp, fresh, and fashionable in a green and red checked satin gown decorated with black embroidered flounces, pagoda sleeves, and green-ribbon-laced undersleeves. Mr. Huntington followed her, his face grim as he leaned against the wall and crossed his arms protectively over his chest. His conservative blue suit clashed with vomit orange, jarring Morgan's ragged sensibilities. Ward's other friend entered behind them. He was taller and thinner than Ward, with a full set of dark whiskers and the devil sparkling in his blue-black eyes. His checkered coat and pants displayed an interest in style.

"I shan't allow you to keep me from your side," Amy said, a determined tilt to her chin as she sat down in the chair next to Morgan's bed. "I did as I thought best for your welfare. Fly into as many passions as you might choose, I should do so again in an instant."

Morgan scowled at her, then lifted her head to fix her gaze upon the stranger. With a short bow and a smile, he said, "Mrs. Montgomery. I'm delighted to make your acquaintance."

"I've forgotten my manners," Ward interjected. "Give me leave, Morgan, to introduce Roland Hathaway, a long-time friend of mine."

She glared at Mr. Hathaway, then dismissed him with an icy shake of her head. "I'm tired," she pouted to Ward.

Wincing, he rubbed her neck. "Then you ought to have been sleeping."

"Wholly impossible in this heat."

"Then you might as well entertain visitors."

"I'll entertain no one, least of all," she snapped, turning to murder Mr. Hathaway with a glance, "a man so lacking in conduct as to visit a woman in her bed."

Mr. Hathaway's eyes flashed, irritation traced with cynical amusement gleaming back at her. "You must have allowed at least one such visit, madam, or you'd not be in this bed."

"Oh, for the love of God," Mr. Huntington breathed, staring at the ceiling. Ward clenched and unclenched his fingers.

"You're very rude!" Morgan spat.

"It appears you could tutor me in those talents."

"I never bade you visit me."

"And yet your flight compelled me to desert wife and child to come to your rescue. After causing such inconvenience, ma'am, you display a shocking lack of manners."

"Oh, for God's sake," Ward growled, "must you provoke her, Ro?"

"Provoke her?" he said, head snapping around to face his friend. "She provoked me!"

"You know better," Edward scolded, "than to rise to that bait."

"She ought to know better than to throw out such bait," Hathaway answered. He focused on her once more, his eyes narrowed, head tilted haughtily. "You, madam, are all my worst fears combined in one. I only wish I'd arrived early enough to prevent this farce of a marriage."

"On that," Morgan snarled, clenching her teeth against the sudden twisting of her heart, "at least we both agree!"

"I assure you that if there's any way I can rectify the circumstances, I shall do so at the earliest possible convenience."

"Then be on your way!" she said motioning to the door. "Nothing could please me more."

Ward rolled his eyes.

"Most certainly." With a short bow, Mr. Hathaway strolled to the door. "I'll await you, Edward, Amelia, in the parlor."

Shaking his head in disgust, Ward flashed a meaningful look at Mr. Huntington and then followed his friend.

With a twitch of his eyes, Mr. Huntington said gently, "Don't mind him, ma'am. Hathaway enjoys behaving outrageously."

"Mind him?" Morgan said, leaning back against the wall. Her head ached from suppressed tears. "He, of all of you, speaks at least some sense."

Mr. Huntington threw his hands up. "Fine. I yield the floor, Amy. I'll see you in the parlor."

A light rain splattered against the windowsill, as Amy's pitying blue eyes searched Morgan's face. Finally she said soothingly, "I wholly understand your depressed spirits, dear, but you must know your poor conduct only adds to the current difficulties."

"It was your betrayal that created the difficulties."

"I make no excuses for assisting in your flight other than to remind you how dreadfully angry I was with Edward. Yet I fancy I corrected my folly when I summoned Ward to your side."

"Amy, you're a bloody fool if you believe this marriage solves anything. It will very likely lead to my hanging."

"Oh fudge! You know quite well that Ward will never let you hang."

"Do I? With what prevention? He's neither a lawyer nor a judge!"

"But he has the money and prestige to hire lawyers and pay for witnesses to extract you from the situation."

"My, that's a lovely thing to pass on to my son, isn't it? Leland, sweetheart, I murdered my third husband, but never fear, your father bribed the witnesses to keep silent!"

Amy looked down at her hands, her eyebrows drawn together. "You killed that beast in self-defense."

"Which, so says your esteemed husband, is a wholly unarguable position since I didn't believe at the time that he meant to kill me."

Her head shot up. "But he would have eventually!"

"Lord, Amy," Morgan said, heaving a sigh of exhaustion. "How can you know that? *I* don't even know that."

"It's of no significance, as marrying Ward will save you," Amy said stubbornly.

Morgan shut her eyes. "Even if that were possible,

Amy, what would be the cost? It would take months before the lawyers settled everything, during which Ward's name would be splashed across the newspapers daily. He'd be ruined," she said, choking back tears when she envisioned Ward's face, tight with pain as he read just such a headline. "Can you not comprehend what that would do to him? To his son? They'd be ostracized, and it would not stop there. It would touch his friends also, you and Edward." She swallowed hard, looking at Amy through narrowed eyes. They'd be obligated to defend Morgan, spreading the scandal further. "And it would all be a waste, for I *did* kill Richard."

"Oh Morgan," she pleaded, leaning forward as her hands fluttered nervously. "Ward is much respected in Boston. The scandal will die in time."

"Indeed it would, if I hanged and he remarried. If not, I should be a constant reminder to Boston of his folly."

Amy sighed and rose. "Edward's right. There's no use talking to you. I've no doubt your brain has been impaired by the exigencies of childbirth. I shall visit again tomorrow."

Morgan widened her eyes, her dark contemplations burning holes in her heart. *Cut Amy off now, before it's too late.* "Don't trouble yourself," Morgan said in her sharpest voice. "I've no desire to see you, Mr. Hathaway, or your precious Edward ever again."

Amy sucked in her breath, as tears jumped into her eyes. She blinked, then turned swiftly and quit the room.

"Good God, Ward," Ro exclaimed in a low, tight-lipped voice. Ward closed the parlor door behind them. "How could you have married such a bloody bitch?"

After weeks of building tension, after three days of restraining himself in the face of Morgan's continual abuse, Ward lost control of his temper. Fire coursed through his veins. "Damn you, Ro, she's my wife! Have some *bloody* respect."

Ro took a short, agitated tour of the room. "She may be now, but we'll cure that soon enough. We shall obtain both a lawyer and an annulment before we leave this God-forsaken city."

"On that score," Edward said, entering, "I'm in agreement. Ward, you cannot stay married to her. She'll ruin you."

"And what would you have me do?" Ward ground out. "Make a bastard of my child and a whore of his mother?"

"Why, you've done the latter already!" Ro snapped. Abruptly, anger reddened Ward's eyesight. Hands curling into fists, he stepped forward determined to shut Ro's large, vulgar mouth permanently. As Ward raised an arm, though, Edward seized it.

"Damn you both for fools! That's more than enough, Roland! Ward, have done! Fighting solves nothing."

"Damn you, Ed, let me go!" Ward snarled, struggling to free himself from Edward's grip. "A fist in his face will solve my temper."

"Possibly, but you'll get blood all over your clothes."

For a second Ward considered belting Edward first, but then his words struck him. With amusement flickering through his rage, Ward snapped, "And yours, too, no doubt."

"Which," Ro said with a small laugh, "is the whole reason he holds your arm. He'd not like mopping up afterward." Ro flashed his rogue's grin and offered Ward his hand. "I apologize, *Mon Capitaine*. It just irks me to see you abused."

Still angry, Ward batted his hand away, but held the bite from his speech. "You irk me in general."

Ro shrugged and Edward fell into a chair. "The problem remains."

"The only problem we have is how quickly Ward obtains a divorce," Ro said.

"Aye, sir, that will add much to her murder defense!" Ward replied.

"Then what *do* you mean to do with her?" Edward asked. "You've not thought this through, Ward!"

"I have thought it out thoroughly. In a fortnight's time I intend to convey her to Beacon Hill. By and bye, I shall publish an announcement of our marriage and the birth of our son." And then erect an invisible fence of concrete about himself and his new family to protect them from the repercussions. And, he thought with a wave of dread, shield society from Morgan's unconventional behavior.

"Oh my God," Edward breathed and leaned back. "I fear to even consider the uproar. Ro, look around, he's got to have some brandy somewhere."

"No brandy. Rum, there, on that shelf," Ward offered.

"Well, one thing's for certain," Ro said with a chuckle. "Whoever's the subject of gossip presently will be grateful. Who is it, Ward? That Renshaw woman, isn't it? Walking in the park after dark without a chaperone, I believe."

Edward smiled. "Well, I think this beats that one to a standstill."

Amy entered the room and leaned against the door. Noting the deep lines around her mouth and eyes, Ward asked, "Is she still bad?"

"She's behaving abominably and her thinking is dreadfully disordered. I've never seen her this way."

"She's never given birth before."

"Hah!" Ro burst out, handing Ward a glass of rum. "Fran was all smiles after birth. The woman's temper has nothing to do with that."

"I agree," Edward said, sipping the rum Ro had given him. "I've yet to see this paragon you described to us, either one of you."

Ward flinched and shoved down the smoldering anger attempting to rise to the surface again. "She's angry right now. In time she'll regain her humor."

"Angry?" Ro asked with a rough laugh. "What has she to be angry about? She's married to a very rich man who may have the capability to save her from hanging for the murder of her third husband. Joyful is what I'd expect."

Remembering those dark minutes when he'd held her hostage, Ward shook his head. "You don't know what you're talking about, Ro. She refused to marry me until coerced."

"She said so to take you in, Ward."

Amy and Ward exchanged harried looks. Amy shrugged. "You don't know Morgan. Is that liquor?" she asked. "May I have some?"

"You may not," Edward answered. "It isn't done, Amelia."

Ward glanced furtively at Ro, who shook his head in disgust. For a moment it appeared that Amelia would argue. Then she sighed her resignation and took a seat.

"And so," Ro said, "Ward, have you considered your grandmother? Do you introduce your paragon to her before or after Boston stones you?"

"I might introduce them first. I'm considering publishing that our wedding took place in November of last year. With my grandmother's approval, we might let leak that we delayed our announcement due to her dislike of the match. Upon meeting her great-grandson, of course, she became reconciled to Morgan."

Edward whistled. "Oh, she'll love playing the monster in your fairy tale."

Ro laughed. "But it suits her so well!"

"What about the murder charges?" Amelia asked.

Ward sipped his rum, frowning. "A marriage announcement isn't legal. I shall enter her name in the papers as Morgan Reynolds. As for the rest," he said, taking a deep breath. Good God, it was so complicated! "That I have yet to answer."

Edward frowned. "Someone will eventually piece it together. When the truth is discovered there'll be the devil to pay, never mind the legal implications."

"Morgan's afraid they'll hang her still," Amelia said fearfully.

Edward shook his head. "The courts don't like hanging women, especially ones of note. Even with Turner harping on in the background, it's very possible they'll only jail her."

"Oh, and that is so much *better!*" Amelia answered with false sweetness.

Edward sighed. "The scandal, Ward—even divorce would be better."

The scandal, Ward thought, panic racing through his veins. The scandal could bring his family to their knees. "We've been over this before," he said firmly, partially to bolster his own faltering courage. "I fully understand the consequences of my actions. Morgan is my wife and she'll hang," Ward said, piercing Amelia with his eyes, "over my dead body."

Amelia sighed. "Which may very well be what she's anticipating."

* * *

"Morgan," Ward said, entering her room. He pulled a chair up to her bed. "We must talk."

Morgan didn't want to talk. Since Lee's birth six days before, she'd been alternately exhausted, irritable, and lonely. Amy hadn't returned after that one dreadful visit. In fact no one had visited but the doctor. The monstrous injustice of her situation still burned in Morgan's heart, so she'd snapped at the doctor, too, making him hate her also. Now everyone hated her. Fine. She hated them too.

"I don't have anything to say to you," she spat.

"Then I'll do the talking."

"You may talk, but I won't listen."

Sighing, Ward reached for her hand. She swiftly hid it under her blanket and stared back at him mulishly. When their eyes met, the hurt she found in his stabbed at her soft heart. Recollect, she admonished it, when his eyes had been jet-black. Recollect the devil-man of her laboring hours, arms crossed over his chest, indifferent to her misery, denying her relief.

"Morgan, you must forgive me at some point."

"Why must I? Have you done anything to warrant forgiveness?"

"You've scarcely given me a chance!"

"That," she said acidly, "is because you've done the unforgivable."

"I did it for your own good."

"You did it for your own selfish reasons, never heeding the danger." She sucked in her breath as fear tightened around her lungs. Lord, if she had an ounce of courage, she'd kill herself now and release everyone from the looming misery.

"In point of fact, you're considerably safer. The law now regards you as my property and cannot, therefore, take you from me without strong justification."

"Rather," she said sarcastically, "like a mad dog, isn't it? Oh, how much better I feel!"

"You've been married three times, Morgan; you know the law. The authorities must go through various channels even to take you to Pennsylvania. With a good lawyer we may forestall your return to Philadelphia for months. During that time we shall undoubtedly devise some sort of strategy to either win your case or have it dismissed."

"Devise a strategy? That's your grand scheme, to devise a strategy? Oh my, Ward, had you explained this all prior to marriage, I should certainly have abided by your wishes with nary a word against you!"

Sighing in frustration, he sat back in his chair. "Even if I fail Morgan, you won't hang. Most courts frown upon such sentences for women."

Puzzled, she asked, "Do they never execute women? But then why does Turner pursue my capture so ferociously?"

"I assume because he believes in the possibility of execution. He has yet to reckon with me."

"And why should he consider you when you've no plan to counter his?"

"You underestimate me, Morgan. Only a month has passed since I first learned of Turner's death, and during that entire time I was too occupied in my search for you to do much else. Had *you* more faith in me, I should have had a better plan by now. At any rate, I had originally expected to return you to Massachusetts, perhaps place you with Ro in Marblehead. After your behavior, however, I doubt your reception. Moreover the police are still searching for you. I've resolved to settle you in Newport."

"The police are searching for me?"

"It started three days after you left. Your departure was at least timely."

Morgan's insides tumbled around as she considered the danger barely averted. Taking a deep breath she asked, "And Newport? Where is that?"

"In Rhode Island. My grandmother summers there."

Her eyes widened in alarm. "Your *grandmother*? Have you gone mad?"

He shrugged. "She'll be difficult, but you're my wife. She'll take you in."

"And where will you be?" she asked, nervous at the prospect of facing the indomitable woman who ruled her captain's life. A woman who could rule such a man—oh, she wished *never* to meet her.

He frowned. "With you, of course. Do you think I'd cut and run?"

But she never would know Ward's grandmother, for she was going to Philadelphia. Oh, but she would much rather join Ward in Newport, much rather meet a hundred of Ward's grandmothers! "It was the way you said it."

"I intend to stay with you for at least a fortnight. Then I must occasionally return to Boston to attend to my business and to your legal case."

She rubbed her eyes, imagining the months of wrangling over a case that was clear-cut murder. Where was the sense in that? "How long, Ward?"

"I expect it'll take a month or two before my grandmother becomes accustomed to our situation. Afterward, with her approval, we shall announce our marriage and Lee's birth, then return to Boston."

"And what manner of welcome do you suppose society will give to a suspected murderess and her family?"

Ward grimaced. "Why would that matter when you dislike society?"

Staring at her hands, at her nails ragged from lack of care, she replied, "You're correct. I truly don't care a rap for its opinions, but I'm not so lost to propriety that I don't understand how much you—and your son—will suffer." Her wayward imagination kept drawing pictures of the cold-hearted Bostonians shrinking from her in disgust, or worse, staring right through her. As Ward's mistress she couldn't care less; as his wife it would kill her. Tears spilled from her eyes.

"Confound it," Ward exclaimed, withdrawing a neatly folded handkerchief from his pocket. He tenderly dried her tears, his eyes glowing so lovingly she hadn't the power to pull away. "Trust me, Mistress, we shall come about."

"I am no longer your mistress."

"But you are—mistress of my home, and of my heart."

Lord, but he was bewitched, besotted by love, viewing all through rose-colored glasses. When had she become the rational one?

Shutting her eyes against the hope sparkling in his gaze, she sank back under the sheets. "I'm dreadfully fatigued, Ward. You may wake me when Lee needs feeding."

"I'm not done talking."

"The doctor ordered me to rest."

She heard him sigh. "He did indeed. We shall discuss it again tomorrow."

They never would. Tomorrow marked seven days since Lee's birth, and for once Morgan had a plan. It required only courage to execute. She'd always had a sizable amount of that.

Chapter Twenty-six

Dressed in a white muslin gown, Morgan sat on the edge of her bed, her ears keenly tuned for the tell-tale sound of the back door slamming, announcing Mrs. Donovan's exit. Stuffed in her pocket, her left hand fingered her diamond necklace. In her right hand, she held a knife.

The door slammed. Morgan closed her eyes and once more roused the dark passion required to accomplish her goal. It didn't prove difficult. For months her disposition had been exceedingly unsteady, and was presently exacerbated by lack of sleep. With but a trifling effort, she fixed her anger on Ward, the perpetrator of all her misery. She must escape him. And she was not Clarissa; she'd not turn the blade against herself.

After carefully hiding the knife in the folds of her dress, she quit the room and descended the staircase, slowly, quietly. . . .

Not quietly enough.

"Morgan?" Ward called from the parlor, and fear lashed her nerves. In her mind, she reenacted the scenes of Ward's brutality—his stony face, his expressionless eyes—and converted fear to anger. Through the doorway, she saw him rise and drop a newspaper on the sofa. Bloody hell. As much as she'd planned for confrontation, she'd truly hoped to escape without his knowledge. Her breath came fast and light as she tightened her grip on the knife.

She was not Clarissa.

"Is there something you require?" he asked, entering the front hall, his forehead wrinkled in concern. "The doctor ordered you to stay in bed, to sleep when the baby sleeps."

"I'm not tired." It wasn't wholly a lie. She wasn't tired; she was utterly exhausted.

Ward frowned and reached for her arm. Jerking it away, she stepped sideways toward the front door. Eyes narrowing warily, he peered at her. "If you insist, I'll allow you to take your rest upon the parlor sofa. When Lee needs feeding I'll fetch him to you."

"I shan't be here for that."

His eyebrows lifted. "No? Where will you be?"

He didn't look alarmed. Why wasn't he alarmed? "I'm leaving you."

"I see," he said slowly. He eyed her speculatively and rubbed his neck. "May I inquire as to where you intend to go?"

Confound it, why was he so calm? Was he so very certain of his ability to overpower her? Oh Lord, but hadn't he every occasion for such certainty? He stood a full foot above her in height, carried at least four stone more than her, and she had naught but a puny dinner knife for prevention.

The knife and his son.

If Leland cried, Ward's loving heart would compel him to attend the baby. Hardening her resolve with fresh anger, she spoke in a loud, carrying voice. "That's not your concern."

"On the contrary, Morgan, upon our marriage knowledge of your whereabouts became not only my concern, but my obligation."

She was only that to him now, an obligation, a duty. Lifting her chin, she glared at him and slid nearer to the door. "How unfortunate for you, sir. I shall, however, be relieving you of that obligation."

His eyes hardened and a forbidding smile curled his lips. He, too, stepped toward the door. "Belay that, Morgan, and return to your room. You're going nowhere."

With that he blocked the door entirely, his legs spread, his arms crossed over his chest, all adding fuel to her anger. He reminded her of her father, bound and determined to force her into submission. She wouldn't! She wouldn't!

"You can't force me to stay!" she shouted loud enough to wake the dead—and one small, sleeping baby. "Move aside, Ward, I warn you." She slid the knife from the folds of her dress. Stab him in the leg, she told herself, to prevent him from following her. And elsewhere for pain. He deserved the pain for all his deception, didn't he?

"I certainly can, especially when your brain is running mad. Please try for some reason, love. You haven't the strength for travel, and your son requires your attendance," he said in his calm, steady voice. For the shortest moment it touched a nerve, calling forth the ragged remnants of rationality. Then Lee's cry turned to a wail, tightening her sore muscles, pulling at her emotions, yanking at her heartstrings. She wanted to rush upstairs and wrap her sweet little boy in her arms—as she simultaneously wanted to flee the tiny creature whose ceaseless demands upon her strength left her as limp and frayed as an old blanket. Those unnatural sentiments struck at her conscience, rousing guilt, then rage, for it was all Ward's fault! If not for Ward she need never leave her son. If not for him, Philadelphia would never have found her!

"I hate you," she hissed.

He flinched. "Your feelings for me are not at issue. We're discussing the needs of your child and your health, which you best serve by remaining with me."

"My needs are best served elsewhere. Step away from the door."

Although the tightness around his eyes proved the effectiveness of her attack, his expression remained impassive. "Your son cries for you. Go back upstairs."

"I cannot!" she shouted, frustration burning in her blood at Lee's pitiful cries echoing in the hall. "You attend him! Bloody hell, Ward, can't you hear him?"

His eyebrows rose. "Certainly. His cries grow with your shouting."

She could bear no more! In one last desperate effort she stepped around him and lunged for the door. Snakelike, his hand whipped out to grasp her wrist. She swung her right arm around, bringing the blade down to his forearm. It pierced his skin. Ward's eyes widened and he yowled, yanking his arm back. "By God, Morgan, you stabbed me!"

But not deeply enough. She swung her arm again, both chilled and excited by the dark red droplets flying through the air, by the flash of steel coated in slick red blood seconds before she plunged the blade into his thigh. No bone impeded its progress; it sliced cleanly through his flesh, buried to the hilt.

"Goddamn it!" Ward rasped through gritted teeth. He took one staggering step backward. "You little witch, what in hell do you think you're doing?"

She didn't reply, didn't take the time to remove the knife or add more wounds. He no longer blocked the door. She was through it and down the steps in a trice. As she fled, Lee's wails rose and Ward shouted for her to come back.

Chapter Twenty-seven

Rubbing bleary red eyes, Ward surveyed the map of Chicago again. As it had before he'd returned to Boston two weeks ago, it yielded no answers. Morgan could reside anywhere in the town, or she might have left it altogether. Damn it, he thought, fear cramping his neck muscles. *Damn it, Morgan, where* are *you?*

He leaned back in his desk chair, clenching his jaw. Two weeks ago she'd vanished without a trace. So many terrible things could happen to a young woman on her own, and Morgan had yet to recover from birth. Granted, she'd survived Boston's streets for a week, but hadn't she surrendered to those dark forces in the end? She'd sold herself to him. Taking a ragged breath, he pictured her in a dank, dimly lit brothel, tears streaming down her face as she fell to her knees and Turner raised a hand to strike—

"Damn it!" he swore, banging a fist on the desktop. He'd kill any man who hurt her, kill any man who touched one single hair on her head.

Abruptly Ward rose, fists at his sides, grappling with the abrupt rage burning in his muscles. This wasn't love. Love was tender; love was civilized.

He took a restless turn around the library, then stopped to lean against the mantel and stare into the fireplace, all the while reminding his overheated imagination that this time Morgan had money and her jewels. This time she needn't resort to any form of prostitution to support herself. With a modicum of frugality she ought to live comfortably for several months.

Unless she was robbed. Even as he lived in the proverbial lap of luxury, his wife could be laying in a gutter, hurt, starving, beaten—he'd kill—

Breathing rapidly, Ward took another turn, stopping this time to stare out a window facing the small garden behind his home. Roses still bloomed, but the leaves on the two maple trees had turned orange-red with the approach of fall. Winter would follow shortly, and Morgan had fled without clothing. Chicago winters were brutal, snow whipping off the lake, howling down the streets. He sucked in his breath as pictures of her cold and alone rose in his mind, replacing anger with icy-fingered dread.

And longing. By God, to touch her, to run his hands through her hair again, hold her against him, safe from the cold, safe from the world's brutality. Every day his arms ached for her, every night he lay awake in his bed, cold as a coffin without her. He couldn't eat, couldn't sleep. He missed her, God how he missed her! To have one more day, one more moment—*Come back to me, love, oh God, Morgan come back*—

Behind him the door opened quietly, snatching him from the vise of sorrow. Ward turned as Herman announced, "Mr. Hathaway to see you, sir."

Ro, damn him to hell. Come to gloat? Or offer consolation? He scorned both, only wanting to wallow in his misery. His body shook with fear and exhaustion, and for a moment he considered telling Ro to shove off. But rudeness signaled weakness in a gentleman. Continuing his perusal of the garden, he rammed his pain back down his gullet and answered, "Thank you, Herman. Show him in, please."

"Of course, sir."

He took a deep breath and set his face into easier lines. A moment later the door opened and Ro entered, dressed with his usual carefree elegance. "Ward," he said smiling. They met in the center of the room to exchange a hardy handshake.

"It's good to see you, Ro. Are you in town just for the day, or are you staying?"

"I'll be here a few days. Fran, Michael, and I are at the Tremont."

"I'd be much obliged, sir, if you stayed with me."

"So polite, Sir Captain," Ro answered with an artificial grin. "Fran wouldn't impose upon you for all the world. I confess, however, that you are the main reason for our visit. How have you been? You don't limp. I take it your leg has healed."

Ward clenched his teeth against the stabbing those simple words provoked. When he could speak evenly he replied, "I'm well enough."

"Well?" Ro asked, raising his eyebrows. "On the contrary, old man, you look like hell. From what I understand you returned to Boston a fortnight ago, and you've yet to leave your house. Don't try denying it; I've been to the Somerset. Nobody's seen you in almost a month. It's causing quite a commotion."

"I've been absent for far longer periods," Ward pointed out.

"But you've never before returned with a baby."

"No," he answered with a small sigh.

"No. And rumors abound as to precisely how that may have happened."

Rubbing the tight muscles of his neck, Ward asked, "Are they bad?" When Ro studied him a moment, as if determining how much to tell, Ward shook his head. "All of it, Ro."

"All right," he said, and crossed the room to pour them brandy. "The best or the worst first?"

Ward sighed and sat in a wing chair. "Let's end on a good note."

"A good note? We might try for one, I suppose. As you might imagine, the worst can be attributed to Reston and his lackey Eames."

Ward grimaced. "Reston blames me and every other Montgomery for his wife's desertion."

"I daresay your father gave him cause for that. At any rate," Ro said, handing him a snifter of brandy, "they, and approximately three quarters of our set, believe the baby is yours."

Ward raised an eyebrow. "Not everyone?"

"Apparently you've never referred to the child as 'Montgomery' in front of your help. I credit your staff— they don't malign you, Ward."

He shrugged.

Ro grimaced at Ward's indifference, then seated himself. "To continue, Reston claims Leland's a by-blow of your abuse of an underage servant girl." Ward sucked in his breath. *Damn.* Like his father. All his years of work, forgotten in a few short weeks. Wasted years, wasted money.

Ro's eyes flashed compassion at him, unusual anger lining his face as his voice turned sharp. "He says that upon learning of her condition you removed her from your home and kept her elsewhere, against her will, for further use. When the mother died—either in child-birth or at your hands—you took the child."

At his hands? "Good God, people *believe* that?"

"That's what Reston claimed. Shaw and I ended the rumor."

"Shaw? Clifton Shaw? He dislikes me as much as Reston."

"Not quite."

For the first time Ward noticed a spreading darkness around Ro's left eye. With a twist of his lips he asked, "And precisely how did you and Shaw accomplish that?"

Ro grinned. "Let us say that neither I nor Reston, Shaw or Eames, shall be found at the Somerset for a fortnight or more. We've been temporarily expelled."

"You belted him."

Ro's grin grew. "Several times. Reston is rather slow."

"You in a brawl—By God I wish I'd been there!"

"You'd have much enjoyed it. Oddly enough, Shaw started it. It's no secret he detested your father, but it seems he dislikes injustice even more than he dislikes your family."

Ward smiled. "Perhaps I ought to have some words with Shaw."

"In time. He's currently indisposed, as are Reston and Eames."

"Apparently you ducked better," Ward said with a smirk, and then took a deep breath. "Thank you, Ro. You have a soul to be saved, sir."

"One of us ought to," he quipped. Then the amusement drained from his face. "I'm sorry, Ward, but the other rumors contain more substance. The majority of our set believe Leland is yours and his mother either died or abandoned the child. Others—and you'll be interested to know Cabot is amongst these—credit your honor and believe you married the woman for the child's sake."

Both relief and comfort eased Ward's tension. Perhaps

not all was wasted. "Even accounting for my father's reputation?"

Ro smiled. "You've long since proven that you're not your father."

"I should think such recklessness proves I am very much his son."

"It proves you're human. In point of fact, Sir Captain, it makes you considerably more likable."

Both bewildered and amused, Ward lifted an eyebrow. "Creating bastards makes me likable? I wonder that I never considered if before. No doubt I should have enjoyed such activities far more than working!"

"No doubt if you had a house full of bastards, you'd be loved!" Ro said with a laugh. "But, in point of fact," he continued more soberly, "they don't think Leland's a bastard. Some believe your wife died in childbirth, thus your absence from public life. The rest contend that you've hidden her away until you make amends with your grandmother. A few expressed willingness to meet this woman before making judgments, and almost all have agreed to receive your son, bastard or not."

Ward jerked in surprise. "You're joking."

Ro grinned. "Shocking, isn't it? You have more friends than you know, old man. Of course, they don't know you like I do." Ward smirked. "As for the ladies, the rumor that we—squelched—has never hit their delicate ears. Amongst *them,* the most prevalent rumor— you'll love this one—is that you left town on business and found the baby abandoned on the streets of New York. With your inherent kindness and compassion, you could do naught but rear it as your own."

"Oh, good God," Ward exclaimed. "Now you are joking."

Chuckling Ro shook his head. "No, it's perfectly true. It seems that presently you're attempting to set a legal adoption in process. Many of the ladies—the prettier ones too!—expressed the opinion that when you choose a wife, she'd be a monster not to accept it as her own."

"A child *off the streets?*"

"It would be her Christian duty of course."

"Half of them are Unitarians!"

Smirking, Ro shrugged. "We Unitarians understand the meaning behind 'Christian duty.' I confess, you make a capital hero, sir. The ladies love you. They always have."

"Hah! With this mug? I scare them half to death."

"You mistake awe for fear." He leaned forward as his voice became serious. "I believe they'd even forgive you divorce. All is not lost, Ward. You—"

"No," Ward snapped.

"Ward, she deserted you."

Heart tightening, Ward took a deep breath. "She was confused."

Ro threw his hands up in exasperation. "She stabbed you, for the love of God! How can you possibly wish to continue with her?"

Attempting to find a suitable explanation, Ward stared hard at Ro. But Ro could never understand. For all his carefree negligence, Ro adhered to the conventions because he *believed* in them. On the other hand, Ward finally admitted that for all his own years of steel-boned discipline he found the rules as frippery and restrictive as Morgan did.

But while Morgan rejected the proprieties, he could not. His family and those he loved—Rob, his grandmother, his son—depended upon him to restore and protect the family name, to prevent them from experiencing the bite of ostracism. He'd endured that grief for many years; he had long resolved that it ended with him. It was his duty.

But Morgan didn't have that duty, and considering her last words to him, he doubted that she wanted it. Overcoming the scandal yet to burst upon Boston would require impeccable behavior, something she'd reject under the best circumstances, never mind for a man she hated.

He sighed, regret settling like lead in his chest. "First I must ensure her safety. All else will have to wait," he said and rose to move to the window, restless again. Ro fell silent as Ward sifted through his mind for ways to keep both his wife and social standing. If he could win back her love—if he could find her—he must find her—

"Where are you looking for her?" Ro asked by and bye.

"I have men in Chicago. And New York."

"New York?" Ro asked, surprised. "Why New York?"

He shrugged, watching a squirrel burying nuts, preparing for a long, cold winter. "I thought she might book passage for San Francisco. As you and Edward pointed out, she could conceivably find safety there."

"If she did, you could, in five years time, sue for divorce under—"

"If she goes to San Francisco, I'll fetch her back."

"Whatever for? She'd be safe, and you'd be rid of her."

"Safe?" Ward asked, turning to lean against the wall. "Perhaps. But what of our son? What," he asked, lowering his voice at the ripping of his heart, "what of me?"

Ward's misery reflected in Ro's eyes, for once bereft of amusement. "And if she isn't in Chicago, or New York, or San Francisco? What then?"

He stared at the floor to conceal the agony he couldn't keep from his face. "I shall search until I find her."

"Good God, Ward, *how*? It's a huge country!"

"And I have many resources at my disposal."

"No one has that many resources! How can you be so certain of victory?"

Ward sucked in his breath, then raised his eyes to Ro's. Fighting back panic, he answered in a rough voice, "I cannot live with the alternative."

"Bloody hell," Ro whispered. "Is it so strong, Ward?"

"Aye."

Ro dropped his eyes to look at his hands. With a sigh he said, "Then you'd better stop searching for her in Chicago or New York or anywhere else. Morgan is in Philadelphia."

A huge, horrible wave of alarm rolled over Ward. "Philadelphia? What, has Edward seen her?"

Ro winced and had the decency to appear chagrined. "We meant to find the girl first and send her away until you lost interest. Neither Edward nor I anticipated the depth of your emotions." He sighed. "Ed has people checking the pawn shops. I received word a few days ago that he found a diamond necklace, which Amelia swears is Morgan's."

Ward shook his head in denial. "But Philadelphia? It makes no sense!"

Ro took a breath, then said in a pained voice, "I'm sorry, old man. Something Morgan said to Amelia led her to conclude that Morgan may be contemplating confession."

"Confession?" he asked, scarcely able to breathe. "No! To what purpose?"

Ro sipped his drink and let out a tired, defeated sigh. "A confession negates the need for a trial, saving you money, time, and the anticipation of her hanging. Moreover, it ensures that the majority of publicity remains in Philadelphia, reducing the scandal you and Leland would endure. Finally, the sooner Morgan is—

gone—the sooner you may choose a new wife and a new mother for her son." He paused. "Amelia believes she loves you that much."

Ward took several deep breaths as his heart repeated the words to his brain. Love—*could* she love him still? She's sworn she hated him, she'd stabbed him—he'd done the unforgivable. But the possibility—

He could scarcely speak. "Morgan's a woman. It's unlikely she'll receive a death sentence."

"Not if the nephew has any say. Even if he's thwarted, she could confess to Weatherly's murder."

"But Weatherly wasn't murdered!"

"If she confesses to poisoning him, they'll believe it. And Ward, if she does, they *will* hang her."

"Why the hell didn't Amy tell *me* this?"

"Presently she's obeying her husband. And Morgan has yet to follow through. She might still leave."

"But if she's found beforehand—"

"That would be unfortunate."

Ward's muscles tensed until they ached. "Unfortunate! Good God, if she follows such a course—and for no reason! Damnation, Ro, my sources tell me Turner had a weak heart."

Ro frowned. "What difference does that make?"

"Morgan's a small woman, if she hit Turner hard enough to kill him it was pure, bad luck."

Alarm rushed across Ro's face. "Bloody hell," he whispered. "I hadn't thought of that. Well then, we'd better board the next train. I warn you, Fran will insist upon joining us this time. She swears that if she wanted to live alone, she'd have married you."

Ward, striding toward the door of his study, laughed a little. "It would have been a short marriage. We'd have bored each other to death in a week's time."

Opening the door, he called for Herman. Ward

found him immediately, across the hall with an expression of consternation on his face as he took the outer garments of two visitors. Ward's heart lurched when Herman lifted his head and without ceremony, announced the arrival of the Earl and Countess of Westborough.

Chapter Twenty-eight

Morgan perused the pages of the newspaper for train schedules. It listed none, but she discovered several ads for Californian-bound clipper ships leaving from New York Harbor. The cost was dear, but the alternative made any cost worthwhile.

Her stomach grumbled and she glanced at the bowl of watery soup next to her. They called it chicken soup, but she was damned if a chicken had ever seen that water. She little doubted that she could have created a far superior soup. In San Francisco that recently obtained knowledge would show to great advantage among its largely male population. San Francisco, where the weather was always warm, the sun always shone and gold flowed from the mountains. Or at least so said the travel guides. She scarcely credited their authenticity, but what did that signify? A continent would separate her from Kenneth Turner—and hanging.

Suddenly weary, she leaned back and rubbed her eyes. Good God, how had she dug herself this hole? What had ever made her fancy the notion of walking into a stationhouse to confess to murder? Exhaustion perhaps, and insanity after the shock of both childbirth and marriage in two hours time. *Oh Ward*, she thought, recollecting with sad amusement the doctor's countenance when he finally, wholly, apprehended the situation. *Only you, my captain, would consider such foolishness. You had to win, didn't you? But neither you nor I won this one. Only Lee won anything at all, and that a trifling win at best— a father and a name, but he lost his mother forever.*

Tears formed in Morgan's eyes. Leaning forward to hold her head with her hands, she sobbed, remembering Lee's sweet little face, his tiny crossed eyes. Did he miss her? Oh, but she hoped he was well! He must be, he *must* be! Ward would provide him the best of care, a nurse with excellent character, of perfect amiability. And he'd explain, wouldn't he, as Lee grew older, about his mother? He'd hold his son near and tell him in his gentle, soothing voice that love, not disinterest, compelled her to flee. *Oh Ward, please, please tell him that! I couldn't bear him to think I merely abandoned him!*

With that, an aching in her breasts reminded her that she hadn't left long. Wiping her tears away, she rose and retrieved a basin from her night table. The aching had started a few hours after leaving Ward, requiring a visit to her midwife, who had shown her how to ease the production of milk and prevent an infection. She'd insisted that Morgan wean herself slowly to prevent shocking her system. And she had—very slowly. Two weeks later she still produced plenty of milk, and damned if she could bring an end to it. Some stubborn part of her heart refused to believe she'd lost either Ward or her baby forever.

On the ship, she told herself as she unbuttoned her bodice. She'd be living between decks without the privacy to care for such needs. And once again she'd be a single woman. In Chicago she'd purchased a red wig and changed her name to Marilyn Ames. When she purchased her passage to San Francisco she'd become Myra Stewart, recently orphaned by both parents, traveling to California to meet her only living relative, her brother.

Who would, upon arrival, have died also.

But first Marilyn Ames must buy those train tickets. Not today. It was raining and she just didn't have the energy to brave the rain, the police, and her own grief-stricken heart. Tomorrow or, if it still rained, the following day. For now she'd remain hidden in this small, back-alley hotel room, fighting back tears and the heavy weariness that permeated her body.

She took a deep breath and reached for the basin.

Shock freezing him in place, Ward stared at the two strangers. Ro came to stand behind him, swearing under his breath. "Bloody hell, what are *they* doing here?"

"Are you Montgomery?" Lord Westborough—Reynolds?—asked in a rough, imperious voice. "It's a pleasure to meet you, sir." He strode forward, offering Ward his black-gloved hand.

Ward glanced over the man. He was a trim, elegantly dressed man of medium height with dark hair and thick side-whiskers. In spite of his politeness, his light brown eyes glinted with irritation as Ward stepped forward to shake his hand. He was far too young to be Morgan's father. Her brother? But then he ought to be Lord Reynolds, not Westborough.

"And for me to meet you," Ward answered. Westborough's grip was strong, belying any impression of foppery. "May I present my good friend, Roland Hathaway?"

Ro, mate that he was, exchanged an amiable greeting with Westborough, who made perfectly polite but perfunctory introductions to his mother, Lady Westborough. Ro and Ward bowed, then Ward boldly claimed her hand, saying with his warmest smile, "It is an honor, madam, to meet Morgan's mother."

The woman stared at him with ice in her sapphire eyes. After a spell she inclined her head slightly in acknowledgement. As cold, Ward thought, as a blue flugen. How the devil had she reared a daughter like Morgan?

"Morgan, as you may suppose," Westborough said, "is the reason we are here. If you would be so obliging, sir, as to fetch my sister?"

Tea, Ward thought rapidly. Women loved tea. Feeling Ro's eyes upon him, he answered carefully, "I'm certain she'd be very happy to see you, sir. Herman, show my guests into the drawing room please. And have a tea tray sent. Ro, you'll stay, won't you?" he asked, turning to avoid the frustration snapping at him from behind Westborough's heavy lids.

Ro, a hooked-fish expression in his eye, nodded. "Of course, Ward. Tea is *exactly* what I'd like right now."

Ward suppressed a grin. "Excellent," he answered as Herman held open the parlor door and ushered them forward, forcing the visitors to either abandon their manners or follow Ward's instruction. Ro started to follow as Ward turned to Herman, saying in a low voice, "Send for Rob. First, however, have Kathleen bring Lee, and quickly please."

"Bloody hell, Ward," Ro hissed, spinning on his heel. "You cannot! Westborough will offer you a facer for certain!"

"Nothing melts a woman's heart like a baby."

"Did you even *look* at those two? The brother is mad as a hornet, and I swear that woman can freeze blood with her eyes! You might as well try to melt the North Pole!"

"I can't think of any other way to reach her."

"Why reach her at all? What in bloody hell are they *doing* here?"

He gave Ro a quick slap on the back. "All in good time, Ro. Come now, let's see to my guests."

Ro scowled at him, but entered the room. Ward followed, eyes flashing over his in-laws. Westborough stood peering at Ward, and his mother sat on the edge of the sofa, her back ramrod straight as if yielding to comfort signaled weakness. She wore black silk. Mourning colors, Ward realized with a jerk.

Westborough asked coolly, "Have you sent for my sister?"

"No. Unfortunately, she's not here."

"Not here?" he asked, glancing uneasily at Ro. "I daresay you know where she is, however. I should like her direction, if you please."

So should I, Ward thought. "That will require some explanation. If you'd be so obliging as to take a seat, we shall discuss it."

Westborough flashed another wary glance at Ro. "I'd rather not. Her direction will suit me fine."

Ward smiled kindly. "You need have no fear of Ro. He knows of Morgan's—indiscretions—and will hold his tongue."

Ward had to credit Westborough. He clenched and unclenched his fists, but held his temper. "Still, this is—"

The door opened, admitting Herman and a maid with the tea. And Kathleen with Lee.

Ro winced and Westborough stared at the bundle in confusion. The countess remained cucumber-cool as the girl stepped timidly forward. With a little curtsy, she presented her bundle to Ward. "He's just fed, sir."

"Thank you, Kathleen," Ward said, taking his son into his arms. The clock rang four, the established time for Ward's afternoon visit with his son, a time he had thus far jealously guarded from all intruders. Today, however, he'd forfeit it for the sake of their future.

Lee's tiny crossed eyes stared up from the depths of the blankets—far too much covering for mid-October. Carefully Ward peeled back some of the layers while peering at his son. Lee's brows drew together in a frown. Ward smiled and the baby's toothless mouth curved into an answering smile, a little dimple popping out in his cheek. The doctor had insisted that at his age Lee could only copy Ward's smile. Ward didn't believe him; Lee smiled from the pleasure of seeing his father.

"What," Westborough said as Herman closed the door behind him, "what is *that*?"

Ward crossed the room to his mother-in-law. "Ro, would you do the tea honors? Lady Westborough," he asked, seating himself carefully next to his mother-in-law, "may I present your grandson to you? If you look closely, you'll see that his eyes are the color of yours." It was a lie. At birth his eyes had been light blue, but of late he'd noted traces of Morgan's sea-green in them.

Lady Westborough's eyes widened; her hand flew to her chest. "Grandson?"

"Your grandson. Leland Reginald Montgomery."

"Good God," Westborough gasped. "Grandson? *Reginald?*"

"Reginald. Morgan's idea."

"After my father," the earl said grimly, stepping forward to view his nephew. He raised his quizzing glass as if Lee were some kind of interesting scientific experiment.

"Named after you, Westborough. Madam, would you like to hold him?"

She stared at Lee as if he were a bundle of snakes, and Ward had a moment of misgiving; Morgan had never discussed her mother in glowing terms. When she finally nodded, Ward shifted Lee into her stiff arms. She stared at him expressionlessly, and Lee's eyebrows pulled together into a confused frown. Waving his fists around, Lee hit himself in the face. The earl's grim expression melted and, chuckling, he dropped his glass. In response, Lee smiled then stuck his fist into his mouth, sucking and studying his grandmother.

"He's so tiny," she said after a minute. "How old is he?"

"Three weeks."

Lord Westborough's forehead creased. "Three weeks? But that's impossible. The last letter you sent was dated but two months ago. . . ." His voice trailed off as sudden comprehension dawned in his eyes.

"I did," Ward answered grimly, "inform your father as to the urgency of the situation. As you see I finally took the matter into my own hands."

"Letters?" Ro asked.

Ward turned to flash Ro a smile, taking the cup of tea Ro offered. Lady Westborough glanced at Ro, then held her grandson out to Ward. Frowning, Ward placed his cup on the table to take Lee. "If you'll excuse me, I shall send for his nurse," he said and started to rise.

Lady Westborough had been reaching for a cup of tea, but stopped to stare at Lee. "You're sending him away?"

Ward lifted an eyebrow. "I thought that's what you wanted." For the first time emotion crossed her face, traces of regret and longing. "You may hold him, madam, if you wish," Ward offered. "You won't offend me if you refuse refreshment."

Disgust flickered in her eyes, no doubt for his complete disregard of tea-ritual, but she held out her arms. Ward surrendered his son once more.

Silence filled the room as Ro finished passing out

plates and cups. Sipping his tea, Ward observed his mother-in-law. She reminded him of his grandmother, without the warmth. After a spell she hesitantly reached in to touch Lee's cheek. The baby—smart, smart boy!—gurgled in response. "But you are such a *happy* baby!" she murmured, a smile floating on her lips.

"Good God!" Westborough suddenly ejaculated, horror flashing across his face, pain shooting through his eyes. "Morgan—the baby—she's not—she's not . . ."

"No," Ward said quickly. "Morgan's fine. She had an easy confinement."

Westborough heaved a sigh of relief, then shook his head. "Oughtn't she to *still* be in confinement?"

Ward eyed him warily. "Before I answer that, I believe you owe me an answer or two. I sent those letters to your father, yet I don't see him. And your mother is in deep mourning. . . ."

Ro scowled. "*What* letters, Ward?"

"My father died six weeks ago," Westborough said.

"Thus, your title," Ward replied.

The earl nodded. "I must apologize, Montgomery, for not responding earlier. I didn't learn of your letters until I was sorting through my father's papers."

"My name is Ward, sir. We're brothers now."

Westborough hesitated, then, his body unbending slightly, he said, "And I am Reggie."

"I'm glad everyone is so polite," Ro interjected. "I, for one, would like to know, Ward, exactly what you said in these letters!"

Ward turned to Ro, whose face was creased in irritation. Bracing himself for Ro's sarcastic wit, he answered coolly, "I requested the earl's blessing in marrying his daughter."

Ro's eyes widened. "Good God, when?"

"A month after learning of Morgan's situation."

"Which one?"

"Which one?" Reggie breathed. "The child, I daresay! Unless you're withholding information. Upon my honor, sir, I would appreciate a truthful answer!"

Ward studied him a spell while searching his mind for the easiest way to convey the information without running afoul of Morgan's brother and embarrassing her mother. Having Morgan's family, English aristocracy at that, on his and Morgan's side during the coming months might check some of Boston's more garrulous gossips.

"Ward!" Ro demanded. "Out with it man! You owe me—us!—an explanation!"

Guilt, Ward decided, would best serve his purpose and keep him on the leeward side of Reggie's temper. Focusing steadily on his brother-in-law, Ward asked, "What do you know of Morgan's life since she left home?"

"I collect you mean since she disgraced us," Morgan's mother said bitterly. Ward felt her glare at him, as if she blamed him.

"We heard," Reggie said, "that she'd married a merchant from Philadelphia." He said merchant with a touch of disparagement, tightening Ward's temper. But, he reflected, Bostonians often expressed similar snobbery.

"You heard this from Amelia Huntington?" Ward asked.

Reggie nodded. "Indeed. Do you know her?"

"Edward Huntington is my good friend. And Roland's."

Hesitating slightly, Reggie said, "Mrs. Huntington's well, I suppose? Has she—has she seen Morgan?"

"They remain friends."

An invisible burden seemed to slip from Reggie's shoulders. "Then she hasn't been completely alone."

Ward glanced at Ro, who grimaced, then with a shrug displaced the blame for Morgan's situation from both their sets of shoulders. With Ro's support behind him, Ward faced Reggie once more. "Mrs. Huntington's friendship wasn't enough to keep Morgan from harm's ways. She's been under my protection for the last ten months. For the two years prior to that, she very much needed the assistance of her family."

Reggie's face creased in irritation, but Ward held steady, refusing to apologize. He'd done his best to correct his mistakes.

"After her disobedience she didn't deserve our assistance," his mother-in-law interjected icily. "We washed our hands of her."

Ro shook his head, frustrated. "Ward never thoroughly explained that. Why would you disown her?"

"She married a sailor," Reggie answered.

"While," Lady Westborough added, "we were planning her wedding to the Earl of Arlington."

"And that is the main source of my confusion. Where would Morgan meet a sailor? Did she love him?"

"She liked him well-enough," Ward said. "More importantly, she disliked her fiancé."

"She hated him," Reggie snapped.

"Her father deemed it an exceedingly suitable match," Lady Westborough said coolly. "Randolph understood Morgan's waywardness and was agreeable to taking her in hand."

"Take her in hand," Ro repeated tightly. "You were going to force her to marry a man she hated?"

"Morgan required discipline. If she'd married Randolph, she'd not have found herself in such dire straits."

"Nor would she—" Ro started angrily.

"Enough, Ro," Ward said gently. "It's past now."

When Ro turned to Ward, his eyes burned brightly,

his face was creased in grim lines. "Whatever assistance you require regarding your wife, you need only ask. I am entirely at your service."

Ward smiled at Ro. "Thank you."

Shrugging, he flashed a chagrined smile. "You needed only to lay the cards on the table, Sir Captain. This is what happens when you hold them too close to your chest."

Ward lifted an eyebrow. "Is that so? How very illuminating."

"Shining light on dark subjects is the very essence of my existence."

Ward opened his mouth to reply when Reggie interrupted in a voice rife with frustration. "Now I'm wholly confused. What sort of assistance might you require? Where *is* my sister?"

Rubbing his aching neck, Ward turned to Reggie. Time for the dead reckoning, regardless of how uncomfortable it would be. "She's in Philadelphia. But understand that if you mean to continue in this vein," he glanced at his mother-in-law, "I won't allow you to see her. She's already paid dearly for her mistakes. She deserves nothing but compassion."

"By mistakes I collect you mean marrying the sailor?" Lady Westborough asked.

"Drumlin was just the beginning," Ward started. "Since then she's displayed a shameful lack of honesty and her choices have been—regrettable. After she married Drumlin . . ."

Sparing neither himself nor Morgan, Ward related all he knew, from Drumlin's death to Morgan's suspected residence in Philadelphia, marching on relentlessly through Reggie's gasps and Lady Westborough's occasional moan. "And so," Ward finished, "as soon as possible, I shall travel to Philadelphia to find Morgan. Ro's agreed to join me, as you may, if you wish."

"Good God," Reggie breathed. "I'm not certain how to face her."

"With compassion," Ward said grimly, "or you'll not face her at all."

Reggie, face drawn, sat down next to his mother and offered her a handkerchief for her glassy eyes. Ward gently removed Lee, sleeping quietly, from her arms. Gray-faced, all arrogance lost, Lady Westborough let him go. She pulled the handkerchief through her hands, whispering, "I had no idea."

"Nor I," Ro said. "If you'd told me this earlier, Ward, my opinions would have been much kinder."

"You ought to have trusted my judgment."

"You ought to have trusted mine."

Ward considered the many hours he'd spend arguing with Edward and Ro, the accusations, the recriminations, for what? To keep his own damned feelings secret? To protect his heart from his two friends, who'd declared—and proved—friendship and loyalty above all else? Wasted effort, wasted time. "You're right."

"If she had not found you," Lady Westborough interrupted. "If you had been on a voyage—"

Ward turned to her. "Don't torture yourself, madam. I've long since retired my command. Let us, instead, look to the future."

Reggie swallowed and said in a tight voice, "She won't truly hang, will she?"

"No, sir," Ward said firmly. "But we're sailing into a hurricane of a scandal. Your support might serve to steer us clear of the worst of it."

"I vow all that's in my power to that purpose," Reggie said.

"Your name may bear some of the taint."

"We've borne up under worse."

"You haven't. This isn't merely a poor marriage. We're speaking of murder, Westborough."

Lady Westborough emitted a tiny, pained sigh, and Reggie's eyes glittered. "For which, I believe, we share some of the responsibility. It's time to make amends for our own mistakes."

"Excellent. As to how to manage the murder charges," he said turning to Ro. "With the help of my lawyers, I've ordered Turner's body exhumed."

"I want to purchase a ticket for the next train to New York, please," Morgan said, sliding several coins through the ticket window.

Behind it, a pox-faced man with a green shade on his close-cropped head wrote out the ticket. "The train leaves in two hours."

Morgan nodded and swallowed the lump in her throat. Next stop New York City and then, in several days time, San Francisco. Good-bye, Philadelphia! Good-bye, East Coast! Good-bye, my son. Good-bye Ward—Oh God, would her heart never stop breaking? How many millions of pieces could it form?

The ticket man pushed her ticket through the window. "Take the platform down to the end there, ma'am."

"Thank you," she said. Lifting her valise, she started toward the depot door.

The clipping of boot heels on tile warned her of someone hurrying along behind her. A moment later a man fell into step beside her, asking rather breathlessly, "Ma'am? Can I talk to ya a minute?"

She slackened her pace and glanced at him. He wore a cheap brown suit and a worn top hat. He carried no cane.

The coarseness of his face and the roughness of his beard marked him as a common ruffian. Shaking her head in denial, Morgan sped up.

The stranger seized her arm and jerked her to a halt. Heart skipping a beat, she spun around to face him. "Unhand me, sir!"

"Lady," the stranger said, his unkempt handlebar mustache wiggling, "you *will* talk to me. See, I know who ya are and I'm hell-bent on collectin' the reward on your head."

Fear coursing through her veins, Morgan attempted to yank her arm from his grasp. "Release me, you fiend, or I shall call a constable!"

She was bluffing but like some waking nightmare, Morgan saw a constable approaching them.

"Now," the assailant said with a yellow-toothed grin, "ain't that just what I was hopin' for."

"May I help ye, mum?" the constable asked in a thin Irish accent.

"Yes, sir," answered her assailant. "You'd best clap some irons on this here lady. She's that Wicked Widow woman, who killed her two husbands. And," he said with a vicious upturn of his mouth, "I'm collectin' that five hundred dollar reward on 'er head."

"You're mistaken," Morgan said, attempting to conceal her British accent. "I'm Marilyn Ames from Chicago. I was visiting relatives."

To Morgan's relief the constable eyed the stranger skeptically. "Ye better be lettin' the lady go. She's got red hair, so she does, and the Wicked Widow's brown-haired."

"She's wearing a wig. Here lemme show ya." The cad yanked on a piece of it.

"Hey, don't ye be doin' that!" the constable said. His ruddy face wrinkled in disgust as he slapped the man's arm away. "By jaysus, you'll leave her be, you scoundrel! Go on, mum, you catch your train. I got 'im!"

"Thank you, sir." Morgan started for the door, heart leaping in relief—

"Mum! Mum! Yer forgettin' your case! Miss Stewart!" the constable called back just as she reached for the door handle. *Oh God, run, run,* a voice yelled in her head. But she could not, for the train wasn't due to depart for an hour or more. She'd have to bluff her way through it. Schooling her features into a bright smile, she pivoted, then swept forward to retrieve the valise from the constable's hand.

He didn't let go. "You said your name was Ames, didn't you, now?"

Gulping, she nodded.

"But I'm seein' the name on this tag, mum, says Myra Stewart."

"It's—it's my sister's."

"It ain't," said her assailant. "I tell ya she's that Turner woman."

"Yer sister's, eh? But ye answered to Stewart, so ye did. And I'm after thinkin', mum, ye'd better be takin' off that bonnet."

"She's wearing a *wig,*" the nasty man said, reaching to grab at it. She gasped at the pain. She'd spent hours meticulously pinning it in place, and the pins and combs scraped her scalp as he pulled both wig and bonnet askew.

The constable's eyes widened. Then he shook his head sorrowfully. "I'm sorry, mum, but I'm gonna be takin' ye to the stationhouse, so I am."

Chapter Twenty-nine

Tired and hungry, Morgan sat on a bench in her jail cell, her mind seething as she eyed the five other women who were her prison mates. Three hours earlier she'd been duly arrested, processed for the murder of her former husband, and cast into this wretched basement cell, with its cracked and dirty plaster walls. The floor was of gray flagstone, the only two lamps burned some acrid-smelling oil, and the chamber-set in the corner stood desperately in need of emptying. Would a permanent jail cell, a prison cell, be better? Would they transfer her to one, or would she pass the days before her trial here with these dirty, unkempt women? No doubt in time she'd come to resemble them.

And why shouldn't she? she wondered despondently. She, too, was a one-time paramour, in addition to being a murderess, runaway wife and mother. Birth and breeding set aside, how could she fancy herself above her cellmates now? Oh God, what wretched folly she'd made of her life! Father had been right. Her willful, hoydenish ways had brought her nothing but ruin. She ought to have obeyed him! She ought to have married Randolph!

Despairing, she shut her eyes and curled herself deeper into her corner, shrinking both from her fate and the eyes of the four prostitutes and one petty thief across the cell. She heard them discussing her crimes in harsh, curious whispers. Only the beginning. During the next months many would whisper both behind her back, and in front of her, as she stood her trial. She easily envisioned the crowded courtroom: newspaper reporters jotting down notes, sketch artists drawing pictures to accompany the papers, a jury listening eagerly to those last dreadful moments of Richard's life, all of them drinking in her shame, her humiliation, and her final, bloody revenge.

And she'd endure it all, for what? For the purposes of acquittal? They never could do so; she'd blood on her hands. Perhaps she might escape hanging, but only to be sentenced to years in prison, while her child grew up motherless, and her husband, name ravaged by scandal, sought consolation in other women's arms—

Morgan gasped at the wrenching in her chest.

"Hey you," a female voice said above her.

Morgan opened her eyes to discover one of the prostitutes standing in front of her. Her eyes were cold, her face wrinkled and hard from years of rough service. "You're that Turner woman, ain't cha?"

Morgan sat up slowly, her stomach sloshing. This was her life now, her bosom companions drawn from the dregs of society. "I'm Morgan Turner."

"I'm Sally Harper." Her eyes, running over Morgan shrewdly, softened as she sat down next to Morgan.

Morgan controlled the urge to shift away, wondering what sort of animal life inhabited the woman's faded brown gown. Lice, perhaps? Fleas? Was this to be her life also? Oh no, good God, no, she hadn't the strength of mind to bear the strain of prison life! Better to make

her confession just as soon as she could persuade a
guard to attend her, confess to Turner's murder . . . and
Weatherly's . . . and Drumlin's . . . and any other man
who'd died within a twenty mile radius. *I've killed them all
sir. I'd kill you too, if I could. Hang me now. You don't have a
rope? You may use the sash to my dress. Truly, I don't mind; I
won't need it where I'm going.*

But where was she going? To hell. Never to heaven,
not with all her sins upon her head. Perhaps confession
wasn't her best plan.

"I knew that Turner. Met him a few years back."

Bloody hell, she'd been with Richard? Had she given
him a disease, passed on to Morgan? No. No, she'd
never seen so much as a sign.

Steps rang through the corridor outside the jail bars.

"Nasty customer, 'im. Liked the hard stuff. After that
once I never would see 'im again. Left Bertha's house
'cuz o' the likes of him. She said I hadta service 'im, but
I tole her I didn't hafta do nuthin'."

So Richard had beaten other women in the same
manner. Why was she so shocked? Hadn't Edward said
something similar? But she'd been his wife, not a prostitute, and Richard had blamed his attacks on her disobedience—

The constable who'd arrested her stopped in front of
the cell door. With a kind smile in his eyes, he asked,
"Mrs. Montgomery?"

She stared at him in dismay. Montgomery? How
could he know? She'd given her name as Turner, resolved to the end to keep Ward free from the taint of
murder.

"Hey, I thought you wuz Turner!" the prostitute exclaimed.

"Was, Sally," the constable answered. "She's remarried, so she is. Mrs. Montgomery, you'll be followin' me now." He turned his key in the lock.

Where? To attend some manner of investigation? Or perhaps to coax a confession from her.

"Gaw! Remarried already! You got a better one this time? Can't be much worse!"

Morgan rose, contriving to smile through her misery. "He's much kinder, thank you." How did the constable know about Ward? Had the police department telegraphed Boston?

Sally nodded and grinned. "Whatcha want her for, O'Hara?" she asked as Morgan slid through the cell door and O'Hara slammed it shut.

"Ain't none o' yer business."

Morgan frowned at his rudeness. "It is *my* business, however."

"Why," he said, "to talk to some people 'bout these murder charges, so they tell me."

"Who?"

"Well now," he said with a shrug. "I don't rightly know, but they're mighty grand folk in that room, so I'll be thinking there's a lawyer or two."

She nodded and smiled again at Sally. Sally beamed her gap-toothed grin. With only that to ease the dread filling Morgan's heart, she allowed O'Hara to escort her down the stone corridor, past men in cages, some hooting, some shouting coarse, vulgar words. Morgan winced, for Ward had taught her the meaning behind those terms, whispered in a warm, husky voice. In his arms they'd heated her blood or made her laugh, but from the mouths of her fellow inmates, they assumed vile, degrading meanings, digging a pit in her stomach. Oh God, what sort of woman was she?

Constable O'Hara yelled back, threatening the worst of her tormentors with dire consequences. Finally they reached the end of the row, climbed stairs out of the basement, then passed through several dimly lit corridors, presently stopping in front of a heavy wooden door. After knocking, O'Hara ushered her into a small room nearly filled by a long rectangular table, around which sat several men. They were all well-dressed, and well-bred enough to rise upon her entrance. Morgan passed her eyes over them until her gaze fixed upon one face, one set of eyes at the end of the table. They held hers steadily, setting her heart aflutter. A flush warmed her face. Ward. *That* was how they knew her name. But how? *Why?*

Out of the corner of her eye, she saw a man across the table from Ward stride toward her. After a courteous bow, he said, "Mrs. Montgomery, permit me to introduce myself. I'm Abner Smith, your husband's lawyer. If you'll give me leave, I'll escort you to your seat, and we shall begin this meeting."

She nodded and floated on a cloud of unreality toward her seat, a wooden chair at the end of the table standing vacant as if awaiting a king—or a murder suspect. It was situated between Smith's and Ward's. Ward—she could scarcely take her eyes from him. He was so achingly handsome it ripped the breath from her lungs, dressed as neat as a pin in charcoal gray, with a black waistcoat embroidered in silver, a snowy white shirt and cravat. All too vividly, she recollected removing those clothes, recollected the feel of his warm skin beneath her fingertips, his chest hair sliding luxuriously between her fingers. Nearly healed from childbirth, her body reacted to the images, desire leaping to life as Mr. Smith pulled her chair out for her. She obliged him, and with a scraping of chairs, the men reseated themselves, talking in low tones amongst themselves.

Oh God, she thought folding her hands to keep them from trembling, what was Ward doing here? He must have searched for her . . . even though she'd stabbed him—fled him—conducted herself as the very murderess these men no doubt believed her to be.

Her foot accidentally brushed against Ward's. She glanced at him. He was staring at her, his countenance holding less expression than a card player. A second later he shifted his focus to the other men, but she continued to look at him, her eyes hungrily taking in the harsh lines of his jaw, the slight darkening of his skin from a half day's stubble. Her hand itched to reach for him, her fingertips to once more run over those familiar, beloved lines, and it required every bit of strength to restrain herself. Clenching her teeth, she too turned to view the assembly.

To fix upon Kenneth Turner.

Contempt pierced her from under his heavy lids, chilling her blood. Oh God, this was a trial! An American trial! No judge, no jury, only these ten men—but that wasn't her understanding of the American justice system—

"Now that we're all present," Mr. Smith said, "I believe the first order of business is to discuss Mr. Roth's coroner's report."

"Oh for God's sake, this is pure balderdash!" Kenneth spat out. "We've seen the report. A coroner's jury accused Mrs. Turner—excuse me, Mrs. Montgomery—of killing my cousin! What's the use of this?"

"The use," a gentleman with a sparsely-haired head and deep-set eyes said, "is to bring to light new information that has been uncovered in this case, and to decide amongst us if the case is worth taking to trial."

"I don't know about this information," Kenneth argued, face reddening, "but I do know that Mr. Montgomery is behind it all! I remind you that he's hardly impartial! He married the very woman responsible for

Richard's death, and is therefore the ultimate recipient of Richard Turner's fortune! Worse still, he did so in the teeth of her confinement, thereby stealing every last cent from Richard's child by claiming it as his own!"

The flush on Morgan's face grew with righteous anger. Of all the nerve, to accuse Ward of all people of such treachery! "No!" she cried out.

Mr. Smith's hand fell on her wrist, squeezing it in warning. The men turned to her.

"No?" asked a tall, lanky gentleman with a full set of whiskers and crow's-feet at the corners of his eyes. "Have you something to add, ma'am?"

"Only that—"

"My client has nothing to say to that," Mr. Smith interrupted, the pressure on her wrist increasing.

"It sounds to me like she does," the man returned mildly.

"And yet," Mr. Smith said, "under my advice she'll keep her own counsel."

"Sir," said the man with the deep-set eyes, "if the lady has something to say that is pertinent to this investigation, then I must insist she say it, else I may, as prosecutor, decide to end this meeting."

Ward spoke up, his voice calm in a sea of increasing tension, as if Kenneth Turner hadn't just offered him the most vile insult. "It's all right, Abner. Let her talk."

Dragging her eyes from Kenneth's poisonous glare, Morgan looked at Ward. His countenance was even, his eyes quiet, soothing her flurried nerves enough that she could address the men with feigned composure. "Mr. Turner is wrong. The child is Mr. Montgomery's, not my hu—not Richard's."

"You're certain of that, ma'am?" the prosecutor asked. "From the records we've been provided, the child's birth came approximately nine months after Mr. Turner's death."

How many times must she explain this? Did men fancy all women imbeciles? Those she'd married had, except perhaps Ward. In all their dealings, he'd conducted himself with the greatest respect for her intelligence. All lost now, for how could any man form a lasting attachment to a woman so predisposed to violence? "Do you wish me to detail the complexities of a woman's person to you, sir?"

The prosecutor's eyes flickered, then sparkled a trifle. "No, ma'am, we'll take you at your word. Now, that resolved, let's discuss this new information. Dr. Barlow?"

"Not so fast," a man sitting next to Kenneth spoke. "My client has a good point. Mrs. Montgomery has been indicted. It's highly improper to conduct such a meeting when our justice system expects her next to proceed to trial, with a judge and jury to determine her guilt."

The prosecutor scowled. "And, Mr. Carter, would you waste the taxpayers' money for a trial when none is necessary?"

"Is justice a waste of taxpayers' money, sir?"

"A miscarriage of justice is. It won't hurt to listen to Dr. Barlow."

"What can he possibly say of any moment?"

"He was," Mr. Smith said firmly, "Turner's doctor. Dr. Barlow, if you would so kindly oblige us by reciting the information you provided Mr. Montgomery."

A man sitting midway down the table spoke through a thick, graying mustache. He was tall, thin, and vaguely familiar. Morgan recollected seeing him at Richard's house once or twice, but had never received a proper introduction.

"Certainly. Mr. Montgomery contacted me via telegram two weeks ago, requesting information as to

Mr. Turner's health. Now that he's dead I trust I won't offend anyone by telling you that his health was very poor. He engaged my services these five years past for treatment of heart palpitations. I prescribed several medications and warned him that should he wish to see old age, he must follow a strict regimen of exercise, continence, and general healthful living. He ignored my suggestions."

"Heart palpitations hardly constitute poor health!" Kenneth's attorney, Mr. Carter, interrupted. "My wife has heart palpitations over a fine piece of lace!"

Heart problems? Morgan's own heart increased its pace in sudden, unexpected hope.

"It began as heart palpitations," Dr. Barlow said. "Over the years his condition worsened. Several weeks prior to marrying this young lady," he said motioning to Morgan, "Turner sought my advice on such a course of action, for, as we all know, he possessed a large fortune. He wished for an heir to pass it on to. I expected that such activities could very well kill him and suggested he make alterations to his will should he insist upon the attempt. And then I increased his medications."

Richard had married her to provide an *heir*? But why hadn't he told her? If she'd known, he might be alive today! She'd believed her pregnancy would anger him, for it would restrict his—activities. And angering Richard had frightened her above all things.

"I don't believe a word of this!" Kenneth burst out. "My cousin was in perfect health. Montgomery paid this quack to lie."

"Mr. Turner judged it beneath his dignity for anyone to know of his illness," Dr. Barlow said placidly. "Moreover, he believed that should his heart difficulties be brought to light, his enemies would prey upon his weakness, seriously hampering his ability to manage either his bank or coal mine. He refused even to make his wife aware of his condition, though I tried to persuade him to reconsider."

The men turned to her, the prosecutor scrutinizing her face as he asked, "Is this true, ma'am? Did Mr. Turner keep this information from you?"

They were all staring at her, including Ward. Twenty eyes, fixed on her face. It unnerved her, then vexed her. What right had they to treat her so uncivilly? Setting her teeth, she said, "Sir, I've answered a number of your questions already, although I've yet to make your acquaintance or that of any man here, save Mr. Smith. All understanding I have of this meeting has been through a few chosen words passed amongst you, and still you cast questions at me without explanation. Before I say another word, I demand at the very least, introductions."

She had the pleasure of seeing several of them flush with embarrassment, and others avert their eyes. Ward, however, said in a low voice, "Touché, Morgan."

Turning to him, she was shocked to observe amusement twinkling in his eyes, mixed with traces of admiration. Her heart jumped. She'd spoken like a harpy, not at all the sort of thing a man would wish to hear from his wife, certainly not her Boston aristocrat husband.

Recovering his equanimity, the prosecutor said graciously, "I apologize, Mrs. Montgomery. It seems we've forgotten our manners in the heat of the moment." With that he went around the table introducing the men and their various reasons for being there, from Mr. Smith to her right, then Mr. Roth, coroner; Dr. Lindberg; Mr. Thompson, chief of police; Mr. Carter, Kenneth's attorney; Kenneth Turner, himself; Mr. Emery, Philadelphia's chief prosecutor; and Doctor Barlow, Richard's physician. "As you know, your husband has recently discovered information that might acquit you of Richard Turner's murder. We're meeting to discuss all the information and," he said, his voice turning severe as he impaled Kenneth with his eyes, "Mr. Kenneth Turner has been invited to join us."

"I may add," Mr. Smith said, "you are under no obligation to answer any question, Mrs. Montgomery. This is an investigation, not a court of law."

"But it ought to be!" Mr. Carter interjected.

Morgan regarded Ward again. Once more he'd shielded the emotion in his eyes blighting her spirits, for she'd drawn her strength and courage from the warm compassion shining in those depths.

"And so, Mrs. Montgomery," Mr. Emery said, "if you would oblige us by answering my question. Did you know of Mr. Turner's heart condition?"

She looked at Ward a moment longer, then focused on Mr. Emery. "No. Richard kept his private affairs to himself."

Mr. Emery's forehead creased. "His private affairs? Isn't a wife at the very heart of a man's private affairs?"

"Not Richard's."

Mr. Emery peered at her. "I see," he said and turned to Mr. Roth, the coroner. "I believe, sir, that after Mr. Montgomery received this information from Dr. Barlow, he approached you."

Mr. Roth flinched, as if disturbed by being selected for the next in line of questioning. "He sent Dr. Barlow to me with a request for exhumation and autopsy. Such a course of action is costly. I refused. It seemed to me and the six men who were on the coroner's jury that the solution to the crime was obvious. I don't like wasting either my time or taxpayer money. I ran my campaign on the latter, if you recall. However, as Mr. Montgomery is the accused's husband, he had a legal and moral obligation to pursue every avenue of defense for his wife. When he offered to pay the shot, I consented."

"And the result?"

"I chose Dr. Lindberg for the autopsy. Dr. Barlow also attended. Both men, upon viewing the deceased's skull, agreed that the blow to the head caused relatively little damage."

"But that was almost a year ago! How can you make such conclusions at this point?" Turner protested.

Dr. Lindberg, a balding man with thickly rimmed eyes and a hooknose, replied, "It takes hundreds of years for a body to decompose so entirely that we should not find damage to the skull. Upon inspection, I noted only the faintest crack above Turner's temple, which would likely cause the headache, but scarcely damage the brain enough to kill him. Even if it did, the victim would take days to die, not the hours the servants' testimony gives us to believe."

Morgan could scarcely believe her ears. How could this be possible. . . . She'd been there. . . . After bashing him in the head, she'd watched Richard collapse in the throes of death. "But . . ." she whispered.

The men nearest to her turned their heads. "Morgan," Ward hissed.

"But what?" Mr. Emery asked.

Breathing deeply, her face growing warm under the scrutiny, Morgan looked to Ward. Mr. Smith advised once more that she need answer no questions, but she scarcely heard him. Ward's eyes gleamed with affection as he whispered in a voice so low no one else could possibly decipher the words, "I brought Lee with me. We're staying with the Huntingtons."

Lee! A wave of longing swept Morgan's tired heart. Oh, her *son*, here in Philadelphia! She wished for nothing half so much as to cuddle his tiny body in her arms, watch him smile as he slept—except perhaps to do so while she sat in Ward's arms—

"Mrs. Montgomery," Mr. Emery called to her. Feeling slightly faint, she turned to him. "You had something to add?"

For just this one time she'd meant to actually tell the truth, that she could not believe herself innocent of killing Richard. She'd *been* there, watching as the light of life in his eyes flickered out.

But Lee was in Philadelphia—

And those soft visions drowned all sense of honor.

"Nothing. I'm shocked, that's all."

"No!" Turner cried out, slamming his fist on the table. "She killed my cousin, I know she did, and she ought to hang! A man can die of a brain injury without his skull being affected. He can be shaken to death. It happens often enough!"

The coroner frowned at him. "I've never seen a man shaken to death. Babies and children, yes, but never a man. Nor did Turner have any signs of such abuse. Mrs. Montgomery, at any rate, could not have done such a thing. To be sure, if we'd known how delicate and frail she was at the time of the inquest, we might have come to different conclusions. I doubt she has either the strength of spirit or physical ability to have swung *anything* strongly enough to kill *any* man. Thus in light of these latest findings, I am changing my report. Richard Turner died of heart failure."

"No!" Kenneth shouted, jumping up, face dark with rage. "You can't change the report once a person has been indicted! A coroner's jury found her guilty and she must stand trial! Tell them, Carter!"

"This is all highly irregular," Mr. Carter objected.

"The whole confounded thing is highly irregular," Mr. Emery snapped as he rose. His eyes pierced Morgan.

"And I place most of the blame on your doorstep, ma'am. If you'd not fled the crime scene this situation would never have developed at all. As for Mr. Roth's report," he continued, addressing the entire room, "it would be best if it were changed. The evidence doesn't support prosecuting Mrs. Montgomery, in any event."

"No!" Kenneth shouted. "You must prosecute! She's guilty, so says the inquest! She shall be brought to justice and hanged for the murder of my cousin. Should you refuse, I shall go to the papers!"

"You shall heed my advice, young man!" Mr. Emery shouted back, stabbing his finger on the table. "This case was going to be devilish enough to win before this new information. I haven't a prayer of it now! How many juries do you think would convict a woman of murder, especially after hearing the circumstances of her marriage? Have you forgotten your cousin's reputation? I promise you, I have not! Furthermore, she is now a mother, married to a man of high standing in Boston, New York, and even here in Philadelphia! From what I understand she's even a member of the English nobility. *No* one wants the responsibility of imprisoning such a lady, never mind hang one! No sir, I shouldn't prosecute Mrs. Montgomery if you sent a blasted battalion of reporters to my office! This case is closed!"

Morgan winced at the shouting, staring wide-eyed at the two red-faced men, appearing on the verge of a fist-fight.

"You'll be a laughing-stock, then," Kenneth replied, fists at his side. "Everyone expected her to hang."

"And you, sir, will be an object of pity," Mr. Emery replied coldly, "which is your own blasted fault for having gone to the newspapers in the first place. No gentleman would have done so." With that Mr. Emery bowed to the other men at the table, most rising hastily. "Thank you all for coming here today. Mr. Montgomery," he bowed to Ward, still sitting coolly in his chair. "Very fine investigative work, sir. I commend you. Mrs. Montgomery." He bowed to her. "It has been—enlightening—ma'am."

He left the room, followed by the doctors and the coroner. Kenneth's eyes followed them, his fists white at his sides. His lawyer leaned across the table to speak soothingly to him. Ward's sea-salt voice rolled across the room. "I should like to have a few words with you, Turner, if you please."

Morgan glanced at him, then noticed that Mr. Smith had not risen, either.

"What, to gloat? Well, it's not over yet, Montgomery! I'll have justice for my cousin, I swear it!"

Maintaining his cool composure, Ward said pleasantly, "I understand your quest for justice. If you allow me a few minutes of your time, you may discover that all is not lost. Contrary to your beliefs, I didn't marry Mrs. Montgomery to lay claim to Turner's fortune."

"Hah! More lies! Your greed is legendary, Montgomery, even in Philadelphia."

"Is it?" Ward asked, raising an eyebrow. "I didn't know. Will you sit, sir? What have you to lose by lending me your ear?"

"Perhaps you ought to hear him out, Ken," Mr. Carter said.

Kenneth stood a moment longer, then shifted over two chairs to slam himself down next to Mr. Smith. "Fine," he said sullenly. "What have you to say?"

Ward eyed him speculatively, his slight smile playing on his lips. Morgan knew that expression; she'd seen it when they'd played chess. He used it to disconcert his opponent before attacking, an attack that was always well-planned, slippery, and painstakingly slow. "First," he said slowly, "you must understand that I believe unequivocally in my wife's innocence. Turner died from his own ill-health. The coroner agrees, and I intend to put that story forth to the newspapers."

"And I shall counter it at every opportunity."

"Indeed," Ward answered. "As you may imagine, I find your insistence of Mrs. Montgomery's guilt distressing. You've not only harmed her, but yourself, your family, and mine. If you continue on this course, you'll force me to employ methods to counteract that damage. I assure you, sir, it shall not be pretty."

"What can you do to me?" he asked with barely suppressed fury. "I'm the injured party here."

"On the contrary, sir, my wife is the injured party. Continue this way and we shall both suffer. I don't suffer well in silence, Turner. At best, your cousin was a barbarian. What he was at worst I may discover from a number of brothels in this city. I need only make the information known to the papers for it to see print. You know how scuttlebutt sells. Should your name be connected with any of those houses, it too, will see print."

"That, sir, is libel! I'll sue!"

"Your suit would prosper only if you proved the information false. Moreover this course of action will only add to the scandal, which I assure you will touch us much less in Boston than you here in Philadelphia."

"I should see it gets into the Boston newspapers as well."

"You'll lose. The Boston newspapers strongly resist besmirching its leading citizens. However, I may yet steer you clear of this storm. To be honest I consider your cousin's conduct reprehensible in all matters. Leaving his entire fortune to a woman he married but months earlier when he'd promised it to you for years was both irresponsible and cruel."

He paused. Kenneth's eyes fixed upon Ward's face.

"Still," Ward continued, "Morgan *did* marry Turner and deserves, we'll call it credit, for bearing with his company during those months. Therefore, while I insist she retain the bulk of Turner's inheritance, I'm willing to remit back to you twenty-five percent of that inheritance, under certain conditions."

Kenneth's eyes quickly calculated. "That would amount to—"

"Quite a bit," Ward said dryly. "First you must promise to cease pursuing Mrs. Montgomery's prosecution—it's a hopeless venture, at any rate—and quit abusing her character publicly. If you refuse, I shall require that twenty-five percent to defend her. And, sir, as Mr. Emery has dismissed the murder charges, I could sue *you* for slander."

Greed suffused Kenneth's features. "I'll abide by those conditions, but I deserve at least half of that inheritance."

Ward shrugged. "Do you think so? No doubt your cousin beat *you* on a daily basis also."

Morgan sucked in her breath, shame burning in her chest. Kenneth reddened with shame also—and guilt. "I couldn't have helped her. Legally a man may do as he pleases with his wife."

"No doubt that helps you sleep at night." Ward paused. "I must warn you, sir, I shall not make this offer again. Accept it now or lose all."

Silence. Then Kenneth nodded.

"Good." Ward focused his gaze on Morgan. "I haven't had the opportunity to consult you on this, my dear. I presume you agree to this bargain?"

"Whatever you fancy is necessary," she answered cautiously.

"Both necessary and proper," he said pleasantly. "Mr. Turner, Mr. Smith has drawn up the papers. If you accompany him to his office, we shall complete this business today. Abner, could you please send for a carriage for my wife and me on your way out?"

Mr. Smith rose and gathered up the papers he'd taken from his case. "Certainly, sir. Mr. Turner, Mr. Carter? My office is two blocks from here."

Kenneth nodded and displayed enough breeding to offer Ward his hand. "Thank you, Montgomery. I apologize for my earlier comments. Apparently your reputation is incorrect. You're very generous."

Ward smiled wryly, shaking his hand. "Sir, all Bostonians are reputed to be greedy and parsimonious. We consider it a compliment."

With that the men quit the room, leaving Morgan to Ward's company. An uncomfortable silence settled in the space between them, filling Morgan with a sort of agitated dread. She regarded her hands, her gloves smudged and dirty from a day's rough use, much like her heart from the years of rash behavior. If only she could cover it too! "I suppose I also owe you my gratitude," she finally said, "and an apology, but truly, Ward, if you had only *explained* it to me . . ."

Ward sighed and leaned back in his chair, holding the edge of the table in his large, black-gloved hands. "I tried, madam, but I'd no specific notion of where my investigations would lead, only that I could open more doors as your husband than as your—captain. Without the bond of marriage you would still stand accused of murder, for I should never have convinced Dr. Barlow to provide me with information on Turner, nor have the body exhumed otherwise." He paused. "I do apologize for resorting to such barbarous methods of claiming your hand in marriage. I hope you understand I did so with the most honorable intentions: your safety and our child's legitimacy. Both being accomplished, Rob is prepared to start divorce proceedings as soon as you require. You need not concern yourself about financial difficulties. I shall settle Turner's fortune on you. God knows you deserve it."

Morgan's heart froze. "Divorce? Do you seek a divorce?"

Ward's eyes were excessively cool. "I expected you would wish for one."

"Me? Why ever would you think that?"

"You made it abundantly clear at our last meeting."

She frowned. Had she requested a divorce? Those days in Chicago were lost in a postpartum fog—

He raised two disbelieving eyebrows. "Is it possible you've forgotten? Good God, Morgan," he hissed, "you stabbed me!"

"Oh! That!" she said, the fog lifting. "I only wished to escape you, but a divorce, Lord, only think of the *scandal!*"

He appeared stunned for a moment, then a tiny sparkle lit his eyes. "Why, we certainly wouldn't want any of that!"

Amusement flickered through Morgan's aching heart. "Certainly not. You must know I am always the soul of discretion!"

A reluctant smile turned up Ward's mouth. "Mistress, if you are the soul of discretion, then discretion is headed straight for hell. Permit me to say you don't appear surprised that I still live."

She bit her cheek. "I—I already knew it. I watched the house in secret and made sure of it before leaving Chicago."

"How very decent of you," he said, lifting an amused eyebrow. "Do you treat all your victims with such respect, or may I count myself privileged?"

She grimaced. "I wasn't so decent to Richard, was I?"

"You could not have saved him," he said, his eyes narrowing.

"Saved him?" she asked, remembering those last awful moments. "Good God, Ward, I—"

"No," he interrupted, raising a hand in warning. "This isn't the place to discuss that. In fact, we ought not," he said, eyeing the half-open door, "discuss our little—uh— altercation, either."

"I should think the stationhouse a prime place to discuss assault and battery."

His smiled slightly and lowered his voice. "These walls have heard enough today. Should Mr. Roth learn of your penchant for knives, my dear, he might reconsider his opinion of you as 'delicate and frail.'"

"Oh, but how could he?" she asked, widening her eyes in feigned innocence. "I am ever so delicate, Captain!"

His eyes sparkled. "Aye, madam, a model of frailty!"

"And discretion!"

"With the soul of discretion," he said chuckling.

"And decency!"

"Best proved in your black negligee?"

"Well, as to that," she said wickedly, "I only meant in public."

"To be sure, we've enjoyed it most in private," he said. A hot gleam touched his eyes, sending desire skittering along her nerves. Memories of his large hands sliding across her skin as he slipped her negligee from her shoulders heated her blood, followed swiftly by the recollection of his kiss, his hard hands gliding over her in sensual exploration.

"I—I suppose so."

The gleam grew, but a tiny ache entered his voice when he spoke again. "You always pleased me, Mistress."

And he, her, but she'd ended that pleasure as surely as she'd ended Richard's life. She swallowed to dislodge the longing dragging at her heart. A useless attempt. "Except, I fancy, in Chicago," she rasped.

"In Chicago you taught me to keep sharp objects from your grasp."

She winced. "Did I hurt you badly? You seem to have healed well enough."

A sharp vulnerability cut across his countenance. "Did you think I suffered only flesh wounds, Morgan?"

Breathe—oh she could scarcely breathe! How deep went those wounds? So deep he could not recover? Aye, so deep he sought a divorce, with all the attached scandal.

A knock on the door interrupted their conversation, and a constable entered carrying packages. "Mr. Montgomery, sir, your cab has arrived. Here are Mrs. Montgomery's possessions, along with release papers to sign." He laid the bundles on the table then lifted his head, eyeing them both in discomfort. "The chief told me to tell ya, sir, that try as we did to stop it, the newspapers have gotten wind of Mrs. Montgomery's capture. Reporters are linin' up outside."

Reporters? Dear heavens!

"You've a back door that empties into an alley, correct?" Ward asked, rising, all pain melting from his features. "Be so kind as to send the cab to the end of the alleyway, please. We'll meet it there." He gathered her bundles together and Morgan scribbled her name on the papers.

"Yes, sir. Of course, sir."

"Then shake a leg," he said, pressing a gold coin into his hand, "before they consider what we're about."

"Fast as light'nin' sir!" he said and sped away.

"Now, Morgan, on with your cloak and wig. We'll put the rest into your valise, all Yankee neat. Now, my hat, my cane, and we cast off!"

Chapter Thirty

Ward shut the door to the coach and it jerked forward. He surveyed Morgan, leaning against the opposite door, her face pale and pinched as she removed her red wig. She smiled wanly at him. "I've caused quite a commotion again, haven't I?"

"We've escaped it for now. Where do you wish me to convey you, madam? Have you a hotel room?"

Her eyes widened, deepening that damned hollow expression she'd regained in Chicago after marrying him under extreme duress—duress supplied by him. "No. I was at the depot when they found me."

"The depot," he repeated. "You were leaving town. Had you decided, then, *not* to confess?"

Her eyebrows drew together. "How did you suppose that? How did you even know I was here, Ward?"

"Amy thought you might consider confession. To that purpose, Edward hired detectives to peruse the pawnshops should you attempt to raise the wind by selling your diamonds. Which," he said, reaching into his pocket, "are here."

She took a deep breath and reached for the necklace. As she ran her fingers over it the sun shining through the window sparkled on the jewels, bringing forth memories of firelight glittering on the jewels and shining on her bare skin. Memories of her laughter, her wanton response to his touch, her eyes brighter than any jewel . . .

"I—I thought never to see it again," she said.

And I feared, replied his heart, *never to see you again.* He didn't speak his thoughts, but studied every movement of her face, every line, every shadow, committing all to memory lest he lose her still. For a short spell in the stationhouse he'd thought she'd forgiven him. But, he thought, his heart weighed down by holystones like a sailor's corpse, more barred their marriage than simple forgiveness.

"Considering our last meeting," Morgan said carefully, "I should have thought Edward would do all in his power to widen the breech between us."

He hesitated. "You've yet to meet Edward at his best. He then believed he had my best interests at heart, but I trust I've corrected his misperceptions."

"He believes I killed Richard."

"That's over now."

She lifted her head. Her eyes were expressionless except for that persistent pain, piercing his heart. He would do anything to remove that pain, even immerse himself in divorce, for the scandal could hardly scratch him in comparison to her suffering.

She looked down at her hands again. "And what do you believe? Were you speaking the truth in the stationhouse or was it all hocus-pocus? Ward," she said, her voice tight, "I was there. Richard appeared perfectly healthy before I struck him."

The stabbing in his chest expanded to a full, throbbing ache. She'd seen far too much of the monkey, his rash, impetuous mistress, and knowing she'd brought much of the punishment upon herself didn't lessen the misery. "We can't be certain. I doubt such a blow could kill him, but it might have led to heart failure."

She heaved a sigh. "It's rather difficult to go through life not knowing if one has killed a man or not."

"He's still dead."

She sighed again and, drawing the necklace through her fingers over and over, turned to stare out the window. After a minute she asked, "Where are we going?"

"I told the driver to take me to Edward's. Unless there's somewhere else you'd rather I convey you?"

"No doubt he'll welcome me," she said, her voice tough with sarcasm, then fading as she closed her eyes. "Lee's there, isn't he? May I see him?"

Bewildered by the question, Ward lifted one eyebrow. "Of course you may."

Presently, she opened her eyes. "He might not wish to see *me* after I abandoned him. I—I haven't been the best mother, have I?"

It required all Ward's strength not to take her in his arms and lend her the comfort her tight voice pleaded for. But if she shunned him it would tear the very heart from his chest. If she accepted him, that would only exacerbate the inevitable agony of parting. "Lee's but three weeks old. He doesn't know what he wants. As for your absence," Ward hesitated and, to ease her suffering, teased gently, "I should not have chosen your precise course of action myself, but I must commend you on actually *having* a plan."

"A plan!" she exclaimed, shaking her head ruefully. He was gratified to see her muscles relax; his own followed suit. "Oh, Ward, I cannot believe I *stabbed* you! For such a scheme as this too! Whatever was I *thinking*?"

He grinned. "I suspect you wished to escape a tyrant of a husband. Do you think, madam, that if I vow never again to withhold a doctor's attention, you might refrain from future violence against me?"

"Oh how could I ever do that again?" she asked, emitting a watery chuckle. "Besides, I am all out of knives. Oh dear," she said, tears springing in her eyes again, despite the levity in her voice. "How can I say such things? I truly am an odious wife."

Comforted by her laughter, Ward smiled broadly. "Ah, Mistress, you're certainly not for the weak-hearted."

"Weak-hearted?" she said, making a noise between a laugh and a sob. "Good God, three dead husbands in three years, Ward! And I am only one and twenty!"

"It *is* quite a record. I, however, am neither inclined to ill-health, nor am I a young fool."

"No," she said, playing with her necklace as the coach slowed. Her face resumed the pinched expression as she took a deep breath, looked out the window, and said with self-reproach tightening her voice, "You are a Boston Aristocrat married to Scandal. This is what, above all things, I had hoped to avoid, the further sullying of your name." Her voice caught, touching Ward's aching heart.

"I had a hand in it also, Morgan."

"Did you? You were, perhaps, hiding behind the curtain when I killed Richard? Did you place the statue in my reach for that purpose?"

The coach stopped and the coachman jumped down as Ward answered, "I helped in the creation of our son. I know of methods to control conception, but I ignored them."

"Because I provided every occasion for you to doubt my fertility. Once more it rests upon me," she said. "How might I wonder that you wish to divorce me? I think perhaps I wish to divorce myself."

"I never—" The coachman opened the door, cutting off Ward's speech. It wasn't a discussion for public ears.

Morgan stood outside the drawing room's double doors, biting the inside of her cheek. Hand on the door-knob, the butler waited as she collected her wits about her. Ward had quite considerately surprised her by bringing both Maeve and her wardrobe to Philadelphia. After tearful rejoicing, she and Maeve had chosen Morgan's most conservative silk day dress in which to meet Edward and his guests. A deep emerald green, it boasted two flounces trimmed with black braids. It but-toned up the front, all the way to its white lace collar; its sleeves were of a moderate width, its undersleeves pris-tine white. And Maeve had arranged Morgan's hair into a conservative knot decorated by a simple turtle shell hairpin. Outwardly she resembled a proper English lady. She'd even donned a black silk shawl, as if the dress itself didn't portray the height of propriety. Rob, she thought with a slight tug of her mouth, would be proud.

Was Rob here? Oh, but how she yearned for the sight of his familiar face, even for his tepid support! Maeve couldn't tell her much about Edward's guests except that Ward had traveled with many people including some Hat Man. Roland Hathaway, no doubt, who'd vowed to end her marriage. And, she thought with a sinking heart, Ward seemed quite prepared to follow that advice.

"Madam? They're waiting," the butler said.

"Yes. Yes, of course they are. All right then. Wish me luck!"

His eyes frowned, but he opened the door and an-nounced her entry. Trembling, Morgan drew on every last bit of training, lifted her head, and entered the room.

The first face her gaze lighted upon stopped her in her tracks. Reggie.

"Oh God, Reggie!" she cried in amazement, then swept forward on winged feet to be folded into her brother's loving embrace. Sweet memories surrounded her in dark wool and the fragrance of his particular brand of snuff.

"Morgan, my dear," he said in his kind, and oh-so-very-*English* voice. "Now don't weep, that's a good girl."

"I'm not weeping!" she said, lifting her head as tears sprang from her eyes and rolled down her face. "All right," she said with a hiccup of a laugh. "I am a trifle. Oh, but Reggie, whatever are you *doing* here? Oh, *how* I've missed you! And I want another hug, even if I've already rumpled your coat beyond repair."

"I can change later," he promised with a slight laugh, and pulled her to him once again. She felt him take a deep breath. A moment later, aware of eyes upon her and hushed conversations taking place around her, she attempted to pull away. He held her tightly rasping, "Not yet, dear. A moment more." Presently he released her and took her measure with his quizzing glass. A lump rising in her throat, she noticed that his eyes had reddened. "Now, isn't that the prettiest gown? Did you wear it for me? Or perhaps for this husband of yours? You ought to be ashamed, my dear. You promised me your heart years ago, and now I hear that you've married no less than four times since last I saw you!"

Chuckling a little, she wiped her eyes. "I've had rather an adventure."

A deep laugh rang through the room, drawing Morgan's eyes away from her brother. Her eyes followed the sound, leaving her with an impression of a large room with numerous floor-to-ceiling windows draped in gold silk, and ornately carved rosewood furniture covered in cream brocade. On one sofa sat Amy and Edward. At the end of another Roland Hathaway stood leaning negligently against the arm, his eyes bright with amusement. "I'm sorry, Mrs. Montgomery," he said, "but it seems 'adventure' is rather an understatement."

"I'm glad I amuse you, sir," she said acerbically.

"Well, it's the least you could do considering the dance you've led us all on," he said, moving toward her, his broad grin displaying bright white teeth through his whiskers. "Still, it's a pleasure to see you safe and sound." He gave her a deep bow, then took both of her hands in his and said with a laugh in his voice, "I must apologize for my deplorable behavior the last time we met, madam. You'll forgive me, won't you? I don't relish being at daggers-drawn with a lady as beautiful as you!"

She frowned, both repelled and drawn to his easy charm. "And if I were ugly, sir?"

"Why then, you could stay angry with me for life! What do ugly women signify?"

"Sir," she said with a reluctant laugh, "I suspect you're an abominable flirt."

Ward came forward from his position near a huge, marble-framed fireplace. "He is, Morgan. And with his wife here, too!" he said with a chuckle.

"Wife?"

"Yes," Ro said, brushing by Ward with a grin as he drew Morgan across the room to a tall blond woman sitting stiffly on the sofa that Ro had been leaning against. "My wife, Frances Hathaway, ma'am, who's most beautiful as you can plainly see, and therefore receives my apologies several times a day. And this woman next to her, I believe you know."

By the time Roland had finished his little speech,

Morgan had long since lost interest. Her eyes widened in disbelief as she stared down at her mother, who sat regarding her with cold, sapphire eyes. In her arms she held—cuddled even—a small bundle of love dressed in a white gown. Lee.

"Oh!" she gasped, tears filling her eyes as she fell to her knees in front of her mother. "Oh, he is so beautiful!" Careful not to wake him, she reached out to run a light finger over his soft, chubby cheek. He lifted one tiny hand and she felt a reaction in her breasts, full after a day's neglect.

"He is, isn't he, Morgan?"

Morgan lifted her head. Incredibly she saw unshed tears and the tiniest glimmer of warmth in her mother's eyes. Myriad emotions tugged at Morgan—anger, resentment, longing. "He's grown since last I saw him."

"Only two weeks, I perceive. I fancy it's not so large a change."

"I—I thought never to see him again, though."

Her mother's throat worked, the delicate white skin of her face creasing as she answered, "It is a difficult thing, losing a child, isn't it?"

Morgan brushed a tear from her eyes. "The most horrible in all the world."

Her mother's face softened slightly. "There are more horrors in the world than that, my dear. But I expect you've learned that, haven't you?"

Vexed once more, Morgan rose and stared down at her mother. She tried to rip away the resentment that blanketed the softer emotions she felt for Lady Westborough, but years of repression held it fast. "No, Mother, I don't. Losing a child is the worst of all things," she said coolly. "Where's Father? I'm shocked he permitted this visit."

Her mother's eyes registered hurt, but she quickly

overpowered it, using the harsh breeding she'd tried to instill in Morgan. "He's dead."

"Dead? When?"

"Seven weeks ago."

"So," she started, while searching her heart for some sort of feeling—sadness, remorse, regret, anything. Nothing surfaced except for traces of relief. Her father had died for her long ago. No, not true. For her, he'd never truly lived. "So, this isn't some sort of rebellion then?"

Coming from behind, Reggie placed a gentle hand on her shoulder. "We didn't know where you were, Morgan. How could we have visited before?"

"And now?" she asked, rigid with tension. She dearly wished to believe they'd continued to love her, miss her, even after her wretched conduct. "Did you come searching for me after Father died?"

Her mother's eyes flickered. Reggie replied, "When I was reviewing Father's papers after his death, I discovered a letter from Mr. Montgomery. Upon learning your location, we immediately booked passage on a steamer."

Ward? Astounded, she turned to him. He stood next to Amy, who had lifted her head to speak to him. Hearing his name, he turned his head to meet Morgan's gaze. He smiled tentatively, so uncommon for her self-assured captain. "You wrote my father? Why? When?"

Ward hesitated and Reggie answered, "He wrote several letters, starting in May, asking for your hand in marriage. However late, we've given him our blessing."

In May? Months and months ago. He'd sent for them, for her family. Confused, Morgan tilted her head slightly. "You requested his approval? In May? But Ward, that was before—"

"We would do better to talk about that later. Presently, we've gathered here to discuss the best way to provide a united front in the face of the publicity of your case, along with the other aspects of our marriage."

"In other words to keep the scandal down to a dull roar," Ro provided good-naturedly.

"Which, if it can be done at all," Edward said, sitting down next to Amy, "will take a deal of planning. We're all grateful for Ward's enviable ability in that area."

"But is it enviable?" Ro asked. "It brings on all that dull, dreary gravity. I daresay I don't envy him at all!"

"Well, neither do I," Edward answered with a laugh. "But we ought to, you know."

"Only if we wish to appear respectable like Ward. Ah, but he's *not* respectable anymore, now is he?"

"Oh, for the love of God, Ro," Ward grumbled. "I swear sometimes you talk only for the pleasure of hearing your own voice."

He shrugged. "You see, I have exceptional conversational skills."

With that Edward barked a laugh, dragging a similar, but reluctant, response from both Ward and Reggie.

"All right," Ward said presently. "Now that you've done your best, Ro, to assassinate my character, may we have a serious discussion? Morgan," he asked placing a hand on the small of her back, "may I find you a seat?"

"Oh, right here!" Amy cried out, patting a tiny space between her and Edward. "Edward will move, won't you darling? Then we may have a nice, comfortable chat."

"Perhaps," Edward reminded her gently, "she'd like to sit with her husband this time. You'll have plenty of time in the coming days for nice comfortable chats."

"Oh, of course. But promise me, Mo! We must catch up."

Morgan smiled warmly at her, her past resentment fading, for when Amy was in a good mood she radiated sunshine. "Tomorrow morning, right after breakfast," she agreed.

"Perfect! I shall refuse all callers for the entire day!" Morgan laughed. "I doubt it will take *that* long."

"Morgan, my love," Ward said, nodding to the empty space next to her mother. "Why don't you sit next to your son. I imagine you've missed him."

My love? Her heart leapt, then took flight. Was she still his love? Or had it only slipped out from force of habit? "All right."

"Excellent," he said sitting down next to her. "First of all—"

"You know I rather fancy a cup of tea. Shall I ring?" Amy interrupted.

"Tea?" Ward asked, confounded.

"Yes. It's coming on four now, isn't it? Morgan must be famished after such an ordeal, and tea is forever refreshing. It won't—"

With that the door of the drawing room opened abruptly. Appearing flustered, the butler entered, announcing "Mrs. Cecil Montgomery." A tall, gray-haired woman in lavender silk entered, carrying a cane, which she scarcely leaned upon. Judging from her wrinkled face, she was quite old, but her snapping black eyes and firm step belied the years.

"Yes, yes, they all know me, or at least most of them. Do go away, sir!" This she said to the butler as Edward, eyes wide in alarm, rose to greet her.

Ro, face comically aghast, rose also, whispering, "Bloody hell."

Amy frowned and Ward's lips curved into a challenging smile. Morgan glanced from him to the old woman and back again, noting a resemblance in the long-lashed eyes, the firm chin. Montgomery—his grandmother? Oh good God, it was his grandmother, the matriarch herself, the only woman who had ever intimidated Ward! A shiver rushed down her spine.

"Edward. Yes, nice to see you young man. I've heard that you married. Is that her? Well, she's pretty enough. Ward, it's you I've come to see—Good God, is that you, Hathaway?" She spoke quickly, her clipped tones making rough commands of every word, so different from Ward's easy cadences.

"Yes, ma'am," Ro replied reluctantly, bowing low.

"Don't try all that pretty nonsense with me. I know what you're about, young man, and it won't work. Ah, is that Frances Sheridan? It is good to see you again, Miss. How is your brother?"

"He's doing well, ma'am."

"She's no longer Sheridan, Mrs. Montgomery," Ro tried gallantly to set himself straight.

But Mrs. Montgomery's scowl only deepened. "She'll be Sheridan to me until you've proven your worth, sir, and not one second sooner," she answered, her keen eyes roving around the room. They flashed over Reggie and Lady Westborough to settle on Morgan. Under her cool scrutiny, Morgan blushed. Good gracious, but those eyes seemed to penetrate skin like a knife through butter, reaching straight into the soul. Morgan's soul couldn't bear much scrutiny.

"Is this her, Ward? You'd better introduce us. What is taking you so long, sir? I've reared you better than this!"

"You've scarcely allowed me a chance, Grandmother," he answered mildly.

"As to that," she snapped, "you've had the last nine months in which to introduce us. When we did talk, you denied contemplating marriage. Had you been honest with me *then*, we might have settled matters better. You've made a mull of it, son."

"I beg pardon, madam," Reggie started bravely. "From what I understand, Mont—"

"Who are you? Have I spoken to you? No. Have you

no better manners than to address a woman several decades your senior without so much as a proper introduction? Don't frown at me. You're in the wrong and you know it."

"This," Ward said, humor dulling the harshness of his voice, "is my brother-in-law, Lord Westborough, Earl of Westborough."

"Ah, so that's who you are. I thought I detected an English accent. I'll have you know that titles don't impress me, especially when they're accompanied by such poor manners. I presume you're the chit's brother?"

Ward's eyebrows rose in amusement. "I must insist, Grandmother, that you refrain from referring to my wife as 'chit' or even worse, 'the chit.' It's disrespectful."

"And has she earned my respect?"

"She's earned mine. No doubt that shall be enough for you. Amy, I believe you were right. Tea sounds like an exceptional idea."

Amy stared, her wide eyes flashing from Ward, to his grandmother, to Edward, who'd raised his eyebrows in shocked amusement. Morgan heard Ro whisper, "Ah, now that is the Sir Captain we both know and love."

"Yes, but this is my home, not his ship!" Edward whispered back, nudging Amy, who, needing no further urging, fled the room.

In the meantime, Mrs. Montgomery peered at Ward. He stood tall under that formidable gaze, his legs spread as if he was balancing on a rocking deck. After a moment a small smile creased the old woman's face. "So it's like that. All right then, would you kindly oblige me, Ward, by introducing me to my granddaughter-in-law? And I believe I have a great-grandson. Unless those rumors are untrue? I warn you, son, so many fly about that it is nearly impossible to find the truth in any of them."

"So Ro has informed me," he said, taking his grandmother's hand in his and leading her to Morgan. Morgan, both awed and appalled by a woman who, since her entrance, had sucked all the strength from the room, started to rise. Mrs. Montgomery waved her hand.

"No, no, sit back down. I can see you well enough, and you've been gallivanting so much about the country you must be close to fainting. Although from the looks of you, you don't faint too often, do you?"

"Are you asking for an answer, madam, or making a statement?"

A slight smile lit her brown eyes. "Not easily intimidated, either. It is an observation. From what I have heard you could scarcely be called namby-pamby. I thought you might lack intelligence, although I don't see that right now."

A touch of merriment lit Morgan's heart. "You can tell that by looking?"

The smile in her eyes grew. "I am considered a keen observer."

"But not very diplomatic, I collect."

"No. And you, my dear, are certainly not stupid, despite your behavior. Merely young and reckless. Time will correct for youthfulness, and I trust Ward can tame the recklessness. I shouldn't have chosen you for him, but I confess I'm not altogether displeased," she said. "Is this your mother? She has your look. Ah, and this is my great-grandson."

"His name is Leland."

"Leland Reginald Montgomery, so says Rob," she replied.

"Rob," Ward asked, humor tingeing his voice still. "Is that where you received your information? Did you torture him, madam, or merely browbeat him into submission? Does he still work for me?"

"Hah. No one with a trace of Montgomery blood would be so paltry. He might, however, be contemplating a short holiday. Lady Westborough," Mrs. Montgomery said in a softer voice, "it is a pleasure to make your acquaintance. I must apologize for my grandson's treatment of your daughter. I assure you that he rarely behaves so rashly. He's a good man in general."

"Why, thank you, Grandmother!" Ward said, his eyes twinkling.

"Don't let it go to your head!"

Lady Westborough smiled. "He seems quite level-headed to me. I fear my daughter must take full responsibility for her difficulties. She's always been a wayward child."

"My own son was much the same. Move over, girl. I wish to chat with your mother. Frances, perhaps you'll join that rogue who claims to be your husband."

"I suppose so," Fran said, rising gracefully. "Do you think he'll ever deserve that title, ma'am?" she asked.

Mrs. Montgomery glanced from Morgan to Ward. "Soon enough, I fancy. The girl may suit us all in the end," she said as she seated herself between Morgan and her mother.

Ward grinned at Morgan. "Well, girl is better than chit," he told her in a low voice.

"Don't talk behind my back, Ward," Grandmother Montgomery snapped. "It's uncouth."

"I was talking in front of you."

"That is ruder still."

"Aye, madam. I stand corrected."

"And don't say 'aye.' This is a drawing room, not a ship's deck. Ah, there's the tea tray. Fetch me a cup, Ward, and something to eat."

Face red, Amy glanced fearfully at Grandmother Montgomery as if hoping she had, like some sort of daytime nightmare, disappeared. Morgan smiled at her and gave her a quick wink. In reply, Amy grinned and took a deep, calming breath before sitting down to pour the tea and distribute it among her guests. Within a short time the food and tea dispelled the tension in the room, allowing several low-voiced conversations to take place. Morgan noted that Ro held his wife's hand as he chatted. An expression lit Fran's eyes that could not be questioned. Love, pure and simple. He returned the look with true adoration, and a lump grew in Morgan's throat, which all the tea in the world could not dislodge.

Ward brought a chair to sit next to Morgan, and they ate in silence while listening to Mrs. Montgomery and her mother discuss the dissipation of youth in general and their progeny in particular. Finally Mrs. Montgomery ended it with, "Well, I shall see to it that my grandson deals better from here on in. You have my word. And now, Ward, explain to us how you shall deal better. We are breathless with anticipation."

Ward carefully wiped his fingers on a napkin before placing his teacup and plate on the tea tray. "All right. I've first resolved to confront the newspapers. The reporters were already lining up at the stationhouse when we left."

Mrs. Montgomery drew in a sharp breath. "Good God."

"Exactly," Ward answered in a cool voice. He dropped his head to smile at Morgan. "I'm sorry, my dear, but I believe it will be best if you grant them an interview."

Her eyes widened; her heart took a hard, frightened lurch. "Interview? But that cannot possibly *help*, can it?"

"It can't," Edward said, shaking his head. "This is mad, Ward. They'll rip anything she says to pieces."

"They'll write the story whether she speaks to them or

not," Ward answered reasonably. "Better that they have the truth."

"But to present my daughter to the company of reporters! To be talking to them about such things!" Lady Westborough protested with a shudder.

Ro shook his head. "Let them make up their own stories. You ought not to add fuel to the fire."

"Let Montgomery speak," Reggie interjected. "He's managed this well thus far. The child is legitimate, my sister is free of all charges—"

"And," added Mrs. Montgomery, "considerably richer. Go on."

Ward turned back to Morgan, his eyes warm as he took her cold hand in his. "Remember, my dear, these reporters are the same men who named you the Wicked Widow. They printed everything Turner said, thus actively participating in the destruction of your honor and reputation. I presume that having discovered your innocence some of them will feel guilty. This is your chance to employ that guilt and paint them a much gentler picture."

"But they're *reporters,* Ward!" Edward ejaculated. "They want a headlining story to sell papers. Blood and scandal!"

His eyes fixed upon Morgan, Ward answered, "Reformation sells also. Well, my dear? What will it be?"

It sounded dreadful, exposing herself to a crowd of men eager to discover the worst in her. "I don't know. I'm—I'm not sure I can."

"Of course you can, girl," Mrs. Montgomery snapped. "You've been married four times. Do you think these men all that different from your husbands?"

Ward's smile grew. "By all means, consider them potential husbands. That ought to loosen your tongue."

She smiled, but her heart pounded. Did he mean it? *Ought* she to be searching for a new husband? But with

Richard's money she'd be capable of supporting herself and her child. No, she'd not need another husband, and after surviving three bad ones and losing this—this good one—

Tears welled in her eyes and she glanced down quickly. "All right. But what do I say? Especially," she took a deep, pained breath, "especially to the more intimate questions?"

"Never fear, I mean to force them to toe the line on those. As for answers." He lifted his head to scan the room. "We must all hold fast to the same story. A united front is necessary to win this battle."

"Of course. Uh, what is the front again?" Ro asked.

"Very funny, Ro. First of all, Morgan," he said, and she lifted her head to regard him. "You must be as honest as possible. One cannot catch honesty in a lie. When asked about your part in Turner's death, you must explain how you hit Turner with the statue. Your fear of arrest compelled you to flee Philadelphia. You needn't elaborate."

"And the reason I hit him?" She drew in a deep breath. "I'm not certain I can—"

"You can. The straight truth. Turner believed in strong discipline and you were afraid."

Oh Lord—oh Lord the humiliation.

In his kindest voice, Ward said gently, "You may breathe easy on that account. By now these reporters know Turner's reputation. If they probe any deeper, we shall explain that further details serve to only embarrass and muddy the Turner name."

"Along with ours!" Mrs. Montgomery spat.

"Yes, madam, but it's infinitely more noble to express concern about the Turner name. Morgan, you must appear a martyr and a victim as much as you may dislike it. I know you're quite capable of presenting yourself that way."

Capable? Of appearing innocent and sweet after all that had happened to her? But she'd caught Weatherly with such a ploy, and this would only last an hour or two. Surely she could keep up the façade that long.

"To that purpose," Ward continued, "we'll present your entire background. Both your mother and Reggie have agreed to it. You'll tell them about your marriage to Drumlin, his death and your marriage to Weatherly, and then your marriage to Turner."

"All," Edward said in a low, tight voice, "without anything aspiring to a suitable mourning period in between."

"You tell them of your family, your falling out, and the fact that you were left penniless in a foreign country. Sound frail and delicate, Morgan. You know how men eat that up," he added dryly.

A smile tugged at the corner of her mouth in spite of the fear yanking at her heart. "Of course. Shall I wear pink? Or white?"

"Pink. I doubt they'd believe the white."

"And your part in all? What will you say, Ward?"

His mouth turned into a grim line just as a tiny squeak interrupted all conversation. Morgan jerked her head toward the sound emanating from her mother's lap. Eyes wide open, Lee waved his arms about and let out another squeak.

"He's wanting his nurse, no doubt," Ward said.

Amy rose. "I'll ring for her."

"Oh no!" Morgan said, taking her hands from Ward's as she rose and stepped toward her son. His face wrinkled up in anger as he squeaked again. "I shall see to him." After having neglected her breasts for hours now, she might possibly have the ability to feed him. Oh heavens, she thought as the truth suddenly struck her completely, she could nurse him herself!

"We've yet to finish this conversation," Ward said firmly from behind her. "And you cannot attend his needs, at any rate."

"We'll finish later." She reached down to gingerly take him from her mother's lap. Lee stared at her a minute, his eyebrows drawn, then started wailing. Morgan laughed, too delighted to hold him in her arms to care for his temper.

"Morgan—"

"I fancy I shall return in time for supper," she said to the room at large. The words came out in a croon as she concentrated on the wailing little bundle in her arms. "Come along, my little love. It is not so bad as you think!" She walked on air across the room, ignoring various protests, then closing the door on them altogether.

Chapter Thirty-one

"Well, that's that!" Edward snapped. "She ignores your orders as always! And what are we to do while we wait? Twiddle our thumbs?"

Puzzled, Ward stared after Morgan. What did she think she could do for Lee?

"At least she's not changed in that regard," Reggie said dryly. "So Montgomery, what will be your part in all this? We'll need to know it if we're to stand behind it."

Ward shrugged off his confusion to concentrate on the matter at hand. "Merely that Morgan came to me for assistance. We met on board ship on her way to America, which anyone can verify. I offered her my services before she married Weatherly, and she sought me out after Turner's death."

"Interesting," Ro said. "And her marriage to you? They'll want to know, Ward. She is, after all, no longer Turner, but Montgomery. As I recall you intended to publish it in the Boston papers as having occurred in November."

"In November!" his grandmother burst out. "But how would that be possible? And how will you explain the time before publishing the announcement?"

"It doesn't matter right now," Ward answered. "I believe she wishes to sue for divorce."

"Divorce!" Lady Westborough cried out, lurching forward in her chair, her face bright with shock. "Good Lord, not even Morgan would do such a thing!"

"Under New York state law, in which I have a residence, she might actually sue for annulment, her consent to the marriage having been obtained under duress. She has both a doctor and nurse as witness to 'duress,' although such action would make Lee a bastard. I expect she'll pursue a divorce."

"But the scandal!"

Ward smiled mirthlessly. "Morgan is accustomed to scandal."

"No!" his grandmother cried out. "I won't permit it, Ward. I have some influence in New York!"

Ward, heart aching, shook his head at her. "I beg you not to use it. If Morgan wishes for a divorce, she may have it."

Amy shook her head. "You wrong her, Ward. She loves you."

"Does she? Has she told you so lately?"

"She did in Boston."

"That was *before*, Amy."

"Has she expressed any change in her regard?"

"She told me," he said dryly, "that she hated me. She's not since denied it."

"At all events," Lady Westborough said in a haughty voice that reminded Ward strongly of Morgan, "you shall prevent her from such a ruinous course of action. You're her husband and you shall bend her to your will. She must—"

Anger burst through Ward's pain. "I will *not* attempt to bend her to my will, madam! Were it possible to do so, I still should not attempt it. It's that very spirit I find so appealing." He rose. "And I warn you now, madam, that if Morgan should remain my wife, you shall only be welcome in my home as long as you remember that. I'll brook no interference from you, or Westborough, or you, Grandmother. And now, if you'll give me leave, it is past time to discover exactly what is on her mind."

As he shut the door Ro said softly, "Touché, *Mon Capitaine!*"

"Oh, he's so beautiful!" Morgan whispered in awe, looking down at the sleeping face of her baby pressed up against her breast.

"That he is mum," answered Kathleen. "I'm surprised you have enough to feed him."

Morgan lifted her head to focus on Lee's nurse, sitting on Morgan's bed. A lump rose in her throat when she thought about how many more hours Kathleen had spent with her son than Morgan had herself. Ward had hired Maeve's cousin for the position, however, and the resemblance between them eased Morgan's heart a little.

"I am too. No doubt he'll be hungry again soon."

"Might be—"

A tapping on the door interrupted Kathleen, followed by Ward's voice. "Morgan, may I come in?"

Morgan's mouth went dry, and it took several moments before she could answer. "Yes, yes of course." Rising, she reluctantly handed the baby over to Kathleen.

Ward entered, his eyes quickly flashing over them as he said in a cool voice, sending chills through Morgan's quivering heart, "Good, you're finished. I'd like a few moments of your time, my dear, if you please."

She nodded at him and buttoned up her dress. Kathleen left. When the door closed, Morgan, heart in her throat, waited for Ward to speak. He regarded her for several moments, his face impassive. Finally he seated himself on the bed across from her and said, "I believe we need to discuss our future."

Oh no, she didn't wish to, not at all! Whatever he said was sure to be heartbreaking and she could not bear any more! What sort of future could she have without Ward?

One with Lee, she told herself. Could she live a full life with only a child to occupy her time? A woman didn't need a man, did she, if she had money to support herself? How many different writers had discussed a woman's disinterest in the warmer side of marriage? She would be one of them—

"If you wish to end our marriage, you have two options," Ward started bluntly, shooting daggers into her heart, "annulment and divorce. I must point out, my dear, that annulment could prove troublesome. It would make Lee a bastard. Divorce is the best course to follow. Despite that, you may sue for either under New York's laws, citing the circumstances of our marriage, the duress you were under when you married me. You might write to both the doctor and nurse—"

"Both would create scandal," she interrupted in a low voice. "And you don't live in New York."

"I have a residence there, left to me by my grandfather. It might take some time, but I believe we should eventually succeed in the suit in New York. As for scandal, you needn't worry too much for that. Once divorced you may move anywhere in the country you choose. The scandal won't follow you. Furthermore, as the wronged party in the suit you may, in most states, remarry."

He'd thought it through so thoroughly! Did that mean he was resolved on this course of action? Perhaps, perhaps not. Planning was second nature to Ward. . . .

"But *you* will still be stung by the scandal, won't you? Without the marriage option?"

Some indecipherable emotion flickered in his eye. "I have no desire to remarry."

"And the scandal? Your name means so much to you, Ward! You've spent all these years of working to wash away your father's stain and now to add to it. . . ."

He shrugged. "I shall live it down. And I have a son in the bargain."

"You mean—you mean to take him?"

This time the emotions were clear—pain and longing. "No. A child needs his mother. I do expect that you'll permit me to see him from time to time."

She took a few deep breaths as that sank in. From time to time meant she would still see Ward. And he would not remarry.

"If you move somewhere not too far away," he continued, a slight plea in his unsteady voice, "you could send Kathleen with him to Boston to stay for several weeks."

She rubbed her hot, burning eyes. "And this—this is what you want?"

His eyes narrowed slightly, and his face turned hard. "No."

"Then why?"

More peering. He crossed his arms over his chest, protectively it seemed to her, and said in an even but tight voice, "Morgan, you refused to marry me three times, and yet I took advantage of your weakest moment and forced it upon you. Afterward you not only claimed you hated me, but proved it quite strongly. I may not be a sensitive man, but even I must understand a knife in the leg."

"I spoke in anger. I don't hate you."

"You may come to if we stay married." He sighed. "When I first proposed marriage, I didn't know about

Turner's death. I expected to paint over our past together without much difficulty. Upon hearing of the murder, I couldn't think beyond your safety. But now we must face the consequences of our actions. Your name has been in the Boston papers. Mine will follow. We may contain some of the damage, but not all."

"Won't divorce only add to it?"

"In the beginning, yes, but once our names are no longer linked the gossip will die down. Should we stay married, however, the murder and our mistakes will hang over us, and only the most exemplary conduct could ever eradicate it."

"Exemplary . . ." she repeated, her voice drifting off as she began to understand.

"Exemplary," he said. Letting out a weary sigh, he rubbed his neck. "You're quite familiar with the sort of society I keep. You lived it in London and Philadelphia. You admit to behaving reprehensibly as Weatherly's wife. Your family has similar stories about your conduct in England."

"But Ward," she said, tears burning her eyes, "you don't like it either! I know you don't!"

He swallowed. "I confess to entering into your sentiments on occasion, but I cannot follow your example. I have duties and responsibilities to my name and those who carry it: Rob, my grandmother, aunts and cousins whom you've never met. Their futures, in business, marriage, education, depend upon my ability to protect and honor that name." His voice lowered, rough with suffering. "It's who I am, Morgan. This is the man you once loved."

He was, a man so dedicated to serving his family, his friends, he spared himself no joy at all. As his wife, as *part* of him, did he expect that from her? Oh, but he'd placed it all on the line for her. How could she ask for more? "How—how exemplary?"

He continued rubbing his neck, his eyes narrowed. "You would have to display complete respect, even reverence for all conventions. No cursing, vulgarity, or improper dressing. My wife shall be expected to attend many different, and often exceedingly dull, parties, balls, and lectures. She must make and receive calls and act as a gracious hostess. You, my dear, would have to be gracious even to those who would slap us in the face over and over again with your past, and our past together, not only in Boston but in New York as well. Bostonians, although often lacking in tact, are very strict about propriety, far more so than the citizens of either Philadelphia or London. Frankly," he said with another weary sigh, "frankly I'm not certain you can do that."

She winced at his doubt in her abilities. But then he knew her well, and when she viewed herself under those circumstances—the subject of gossip, the burning humiliation and stares, the constant bitter necessity of biting her tongue—she wondered if she *could* do it. *Would* she do it? The thought created a lump in her throat. "Might I choose not to attend functions where the gossips will be?"

He shook his head firmly. "No. The more one runs from scandal, the harder it follows. I have had many years to learn that lesson."

She narrowed her eyes. "No cursing at all? Ever?"

His lips twitched. "Not in public, at any rate."

"But in private? And the vulgarity? And my negligees? I don't have to give them up, do I?"

The twitch became a reluctant grin. "I'd rather you didn't surrender either in private, Mistress, but they would belong to the bedroom, not the dining room, drawing room, or any other part of the house." The gravity returned to his face.

"Might I go on holiday to escape occasionally?"

"By and bye," he said, regarding her with a sudden gleam in his eyes, "but presently we have much to prove to society. Separating would only add to the gossip mill. Moreover, your son needs you, and you ought still to be in confinement. Are you considering this, Morgan? Marriage to me?"

"I—I am. You might join me on holiday, you know."

He paused, hope smoothing the lines on his face. "And your son?"

"I should never leave *our* son behind."

The gleam grew, accompanied by a slight smile. "And would you leave your negligees behind?"

"I should pack nothing else!" she said with a laugh.

His face turned grave, the gleam vanished. Disappointment drew a cold steel edge in his voice. "That's exactly what I was talking about. If you mean to conduct yourself thus, Morgan, you'd be happier suing for divorce."

"I was quizzing you!"

"I am deadly serious."

Her heart shook. He was painting her into a deep, black corner. "If I did misbehave, what would you do?"

His eyes pierced hers, suffering settling into the creases of his face. "What do you think I should do? Beat you? Hit you? I could not, love, even if I believed it would correct your conduct."

"Love," she repeated, her heart flying hopefully in her chest as she scarcely heard the rest of his speech. "You called me love."

He flinched, glanced away, then focused on her once more. His voice was low and pained. "Did you think I ever stopped loving you, Mistress?"

"Yes!" she said, tears forming in her eyes. "Of course I did! Here you talk about divorce and—and remarrying as if it doesn't hurt you at all. But it's killing me, Ward! I cannot imagine ever spending my life with another man."

He took several deep breaths as an awful vulnerability spread across his face. "Morgan," he said in a soft, pained voice, "Boston will not forgive you a second time; it might not forgive you this time. The freedoms you cherish will vanish. I cannot change that. I'd rather see us divorced than see you unhappy."

"Then you cannot possibly divorce me, because I should stay in Boston and haunt you with my miserable, unhappy face daily! Oh Ward, if you love me I can do anything! I shall even," she said as tears freely flowed down her face, "I shall even bear the company of the triple-dog-damned Mr. Cabot."

And with that, no longer able to stand the distance between them, she threw herself in his arms, sobbing pitifully for all the pain of the last years, and all the pain of the last weeks. "I love you, Ward."

"And I love you," he said, clutching her fiercely against him, his arms steel bands as he kissed the top of her head, murmuring, "Hush. . . . Hush, love . . . . It's all right now. . . . Don't cry, Mistress. . . . Hush, hush. . . ." Her sobs subsided and she stood leaning against him, listening to the beating of his heart, his quiet breathing. Oh he loved her, in spite of all, loved her and it couldn't be possible, but what did that signify? He loved her.

"And so," he said at last. "And so you wish to stay married? Have I finally an affirmative answer after asking you four separate times?"

She laughed a little and lifted her head to view his lovely, carved countenance softened with affection, eyes so warm they could melt a woman's heart. "Aye, sir. I will stay married to you."

"Even under the circumstances?" Anxiety flickered in his eyes. "You must be certain, for if you cannot . . ." He closed his eyes and drew a shaky breath. She felt his large, hard body tremble like a child in the midst of a nightmare. "Then you must leave now and we—we—*damn it.*" Another horrible shudder as he opened his eyes, aching vulnerability staring down at her. "I can't lose you again. I can't. . . . This last time, I couldn't eat, couldn't sleep. I thought you might be hurt or dead and—if anyone hurt you I would kill them. Do you understand? *I would kill them,*" he said, roughly, lifting his hands to hold her face steady while he peered at her.

"Yes," she said slowly, tears filling her eyes. Oh, she'd not known how badly she'd hurt him, but it shone in his eyes and sent fissures through her heart.

"No," he said, roughly. "You don't. When I first fell in love with you, I thought love was a beautiful thing, soft and gentle as goose down. I thought I was a man entirely in control of my emotions, entirely in control of my life. Well I am neither—and love is sometimes hard, possessive, and jealous. I promise you, I shall always try to restrain those passions—"

"Not all of them, I hope!" she exclaimed in a watery voice.

"The rougher ones, but you must promise me this, that you'll abide by the rules, for if I lost you again—" His voice cracked and she noted a suspicious wetness in his eyes. "If you left me again, Morgan—I could not bear it."

"I promise."

He searched her eyes, that vulnerability stabbing her heart. "You've promised before, and broken it," he rasped.

"I promised because I could not bear to hurt you."

"You could not have hurt me more."

"I had no notion how deep your feelings went—"

"I'm not a man prone to making passionate declarations of love. In fact," he said, kissing her forehead, "I've not declared it to any other woman, not even Fran, although I was once—no twice—engaged to her."

"To Fran? *Ro's* wife?"

"Aye," he said with a wry smile. "That's a story for another day, however. And so," he said tenderly, wiping her tears away with his thumbs. "May I have a kiss to seal it, then?"

"You may have far more than that! Ought we not to consummate our marriage?" she asked saucily.

He laughed, eyes twinkling. "Ah, I do love you, Mistress, and I've missed you more than I can say. But the doctor said we must wait six weeks past birth at least, and I won't jeopardize your health."

She smiled and reached to trace his jaw-line. "I suppose I'm not quite healed yet. Then shall we wait until we return to Boston? As I'll still be in confinement and unable to entertain, we might consider it a sort of honeymoon."

"To Boston then," he said and gave her a long, thorough kiss.

Afterwards she chuckled. "Ah, your kiss is as wonderful as ever. I suppose you *have* healed."

"I have and let me say I'm particularly glad you didn't take your stabbing to the extremes you read of in *The Lustful Turk.*"

"But I wouldn't destroy my own pleasure by cutting off your parts, would I? Oh God, Ward, how can you want to stay married to me? What kind of woman says such things?" she asked, tears springing to her eyes.

He smiled and kissed them both. "The sort of woman, Mistress, who could bring a staid and sober sea captain, of long Boston lineage to his knees. Now, shall we tell our friends that the Wicked Widow has found yet another victim?"

She smiled. "Aye, aye, Captain."